SARAH LOVE

GERALDINE O'NEILL

POOLBEG

Published 2011
by Poolbeg Press Ltd
123 Grange Hill, Baldoyle
Dublin 13, Ireland
E-mail: poolbeg@poolbeg.com
www.poolbeg.com

1

A catalogue record for this book is available from the British Library.

ISBN 978-1-84223-453-2

Typeset by Patricia Hope.
Printed by CPI, Cox & Wyman, UK

www.poolbeg.com

NOTE ON THE AUTHOR

Born in Scotland, Geraldine O'Neill lives in Co Offaly, Ireland with her husband, Michael Brosnahan. She has two adult children, Christopher and Clare.

Sarah Love is her eighth book.

ALSO BY GERALDINE O'NEILL

Tara Flynn

Aisling Gayle

Tara's Fortune

The Grace Girls

The Flowers of Ballygrace
(Also published as A Different Kind of Dream)

Tara's Destiny

Leaving Clare

PUBLISHED BY POOLBEG

ACKNOWLEDGEMENTS

Once again, thanks to Paula and all the lovely staff at Poolbeg for their work and expertise on *Sarah Love* – and Gaye for her excellent editing skills.

As always, I'm very grateful to Mandy and the staff at Watson, Little, who look after my literary world in such a professional, warm and supportive manner.

I really enjoyed writing *Sarah Love,* and it was wonderful to take a trip down the memory lanes of Newcastle-Upon-Tyne – although Pilgrims Lane and the shops are purely fictitious, as are the characters. Newcastle is special to me as I trained as a teacher in Ponteland College of Education in the mid-1970s. It is also where I met my husband, Mike Brosnahan, and I am eternally grateful to Newcastle for that! Writing *Sarah Love* brought back happy memories of our student days and all the friends we made there, including Ann Shaftoe and Phil Read, Kathy Bowes, Dave Rumney, Steve Hall. And of course, memories of my sister, Kate.

I'd like to pay tribute to the late, great Catherine Cookson whose many books gave me hours of happy reading in the college library when I should have been studying!

Thanks to Alma McManus, the style guru from *Clothesology* in Fermanagh, who patiently taught me the basics of sewing, shared her expertise in dress design and miraculously helped me make my first skirt!

Also, thanks to Judi James from Fenwick Department Store in Newcastle-Upon-Tyne for helping me with the history of the store in the 1960s.

Go raibh míle maith agat to Tullamore artist, Siobhan McCormack-Ryan for inviting me to join her in *Duan,* the Celtic Celebration in New York, for St Patrick's Day 2010. Siobhan exhibited her exciting, vibrant paintings at the event in the Irish Consulate whilst I read from recent work. We had a wonderful week exploring New York before the event and are very grateful for the support of our families and around fifty friends who travelled from Offaly. Warm thanks also to the lovely staff in the Irish Consulate.

Thanks to the New York Offaly Association who invited us to join them in the St Patrick's Day Parade, and to Page and Mae from Annapolis and Rod and Nancy Girvin from San Diego (and daughter, Allison!) who travelled to New York to meet us.

I'm indebted, as always, to Mike, Chris and Clare for their loving support in all I do.

Congratulations to John and Adele on their forthcoming wedding in an Irish castle!

Finally – a heartfelt thanks to all my readers near and far who make all the solitary hours at the computer worthwhile.

Sarah Love
is dedicated to my sisters,
Teresa, Kate, much missed Patricia, Berni
and my brother, Eamonn.

The family I was born into and the family
I would have chosen.

Take your needle, my child, and work at your pattern;
It will come out a rose by and by.
Life is like that; one stitch at a time taken patiently
and the pattern will come out all right, like embroidery.

OLIVER WENDELL HOLMES

CHAPTER 1

Tullamore, County Offaly

September, 1964

When the morning sky gave enough light to see clearly, Sarah Love checked her watch. She slid out of the narrow single bed and walked barefoot on the cold, cracked linoleum over to the old wardrobe. She opened the door inch by inch, wary of the loud creak it made when opened quickly.

She tucked a long strand of white-blonde hair behind her ear, then carefully lifted out the heavy hanger. It was weighed down with the long white lace wedding dress she had been working on for the last few months. She often did alterations and made items for local people, but this dress was different. It was the first wedding dress she had made – and it was her own.

She hung it on the outside of the wardrobe and then sat back on the bed, scrutinising it for any flaws. So far, she had found none. The pattern had been ordered through a shop in Dublin and then she had waited two weeks until it arrived from London. It had been worth the wait. No bride in Tullamore would have a dress like it. She still had a few small details to finish – loops for the pearl buttons on the back and the cuffs, and some small white roses to sew on the neckline. But she had plenty of time. The wedding wasn't for another two weeks.

A door creaked somewhere in the cottage and then the familiar

1

rattling in the kitchen told her that her brother James and his wife Martina were up. It would be another half an hour or so before she would feel comfortable about joining them.

When Martina moved into Loves' cottage eighteen months ago, she had made it perfectly clear that she liked to have the mornings alone with her husband. When Sarah joined them, the stilted conversation indicated that Martina didn't want her sister-in-law around until she and James had their first cup of tea together and eased themselves into the day.

At the beginning it had upset Sarah, being made to feel like an unwanted lodger in her own home. But there was nothing she could do about the situation. As the oldest and only boy in the Love family, James had been left the cottage and she was now living there under sufferance.

She had endured it, and in a few weeks she would have her own kitchen and would be sitting down to breakfast with her own husband every morning.

Sarah wondered whether it was worth starting work on the dress now or whether she should wait until after breakfast. She glanced at a book on the cabinet by her bed, and then her gaze moved to the sewing table beside the window with her collection of needles and threads, and the new boxes of trimmings for her dress.

She went over to the wrought-iron stand where she washed every morning. She lifted the white tin jug and poured water into the basin. Then she took a bar of soap and washed her hands in the cold water and dried them on a rough towel. She wouldn't risk marks on the white material.

As she worked away, stitching the satin rosebuds around the neck of the dress, Sarah lost herself in the details of her wedding day. She rehearsed every minute of the morning from leaving the cottage on James's arm until she was walking up the aisle with her two friends, Sheila Brady and Patricia Quinn, walking behind her in the pink dresses she had made for them.

Then, she saw herself standing at the altar beside Con Tierney – the local lad she had been courting for the last three years. They would take their vows in front of nearly sixty people, and after that they would go to Butler's Hotel for their wedding breakfast.

Later on that evening they would take the train up to Dublin, and spend their first night together in a small hotel in Bray.

Sarah's thoughts always came to a halt after that. She couldn't begin to imagine herself and Con alone in the hotel room for a whole week. Herself and Con in a big double bed for the first time. She supposed she would just handle it like every new bride. Take it a night at a time.

When she decided that it was safe to venture out into the kitchen, Sarah finished the rosebud she was on, hung the dress back up, slid her feet into her slippers and went into the kitchen.

Martina was over at the stone sink, washing the plates and mugs.

"Good morning," Sarah said. "It doesn't look too bad out."

Her narrow-hipped sister-in-law turned towards her. "Are you on a split shift in the hotel today?"

"I finish at four and then I'm back on again at six for the evening."

"We need flour and tea."

"I'll get them," Sarah said. "But can it wait until tonight? I wasn't going to come home because Sheila invited me to have dinner out at their house." Sarah's old school-friend lived with her elderly parents in the middle of Tullamore and was always happy to have Sarah's company for a few hours.

Martina turned back to the sink without answering, the way she often did.

Sarah's chest tightened. "We're not that short of tea and flour, are we?" She went over to check the flour bin. "There's enough for three or four loaves, and the caddy is half full."

Martina took up a linen teacloth and began to dry the wet cups and plates.

Sarah waited for a few moments, to see if there would be any more to the conversation. There wasn't. The silence hung in the air, making her wonder if she should change her plans and come home with the tea and flour during her afternoon break.

Then, she caught herself. If her brother's wife wanted her to bring the things home, she could ask like a normal person. Trying to read Martina's mind had got her nowhere in the past. Her moods were so changeable that Sarah could cycle all the way back home with the flour and tea to be met with a bemused half-smile.

Having a nice hot meal put down to her in Sheila's welcoming house was a far better option. She put the kettle back into the middle of the range to boil and then cut two slices of brown bread and buttered them.

As she poured hot tea into her mug, she looked over at Martina who was now scrubbing the sink. "Will I pour you a cup of tea?"

The scrubbing continued for a few more seconds. Then eventually she said, "No . . . I've had enough."

Sarah lifted her plate and mug and headed towards her bedroom where she could relax with her breakfast.

"Thank God the timing has worked out well," Martina suddenly said.

Sarah halted in her tracks. "Timing for what?"

"The wedding . . . we're going to need your room."

Sarah turned to look at her.

"We've a baby on the way now, so we'll need more space."

Sarah's face broke into a smile. "That's great news!" She turned back to put her breakfast things on the kitchen table. "You both must be delighted."

Martina leaned against the sink. "I suppose we are . . . I'm still getting used to it."

"It'll be lovely for you to have a baby around the house." She suddenly noticed her sister-in-law's pale face. "Are you feeling okay?"

"I'm not too bad."

"Do you feel sick in the mornings? Do you know when it's due?"

Martina's face tightened. "I'm grand – I'm not making a big issue of it and I don't want you to be going around telling everybody."

Sarah caught her breath at the assumption. "I wouldn't say a word until you –"

"It's private business," Martina continued. "And I'm keeping it in the family for the time being. I've my mother warned to say nothing for a while, and I'm not telling the sisters yet because they're nothing but a pair of yaps."

"Well, I'm delighted for you and James." Sarah lifted her mug and plate. "I'll be in the room sewing until it's time to go to work."

"Sarah . . ." Martina said. "Have you decided what you're doing with your hair yet for the wedding?"

"I've had a chat with the hairdresser," Sarah's voice was deliberately light, "and she's going to try the head-dress with my hair loose or up in a bun."

"You've far too much hair for a bun," Martina stated. She narrowed her eyes. "I thought you were going to have a good bit cut off it?"

Sarah shook her head. "I never said that. You suggested it to me last week and I told you then I didn't want it cut."

"Please yourself!" Martina snapped. "I just think you're going to look like a ghost in a white dress with all that whitey hair around you. If you had it cut to an ordinary shoulder length, the head-dress would sit better."

"I'm not having it cut." Sarah went into her bedroom and closed the door. There were a lot of things she wasn't confident about, but the one thing she knew was that she had nice long hair. Since she was a little girl, people had commented on the colour and the fact it was so long she could sit on it. Occasionally she found herself on the receiving end of snide remarks from other girls. She remembered being teased by two particular girls in school, that even though she didn't have pink eyes, the colour of her hair meant she was half-albino.

When she came home crying, her father had told her that they were only jealous of her unusual, beautiful hair and she must learn to ignore them. Sarah now recognised that same jealousy in Martina and was determined to ignore her advice.

* * *

The hotel dining-room was busy at lunch-time as it was a market

5

day for the farmers who had travelled earlier in the morning into the town. Sarah went back and forth to the kitchen carrying plates of cabbage and bacon, roast beef and chicken. She then brought out dishes of potatoes and vegetables and jugs of gravy. This was followed by apple tarts and trifle.

When the rush quietened down, her time was spent clearing tables and setting fresh tablecloths and cutlery for the evening meals. It was hard work, but the hotel was a nice place to work in, and she was more grateful for it than ever since Martina had moved into the house. The staff were cheery and friendly, and there was always a bit of banter in the kitchen with the other workers.

Sarah could find herself working anywhere depending on how busy things were. She was often asked to come in on a Friday or Saturday morning to help with the bedrooms after the commercial travellers who usually stayed mid-week had departed. She found the work in the bedrooms satisfying, and enjoyed looking at the shiny sinks and taps and freshly ironed sheets on the bed when she had finished. But any time she had a quiet minute to herself, Sarah drifted off into daydreams about the dresses she was making and the ones she planned to make after her wedding. At some stage in the future she would love to work for a good-quality dressmaker where she could spend all day working on the small details that made a garment stand above the rest.

That was one of the things that she and Con had in common – dreams for the future. He worked as a painter and decorator, and had plans to open his own shop one day, selling wallpaper and paints and, further down the line, carpets and furniture. He had saved up and bought a van in the last year, so that he could travel further afield, and often worked late into the evening.

Over the last few months, Con had been busy doing up the small cottage just outside the town where he and Sarah would live. It was within easy cycling and walking distance for work. An old uncle had left it to him and his three brothers. Con had given the others the price of their fares over to England and a bit extra to tide them over until they got settled in jobs, and they had willingly given him the run-down cottage.

Sarah had made curtains for all the windows while Con had plastered and painted and hung wallpaper. Over their year-long engagement, they had saved up and bought rugs for the stone floor and had put a new range in the kitchen for cooking and to keep the place warm, and a sturdy pine table and chairs.

Now that it was almost ready to move into, Sarah was doing her damnedest to keep out of it until they were married. Con had a different view of things. He would have been happier if they would meet up in the cottage regularly to do – as he called it – "a bit of courting". But once they had got somewhere on their own, Sarah found out that the kissing and cuddling wasn't enough for him.

She had walked out on him on several occasions recently, once when he had tried to take her blouse off, and on another occasion when he had forced her hand on top of a part of his body that was out of bounds for a single girl.

"If you don't stop this carry-on, I won't come down here any more when we're on our own," she had warned him. "It's only a few more weeks until we're married. Don't go spoiling things now."

He had gone stomping off out the back door and down into the overgrown garden. Ten minutes later he had returned. "I'm sorry, Sarah," he said. "I promise it won't happen again." He'd run his hand through his dark hair. "It's just that you're so lovely. It's only natural I can't stop thinking about you. Every night recently, I keep imagining what it will be like when we're actually married." He'd gone over and stroked her hair, then he had pulled her close and murmured in her ear. "I keep thinking what it will be like with your long blonde hair hanging down over your face and your breasts – like Lady Godiva."

"Don't!" The picture he described terrified her. "If there's any more talk like that, there will be no wedding."

Con had reassured her that he would keep his hands to himself until they were married, but the incidents had made Sarah wonder whether she actually loved him, because she had felt nothing but panic on both occasions. It worried her, because in most other ways they got on fine. Con had a good nature and locally was held in high regard, although he was inclined to be a bit loud when he'd had a few drinks.

She'd had to bite her tongue on a few occasions when he got carried away, enjoying being the centre of attention and hogging the conversation. If it continued when they were married she would have to have a serious word with him about it, because she didn't want to be one of those wives who sat in the background afraid to speak out. The other area of concern was more intimate. She had heard from friends that when you really loved somebody the sex thing came naturally. She hoped they were right. She would find out in a few weeks' time.

* * *

Sheila had a corner cleared for Sarah at the cluttered old kitchen table, and the two girls sat chatting as Sarah ate a pork chop, fried potatoes and cabbage. Sheila had had her own meal earlier, and now sat opposite her friend eating a slice of apple tart. As usual, her elderly parents were seated at either side of the fireplace, "like two bookends" as Sheila often wryly referred to them.

Every time Sarah visited they would be in the exact same spot, sometimes dozing and sometimes chipping into the girls' conversation, although their poor hearing often meant they got the wrong end of the stick. Most of the time they all rubbed along together, but there were often occasions when Sheila felt the lack of privacy in the house. The only place she could have brought Sarah was into her bedroom, but her mother and father would have seen it as odd, and couldn't imagine that the girls would have anything to talk about that couldn't be said in their presence.

"How are things going for the wedding?" Sheila asked. "It's not long now."

"Grand," Sarah said smiling. "I've only another few evenings' work on the dress and it's finished."

"What I've seen of it, it's absolutely beautiful," Sheila said, "and I'm delighted with the bridesmaid dress. You made a lovely job of it. I don't know why you don't go into it professionally."

A slight tinge of embarrassment came into Sarah's cheeks at the praise. "I think Patricia was pleased with her dress, too."

Sheila rolled her eyes. "Well, if you can please that one, you can please anybody! She's the fussiest girl you could come across."

"Oh, she doesn't mean any harm," Sarah said. "It's the way her family are. They just worry about every little detail."

"The last time we were over at your house together, she kept going on about the dress being too loose at the front, and it looked perfect on her. She was breathing in and trying to grab handfuls of the material but there was nothing to grab." Sheila sucked her breath in through her teeth. "I'd swear to God she's only saying it to make the point that I'm stouter than her."

"Ah, she wouldn't do that," Sarah said, wrinkling her brow. "In fairness, she has lost weight. I'd say she's gone down about half a stone between the first fitting and the last. She came over one night last week and I took it in a bit at the side seams, and it looks better now." She paused for a moment. "I didn't think she looked too well, between the loss of weight and looking very pale."

"Patricia's the lucky type that's more inclined to drop weight than put it up." Sheila looked down at her half-eaten apple pie and shook her head. "I think I'd better start cutting out the sweet stuff or you'll be letting the seams out on mine as opposed to taking them in."

"You're grand as you are," her mother commented loudly. "It's better to have a bit of weight on you than to be looking all thin and pinched like Patricia Quinn. Her mother is the very same – you'd wonder if they ever eat a bite at all."

"Men like a woman with a bit of meat," Jimmy Brady chipped in.

Sheila clapped a hand over her mouth to stop herself from laughing out loud.

She leaned across the table and whispered to Sarah. "You can't say a word in this house without it becoming a free-for-all!"

Sarah smiled. She was well used to the Bradys' ways, as she was with her friend Patricia's family. Both families were very pass-remarkable. Patricia's mother was forever commenting about Sheila Brady, saying would the girl never think of getting out for a bit of a walk to lose the weight around her hips. Behind all the comments there was no real malice, and Sarah usually let it all wash over her with a smile.

"How is the little cottage coming on?" Mrs Brady asked.

"Grand," Sarah told her. "We've the inside more or less finished. It's all papered and painted."

"Oh, you're lucky having a man that's good around the house," the old woman said. "Con Tierney can turn his hand to anything."

Sheila gave a low giggle and whispered to Sarah. "I hope he keeps his hands to himself before the wedding . . . I've heard a lot of men find it harder the nearer it gets." She was not speaking from personal experience, as she had never had much luck with lads.

"He'll keep his hands to himself all right," Sarah whispered back. "I've warned him if he doesn't there won't be any wedding!"

"And no better woman to put him in his place. He's a changed lad since he met you."

Sarah suddenly felt uncomfortable at the way the conversation had turned. She knew Sheila meant no harm, but her chatter had touched a raw nerve. She changed the subject to something more inane, and tried to put Con's reputation as a ladies' man before they met out of her mind.

She spent over an hour at Sheila's, cycled back into town to collect the items that Martina has asked for, then headed back to the hotel.

She would keep busy for the next few hours, serving meals and clearing and setting tables for breakfast in the morning. When she got back home around ten that night, she would go straight to her room to continue working on the rosebuds and button loops on her dress. She would then cross off another day on her calendar – counting down to her wedding.

Another day less until she was gone from the home she was no longer welcome in.

CHAPTER 2

The following afternoon Martina stuck her head into Sarah's bedroom. "Are you working this evening?"

"No," Sarah said. "Patricia said she might call up to try her dress on again."

Martina made a derisory snorting noise. "That one! She's never satisfied. She's been up and down here like a fiddler's elbow. She must have tried that dress on half a dozen times and she's still complaining that it needs taking in here or taking up there. She's one visitor I won't miss when you have your own house to entertain your friends."

Sarah stiffened up. Sheila and her mother had moaned about Patricia yesterday, but it was really just light chat. Martina saying the same thing sounded far more vicious. She didn't know how much longer she could tolerate her sister-in-law's manner. If it wasn't for the trouble it would cause with James, she would wipe the floor with her.

Martina had always been outspoken but she was now becoming blatantly rude – forgetting that the house she was living in was the only home Sarah had ever known. It was the house where there had always been a welcome for her friends from her warm-hearted mother. After she had died when Sarah was only thirteen, her father had done his best to keep the house running in the same way. There was always a cup of tea and some home-made bread or cake for anyone who called. Then, her father had dropped dead of a heart attack three years ago, and when the family picked themselves up again, they continued the same way of doing things. Shortly afterwards, Martina arrived.

It was changed days.

Martina crossed her arms high over her stomach now and said, "Was it chicken you ordered for the wedding meal?"

Sarah looked up at her sister-in-law, surprised she was actually showing interest in her plans. "Well, a choice of chicken or roast beef . . ."

There was a sudden awkward silence and Sarah turned her attention back to the white lace dress.

Martina cleared her throat. "James wants to pay for it."

"For what?" Sarah asked.

"The wedding breakfast."

"He wants to pay for it? He never said anything about paying to me . . ."

"He's a typical man; he always leaves those sorts of things to me."

Sarah bit her lip as she digested this unexpected news. She knew she should be delighted at the offer, but the way it was delivered made her unsure how to react. Martina should have given her the good news in a warmer tone and kinder words, but because of James Sarah couldn't voice that opinion.

"That's very good of you . . . I wasn't expecting it. I'll have to let Con know. He'll be delighted."

"We had to give you a decent present. It would look bad if we didn't. He's your only brother . . ."

Sarah told herself to keep calm. There was no point in responding in the same manner as her sister-in-law had spoken to her – it had always backfired. And besides, she had promised herself that no matter what Martina said, she wasn't going to take things personally. When Martina was in this type of mood, no one was spared from her sharp tongue.

Sarah took a deep breath and smiled. "You're both very good."

* * *

She was standing by the bedroom window deep in thought when she caught sight of Patricia Quinn, pushing her bike up the hill. She was just turning away to walk down to meet her when something made her stop and watch. There was something unusual about the way Patricia was moving – something that wasn't quite right. Her usual purposeful step had slowed down as if pushing the bike was a great effort, and she was looking around her in a strangely distracted manner. The small, slim girl always had a confident air about her, but the closer she came to the house, the more curious Sarah felt. She went out of the bedroom and through into the kitchen where Martina was stirring something in a pot, and then to the cottage door.

She expected Patricia to have reached the gate by the time she got there, but there was no sign of her. Sarah went over to the stone wall to look down the hill, and saw her bridesmaid-to-be sitting on a rock with her head in her hands. She opened the gate and set off at a run down the slope to meet her.

"Are you all right, Patricia?" she called.

Patricia's head jerked up when she heard the voice. She quickly moved to her feet and then gave a broad smile. A smile that didn't reach her eyes. "I'm grand . . ." she said, straightening up properly. "I just got a bit of a stitch in my side . . ."

"You look very pale," Sarah said, looking concerned. "And you were walking – you usually manage to cycle the bike up to the house."

"It's only a stitch." Patricia smoothed her navy-and-white spotted dress down and fixed the edges of her white cardigan, then she stooped to lift her bike up.

"Well, I'm glad you're okay now," Sarah said, sensing that her friend didn't want a fuss made. "I'm looking forward to seeing you in your bridesmaid dress. I think it's going to be grand on you now."

"You're not working in Butler's later tonight, are you?" Patricia asked.

"No, if I work in the evenings it's from six o'clock to help serve the meals. I'm glad to have the night off to get my dress finished."

"Have you much left to do to it?"

"Just the trimmings." She smiled. "I've enjoyed doing them the most. I stitched some little roses in pink around the neck of your dress since you last saw it." She waited for some sort of reaction – a sense of looking forward to the wedding – but there was none. "Are you sure you're okay?"

Patricia nodded. "I had fried potatoes before I came out, and I must have eaten them too quickly. It's probably only a bit of indigestion or something."

"You'd want to be careful," Sarah told her, as they started to walk along, the bicycle between then. "I've never heard you complaining of it before."

"I'll be grand. How are the wedding plans coming on? You can't have much more left to organise."

"Okay. But you're never going to guess what's happened."

"What?"

"Martina told me that James is going to pay for the wedding breakfast. Imagine leaving it until a week before the wedding to tell me! I had it all organised that I would pay for it out of the bit of money that Daddy left me."

"Did you have to pay it in advance?"

"No, they said it would be fine to pay it any time around the day of the wedding – before or after. I was going to go to the bank next week."

"And didn't Con offer to pay for it?"

Sarah's eyes widened. "I wouldn't let him. It's the bride's family's place to do that."

"Well, since your parents are both gone . . . God rest their souls."

14

"He's had to pay for a lot of the work at the house," Sarah said. "He's paid for all the plastering on the walls, the new doors, paint and wallpaper and everything."

"Did he offer to pay for the wedding or did he just leave it to you?"

Sarah suddenly felt awkward, as though Patricia was suggesting that Con was mean or that she was so desperate to get married that she was paying for her own wedding. She knew she was more anxious than normal with all the arrangements and the strain of living with Martina and James. Maybe she was being too sensitive and picking things up the wrong way. The last thing she needed now was a falling out with one of her bridesmaids.

"Oh, we chatted it out," she said, in a deliberately light tone, "and I told him I was happy to pay for the wedding with Daddy's money, because that's what would have happened if he'd been alive."

"Under the circumstances I would have let him pay."

"It makes no odds," Sarah said. "When we're married what I have will be his anyway and vice versa." She wasn't exactly sure what money Con had, but he had a half decent job and never seemed too badly off.

"Have you paid for the flowers and the wedding cars as well? Did you have to pay for those in advance?"

"We paid deposits," she said briskly. "We don't need to pay the rest until next week." Then she pointedly changed the subject. "I'm looking forward to seeing your dress on you. I hope you like the little roses."

Patricia parked the bicycle at the side of the house and the two girls went in.

Martina greeted Patricia with a nod and then turned to Sarah. "I brought our own bits of washing in from the line, but you still have things left on it."

Sarah gritted her teeth. It wouldn't have killed her to take two blouses and a brassiere from the line. "I'll get them later, thanks." She turned to Patricia. "Will you have a cup of tea?" She knew that

Martina had boiled the kettle only a short while ago, but it was unlikely that her sister-in-law would offer her friend a drink.

"I won't. I had one before I came out."

"It's not like you to refuse a cup of tea." There was a deliberate teasing note to lighten things. "I know you don't care for cake or biscuits too much, but it's not often you refuse a cup."

"We'd better get on with the dress," Patricia said. "We need to get that all over and done with."

They went into the bedroom and closed the door. Patricia unbuttoned her blouse and then took off her skirt, leaving on her white, lace-edged petticoat.

When she zipped the bridesmaid dress up, Sarah was relieved that it now fitted her friend's narrow waist and hips perfectly. It was another thing to tick off her list of things to do before the wedding. "That's it," she said. "We can hang it up now and forget about it until the wedding."

"Grand," Patricia said, reaching behind to unzip it.

"Don't you want to see yourself in the mirror?" Sarah was surprised as most people automatically moved to check how they looked in something new – particularly when it was something as special as a bridesmaid dress.

Patricia looked down at herself, smoothing the satin over her stomach. "I can see it's fine." Then, she caught sight of her friend's disappointed face and must have realised how little effort she was making. She moved over to the wardrobe and looked in the mirror. "It's more than fine, Sarah, it's beautiful. You've made a lovely job of it."

"You're not yourself, are you? Have you still got the stitch in your side?"

Patricia slipped the dress down from her shoulders. "It's easing. It's not as bad."

A knock came on front door of the cottage, and they heard Martina answering it.

"I think that's Con's voice," Sarah said. "I wonder what's brought him up here. He's supposed to be painting down at the house." She gave a little sigh. "Well, he may wait with Martina until we're finished." She turned to help Patricia step out of the dress, and as she put it on the hanger, she again noticed how pale she was. "Are you sure you're okay?"

Patricia did the zip up on her skirt, and then lifted her blouse. "I think I need to sit down for a few minutes . . ." She moved over towards Sarah's bed, fumbling to do up her buttons. "I feel a bit faint." She sank down on the single bed, and then, just as she had done earlier when she was coming up the hill, she put her head into her hands.

Sarah felt her heart quicken. She had never seen Patricia sick before, and there was definitely something wrong here. "A glass of water might help you," she said.

"Thanks," Patricia said, "and if you have a tea biscuit or a digestive . . ."

Sarah rushed out into the kitchen where Con was standing chatting to Martina, dressed in his decent clothes. He always made a point of giving her and James their place, and was always friendly and polite to them. He often gave James a hand with odd jobs around the house or farm, and if there was any atmosphere in the house between the two females when he called, he could be depended upon to diffuse it by telling some old joke or yarn. Sarah was grateful for it, as it was one less area of awkwardness between her and her sister-in-law.

"Patricia's not feeling too good," she told Martina and Con as she went over to the cupboard above the sink for a glass. "She looks as though she could faint any minute."

"Jesus!" Martina said. "That's all we need."

Con took a step towards the bedroom door. "Will I go in to her and see if there's anything I can do?"

"It might be no harm," Sarah told him. It crossed her mind for a moment that he was in his smart shirt and trousers and not dressed for painting, and presumed something had come up. She filled the glass at the tap.

"I thought she was pale when she came in," Martina said, her manner more pleasant than before. "Do you want me to get her a sup of brandy?"

Sarah tried not to look surprised at her sister-in-law's concern. "It mightn't do her any harm. She said she would try a dry biscuit – do you know if we have any digestives?" She reached up for the biscuit tin.

"There's a new packet up there," Martina told her. "She must be bad if she's looking for a biscuit. I'd say she's not had any lunch or anything. You never see her eating much, that's why she's like a whippet." She bent down to the cupboard to get the brandy bottle which was kept for emergencies. "I'd say she's gone too long without eating." Although thin, Martina prided herself on having a good appetite.

Sarah found the biscuits and then rushed back to the room with them and the glass of water. Patricia was still sitting on the bed, her arms folded and her gaze directed at the linoleum floor. Con was standing by the window, one hand cupping the lower part of his face, as though unsure of what to do or say. For a moment Sarah wondered if Patricia was embarrassed with a man around when she felt sick.

Sarah handed her the glass. "Drink this," she said gently, "and try to eat the biscuit, it might help." She looked over to her fiancé. "How does she look to you, Con? I was saying earlier that I thought she looked very pale."

"I'll be grand," Patricia said abruptly. She took a sip of the water and then bit the edge of the biscuit.

The conversation came to a halt as Martina came through the door, solemn-faced and carefully carrying a small gold-rimmed brandy glass in both hands. "This will pick you up."

Sarah was reminded of the priest in Mass dramatically holding up the chalice at the Consecration. She had to stop herself from smiling, because she knew they were expensive glasses that Martina got as a wedding present, and had never had the occasion to use. Knowing her sister-in-law, Sarah guessed that she was hoping that the fancy glasses would impress Patricia and be commented upon.

Patricia took the small, balloon-shaped glass and lifted it to her lips. She took a sip and then shuddered. "Oh, no . . ." she said, pulling a face. "I couldn't drink that stuff."

Martina moved to take it swiftly from her. "You'll have it, won't you, Con?" she said, turning towards him. When he looked hesitant, she thrust the glass in his hand. "It's too good to waste." She raised her eyes to the ceiling as though despairing of Patricia. "Go on, you might as well enjoy it as have me pour it down the sink."

Con shrugged, then lifted the glass to his lips, downed the brandy in two large mouthfuls and handed the glass back to Martina.

"If you two want to go back into the kitchen, I'll stay with her until she's a bit better," Sarah said, in case her friend was embarrassed at being the centre of attention.

"I'll make a cup of tea," Martina said, and she and Con left the two girls alone. Patricia took a few more sips of the water and managed half of the biscuit. "I'm really sorry . . ." she said several times, unable to meet Sarah's eye.

"Sure, you can't help being sick," Sarah told her. "Just make sure you take it easy now."

Gradually, Patricia's colour came back to normal. She got to her feet. "If you don't mind, I'm going to head off home." She looked slightly shaky but had a determined look on her face.

"Stay and have a cup of tea."

"I won't, thanks. Con has called down to see you and I'll only be in the way."

"He's not staying," Sarah said. "He'll be going shortly – he has work to do down at the house." She looked at her friend. "Don't be worrying about Con – he won't have called about anything in particular. He's up and down here regularly."

Patricia's eyes flitted towards the window. "I've tried the dress on and it's grand, so I'll head back home and get an early night," she said. "We have a meeting in work in the morning."

They walked out into the kitchen where Martina and Con were chatting. "She's feeling a bit better now," she told the other two.

"I think I just need an early night," Patricia said, not looking directly at them.

As they walked towards the outside door, Sarah said, "Are you up to cycling the bike back, or will I ask Con to walk it down for you?" She glanced back at her fiancé. "You won't mind wheeling Patricia's bike down for her, Con?"

"No," he said quickly. He put his teacup on the table. "Do you want me to bring it now or later?"

"No, no . . . I'm grand now, thanks," Patricia said, going outside now, "and I'll be fine cycling home."

After she waved her friend off, Sarah came back into the kitchen. "What brought you up this evening?" she asked Con. "I thought you had a lot to do down at the house."

"My mother asked me if you could go down to take a look at her wedding costume." He rolled his eyes to the ceiling. "She thinks the dress is too long and might need a bit taken off of it, and she said something about letting the seams out somewhere." He looked at Sarah, a strangely perplexed look on his face. "I don't know what she was talking about, but she asked me to tell you anyway."

Sarah's brow deepened. This was all she needed in the week coming up to the wedding. She hadn't even seen Mrs Tierney's dress and jacket. She was a big woman and God knows what sort of work the taking up and letting out would entail. She hoped it wasn't going to be as complicated as the last job she had done for her. "Does your mother want me to come down this evening?"

He shrugged. "I think so . . ." He looked over at the window. "I thought we might walk down together and then you could take a look at the wallpaper I put up in the cottage last night."

Martina made a little snorting noise. "Don't you be getting any ideas, tryin' to get her down to that house when ye're all on your own, Con Tierney!" she laughed. "Ye may wait another couple of weeks until it's all official. You don't want to give everyone room to be talking about you."

Sarah whirled around to face her sister-in-law. "Indeed he

doesn't have any ideas like that," she said, "and I'm surprised at you saying such a thing."

Martina raised her eyebrows, laughter still in her eyes. "God, you're surely very touchy," she said. "And wouldn't Con be the strange man if he didn't have ideas like that in his mind?"

Sarah acted as if her sister-in-law hadn't spoken. She went and got her light jacket from the coat-hook at the side of the door. "We might as well go now," she said to Con, "so that I'm back before it gets dark."

They set off walking down the hill towards the town where they would come upon Con's family house first and then, just a field further on, the cottage they would live in as man and wife.

"I'm glad to get out of the house," Sarah said, taking a deep breath of the cool dark air. "It's been one of those nights where nothing seems right. First Patricia feeling sick and showing no interest at all in her bridesmaid dress and then Martina making her usual nasty digs."

It struck Sarah that Con was unusually quiet, and she wondered if she was complaining too much. He often commented on his mother's moaning. He might be thinking that when they married she would turn out to be like his mother or Martina – or a lot of the married women they knew. She would have to be careful not to go down that road.

She glanced at Con now, and suddenly pictured him tall and broad in his wedding suit. He was a good-looking lad and a lot of girls would be proud to have him. She would make more effort. She would lighten up. If it wasn't for Con she would be stuck in the house with Martina and James forever.

"How are things going on down at the cottage?"

"Grand . . ."

Sarah noticed that his manner was distracted and he was rubbing at his chin again.

A strange feeling suddenly came over her. A feeling that something wasn't right. "Are you all right, Con? Is there something the matter?"

There was a few moments' hesitation. Then, a cold hand struck at Sarah's heart.

He came to a halt. His body was turned towards her, but he wasn't looking at her. Wasn't meeting her eyes.

"I don't know how to say it . . . I was waiting for the right minute."

Sarah stood still and waited.

"It's Patricia," he said. "She was going to tell you if I don't tell you first."

The dress, she thought. *She doesn't like the dress and she doesn't want to wear it.* Her mind raced. There was no time to make a new one, and more material would cost a fortune. Surely the dress couldn't be that bad or Sheila would have complained?

Their eyes met, hers confused – his tortured.

"Seemingly . . . she has a child on the way," he told her.

The night came to a standstill.

"Patricia has a child on the way?" she repeated. Her voice was a dull echo in her ears. "Are you sure?" And when he responded with a bare nod she said, "How do you know all this? Why has she told *you*?"

He closed his eyes tight and then moved his head upwards so that when he opened them again he was staring at the sky. "Oh, Sarah . . ." he said. "I've been a fecking eejit and I can't tell you how sorry I am . . ."

Why is he apologising? she thought. *What has Con got to do with Patricia? Why is he speaking on her behalf?*

"I never imagined any of this would happen. It was stupid – a kind of madness. It was you I really wanted, but she turned up after you went home." His voice seemed to disappear, and when it returned, it sounded like a stranger's. "Honest to God – I have no feelings for her. It's only you I love."

And then she knew. Her heart dropped like a heavy stone and barbed wire tightened around her throat. She couldn't speak. She could hardly breathe.

"I've been trying to work out what to say to you," he went on, filling the huge silence from her. "But she was going to tell you this evening if I didn't come up, and I didn't want that to happen. I wouldn't do that to you . . . you deserve better than that."

She could hardly hear him now. All that was sinking in was that Con was telling her that her whole world – her whole future – had come crashing down upon her head.

All that she knew to be true and decent were no longer there.

She now knew the reason for Patricia's strange reluctance coming up the hill to the house. For her nervousness and sickness. For her disinterest in the bridesmaid dress. For her concern about how far the wedding plans had gone.

Her supposed best friend knew that there was never going to be a wedding and now there was no house for her to escape to, to get away from Martina and James.

The thought hit Sarah like a bolt of lightning, and she suddenly felt faint at the enormity of it all.

Patricia Quinn had been sick because she knew what devastation her news would bring. How the wedding plans would all have to be halted. Or maybe she was working out how quickly she could put her own nuptial plans into operation. Because there was no doubt that she and Con would have to marry if she was having his baby.

"It only happened the once," he said, as if he thought it made a difference. "It was the night we had the row . . . the night you ran out of the cottage."

"You're referring to the night you tried to get me drunk so you could take my clothes off me?" Her voice was tight and strained. "The night you wanted me to have sex with you?"

His face crumpled and he put his hands up over his eyes.

"Was Patricia just handy that night or did you have an eye for her all the time we've been courting?" She wondered that it sounded even vaguely normal. She wondered that she was able to hold this conversation with him.

"Honest to God, Sarah, I never thought of her before that night – and I never have since. She came up to the cottage just after you left. She was looking for you. We started chatting and then we had a glass of beer and then . . . I don't even remember who made the first move or how it happened." He closed his eyes and shook his head. "Christ Almighty, Sarah . . . what have I done?"

"It's simple enough, you've ruined everything," she told him in a slow and measured voice. "You've ruined us. It's all finished."

"No, no . . . We can sort it," he said, "I'll do whatever it takes. I'll explain to Patricia and her family – I'll sort things out and make it up to you. Oh, Sarah . . ." He reached towards her.

She immediately slapped his hands away and then folded her arms tightly across her chest. "You'll make nothing up to me," she said. She gave a bitter little laugh. "There's no fixing of this situation. Don't cod yourself."

"Don't say that," he pleaded. "For God's sake give me the chance to sort it out."

Sarah looked at him and she saw tears in his brown eyes. Tears mingled with fear. Then, as she looked past him into the darkening sky, she felt her heart harden. Everything had changed. Con Tierney was no longer the person she thought he was, and she couldn't even allow herself to think of Patricia Quinn, her supposed friend.

Everything that had been sure and certain was gone, taking her future along with it.

She unfolded her arms and took a step towards him.

His eyes lit up as he saw what might be a thaw in her.

She met his gaze for a few moments and then she drew her hand back and slapped his face with a greater force than she had thought herself capable of. Strong enough to make the six-foot, broad-shouldered Con Tierney sway on his feet.

"I hate you!" she told him.

His hand came up to the reddening circle just below his eye. "It's okay, I deserve it."

"I hate you!" she repeated. "And I never want to see you again for the rest of my life." She suddenly felt an overwhelming urge to keep slapping him over and over again. To give vent to all the anger and humiliation she felt. Then, shocked at the ferocity of her feelings, she took a deep, shuddering breath to control herself. She held her head high, turned on her heel and started walking back towards the cottage.

"Whatever happens," he called after her, realising there was no point in following, "I'll love you – for the rest of my life."

Sarah kept on walking.

Con and Patricia Quinn had betrayed her in the most humiliating way, and as she walked along she realised this was only the start. With almost every step she thought of another hurdle she would encounter over the coming days and weeks.

She would have to face telling people now – starting with her sister-in-law and brother. She couldn't bear to even contemplate Martina's reaction to the fact that she would now be staying in the cottage with them indefinitely. She would have to tell Sheila that her bridesmaid role was now redundant, and she would have to inform all the people who had been sent invitations that the wedding was off.

Then she suddenly came over all dizzy as she realised that she would have to cancel the wedding breakfast in the hotel, the wedding cake and the flowers. Her heart gave a sickening lurch as she thought of walking down to tell the priest that the wedding was off and the reason why. And even if she contacted Con and told him that he could do some of the dirty work he had caused, she knew she would still have to face the priest at Mass on Sunday.

Oh God! she thought. The utter humiliation.

These were only the obvious things that had jumped into her mind, and she knew there were probably other things she hadn't even thought of. Within a few seconds she had wondered how on earth she was going to face the people in work. All the girls in the hotel who loved hearing all the details about how her wedding dress was coming on and how much more work Con still had to do in the cottage. And worse still, she had walked in on them only yesterday as they were discussing how much they had collected for her wedding present.

She felt so dizzy and overwhelmed by it all that it reminded her of the time she had drunk a glass of sherry much too quickly one Christmas.

When she had turned a bend in the road and was out of view of Con and any of the neighbouring cottages, she sank down on the stump of a tree-trunk and put her head in her hands.

She now knew how people felt when they contemplated killing themselves.

If it wasn't for the fact that it was a mortal sin, it appeared an almost attractive alternative to facing the days, weeks and months that lay ahead.

CHAPTER 3

When she reached the cottage, Sarah stood at the gate for a few minutes trying to compose herself. Compose herself when her life had just fallen apart. Compose herself when all she felt like doing was screaming and roaring. And the very last person she wanted to explain herself to was Martina but there was no escaping it.

Her sister-in-law was sitting in an armchair by the fire, knitting a baby jacket.

When Martina heard Sarah open the door, she dropped the needles and wool to the side of her chair. She wasn't taking any chances in case Sarah had brought a friend home who might spot the tiny garment and guess her secret.

"What's brought you back?" Martina snapped. "I thought you were gone out for the evening."

"I changed my mind." She planned on getting her news over and done with as soon as she stepped in the cottage, but she suddenly found herself heading for her bedroom.

"And where's himself?" Martina said, reaching down for her knitting again.

Unable to say the words that would eventually have to come,

Sarah rushed into the bedroom and, after closing the door behind her, she threw herself down on the bed. Her breathing came in short, sharp pants as she ran the whole scene between her and Con over in her mind again like a film.

How had she not seen this catastrophe coming? Had there been clues there that she had missed? Had there been a change in either Con or Patricia that she had missed? Surely they had been engulfed in guilt and worry about what they had done? Up until this evening she had been totally unaware of anything wrong with either of them.

She pressed a fist tightly over each eye, to stop the tears that she anticipated would come – but she felt only a hollow darkness.

She lay there for a while, her mind a whirl of black thoughts, and when she had tortured herself enough, she decided to gather herself together and go into the kitchen to face the first of her judges.

As she turned to move into a sitting position, her gaze fell on the white, lace creation she had worked so hard on over the last few months. The sight of it made her stomach heave and she brought her hand to cover her mouth. She stared at it with wide eyes until she could bear the sight of it no longer, and then she flew from the bed to rip it from its hanger. Her hands tore at the tiny roses, scattering them across the stone floor like confetti, and then she wrenched at the shoulder seam until a tattered sleeve had joined them. Her strength grew with each tug at the dress, and within minutes the stone floor was littered with remnants of lace and satin.

In the midst of her misery she paused to look at the white wisps and wondered how something that had taken all those months to painstakingly cut and stitch and measure, could be destroyed in minutes. Something from the Sunday gospel about building a temple and tearing it down in three days came to her mind.

Where was God now? she thought bitterly. Where was the Sacrament of Matrimony that had gripped her in its thrall for the last year? Where was the power from all the candles she had lit to help her refuse Con Tierney's advances and help hold her tongue with Martina? How persuasive had all her prayers been that Patricia Quinn could cancel them out with a few minutes of lust?

She knew now that God was not on her side.

She had done everything the right way – done it according to the Holy Book. And what had she received in return? Nothing, only shame and humiliation.

She was just finishing off the bigger pieces with her pinking shears when a knock came on the door.

"Are you all right in there?" her brother's voice called from the other side.

Sarah froze.

The door handle twisted.

"Can I come in?" he asked, opening the door.

Sarah moved to block his view, but it was too late. James stood open-mouthed, looking at the sea of white on the floor, bed and furniture.

"Jaysus!" Martina said, looking over her husband's shoulder with wide eyes. "What have you done to the dress? It's in flitters!"

Their shocked gazes came to rest on Sarah now, and she knew there was no point in prevaricating. "It's off," she told them in a dull voice. "The wedding is all off."

"Have ye had a row?" Martina's brow wrinkled in confusion. "Ye both left here happy enough. It must have flared up very quick." She looked at the shreds of white lace and satin. "Mother of God, Sarah – you were a bit quick off the mark in destroying the dress over a silly row. There's no way you'll be able to sort that out before the wedding." She shrugged. "You'll have to buy a new one."

"It's off," Sarah repeated. "There isn't going to be any wedding. I wouldn't marry him now if he was the last man on earth."

Martina looked at the floor again. "You definitely lost the head with him. It must have been a serious row."

There was no point in dragging the whole thing out. They would have to know sooner or later.

Sarah took a deep breath.

"Patricia Quinn is expecting Con's baby."

The colour drained from James's face, and, for once, Martina Love was dumbstruck. Sarah had wished for this on many occasions, but fate decreed that on this occasion she hardly registered it, far less was able to enjoy it.

James recovered himself first. "Jesus Christ, Sarah . . ."

"My God!" Martina said in a low whisper. "My God . . . I don't believe it. I knew I was right about that one! I never liked that Patricia Quinn from the first time I clapped eyes on her." She paused. "But even so, I never thought she was capable of anything like that. Imagine her getting up to no good with an engaged man! She's nothing but a trollop and a whore!"

"Now, now – there's no good in name-calling," James told her. "And don't forget, there's two of them in it. It takes two to tango. Con Tierney has a lot to answer for."

Sarah sat silently on the edge of the bed, her shoulders hunched over.

"Come up into the kitchen and tell us all about it," Martina said, in a voice that was surprisingly kind.

"I don't really feel up to talking," Sarah said.

Martina came into the bedroom now, and went over and took Sarah's arm. "Come in now, and get it all off your chest."

When the two women were seated at the kitchen table, James went over to the cupboard next to the sink. "A drop of brandy might do us all no harm," he said, reaching for three mugs.

He poured a measure into each one, then three large spoonfuls of sugar, and then he lifted the recently boiled kettle and filled them up with hot water and brought them over to the table.

"I knew well there was something wrong the minute you came in," Martina told her, handing her a mug across the table. "I could see it on your face, and then I could hear all the ripping and pulling of the material. I thought you were going mad – I was so worried that I went out to the field to bring James in."

Sarah lifted her mug and took a sip of the hot, sweet drink. The first taste made her screw her face up, but as the warming golden liquid went down her throat, she found a comfort in it. She took another drink then said, "I can't marry him now. He's going to have to marry Patricia Quinn."

"The deceitful bitch," Martina started again. "I never liked her – nor anyone belonging to her." She sucked her breath in through her teeth. "Who told you and how long has their dirty business been going on?"

Sarah took another mouthful of the comforting drink and then started off.

Half an hour later when Sarah had said all there was to be said, James went off back into the field to finish off fixing the fence.

Sarah was relieved that no mention had been made of her having to stay on in the house with them now that her wedding plans were smashed. And, in all truthfulness, she had to admit that Martina had been much more supportive than she could have expected, given that she had always liked Con.

"I didn't like to say it in front of James," Martina said, thumbing towards the field outside where James was working, "but I've heard from various sources that she'd lie down with anyone. Sure, I know it myself – I've even caught her giving James the eye when she thought I wasn't looking." She rolled her eyes incredulously. "As if he would look at a scrawny, stuck-up thing like her."

Sarah nodded in agreement, knowing perfectly well that Martina was flattering herself. Patricia Quinn certainly wouldn't have been casting licentious glances at her old-fashioned, hen-pecked brother. Martina was safe enough. Unlike herself, who now had to live with the fact that her own future husband obviously hadn't any qualms going with the scrawny, stuck-up Patricia.

She thought of the red mark she'd left on his cheek and felt the tiniest flame of satisfaction.

"What are you going to do about all the wedding arrangements?" Martina asked. "You'll have to cancel everything . . ." She paused. "Is there no way you'd take him back and try to sort things out between ye?"

"Never," Sarah shot back. "Never in a million years. How could you sort out a situation like that? The best thing he can do now is marry Patricia Quinn and have done with it. As far as I'm concerned he's dead and gone."

Martina took a sip of her brandy then said, "Aren't you going to find it very awkward bumping into them around the town?"

Sarah looked blankly at her. "Of course I am, but what can I do? It's not my fault and I'm sure people will know that."

"Do you believe they were only together the one time, or do you think they were at it all the time?"

Sarah felt her throat tighten. She hadn't thought of that. "I don't know . . ." she answered, "and I don't care. Once is more than enough for me. There's no turning back now." She drained the last of the brandy from her mug and pushed her chair back. "If you don't mind I'm going to go into my bedroom now and tidy all that mess up."

"I was just thinking," Martina said, "you'd be better off starting with the priest. He'll have to know the wedding is off, and it would look bad if he hears it from someone in the town."

"Tomorrow," Sarah sighed. "I'll think about it all tomorrow."

CHAPTER 4

Father Kelly reached across the dining-room table in the Parochial House to pat Sarah's hand with his own broad-fingered one. "You'll be grand," he told her. "In a year or two's time you'll be thinking that it was all for the best. There are plenty of nice men who would be delighted to have a lovely girl like you."

The kind, elderly priest had dealt with numerous girls in Sarah's position over the years. Time, with the support of family and friends, was the only cure.

Tears engulfed Sarah's eyes. She couldn't imagine ever feeling anything other than shame, and the thought of feeling like this for the next year or two horrified her. "He's made a holy show of me, Father," she said, her voice frail and weary. "They've both made me look like the biggest fool in Tullamore."

She had hardly slept in the last forty-eight hours, and it showed in her pale face and the dark circles under her eyes. She hadn't been in to work in the hotel either. She came out in a cold sweat every time she pictured herself standing in front of the hotel manager explaining how her wedding was all off. She had avoided telling anyone so far, as James had been good enough to drive into town to let the hotel know she was sick and would be out for the next few days.

"Now, don't be saying things like that," Father Kelly told her. "Sure, it's only a nine-day wonder. They'll find someone else to talk about soon enough. If you heard the things that I've been told over the last number of years, your head would be reeling. Everyone has their own troubles."

But they're not public, Sarah thought. She couldn't say it to his face. It wasn't in her to contradict a priest.

Father Kelly studied her for a few moments. "How are things back at the house with James and Martina? I suppose Martina's not the easiest to live with at the best of times?"

Surprised, Sarah lifted her head to look at him. She had never talked personally to him before, and she certainly wouldn't have said anything to him about her sister-in-law. "She's been very good, considering they're now stuck with me."

"Ah, she's a decent enough woman," the priest said tactfully. "And your brother is the finest, but I suppose they'd like to have the place to themselves. "Have you thought what you're going to do now?"

Sarah wasn't sure if the priest was referring to her immediate problems over the wedding or her longer term plans – which she'd given no thought to. "I'm cancelling everything," she told him. "I've come to tell you first and then I'm going to go into town to let the hotel and the flower shop know."

"Wouldn't it be easier on you to tell them over the phone?" He nodded out towards the hall. "Why don't you use the phone here?"

Sarah looked at him. "I wouldn't be sure of the number or anything . . . or what to say." Although she occasionally answered the phone in the hotel reception if there was no one else around, she had rarely had the occasion to actually dial a number herself.

Father Kelly stood up. "Sure that's no problem, I'll do it for you," he said. "It's just a matter of looking up the number in the book."

As he went out into the hallway to get the directory Sarah felt a great sense of relief. A phone call would save her the embarrassment of explaining the situation face to face.

A few moments later he came back into the dining-room carrying the phone directory. "That's all sorted with the hotel. Jimmy Butler is an understanding man so I didn't have to say too much." He raised his eyebrows. "He said you might call in when you feel up to it and he'll do what he can regarding the deposit on the meal."

Sarah's eyes filled up with tears. When would she ever feel up to facing people? She nodded her head. "Thank you, Father. I'm very grateful."

He put the directory down on the dining-table and then he opened it and started to search through it. "There's the florist's phone number now," he said, stabbing a finger at a point on the page. "Now, be a good girl and go out into the hallway and give them a ring."

Her throat tightened. The woman in the flower shop had been very chatty and friendly, asking her about her dress and giving advice on which flowers would look best.

Father Kelly moved towards the door. "I'll call the number out to you, and you dial it," he told her. "You just have to tell them that due to unforeseen circumstances the wedding has been cancelled, and you wanted to be sure to give them plenty of notice." He saw the hesitation on her face so he went over to the phone table in the hall and picked up the receiver, then held it out to her. "Good girl!" he said, winking at her when she eventually took the phone off him.

Fifteen minutes later as Sarah cycled back up to the cottage, she felt a slight sense of relief. She had now started the process of dismantling all her wedding plans but she still had a number of things to sort out. Her next task was to visit her other bridesmaid Sheila and tell her the humiliating news. She supposed she should be comforted by the fact that anyone who knew her and Con well would be as shocked as she was. Con's family would be disgusted by the carry-on between him and Patricia Quinn and his mother wouldn't waste any time telling him. She would be straight down to the priest asking him to come up and talk to Con and hear his confession of the terrible thing he had done. His sister, Orla, who was two years older than Sarah – and got on great with her – would be devastated.

Whilst Sarah knew everyone would be on her side, it did nothing to assuage the feelings of rejection and failure which overwhelmed her.

She got off the bike at the cottage and took a deep breath before going inside to face Martina's interrogation about the latest developments. At least she could tell her that she had cancelled most of the bookings to do with the wedding and say how understanding and helpful Father Kelly had been.

Then they would both do their best to tip-toe around the subject of Sarah's future living arrangements.

* * *

Sheila was of the same opinion as Martina. "The skinny, sharp-nosed fecking trollop!" she said, banging the kitchen table when she heard the news.

Sarah had to tell her to keep her voice down as she couldn't face going over the whole story with Mrs Walsh.

"Tell me you're kidding me? Surely Con Tierney wouldn't look twice at that rake of a thing when he has a far lovelier girl?"

"It obviously wasn't just a lovely girl he was looking for," Sarah said, her face white and tense, "it was a girl who would give him what he wanted."

"You poor oul' divil," Sheila said, coming to put her arms around her friend. "Are you all right?"

Sarah shrugged. "It's like being in the middle of your worst nightmare, but you wake up and you're still living it. I just keep hoping that it will all go away."

"I can't believe it," Sheila said, remembering to lower her voice again. "Patricia fecking Quinn – who thinks she's better than everybody else – getting up to no good with her best friend's boyfriend a fortnight before the wedding! It would have been bad enough if it she had been expecting to her *own* boyfriend – she'd still be the talk of the town. But it takes some class of a girl to do what she's done with a lad she hasn't been courting." She shook her head. "How would you go baring your body to a lad you've never even kissed?" She had little or no experience of men and from what she had heard of the sex act, it was something she was in no rush to try. "I'll tell you, Sarah, she's no better than a common whore and now the whole town will know it."

"She's not the type to care too much what others say."

Sheila raised her eyebrows. "Can you imagine what her mother had to say about it? She'd have no doubt tried to put a good face on it if Patricia had a boyfriend. She's the kind who would have arranged a hurried wedding, pretending it was a honeymoon baby, but she'll have a hard time talking her way out of this one."

Sarah gave a weary sigh. "I'd imagine she'll talk them into getting married as soon as possible."

"Do you think so? Now, no offence or anything, but I would have imagined that Mrs Quinn was looking for someone a cut above Con Tierney as Patricia's husband." Then, she caught the look on Sarah's face. "I think a painter and decorator is fine, but if she had her way, Patricia would be marrying a teacher or a doctor or someone like that." Her eyes narrowed. "Mind you, I wouldn't be a bit surprised if Patricia had her eye on Con all along. Any time we were all out together she was always laughing at his jokes and hanging on every word he said."

"I never noticed," Sarah said quietly. "I never imagined for a minute that there would be anything between them." She looked over her friend's shoulder to the window and the green fields beyond. "It makes you realise you don't know anything in life – I think nothing will ever shock me again." She turned back to Sheila. "All the months of me making sure that Con kept his hands to himself. I thought we only had a few weeks to get through and then I'd put up with whatever I was supposed to do. If the truth be told, I was dreading our wedding night. The thought of it frightened me." Tears welled up in her eyes. "I just can't understand how someone would just do it on the spur of the moment the way Patricia did."

"I wonder was he the first?" Sheila mused. "Or whether she's had other lads before? I suppose we're never going to know."

Sarah's gaze went back to the window again. At times she felt she was still in a weird dream, and that she would wake up and things might just go back to normal again.

Sheila sighed. "Well, they're stuck with each other for life now whether they like it or not." She drummed her fingers on the table now, thinking. "If they get married, I wonder if they'll stay here in Tullamore or move away. It would be the right and decent thing for them to go and not have you constantly bumping into them around the town." She paused. "If they do decide to brazen it out and stay here, what will you do?"

Sarah looked over at her, wondering if her friend was actually enjoying all the drama. "I haven't thought about it," she said. "I'm still going around explaining that the wedding is off, and I haven't thought beyond that yet."

After a cup of tea Sarah stood up to go, weary from going the whole thing over and over again. And she still had to make the journey back through town to get home without meeting anyone.

The whole scenario was never-ending, as each person she told wanted to express their shock and indignation over it, and then ask her further questions she hadn't even thought of herself.

She supposed couldn't really blame them. It was only human nature. And amazingly, the more people she spoke to, the more matter-of-fact she heard herself sounding. She was getting used to people knowing what had happened. Maybe Father Kelly was right. Maybe it was only a nine-day wonder.

Maybe sometime in the future she might have a conversation again that didn't centre around Con Tierney and Patricia Quinn.

CHAPTER 5

The town was quiet and Sarah cycled back with her gaze kept firmly ahead. She parked the bike at the side of the house and, just as she went towards the cottage, Martina came rushing out.

"I thought I heard the bike on the stones," she said, looking all flustered, "and I thought I'd better warn you. You've had nothing but visitors since you left."

"Who?" Sarah asked.

"Con Tierney called up an hour ago, saying he needed to talk to you." Martina rolled her eyes. "As you can imagine, I gave him a very cool reception."

"Thank God I missed him," Sarah said, giving a weary sigh. "He's the last person I want to speak to."

"He said he'll call back later," Martina informed her, as they started walking towards the front door. Martina indicated towards the two black bicycles which were parked against the wall. "And Father Kelly and Miss Reynolds are here to see you."

Miss Reynolds was Sarah's old National School teacher who lived nearby. She was retired now, but she still kept a keen interest in her old pupils.

"*Miss Reynolds?*" A feeling of shame and humiliation washed over Sarah. It was bad enough that the priest knew all that had happened, but the thought of facing her old schoolteacher made it worse.

"They arrived about ten minutes ago and I've made them a cup of tea." Her eyes shone and Sarah realised that whilst Martina was horrified by her sister-in-law's public jilting – and its future implications for her and James – there was a part of the drama she was actually enjoying. "Father Kelly is such a lovely man, and Miss Reynolds has been very nice too," she prattled now. "She was saying what a great seamstress you are, and what a lovely job you made of her tweed skirt last winter."

Sarah nodded, hardly noticing the fact that Martina had paid her a rare compliment. She walked towards the kitchen, offering a silent prayer that she would have the energy to cope with yet another excruciating conversation.

The visitors were seated at the kitchen table. The priest stood up when Sarah came in. "I was talking about you to Miss Reynolds, Sarah, and we thought we'd take a trip up to see how you are today."

"I'm grand, Father." Sarah was aware that her strained voice sounded anything but grand. "I'll survive." She looked over at her old teacher. "Hello, Miss Reynolds. It was nice of you to call up."

Kitty Reynolds stood up now and came around the table to take her old pupil's hands in hers. "Well, Sarah, I know underneath it all you're a strong girl, and I know you'll get through this. In fact, it could be the making of you."

Sarah gulped. Whilst the old-fashioned, strict teacher had always been encouraging towards her – even after Sarah had moved on to secondary school – she had never shown her any kind of physical affection before.

When the teacher let go of her hands, Sarah sat down at the table. "I've sorted out a few more things," she said looking from the teacher to the priest. "So it's a case of trying get back to normal now."

Father Kelly studied at her closely. "Take it easy now – don't be too hard on yourself. You've had a hard knock and it could take a while to get over it."

"I was thinking the very same thing myself," Martina chipped in, as though anxious to be included in the conversation.

Sarah nodded slowly. There was something about priest's demeanour that made her think he and Miss Reynolds wanted to say more. Then she wondered if he didn't want to speak out in front of her sister-in-law. She looked down at his empty teacup. "Would either of you would like another cup of tea?" she asked, getting to her feet.

"I've had plenty," the teacher said.

"And you, Father?" Sarah checked.

"No, no," he said, holding his hand up, "Martina has looked after us well. I've already had two cups and a big slice of apple tart." He patted his stomach. "Sure, I have to look after me figure!" He gave a big hearty laugh.

"What about a drink?" Martina asked, looking from the priest to the teacher. "A little whiskey or brandy?"

"Not at all, we have to be going," he said, speaking for them both. "I'll take you up on the drink another time. I have to make a few sick calls in the evening, and it wouldn't look well if I was breathing alcohol fumes all over them." He laughed again, then he looked at his watch and got to his feet. "We must go now. I have to look in on old Mrs Doherty on my way back."

They thanked Martina for the tea and cake, and Sarah went outside to see her guests off. They collected their bicycles and then Sarah held the gate open wide for them to walk the bikes out.

When they got out onto the road, the priest looked back at the cottage. "We were hoping for a private word," he told her. "We didn't like to be talking in front of Martina . . ."

Miss Reynolds looked at Sarah. "I have an idea that might help you out of your difficulty." The teacher took a deep breath. "I wonder would you consider taking a little break away from Tullamore. Away from Ireland?"

"What kind of a break?"

"I have a distant cousin over in England – Newcastle-upon-Tyne to be exact. Lucy – an unmarried lady in her late thirties. I was speaking to her on the phone only last night. She has a business – a wool and sewing shop – in the centre of Newcastle city. I've been over there to visit her several times." She waved her hands. "I won't waste time going into unnecessary details. Anyway, it seems she has a vacancy for a young woman in the shop at the moment, and I wondered if you might be interested. I told her I could vouch for your sewing skills, and that you've made me various things over the years." She raised her eyebrows in question now.

Sarah's stomach lurched. She had only been to Dublin twice in her life and a few times to Galway. The thought of going to England seemed like being asked to fly to the moon.

When he saw the look of shock on her face, Father Kelly tried to reassure her. "Newcastle is a nice, friendly place in the North of England. I've been there once myself. It has a beautiful cathedral."

"There are plenty of Irish over there," the teacher went on. "The woman who usually works in the shop has to look after a sick relative. It might only be for a few months, but I thought of you straight away . . . I thought it would get you over this awkward period."

Father Kelly smiled encouragingly. "By the time you come back, things could be settled here and the wedding business all forgotten."

If only that was true, Sarah thought. He obviously didn't know how small-minded and vicious people could be. If he spent a few days in Martina's company he might just get an idea of how things really were. Lying in the dark at night, she had wished she could just disappear for a while – maybe even forever – but in the daylight, the reality of moving to a big, strange country was every bit as frightening.

"I'm not sure, Father . . . I've never been to England. I wouldn't know where the place was or anything."

"Ah, sure that's no problem." He smiled reassuringly at her. "If you decide you are interested, Miss Reynolds can easily advise you on the boat times and all that kind of thing."

The teacher looked her in the eye. "I'm not expecting an answer immediately. I told Lucy about you – said what a talented, clever girl you are. Exactly what she needs. I said I'd have a word with you, and get back to her in the next few days when you've had a chance to think it over."

Sarah nodded her head. "Thank you for thinking of me."

Miss Reynolds lifted her calf-length dirndl skirt up a few inches and put a leg onto her sturdy old bike. "Take your time and drop down to me when you've decided one way or another."

"I will . . ."

The priest put his black hat on. "Look after yourself now, and I'm keeping you in my prayers. We'll find some way to help you out of this situation, one way or another."

Sarah suddenly realised that the priest had obviously been racking his brains and had gone to ask the teacher for her assistance. Tears suddenly welled up in her eyes at their concern and kindness.

"Drop down to the Parochial House if you want to chat anything over," he said, tipping his hat.

The elderly pair set off cycling in a rather unsteady manner, but straightened up as they gathered speed and disappeared down the hill.

As Sarah went back into the cottage, she decided to say nothing about the priest's suggestion. Her situation was certainly desperate, but to move to another country to escape from it was surely too drastic? Although even as she thought it, she realised that neither the priest nor Miss Reynolds reckoned it was too drastic.

Martina was washing up at the sink. She turned to Sarah. "Wasn't that nice of them coming up to see how you are?"

"It was. I have a headache and I'm going to have a lie down for an hour."

As she put her head on the pillow, Sarah realised that she had been afraid to mention the visitors' suggestion to Martina. She knew that it would suit her sister-in-law very well if she had somewhere else to go, whether it was in Ireland or further afield.

Neither she nor James had said anything outright about being stuck with her now, but Sarah knew it was only a matter of time.

As it was only a matter of time until she had to face other people. She would have to go into work the day after tomorrow and suffer the sympathy and questions she knew would be showered on her by the other staff.

And she now had to face another visit from Con again. She would have to make sure she was geared up for him whatever he had to say.

Sarah buried her face in the pillow. When would it all end?

* * *

A knock came on Sarah's bedroom door. Martina stuck her head in. "You have visitors again," she said. Her voice dropped to a whisper. "It's Con along with his mother. Me and James are going out for a short walk to let you chat on your own."

Sarah's heart sank like a stone in shallow water.

She had prepared herself for another visit from Con again – had rehearsed what she was going to say – but what on earth was his mother coming up to the cottage for? She had never had any reason to set foot in it before. She dragged herself into a sitting position and then got up to check her appearance in the dressing-table mirror. Her face looked paler than she'd ever seen before. She lifted her powder compact and rubbed the little velvet pad over her face and she gave her hair a quick brush. Then she took a deep breath and went out to the kitchen. The tall, dark-haired Con and his shorter, sturdy-looking mother were standing by the kitchen table.

"Sarah . . ." Con said, moving across the floor to greet her. "We need to have a good talk."

Sarah side-stepped him and put her hands behind her back. "We've done all the talking that needs to be done." Ingrained good manners made her look over to acknowledge her other visitor. "Hello, Mrs Tierney. I suppose you know the whole story?"

"I do," she said. "But there's news you don't know yet, and I've come up with Con to make sure you hear the right story."

Sarah looked at the woman who would have been her mother-in-law. She straightened up, her arms folded defensively in front of her. "I don't want to be disrespectful to you, Mrs Tierney, but there's no point in wasting your breath."

Mrs Tierney's eyes flitted over to her son and then back to Sarah. "What went on was disgraceful," she said, "and there's no excusing it. But from what Con tells me, it was a moment of madness that he'll regret for the rest of his life."

Sarah nodded her head, deliberately keeping her gaze away from him. "We'll all regret it," she said, feeling the same hot anger beginning to rise inside her that she'd felt the night she had slapped his face.

"But things have changed," Mrs Tierney said. "She's . . . Patricia Quinn went into hospital yesterday morning and she's lost the baby."

Sarah caught her breath – and then realised she felt no raging anger, no confusion, no great waves of emotion. Just a dull, flat nothingness. What happened to her the night that Con told her about him and her bridesmaid had killed off any feelings for him.

"If you are willing," Con said in a low voice, "we can go back to where we were before this business all happened. I promise that I'll make it up to you, I'm not saying it will be easy for you but –"

"This *business*?" Sarah snapped. "Is that what you call it? *This business?*" She started to laugh now – a high hysterical laugh. She looked from mother to son. "You honestly think I would even consider taking you back?"

Mrs Tierney came over to touch her arm. "Now, Sarah," she said, a slight tremor in her voice, "there's no point in throwing everything away. Apart from this one mistake – this one *bad* mistake – you and Con have got on just grand. And the family all think the world of you. Poor Orla is devastated by all this carry-on." Tears suddenly came into her eyes. "He's been a stupid, stupid lad . . . but if you can just see it in your heart to forgive him, he'll make it up to you." She looked over at her son – her eyes appealing to him.

"I'll do anything," Con said quickly. "You've no idea how much

I regret what happened, and I'll go on regretting it for the rest of my life."

Sarah's eyes narrowed. "And Patricia Quinn? Does she regret it too? Have you both talked about it? Have you been to see her since she lost the child?"

Con lowered his head. "I went up to the house to see her this morning."

"It was only the decent thing," his mother said. "I made him do it. He had to see her face to face – there were the two of them in it – and he had to see her and make things right before coming to see you."

Sarah imagined the scene with Patricia and her mother up at the house, and knew without a doubt that there would be no welcome for him. She sat down on the old pine chair, folded her arms, and then looked at the man who she had thought would be her husband. "Tell me what was said. Tell me what you and Patricia discussed."

Con's hands came up to his face now. "Oh, Sarah . . . do we have to go through this? Is it going to make it any better?"

"I want to know what you both said." Her voice was cool and calm. She knew he would find the explanations excruciatingly embarrassing, but she didn't care.

He took a deep breath. "It was all said the other night, even before she went into hospital," he told her. "We both knew we had made a mighty mistake . . . I think she's relieved now it's all over, and I know I am."

"That's very convenient for you," she said. "But no matter what you both feel now, you'll always know that you had that between you. It will always be there."

"There's plenty been in the situation before and got over it," Mrs Tierney said. "There's only ourselves and yourselves, and the Quinns, who know anything about it."

"And Father Kelly," Sarah said, "and all the business people I had to cancel for the wedding."

"*Cancel*?" the older woman said. "Have you been to the priest

46

already? Have you cancelled the wedding breakfast and everything?" She shook her head. "Oh, dear God!"

"I have," Sarah told her, feeling a stab of satisfaction that they hadn't even considered she might do that.

"You were very quick off the mark," Con said.

"Not as quick as you were to ruin all our plans," Sarah retorted.

There was a most uneasy silence.

Then, Mrs Tierney, undaunted, started again. "What we need to keep in mind here," she said, "is that there was only *one* occasion of madness, and it's all over and done with. Both Con and Patricia Quinn want to forget that it all happened and get on with their lives, and both the families want to put it behind them." She gave Sarah a little reassuring smile. "It's you and him that belong together – and always did. Con wants the chance to show you how much he's learned from the mistake, and he'll spend the rest of his life making it up to you." She looked over at her son. "He's a hard-working lad, and he'll make sure there's always food on the table and turf on the fire. He'll never look at another woman as long as he lives."

"How can you ask me to forget what's happened?" Sarah said, an incredulous look on her face.

She looked over at Con now and his gaze caught hers. In that moment she saw the pain and the guilt in his eyes and she knew with an inexplicable certainty that he had learned his lesson, and she would never have to worry about him being unfaithful again. His whole demeanour told her that the last few days had devastated him and made him realise that he had risked their whole future together.

She knew that if she could find the strength to forgive him that she would have the upper hand with him – that he would always be trying to make up for his terrible mistake. If she could remind herself that his relationship with Patricia Quinn amounted to nothing more than a few minutes of madness out of a few years of a good steady courtship. If she could forgive Con, she could go ahead with the wedding plans – the date for the church and the hotel would be unlikely to be snapped up by someone else since yesterday – and she could escape from Martina and James as she had been so desperate to do.

Why should she throw everything away for the sake of one indiscretion? Other people got over things – and so could she.

"If you agree to put this behind us," Con said, "I promise you that you'll never regret it."

"I'm glad you came up today," her voice was steady, "as it's helped me to see things more clearly. I need to get away from this house . . . I need to have a fresh start."

"We *will* have a fresh start," Con reassured her. "We'll have a whole new life together."

"Yes, we will . . . but it won't be *together*."

"Now don't be talking like that," Mrs Tierney pleaded.

Sarah held her hand up. "It's all finished between you and me, Con. I can never forgive you or Patricia Quinn for what you've done."

"You can't mean it," Mrs Tierney gasped. "You can't throw everything away!"

"It was Con who threw it away, not me."

There was a short silence during which things suddenly seemed clear to Sarah. Glaringly clear.

She went across to the door and opened it wide. "I'd be grateful if you left now as there's nothing more to be said."

Mrs Tierney walked out first, dabbing her eyes.

Con halted at the door. "I'll give you time," he said. "I'll wait as long as it takes for you to forgive me."

Sarah looked him straight in the eyes. "Don't waste your time," she told him. "I wouldn't take you now if you were the last man on earth."

CHAPTER 6

Newcastle-Upon-Tyne

On Saturday afternoon Lucy Harrison locked the door of her sewing shop and then turned towards the lane, her head bent against the slight breeze that lifted strands of her long, curly dark hair. She walked up the cobbled Pilgrims Lane, giving a brief greeting to any of the other shopkeepers she met on her way. She never stopped to chat to any of them. No one would have expected it, as by now they were used to her quiet, self-conscious manner.

As she walked towards the busier streets at the centre of the city, she was preoccupied with thoughts of the girl who would be travelling tonight from Ireland to begin work in the shop on Monday.

Lucy felt she had been caught unawares by the phone call from her father's cousin, Kitty Reynolds, and almost railroaded into making an instant decision about taking the girl on. When Kitty realised that Lucy was running the sewing shop on her own, she had said that she had the perfect assistant for her – Sarah Love. The elderly teacher had briefly explained the girl's position – something to do with a broken engagement very close to the wedding – and how it had caused a lot of bitterness and gossip. She said it would be better for Sarah to move away until the dust had all settled.

Lucy wasn't at all sure she wanted a young girl working in the shop with her. At times she had even found the presence of Mary – her previous helper – to be intrusive. It wasn't that there was a single thing wrong with the pleasant, middle-aged woman; it was more the effort of having to talk to her when she didn't feel like it and pretend to be interested when she had more serious things on her mind.

Working on her own might be harder some days, but at least she could retreat to the kitchen at the back of the shop without feeling she had to explain herself.

When Lucy had hesitated about taking on the responsibility of a girl leaving Ireland for the first time, Kitty Reynolds had reassured her that Sarah Love would be no trouble.

"Once she gets over this bit of an upset, Sarah will be grand," the teacher said. "It will do her the world of good to see a different country and different people. And you can rest assured that she is a hard worker and the finest seamstress you could ever come across."

"But won't she miss her family and friends?" Lucy had said. "And she might find a big city very hard to adapt to after living all her life in the country."

"She only has a brother and his wife at home," Miss Reynolds had said, "and they can't wait to be rid of the poor girl."

Lucy had given one last shot at trying to put the teacher off. "To be honest," she had said, "I'm more used to working with an older woman. I'm not sure how good I would be at handling a young girl. It's something I have no experience of."

But Miss Reynolds was determined in her plan. "Sarah's not a giddy sort. You couldn't have anyone better. I taught her and she was one of the brightest girls in the school. She learns quickly and easily and has a great way with people – young and old. And if you put that together with her sewing skills, it makes her the perfect shop assistant for you." The teacher had paused for a few moments to let it all sink in.

"I'm just not sure . . ." Lucy said.

"Give her a try," Kitty said, "and if it doesn't work out you can just send her home again. It's as easy as that. If you can even keep her for a few weeks it would be a great help to the girl, to get her over this. God knows she needs someone to give her a helping hand and I know you're the right person to do it."

Lucy wasn't at all sure about that, but in the end she found herself agreeing, just to end the uncomfortable phone call.

It was only when she hung up the receiver and went to make a cup of tea that it dawned on her that the teacher had meant the coming weekend which was only a few days away.

Sarah Love would be travelling overnight on Saturday to arrive on Sunday.

CHAPTER 7

It was a clear, dry Saturday evening when James drove Sarah up to Dublin for the boat to Liverpool. He parked the car outside the terminal and then carried her new case over to the ticket office. It was a big case, packed to capacity with the winter clothes she had stitched the previous year, and as many summer outfits she could squeeze in. The trip was not a holiday and she didn't know if or when she would return to Tullamore.

"I'm fierce sorry for the way things have turned out." James put the case down between them. "I'd never have thought that Con Tierney would have done the dirty on you like that." He rubbed his chin. "Who would believe it? Just over a week ago we were all talk about weddings, and now you're leaving for England."

Sarah looked at her brother. She couldn't remember a single time when he or Martina had been "all talk" about her wedding. Is that what he really thought? He had said very little about the wedding, and had even left it to his wife to say he would pay for it.

James suddenly touched her arm. "I hope you're not going because of the new babby? We could always have made space for you . . . maybe built another room on or something. I wouldn't like you to think we wouldn't give you a home."

Sarah swallowed back the bitter response on her tongue. He had said nothing of that in the last few days. He had made no effort to talk her out of going. He had sat silently while his wife did all the talking. Just listening, while Martina said what a great opportunity it was for her, and how England would be the making of her.

He hadn't argued when Martina said that people would only be talking and laughing behind her back about what Con Tierney and Patricia Quinn had done, and that she'd be better off finding herself a decent fellow over in England.

The one redeeming thing that James had done was give her two hundred pounds when they stopped off for a cup of tea in Kinnegad this evening. He'd slid the folded envelope across the scratched wooden table, saying, "That will help you to get on your feet. I'd put some of it by for your wedding and I added a bit more to it."

Sarah had opened it and when she saw all the ten-pound notes she realised that this was her "Goodbye and Good Luck" money. That this was James's way of easing his conscience about turning her out of the family home.

It was better than nothing, and more than she had expected of him. She didn't protest.

After giving her the money, James had turned towards the window. For a few moments he appeared to be thinking deeply.

"It's a fine evening," he said then, looking off into the distance. "A red sky coming up. You'll have a good crossing."

Sarah remained silent. What did her brother know about good crossings? What did he know about *anything*? He'd never been out of Ireland in his life. He had rarely been out of Tullamore. The odd trip to Dublin and Galway had been his furthest travels. And yet, here he was, waving her off to a new life on a cattle-boat full of strangers.

* * *

She had decided not to book a berth on the overnight boat, as Miss Reynolds had warned her that you never knew who you could end up sharing with. The teacher said she had once travelled with a drunken Dublin woman who had alternatively sung or been sick all night. Better to find a quiet corner on the boat beside decent people, who would keep an eye on your things while you slept or went to the toilet. Sarah had also taken her advice about keeping her purse inside her clothes, and had worn a jacket with a zipped inside pocket under her coat.

When she arrived up in the passenger lounge, Sarah had looked around her, and then spotted an empty, vinyl-padded bench behind a well-dressed couple with two sleeping small children. It looked as good as she was likely to get. It was away from the bar and out of the main passageways where people would be wandering, or staggering, up and down.

After a cursory conversation with the couple – who told her they were from Carlow and going over to a wedding in Liverpool – she settled down on the bench. She sat for a while, reading her book and watching the other passengers. Then, when the boat moved off, she looked out of the porthole behind her until the land had disappeared and all she could see was grey water. As the dim evening slipped into complete darkness, Sarah decided she might as well try to get some sleep. She took a thick cardigan from her case and wrapped it around her handbag to use as a pillow, and then she put her coat over her as a blanket.

The trip was long and tedious, but calm and relatively quiet. She ate little and slowly to make sure she didn't feel sick, and even though the boat had given the occasional lurch, she had been fine. The only problem was the drunks who did the rounds of the floor – whistling or singing – to see who they could engage in chat. Most of the time Sarah had kept her eyes closed – even when she wasn't trying to sleep – so as not to encourage anyone to sit beside her.

She must have slept for a few hours, because when she woke the boat was totally silent. All the noisy drunks and singers were asleep. Sarah shifted into a sitting position, turned to look out of the porthole behind her and saw the sun coming up over the sea. It was such an unexpected, beautiful sight that she blessed herself in thanks. Then, she lay back down and murmured *The Memorare* prayer to Our Lady, asking her for a safe journey to Newcastle and the strength to cope with her new life.

CHAPTER 8

After queuing for ages to disembark, Sarah arrived at the docks in Liverpool and then took a double-decker bus into the city centre. She was tired as she had slept little, and felt in need of a proper wash. Before the boat had docked she had gone to the ladies' toilets and changed her underwear and done her best to freshen up with a facecloth.

The bus dropped her off outside Liverpool Lime Street station, and after a two-hour wait she caught the train up to Newcastle-Upon-Tyne.

Being a Sunday, the train was quiet, so she dozed on and off and was almost startled when she heard her stop being announced. She quickly pulled her coat and hat on, and then lifted her handbag and book and made for the luggage area to retrieve her case.

When she stepped out onto the platform, she had to stop for a few minutes to take in the size of Newcastle station, and negotiate her way out. She asked a porter and he told her to go up the steps and across the bridge to the entrance, which took her another five minutes as she struggled with her heavy case.

Lucy Harrison was waiting for her outside the ticket barrier as arranged. Miss Reynolds had described her cousin accurately –

medium height, very slim with shoulder-length, black curly hair. She was wearing dark slacks under her Burberry raincoat.

Sarah's heart quickened when she got closer to the barrier. The teacher hadn't mentioned the deep frown-lines on the shopkeeper's forehead and the fine but noticeable streaks of silver through her black hair. But those features concerned Sarah least; it was the pale face and the distracted, heavy look in her eyes as she came forward to greet her that bothered her.

"How do you do? I'm Lucy Harrison," she said, in a clear clipped English accent. Her hand came out to shake Sarah's. She gave a brief smile which went nowhere near her dark eyes.

"I'm Sarah . . ." Her throat felt hoarse. "Sarah Love."

"I hope your journey wasn't too bad? It's a long haul from Ireland, isn't it?"

"It was grand," Sarah said. There was no point in starting off on the wrong foot by complaining about how little sleep she'd had. She had arrived safe and well and that was all that mattered.

"I see a trolley over there." Lucy pointed. "Your case looks very heavy and I think it would be easier if we wheeled it out to the car. Stay there and I'll get it for you."

While she was gone, Sarah looked up at the big station clock and saw that it was half past three. She had lost all sense of time, and suddenly realised it was Sunday and she hadn't been to Mass. Her heart sank. It was too late now. There was nothing she could do, and it hadn't been deliberate. She would visit the nearest church or the cathedral as soon as she could to make up for it.

Her mind flitted back to Tullamore and she wondered if people had stood outside the church in Harbour Street this morning discussing her absence. News travelled very quickly, and it would only take a couple of weeks of her missing Mass, for people to know that she had moved away. By now, more and more people would know the reason behind it.

She wondered if Con and Patricia Quinn had thought of her this morning when they knelt at the altar. She wondered if they would see or even acknowledge each other if they met. For all she knew, they could be back together, safe in the knowledge that she was on the other side of the Irish Sea.

James had sorted things out with her job in the hotel and had gone in to pick up her wages. The only person she had told face to face about her move away was Sheila who had not tried to dissuade her or tell her she was mad for leaving. She had just put her arms around her and said she would miss her, and promised to write to her every week.

Sarah could imagine the local postman, Kevin O'Reilly, delivering the letters she would send back to her friend. "That's one from over the water," he would state, "Going by the handwriting, I'd say it's from the young Love girl. Wasn't it a terrible pity about the wedding?"

Tears welled up in her eyes at the thought of all the familiar people and places she had left behind.

Sarah suddenly caught herself and drew her thoughts back to the present.

The shopkeeper came back a few moments later and helped Sarah to lift the case onto the trolley and then they walked across the expansive station and through the portico entrance, to where Lucy Harrison's blue Austin Somerset car was parked.

"I've organised a room for you in Victoria Street," the shopkeeper explained as they turned out of the station and left up the main road. "A business acquaintance of mine owns it, and it's a fine big house with five or six bedrooms and a bathroom. I think he has four already sharing it at the moment." She paused. "It must be three if he has one of the rooms to spare. He has nurses in it and two students from the Medical College."

Sarah felt a pang of alarm. What would medical students feel about sharing a house with a shop assistant? She didn't mind the nurses so much – theirs was a more ordinary sort of job – but sharing with a trainee doctor was a different matter. That was much more professional and educated. Then, she told herself not to be so silly. Lodgers from all kinds of background shared houses. One of the teachers at her school back in Tullamore had lodged with people who owned a shop. She would make sure there was no problem sharing with whoever else was in the house. She was as respectable as anyone else and she would be quiet and tidy around the place which was all anyone could ask.

The house was in a small cul-de-sac, just off the main road, in a row of around ten large houses on either side of the street. The Austin pulled up outside the second house from the top. Whatever fears Sarah had concealed on her journey over from Ireland, she felt them rise to the surface as she walked up the path, then climbed the half a dozen steps to the front door of the tall, grey-stone building. From what she could see, there were three floors plus a basement with windows under the stairs.

Lucy Harrison lifted the heavy brass knocker and tapped it three times. They waited a minute or so and then she knocked again – louder this time. The door was opened and a young woman with short brown hair and dark-rimmed spectacles stood looking at them.

"I've brought your new lodger," Lucy said, indicating Sarah.

The girl's eyes widened as she took in the heavy suitcase. "We weren't told anything about a new person . . ."

"Mr Spencer organised it. He said there was a spare room?"

The little knot of anxiety in Sarah's stomach suddenly grew, making her feel she was either going to be sick or need to use the toilet very soon.

"I was away yesterday," the girl said. "Maybe he told one of the others. Why don't you come in and wait while I check?"

As she went off down the corridor, Lucy motioned to Sarah to come into the hallway with her.

As they waited, Sarah looked to her left at the dark wooden staircase, which she could see went up two more floors. Her gaze then went directly in front to the hallway which had two wide, painted doorways leading off into rooms and another staircase at the bottom, which she deduced led down into the basement.

The short-haired girl came out of the room at the bottom of the corridor. She smiled and held her hands up as she came towards them. "Sorry about that. Apparently Mr Spencer was out at the house yesterday with a helper and they've sorted one of the rooms upstairs. I was working and didn't know anything about it." She stretched her hand out to Sarah. "I'm Elizabeth Appleby, pleased to meet you."

Just as Sarah was shaking hands with her, another girl appeared behind her with blonde curly hair.

"And this is Jane – Jane Phillips. We're both nurses in the Infirmary."

"And I'm Sarah Love." A flush rose from her neck to her face as she introduced herself, knowing that the questions about why she had moved to Newcastle would inevitably follow.

After Lucy Harrison left, the girls showed Sarah up to her room. Although she was tired and anxious about everything, she felt a real sense of relief when they opened the door. It was a much bigger bedroom than she had expected and well furnished, with a double bed, dressing-table and stool, wardrobe and tallboy. There was also a bedside cabinet with a small lamp, and a deep-buttoned, blue velvet armchair by the bay window.

"This is lovely." She put her case down in a corner.

It was much better than anything she had hoped for. She cast her eye over it again, and quickly reckoned it was at least three times the size of her bedroom back home. On a second look, she could see the furniture was slightly scuffed and scratched in places, and the velvet chair and the cream and blue curtains were faded. But they had been good quality in their day and had been reasonably well looked after. The bay windows were tall and wide, and Sarah liked the way the light came through the coloured stained-glass panels at the top.

She followed the girls back downstairs, and they showed her the bathroom. Sarah looked at the white bath with the curved legs and the big white porcelain sink, and the toilet with the chain and handle for flushing. She said nothing about the toilet facilities she was used to back home – the makeshift dry toilet they used in the wooden structure out the back of the kitchen, and the big tin bath she carried into her bedroom twice a week.

"We buy our own soap and shampoo," Jane said, "and each of us has our own towels. We have a big double sink and spinner in the kitchen for doing our washing, and there are two lines outside to hang it out to dry."

The nurses then took her into the big kitchen which also served as a dining-room and sitting room.

Sarah pointed to a polished wooden cabinet. "Is that a radiogram?"

"Yes, aren't we terribly posh?" Elizabeth laughed. "Mr Spencer brought it round last Christmas when he heard that two of us were working over the holidays. They were buying a new one and said we could have this for the house, as long as we looked after it. It's the one thing in the house that gets a daily polish."

Sarah suddenly felt the tension starting to drain out of her. The girls were obviously nice and friendly, and making her as welcome as they could. She quickly got the explanations about leaving Ireland out of the way. The conversation turned out easier than she had imagined, as both girls had moved up to Newcastle from Liverpool and Durham, and accepted the fact that she'd moved for work easily.

Jane made a pot of tea and Sarah was impressed with the handiness of the teabags which she had never used before.

"Quicker and easier than tealeaves," Jane told her, demonstrating how you could put a bag in a mug and pour the boiling water on top. "In the mornings we never have time to make real tea here. We're always running." She went over to a cupboard. "There's bread and biscuits there, and there's ham and cheese in the fridge. I'm going to make us both a sandwich now if you fancy one."

Sarah realised she hadn't eaten since early that morning in Liverpool. "I'd love a sandwich, please." She thought for a moment. "I'll have to go out and get some shopping. I never even gave it a thought . . . Does everyone buy and cook their own food?"

Elizabeth nodded. "It's the best way. We share things like toilet rolls, sugar and washing powder. We tried buying the food communally, but it didn't work out. We often work different shifts from each other, and so do the medical students, Vivienne and Anna, and sometimes we eat in the canteen at work. But there's no problem about taking a few slices from a loaf or a drop of milk. We're all glad to borrow from time to time."

"I'll get some shopping during my lunch hour tomorrow," Sarah told her. "I'm going to have to sleep for a few hours, so toast or something light will do me later."

"I'm doing a chicken later, so you can have some of that if you fancy when you get up. If we don't fancy cooking we're never stuck – there's a great chip shop around the corner and we often use it."

"A chip shop?" Sarah's eyebrows lifted. "We don't have anything like that back home. You have to go to Dublin or one of the bigger places. I've been a few times and I really enjoyed it."

"We have everything we need in Newcastle," Elizabeth said, "apart from the right man. Have you left a boyfriend back in Ireland?"

Sarah shook her head. If she'd been asked that question a week ago it would have been a different answer.

"Well, you won't have any trouble finding another with that lovely long blonde hair you have." She laughed and held up crossed fingers. "Hopefully we'll all meet the right man. It won't be for the want of trying!"

Sarah looked down at her cup. The last thing she wanted was the right man – or any man. She took a sip of the tea. It was strange-tasting, but she drank it.

Like everything else in her new life, she would get used to it.

CHAPTER 9

Sarah opened her eyes, for a few moments unsure where she was. Then her gaze fixed on the bear-shaped stain on the ceiling and she suddenly remembered that she was in a different room in a different country.

A pang of anxiety struck her chest.

Before the dark memories of why she was here could take over, an ambulance siren, which had started during the last few moments of her sleep, gathered momentum. When the screeching noise had reached its peak, the vehicle came to a halt disturbingly close. Sarah sat bolt upright.

Ambulance sirens meant bad news.

She threw the bedcovers back and rushed over the cold wooden floor to the corner of the bay window, to look down on the street below. The ambulance had pulled up on the opposite side of the road, beside a house with a green door. Sarah watched as the driver and his mate jumped out and then went to the back of the vehicle to open the double doors. A few seconds later they appeared carrying a stretcher.

She felt her heart begin to pound. She had never experienced anything as dramatic at such close quarters. By the time the ambulance men got to the door of the house it was open, and a slim, fair-haired woman in a dressing-gown let them in.

Sarah stood, her gaze fixed on the open door of the house.

Several people passed up and down on both sides of the street, and then there was movement again at the house opposite. The ambulance men came out carrying a figure on a stretcher. They were followed by the woman, a fair-haired boy of around fourteen and, surprisingly, a tall, dark-skinned girl with long black ringlets who looked a bit older. They were all dressed in nightwear. The girl came forward to put her arm through the woman's and Sarah instinctively knew from the way they were with each other that they were mother and daughter. Sarah could see the woman's shoulders shaking as the stretcher was manoeuvred into the ambulance. The girl huddled into her side and then the boy came over to stand close beside them. After a while, he placed a comforting arm around his mother's shoulder, as though he was trying to behave like a grown man.

Sarah stood watching as the ambulance doors clanged shut and then the siren started up again, leaving the three figures frozen on the doorstep as it hurtled down the street.

Sarah suddenly realised that not one person who had passed by had stopped to offer a word of concern. And none of the neighbours had come out of their houses to check what was happening.

A dark feeling washed over her. *What kind of a place have I come to?* she wondered. *Do people not care about what happens to their neighbours?*

She went slowly back across the room and got back into bed. She pulled the covers up to her chin and lay there trying to block out all the fears whirling around her. The thoughts of the frightening future she had walked herself into, and the humiliating thoughts of the past that had driven her towards it.

She had been chased to a precipice with no way forwards or back.

The worst bit was having no one familiar to turn to. She turned on her side and caught sight of her anxious face in the mottled wardrobe mirror. She stared at herself, then thought, *What did I do to deserve all this?*

She turned again, towards the blank wall.

Shortly afterwards there were noises around the house – the nurses had an eight o'clock start. She would let them get up and out before going down. The front door banged, and then a short while later she shifted herself, the heavy feeling still gripping her chest.

She put her dressing-gown and slippers on and went out into the hallway and downstairs to the bathroom. Although it was a big house, Sarah noticed that it felt warmer than the cottage would first thing in the morning.

When she had finished washing, she went into the kitchen. She went over to the cooker and felt the side of the kettle. It was cold; the girls must have gone out without any tea or breakfast. She wondered about the medical students she hadn't yet met. The nurses hadn't said where they were last night. They could have come back late for all she knew, as the walls in the house were thick and you couldn't hear every sound. She fiddled with the gas knobs on the cooker, and after a few false starts and several matches, finally got it lit. She put the kettle on to boil and then turned the grill on. She felt a small surge of success when it lit first time. She took two slices of bread from Elizabeth's loaf and put them on to toast. She used the girl's butter and marmalade, and put a teabag in the mug of boiling water as she had been shown last night.

After eating, she went back upstairs and over to the window to check the weather. The sky was a non-committal grey, but it was dry. She was just turning away when she noticed a middle-aged woman go out of the gate from the house next door and cross the road. She went over to the house where the ambulance had been and knocked on the door. Sarah stood and watched. The door was opened and the mother of the children came out to stand and talk on the doorstep. At one point, the other woman put her arms around her, comforting her. Then, an elderly man wearing a soft cap came down the street on a bike, and he slowed up when he saw

64

them. The woman from the house next door said something to him, and he dismounted the bike and went over to the door.

The two children came out and the man ruffled both their hairs, and said something that made them laugh. As she watched the little group, Sarah felt her heart start to lift. There were obviously people about who did care. *Maybe they hadn't heard the siren earlier*, she thought. *Maybe the other neighbours hadn't realised the ambulance had stopped outside the house*. It didn't matter now. She felt much better that someone had stopped to show their concern. She felt there were good people around like the ones back home.

She decided on a navy skirt and matching half-belted jacket she had made the previous summer, with a navy and white short-sleeved sweater underneath.

Since she had time to kill, she pondered over her hair and make-up. Lucy Harrison had been tidy but plain, her thick, curly black hair restrained with two clasps above either ear. Sarah decided on a half pony-tail, which swept her blonde hair up at the sides, and left the rest flowing neatly down her back.

She killed another ten minutes making her bed and tidying her room.

She left the house carrying her bag and umbrella, and a scrap of paper in her pocket with directions to her new place of employment. At the bottom of the hill she halted to examine the paper which Lucy Harrison had given her when she left her at the house in Victoria Street.

"You'll find it easy enough," she had said, scribbling the address down. "Just make your way down to the railway station and then up to Pilgrims Lane. It has '*Harrison's*' above the door. If you get lost, just ask anyone to direct you from the station."

There was little or no traffic apart from a few parked vans and cars. Sarah picked her steps down the cobbles, checking the shop names on either side as she went along. Pilgrims Lane was longer and wider than any lanes she knew back in Ireland. She stopped and sighed. She had to keep reminding herself that she was in a big city now and not a small town. She passed a jeweller's and next door to it a pawnshop, then a butcher's and a cobbler's. As she passed the doorway hung with dead pigs and rabbits, the smell of fresh bread alerted her to a baker's shop further along.

She knew from the walk down to the station that this was only a small part on the edge of the city, and Sarah found it surprising that there were all these shops. Her eye caught a sign for Thomson's Bookshop and just as she got near to it, a dark-haired young man of medium height in a pinstriped suit came out. He stopped to check something in the window, and then he suddenly walked backwards and bumped straight into her.

"Blidey hell, man!" he said, finding himself knocked off balance. He turned to look at her – then stopped and just stared in a mesmerised fashion. "I'm awful sorry," he finally said. "I was so busy concentrating on the window . . . I wasn't looking where I was going. Are you all right, pet?"

"I'm grand." She felt a blush starting. He was still standing, staring at her. "You don't happen to know where Harrison's shop is?"

He raised his eyebrows, then he started to laugh. "Are you havin' me on?"

Sarah looked at him, confused.

He pointed to the shop opposite. "You're right in front of it. Although, I don't blame you for not noticing, the name plaque could do with a good clean!"

Sarah turned to face a double-fronted, drab, old-fashioned shop. The locked and padlocked double doors looked as though they hadn't had a wash or a lick of paint in years. The window to the left of the door was empty apart from a couple of bare shelves and a half a dozen balls of wool. The right-hand window had a variety of faded knitting patterns and sewing patterns thrown on top of sheets of dusty brown paper. A basket with plastic daffodils sat sadly in the middle of it.

"Miss Harrison is a nice lady." His voice was low and confidential. "But the shop's a bit of a tip inside and out. She's not what you would call an astute businesswoman."

Sarah felt her stomach clench at the disclosure.

He tapped a finger on the glass of his watch. "Half-nine and she's not even here yet. Tut – tut – tut!" His dark-brown eyes met Sarah's again and she could see the amusement in them. "Have you other shopping to do until it opens? She'll probably be here in a few minutes."

"I'm not actually shopping," Sarah told him. "I'm here to start work in the shop."

His eyes widened. "I've just put my foot in it, haven't I?" He started to laugh again. "Don't tell her I said anything about the shop – she might come across and stab me in the heart with a knitting needle!"

Before she could help herself, Sarah started laughing too. Something she hadn't done for days – since the night Con Tierney had shattered their wedding plans. "Oh, don't!" she said, biting her lip to stop herself. She looked over her shoulder. "If she comes and catches me standing here laughing I'll be in trouble."

He stretched his hand out. "David McGuire – pleased to meet you."

"Sarah Love," she said. As they shook hands, heavy drops of rain began to fall.

"Well, Sarah Love," he said, "you're obviously not a native of Newcastle, are you? That's a fine Irish twang you have there."

Sarah's face reddened further. "I've just come over . . . I arrived yesterday." She wiped a few raindrops from her face.

He checked up and down the lane, then he took her gently by the arm. "Come in, come in," he said, guiding her into the shop doorway. "You don't want to get that lovely long hair all wet, now, do you?"

Sarah was flustered at the compliment. She wished she'd tied her hair up or plaited it. "I don't want Miss Harrison arriving and thinking that I'm late."

"She wouldn't want you to get soaked through on your first day," he said, raising his eyebrows. "We can watch from here." He paused. "Would you like a cup of tea? Mrs Price just made a pot ten minutes ago." He thumbed into the shop. "We have a handy little kitchen at the back."

Sarah shook her head, feeling awkward and embarrassed at her predicament. "Thanks, but I won't . . ." She moved a few steps forward again to check if there was any sign of her new employer, but there wasn't.

"Do you like books?" He gestured towards the first set of shelves behind the door.

"I love them," Sarah said, "when I can afford them, and when I have the time to read." A picture of the library in O'Connor Square in Tullamore flew into her mind. She usually borrowed books as opposed to buying them.

"Miss Harrison is one of our best customers actually. She's a great reader." He was silent for a moment. "So what do you do with your time instead of reading, like?"

The picture was replaced by one of her nearly finished wedding dress. "I sew and knit." She turned back to look out of the window.

"Well, I suppose that's handy if you're going to be working in a shop that sells all that kind of stuff." He studied her now. "So . . . what brings a lovely colleen to Newcastle-*Upon-Tyne*?" He put a funny, heavy accent on the last two words, and Sarah wondered if his way of speaking was typical of people from the North East of England. She had been told by Father Kelly that they were often referred to as 'Geordies'.

Sarah's expression went blank now. She hadn't expected him to ask her that. .

David McGuire looked at her curiously. "I'm only chatting – I don't mean to be nosey . . ."

"I know Lucy Harrison's cousin . . ." Her words came out stiff and stuttering. "She thought working in the shop might suit me."

He nodded slowly. "Lucy . . . is that her name, like? I don't think I've ever heard her called anything but Miss Harrison around here, and the older one that was there was a 'miss' as well."

At that very moment Sarah heard footsteps coming up the cobbled lane and seconds later Lucy Harrison appeared, the shop keys jingling in her hand.

A wave of gratitude washed over her. "I have to go. Thanks for letting me stand out of the rain."

"Any time," he told her. "And we sell second-hand books as well."

"I'll be too busy with work for reading," she said as she walked away. *And far too busy for men.*

CHAPTER 10

"I'm sorry you had to wait." The shopkeeper looked flustered as she located the right key. She took a few moments to get the padlock open. "I didn't sleep too well last night, and then I overslept this morning."

"It's not a problem, I've only just arrived," Sarah told her.

David McGuire was right – the interior of the shop, while bigger than she had imagined, reflected a similar standard as the neglected window. Sarah's heart sank as she glanced around as she followed her new employer across the floor to the long, wooden shop counter. There were dozens of rolls of material leaning higgledy-piggeldy up against a wall, and a few – obviously having fallen – lying on the floor. The two walls on either side and the back wall had shelves stacked precariously with various colours of wool.

Lucy indicated a door over in the left-hand corner. "We have a back area here," she said, going across to it, "with a stock-cupboard and a kitchen and toilet."

Surprisingly, the area hidden from the public was the tidiest area of all. The stock-cupboard was a reasonable size and the rolls of material and packs of wool were all laid out on shelves, while the kitchen had a small clean Formica table with four wooden chairs tucked under it. There was a sink unit with a couple of cupboards and a worktop with an electric kettle and toaster, and three matching jars for tea, coffee and sugar. There was even a small fridge. But the thing that surprised Sarah the most was the filled bookcase which stood against the wall beside the window. She opened her mouth to comment on it, and then thought better of it. The small toilet and sink were spotlessly clean and smelling of bleach and disinfectant.

"This is a lovely area." Sarah was glad she could say something good.

"I know the rest of the shop isn't up to scratch," Lucy said in a defeated tone, "but I've been on my own for three months." She went over to the tap to fill the electric kettle. She brought it back to the worktop and plugged it in. "It's since Mary left to look after her mother, and I thought I could manage everything on my own until she came back."

Sarah wondered if the shop and the window display could have deteriorated that much in three months. Perhaps Mary hadn't been so fussy about things either.

Lucy gave a short sigh. "But it hasn't worked out too well. Mary – Miss Shaftoe – it seems will be gone permanently, as her mother isn't fit to be left on her own during the day. It's difficult really, because while her mother is in her eighties Miss Shaftoe is over sixty herself. I think she's probably going to retire now, and I can't say I blame her." She motioned towards the door. "I haven't really got on top of things in the shop since she left."

Sarah wasn't sure whether her new employer was referring to the untidy state of the shop or to the business in general.

"I'll be very happy to do anything you feel needs sorting out." She was trying to pitch her response very carefully, so as not to imply any criticism.

Her job routine in the hotel back in Tullamore had run like clockwork – setting tables, checking menus, helping out in the kitchen until the customers started to arrive, serving and then clearing up. The same, day in day out. It was hard work but in a way she had enjoyed putting things back in order again after the lunchtime mess, and had felt a satisfaction seeing the tidy, set tables at the end of her shift. Of course there had been days when the job was so mindless that she could plan her sewing projects in her head as she went about her work. Sarah felt working in the shop was much more to her liking, and if Lucy Harrison would let her, she could put all her energy and enthusiasm for sewing into this new job,

"We'll have a cup of tea," Lucy said, "and then I'll show you where everything is, and how to work the till."

The customer bell sounded and Lucy looked up at the clock. "That will be Harriet – Harriet Scott. She calls in at this time most mornings."

Sarah heard the quick, light footsteps coming across the shop floor and around the counter towards the kitchen. A small, slim girl of indeterminate age came in wearing a navy and red nurse's cape and hat.

"Terrible morning, isn't it?" She gave Sarah a beaming smile. She took the hat off to reveal a neatly tied bun of red hair. "So, this is the talented Irish dressmaker you were telling me about?"

Sarah thought the nurse's accent was more like the lad's from the bookshop than Lucy's.

"This is Sarah Love," Lucy said, then she turned to the visitor, "and this is Harriet Scott. Harriet is a District Nurse."

The girls shook hands, and instinctively Sarah knew she was going to like Harriet.

"Have you time for tea?" Lucy went over to the teapot. "I'm making some now." She poured some water from the kettle in to scald it, and then she opened the tea caddy and put three spoons of tealeaves in the pot.

"I suppose I could have a very quick one," Harriet pulled a chair out from under the table, and then she sat down to face Sarah. "Haven't you got gorgeous blonde hair? Tell me, what do you think of Newcastle so far?"

"Grand," Sarah said, nodding and trying to smile as though she meant it. "I haven't really seen that much . . ." She could hear her voice giving away her anxieties. "But I like the buildings and I've heard the cathedral is lovely."

Harriet raised her eyebrows "Are you a Catholic? I suppose you are, being Irish."

Sarah couldn't remember ever being asked this before. "Yes," she replied, "I am." For some reason she thought that Lucy would have automatically told anyone this when she was discussing her new employee. Obviously not. Back home almost all the people she knew were Catholic, and everyone knew the small numbers who were Protestant.

Lucy put a mug of tea down on the table in front of her and another beside the nurse, then she brought over the sugar bowl and milk jug.

"I'm C of E," Harriet said, matter-of-factly, stretching over for the milk. "Although I don't get to church every Sunday. There are times when it's too big an effort if I've been out dancing on Saturday night."

Sarah caught her breath. Nobody she knew back home would ever say that they couldn't make Mass because they had been out too late the night before. If they ever did ever miss Mass for such a reason, they would pretend they had something dramatically wrong with them as an excuse.

"Churches don't matter – we're all God's children," Lucy said. She paused as though she was going to say something else, then she shrugged her shoulders. "Although there are many days when I wonder if He even knows we're here."

"I suppose that's when our faith is tested," Sarah said, thinking of how angry she felt with God last week. Thinking how angry she felt with God every time she went over her situation in her head.

There was a small silence and then she remembered Miss Reynolds' advice when she left her at the boat in Dublin a few days ago. She'd warned Sarah that she would be in a big city with every kind of religion in it. For all she knew, Lucy Harrison might not even be a Catholic. Her cheeks started to flame, realising that her comments might infer that she thought everyone believed in God and went to church. She reached for the milk jug, trying to look confident and relaxed. Trying to look as though she didn't regret speaking out.

Lucy put a plate with half a dozen digestives on the table and then sat down. She glanced at Harriet. "Have you a busy morning ahead of you?"

"Yes," she said, reaching for a biscuit. "I've a new mother on the round, the little five-year-old fellow who has polio in his legs, and the usual elderly patients. When I'm finished I'm in the clinic in the afternoon."

"It sounds like a really interesting job," Sarah said.

"And she's good at it," Lucy Harrison said. "For a girl so young, she has a very wise head on her shoulders."

Harriet smiled and shook her head, embarrassed. "I love it, so I'm very lucky doing something I really enjoy."

The shop bell sounded and Sarah went to stand up.

"I'll get this," Lucy said. "You finish your tea"

When Lucy went out into the shop, Harriet gave Sarah a sympathetic but friendly grin. "It must be very different for you over here. Have you worked in a shop before?"

"No, I worked in a hotel, but I love sewing and knitting."

"Well, that definitely helps when you're in a place full of needles and wool," Harriet laughed.

"Do you knit yourself?" Sarah asked.

"A bit, it depends on my time and my moods. I'm more of a reader."

"There's a bookshop just across from here."

"I'm one of their best customers," Harriet said. "I buy loads of books, although mainly second-hand." She lowered her voice. "The manager – David McGuire – is really lovely."

"I think I met him this morning." Sarah was deliberately vague about meeting him, as she didn't want anyone to think she was only here five minutes and was already making herself familiar with people.

"He's gorgeous, isn't he?"

"He seemed a nice lad," Sarah said. "I was waiting outside the shop for Lucy this morning and it was raining. He saw me and said I could wait inside the shop for her, which was decent of him."

"He's that kind, he'd do anything for you," Harriet said. She glanced towards the door, checking that Lucy couldn't hear. "I've been trying to find out if he has a girlfriend, but he just laughs and jokes and you can't ask him anything serious."

"Doesn't Lucy know? She must see him every day."

Harriet rolled her eyes to the ceiling. "That's not the kind of thing that you could ask Lucy. She has no interest in men – especially not lads our age. What about you? Have you left a boyfriend behind in Ireland?"

Sarah's heart quickened. Lucy Harrison obviously hadn't told her. "No . . ." She couldn't lie as the nurse would probably find out. "Well, actually, I was engaged . . . I was supposed to have got married . . ." Without warning, her eyes suddenly filled up. She reached in her jacket pocket for a hanky.

"Oh, Sarah . . ." Harriet reached over to touch her arm. "I'm sorry I asked. I didn't mean to upset you."

Sarah rubbed her eyes with the hanky. "No, not at all," she said. "How could you know?" She halted. "I should have been married this coming Saturday." She took a deep breath. "But he did the dirty on me with one of my best friends."

"Oh, no!"

Sarah nodded. "I just found out last week. And it was even worse. He came up to tell me she was expecting his baby."

Harriet gasped. "You poor thing!" She took Sarah's hand in both hers. "No wonder you're upset. Imagine them going off together like that!"

"But they didn't," Sarah explained. "She lost the baby, and then he and his mother came up to see me – to try to get me to go ahead with the wedding."

"I don't believe it! Tell me you're joking?" Harriet's eyes were wide.

"I wish I was. I had no option but to leave – I had to get away."

"You did the right thing." She patted Sarah's hand. "You'll get to like it here. Lucy is quiet but she's a good decent woman. You'll get on fine together."

Sarah nodded. "I hope so . . ."

Harriet took a final mouthful of her tea. "I've got to go." She stood up and reached for her nurse's hat. "I hope the rain keeps off." She walked towards the door. "It was lovely to meet you, Sarah."

"It's lovely to meet you, too. It's nice to see a friendly face when you're in a strange country."

"Oh, Newcastle has lots of friendly faces, and you'll be sick of the sight of me soon." The young nurse smiled. "I call in here most days, depending on my round."

Sarah followed Harriet into the shop. They chatted as Lucy put the customer's wool and knitting needles into a paper bag, then put her money in the till and gave her change back.

Lucy joined them when the woman left.

"I'm off to brave the rain," Harriet said, pulling her hat down over her red bun.

Lucy walked to the door with her. They started talking in low voices, and, feeling that their conversation might be private, Sarah walked back to the kitchen.

Then Sarah heard Harriet say, "If you don't feel the sleeping tablets are mixing well with your other medication, you might have to go back to the doctor."

Sarah went over to the sink and turned the water on to make sure she couldn't hear any more.

Then the shop bell sounded as Lucy closed the door and, shortly afterwards, Sarah went back into the main shop.

Sarah noticed her new employer had a despondent air about her. Sarah bit her lip. She had something to ask and she needed to do it sooner rather than later.

"Can I just check something with you, please?" she ventured.

"Yes?"

"I was just wondering . . . what should I call you? You didn't say . . ."

"Call me? What do you mean?"

Sarah felt her neck start to redden. "Should I call you Miss Harrison or should . . ." She shrugged, feeling like a silly schoolgirl.

The shopkeeper's eyes narrowed as she pondered the question. "Actually . . . Lucy will do. Mary – Miss Shaftoe – who was here before you, preferred us to use our surnames, but personally, I don't think it matters."

The doorbell went and a customer came in and Sarah watched and listened as Lucy showed the woman patterns for a baby's matinee jacket. After that a woman came in looking for needles for a sewing machine and while Lucy served her, Sarah attended to a young girl who was looking for three balls of blue wool.

Sarah waited until Lucy had finished with her customer, then she gave her the bag with the wool in it so she could ring it up on the till.

During the next quiet spell Lucy showed Sarah the drawers that held knitting and sewing needles of every length and thickness, crochet hooks, hooks and eyes, press-studs and a variety of sewing implements she had never seen before. Then she showed her how to measure the yards of material on the counter using the long copper ruler on the top and edge.

She was in the middle of showing her how to use the till when the bell went. Two elderly women – obviously sisters – came in, linking arms. They were both white-haired and small.

"Will I serve them?" Sarah asked.

"If you like. I'll be through the back if you need me." Lucy hesitated. "Will you be okay about the money? Do you know all the different English coins and notes?"

"Yes," Sarah said, "I made sure I got used to them travelling over. I'll be careful not to mix them up."

"And if you remember not to speak too quickly."

"Was I? I didn't realise . . ."

"It's probably me." The shopkeeper's tone was apologetic. "It's just occasionally I find it difficult to catch certain words."

"I'll make sure I slow down." It had never occurred to her that anyone would find her difficult to understand.

She went towards the two elderly ladies. "Can I help you?" She enunciated each word carefully.

"I'm looking for a pattern and wool for a nice thick cardigan," the taller of the women said.

Sarah felt her heart lift on hearing a familiar Irish accent. "Oh, which part of Ireland are you from?"

The smaller woman beamed. "Kildare – and where are you from yourself? I didn't catch the accent there."

"Tullamore." Just as she said it, Sarah suddenly realised that they might know someone who knew her or Con's family. She held her breath.

"Tullamore! It's not that far from us really, but it's not a place we'd know very well."

Sarah was relieved.

"And I'd say you're fresh off the boat?" The woman's eyes were bright and friendly.

Sarah nodded, a warm feeling spreading through her now. The old lady reminded her of Sheila Brady's old mother back in Tullamore. She suddenly felt rescued from the cloak of unfamiliarity all around her. "I just came over yesterday."

"Yesterday? Imagine . . . You'll still be getting used to things so. Big difference. What's your name?"

"Sarah – Sarah Love."

"Love? That's unusual, isn't it, Agnes? We're Bradleys." She gestured to her sister. "Agnes and Bridget."

"I hope you're staying," said Agnes, "because it's nice to see a cheery face in here for a change." She nodded towards the back shop. "That one never smiles," she said in a low voice. "There are times when you'd dread coming in, only you'd need something."

Bridget dug her in the ribs. "She'll hear you, big gob!"

Sarah almost laughed out loud. This was exactly the kind of banter that went on with Mr and Mrs Brady back in Tullamore. She suddenly felt lighter and more at home. "I'll show you the cardigan patterns I have," she said, lifting the large, heavy pattern book from the counter. She thumbed through it, until she came to the cardigan section, and then she opened it flat and turned the book around to face them. "What type of sleeve did you want? Raglan or set in?"

"Raglan, of course." Agnes Bradley's voice was high with surprise, as though Sarah had known her preference of sleeve type for years. "I was in Tullamore a few years ago when I was home on holiday. I suppose it's a nice enough place."

Again Sarah had to stop herself from smiling at Tullamore being damned by faint praise. "How long have you been in Newcastle?" she asked.

"Over forty years. We never imagined we'd be here that long, did we, Bridget? If you'd told me that when I first came over, I would have died."

Sarah felt her jaw clench.

"We only came over for a year to see how we liked it." Bridget laughed and shook her head. "And then we stayed on for another year and another year. But that's life – that's the way it was meant to be."

Sarah didn't know whether to be comforted or horrified at the thought of living in this strange city for the next forty years. She hadn't thought any further ahead than the next few weeks. She hadn't even thought about Christmas which was only a few months away. "You obviously settled . . ."

"Oh, aye, we did that," Agnes agreed.

Sarah noticed that the last sentence was spoken in what she now recognised was the Geordie accent. Most of the people who had come into the shop spoke that way. She supposed they were bound to have picked it up having lived here so long. The sisters spent a good half an hour in the shop, choosing a pattern and wool, then, as Sarah was totting up their bill, Bridget indicated towards the door behind the counter.

"Would you ask herself if she found the name of another seamstress for us? Since Miss Shaftoe left, we've had nobody to do any alterations for us." She looked over her shoulder, and then said in a low, conspiratorial voice. "We know a very good second-hand shop that sells beautiful clothes, but because we're smaller than average we often have to get them altered."

"Is the second-hand shop near?" Sarah also spoke quietly, not wanting her employer to hear her making chit-chat with the customers. "I wouldn't mind paying it a visit, myself."

"Oh, we'll give you the address," Agnes said, digging into her handbag for a small notepad and a pen. "It's only five minutes' walk, just the other side of Grey Street, and the woman who serves in it is lovely." She wrote the address down and drew a little map.

Sarah suddenly thought. "I could do any alterations if you like . . ." Then she hesitated. "Just let me check that Miss Harrison hasn't organised anyone else to do it."

She tapped on the backroom door and then went in. To her amazement, Lucy Harrison was sitting engrossed in a book. She looked up startled when Sarah came in.

"I have some customers asking whether you've taken on another seamstress to do alterations?"

Lucy's brow deepened in thought. "No . . . I haven't. Not yet."

Sarah looked at her. "I can do alterations if you like. I noticed you have a sewing machine in the stock-room."

Lucy looked blankly at her.

Sarah suddenly thought that her boss might feel she was trying to get out of serving in the shop during working hours. "I can buy one to use at the house in the evenings as well." She presumed it would be relatively easy to find a second-hand machine in a city of this size.

"Are you sure?" Lucy said. "We'd have to work things out . . ."

The shop bell went signalling another customer.

"Is it okay if I tell the ladies to bring their suits in?"

Lucy lifted her dark eyebrows. "You decide . . . If you don't mind doing the work, then that's fine by me."

Sarah went back to the two sisters. She felt a little surge of achievement that she'd sorted this out. Doing alterations back at the house would fill the long, empty autumn evenings and take her mind off her old life. And it would also give her something to do when the shop was quiet, which it seemed to be most of the time.

There was another lady waiting to be served, so Sarah quickly told the women her news and then wrapped up their items and totted up their bill.

"We'll drop our stuff off in the morning," Bridget told her as she took the change. "We'll sort through our wardrobes this evening and see what needs altering." She shifted the handles of her shopping-bag further up her arm, as though rolling her sleeves up, ready to get stuck into the work.

"See you tomorrow so," said Sarah happily.

As she measured out two yards of curtain lace for her following customer, the woman said: "Did I hear you talking to those other ladies about alterations?"

"You did," Sarah said confidently.

"It's my first time in this shop," the woman said, "and I didn't realise there was a seamstress working here. I have a coat that needs altering and my husband has a pair of heavy work trousers that needs a new zip. Would you be able to do it?"

"Of course." Sarah said it as though she had been doing alterations in the shop for years. Inside, her mind was racing. If she was going to have to measure clothes on people for taking up or letting out, she would have to provide a place for them to try the garments on with a mirror. She would have to ask Lucy Harrison if she could make a space in the back-shop somewhere. She would suggest curtaining off an area of the stockroom and putting a full-length mirror and a chair in it. It would take no time to do. It was just a matter of finding a suitable remnant of material for curtains and using one of the chairs from the kitchen until she found time to pick a nice one up in a second-hand shop.

But she couldn't do anything without checking with her new employer.

The door clicked shut after the customer and Sarah took a deep breath and walked towards the kitchen. She was slightly anxious about looking as though she were trying to run before she could walk, but it was outweighed by the feeling of doing something she loved with all the empty hours that loomed ahead.

"Lucy, I was just wondering . . ." she started, then halted at the door.

Her employer was sitting at the table with her head on her folded arms, fast asleep.

Sarah stared at her for a few moments. Then, remembering the conversation she overheard with the young nurse, she tip-toed out backwards into the shop.

She served six customers as the morning went by and Lucy Harrison still had not appeared. Sarah had also spent time gazing silently out of the shop window, thinking about what she had been doing this time the previous week and all the weeks before. The weeks when she was planning her wedding to Con Tierney. The weeks when Patricia Quinn was being fitted for her bridesmaid dress.

The door to the back-shop opened.

"I'm very sorry . . ." The shopkeeper blinked the tiredness out of her eyes. "I don't know what's wrong with me at the moment. I'm awake at night and then tired all day. Did you manage all right by yourself?"

"I did," Sarah quickly reassured her. She could tell her employer was embarrassed. "Most people were looking for wool, but I measured and cut material for two customers as well."

"And the till?"

Sarah nodded. "Yes – I think I've got the hang of it." She lifted a small square receipt book with a navy carbon-copy sheet. "I wrote down everything I sold down in the book, and gave the customers one copy and kept the other in the book like you told me. The money is easy enough once you get used to it. I just have to stop myself from comparing it to the Irish coins."

The shop-keeper's face brightened. "Well done, Sarah," she said. "For a first day, you've got off to a flying start."

Sarah felt a little wave of relief, and then decided to take a chance. "Can I suggest something, Lucy?"

"Go on . . ."

"You know we talked about me doing alterations?" She went on then to explain that if she could spend an hour in the back-shop, she could set up an area where she could do the alterations and beside it, a small changing-room.

Lucy looked dubious. "Wouldn't it be a lot of extra work for you?"

"I thought I could get on with sewing when the shop was quiet." If this morning was anything to go by, there wasn't enough work for two of them. And yet, there was something that made her think her employer wasn't sure about her suggestion.

"It's just that there will be times when I've got to go out . . . and did I tell you that I always have Thursday off? I can change my arrangements this Thursday, if you feel you need me. Since it's your first week, I understand you might need me around."

"I'm sure I'll be fine to be left on my own by then," Sarah said. "If we're quiet and I'm working in the back, I'll hear the shop bell and come straight through. On the other days when we're both working, if it suddenly gets busy you just have to call me and I'll come to help."

Lucy nodded, still thinking. "I suppose we have nothing to lose." She glanced at her watch. "Gosh – it's nearly half past twelve. Would you manage here if I pop out to the bank? I might stop off and pick up a pie or a sandwich when I'm out, but I'll probably get back around one o'clock. We close between one and two, so you can take an hour for your lunch then. Did you bring anything for your lunch?"

"I haven't had time to get to the shops yet," Sarah told her. "I'll take a walk out and see what there is."

Lucy went into the back-room and got her coat and handbag. "Are you sure you'll be okay on your own?"

"I'll be grand," Sarah said. "I'll give the shop a tidy around while you're gone if it's quiet."

Lucy put her rain-coat on and then went towards the door to check if she needed her umbrella. It wasn't actually raining, but the sky was overcast so she went back into the kitchen to collect it.

Sarah watched as the slightly built, dark-haired figure went towards the door and noticed a definite slump of her shoulders. She found it confusing that although Lucy Harrison's face looked like someone in their late thirties, her posture and movements were that of an older woman. And then it struck Sarah. Her demeanour was that of an older, *dispirited* woman. Sarah wondered if she had always been old for her years, or if something might have happened that had suddenly made her like that.

Sarah stared after her for a few moments, then her mind turned back towards Tullamore. Back to the fiancé and friend who had betrayed her. Back to the family who didn't want her.

A feeling of determination rose inside her. She would not let what had happened hold her back. No matter what – she would keep going. She would make the best of this fresh start in a new country. She would work hard at her new job, and she would help Lucy Harrison to build the dilapidated shop back into a good business.

CHAPTER 11

Sarah walked to the door to look at the windows on one side and then the other. The windows were the first thing that customers saw when they came up to the shop. They had made a terrible impression on her – and they would obviously do the same for the customers. She would start on them first.

She went into the kitchen and filled the electric kettle to the top and put it on to boil, then she found a clean navy and white apron, a brush and pan and an empty waste-paper bin. She went to the window that held the piles of wool first and picked the balls out. She held them one by one over the bin and brushed each down before placing it on the counter. Then she started brushing the dust and the cobwebs and the dead flies, and when she had cleared it all, she gathered up the dusty sheets of brown paper and rolled them up tightly and put them in the bin. She took the bin through the back to empty it into a bigger one, and then came back with a basin filled with hot water and disinfectant to wash the window and shelves down.

She made several more trips to renew the water, finished the shelves and afterwards climbed into the window. She was just polishing Windolene off the glass when she saw a figure gesturing to her from the door. David McGuire was standing, smiling at her. He pushed the door open, making the bell ping, and came in.

"I saw your boss go off a few minutes ago, so I thought I'd look in and see how you're getting on, like." He grinned and pointed towards her apron. "I see she has you working hard already."

"She didn't ask me to do this, I offered," Sarah said, stepping out of the window and down onto the floor beside him. For a moment she wondered whether to be curt with him to make him keep his distance, but there was something about him that made her think of the harmless, friendly lads at home. "I feel the whole shop needs a good clean, and I can't relax inside while I know the windows look a mess."

"Well, it looks a whole lot better to me already," David said. He put a finger on his chin. "I'm just thinking . . . I have some lining paper I could give you for the windows." He gestured across to the bookshop. "The boss sent stuff up from the shop in London and we've got a good bit left over, like. It's quite nice, a striped sort of design in different colours."

"That would be great."

"I'll get if for you now."

By the time he came back with the paper, Sarah had finished polishing the window and had gathered up balls of bright red, green, yellow and blue wool and stuck needles through them. She had also got a few cheery-looking knitting patterns for children's hats and scarves and sweaters, and had thought of a few more ideas for the display.

"Do you sell things other than books in the shop?"

"We sell stationery and pens and pencils and all those sorts of things."

"Would you have any of those plastic things with the letters of the alphabet for making signs? I think you can get them in capitals and small letters."

"Yeah," he said, "I think we do."

She had just put the fresh lining paper in the window when she had to stop for a customer. The lady was looking for crochet needles and wool, and had brought a pattern with her. Sarah was relieved that the woman knew what she needed, as crocheting was one of the areas she had no experience in. She made a mental note to buy a beginner's book about it, so she would have some idea if any of the customers asked her advice.

She was back at the window finishing off her display when David came back, with two letter templates and three large pieces of card in black, red and white, a thick black pen and a small container of glue.

"That should be everything you need to make signs," he told her.

"Oh, that's grand," Sarah said, delighted. "How much do I owe you?"

He winked at her. "I'll sort it out later. I might be able to get you a bit of a business discount."

"Are you open during lunch?" Sarah asked. "I was going to come in after one o'clock to buy a book on crocheting, and I can sort out what I owe you then."

He clapped his hands and rubbed them together. "Another new customer! I'm glad my business charm still seems to be working." Then he looked at her serious face and said, "Aw, I'm only kidding, like. We stagger our lunch breaks so we don't have to close the shop. We sell weekly and monthly bus tickets, and folk often come in to buy them when they're out for lunch."

"That's grand," she said.

She glanced past him now, to see if there was any sign of Lucy. She wanted to get at least one of the windows finished before she came back, and she also didn't want to be caught chatting to a lad on her first morning at work.

He seemed to sense her thoughts. "I'll leave you to it then . . ." He looked at the freshly washed shelves and the gleaming glass in the window. "You're doing a great job there – it looks like a different place already." He moved towards the door. "Aw, look at that! The flaming rain is on again. Don't go wasting your time washing the outside of the windows 'cos they'll only get ruined." He paused.

"Come to think of it, the lad who does the shop windows every month is due round Thursday, so there's no point in doing them any road."

Sarah gave a little sigh from all her exertion. "That's good. It'll really finish the windows off nice having the outside done as well."

Sarah was through the back emptying a basin of dirty water from the second window when the bell went. She quickly took her apron off and went through.

A tall, elegant young woman came into the shop. She stopped at the door to shake the drops of her umbrella, and then left it leaning against the edge of the doorframe where it wouldn't be in anyone's way.

Sarah's gaze immediately fell on the light wool navy suit with the white piqué over-collar, and the flattering three-quarter-length sleeves with long navy leather gloves. As the young woman came towards her, she quickly took in the details of the outfit: the skirt length – falling fashionably just below the knee – the dark grey rows of pearls, the navy shoes with the white button trim. Her accessories were equally impressive, a brimless navy hat over a sharp, dark bob and a matching navy leather bag with a rolled handle and clasp. Sarah had only ever seen similar outfits in a magazine before, or on the cover of a pattern. The outfit topped anything Sarah had seen worn by any of the well-dressed women she saw at Mass in Tullamore, or by the fashion-conscious women she saw in Grafton Street in Dublin.

"Do you have black sequins, please?" the woman asked, coming towards the counter. She removed a glove, then opened her handbag and brought out a small paper package. Carefully, she spilled a few sequins onto the counter. "Like these if you have them, or something very similar."

Sarah tore her eyes from the outfit to look at the sequins. "Yes," she said, nodding. "I think we have some. I'm sure I saw black sequins in a drawer earlier this morning." She moved across the floor to the trimming drawers.

"Oh, wonderful!" The woman's eyes followed her anxiously. "I travelled up from London last night to do a fitting for a dress, and the only thing I hadn't finished was the hem. When I looked at the outfit on, I suddenly realised that a row of sequins at the bottom of the dress would really pull the whole thing together." She tapped the side of her forehead. "And of course I didn't think to bring my little bag of sequins with me."

Sarah looked at the vast array of boxes filled with buttons, press-studs, hook and eyes, beads and pieces of ribbon. She pulled another drawer out and immediately her hand fell on a row of boxes holding different-coloured sequins. "Was it plain black, or black with navy?"

"Oh, plain black, please – best to stick to the same all over. I'm absolutely sick of the bloody little things – I've hand-stitched hundreds of them on this dress."

Sarah was shocked to hear such an elegant woman swearing, but she didn't show it. She brought a box across to her. "Is it for a special occasion?"

"A wedding." She took her purse out of her bag. "I don't usually travel for fittings, but it's my old school-friend's wedding – I grew up in Newcastle – and I've made the dresses for her mother and aunt. They've been down to my rooms in London twice already for fittings." She rolled her eyes. "Two of the most glamorous women you've ever seen – like Jackie Kennedy and her sister. The dress I'm making is for the bride's mother, for the evening of the wedding. She has a beautiful coat and dress for the actual day."

"Did you make that too?" Sarah lifted the small bags of sequins out of the box.

"No," the woman's voice was low and confidential. "She bought a Chanel design from one of the London stores when she was down for a fitting. I was relieved actually – it took me long enough making the two dresses."

Sarah was very curious now. Although she had never seen an actual outfit, she had certainly heard of Chanel and knew it was the sort of design only very rich women could afford. She had never met anyone before who talked about high fashion designs as though it was an ordinary thing.

"If you don't mind me commenting," Sarah ventured, "your own outfit is beautiful. Did you make it yourself?"

The woman's eyes widened and then she smiled. "Thank you. As a matter of fact, I did. It's one of my own designs." She checked her watch and then moved her attention to the sequins again. "I'll take a full box of sequins," she said. "I don't know how many I'm going to need. I might have to do several rows on the hem, and I won't know until I've started."

Sarah bent under the counter to get a small paper bag.

"Your own suit is well stitched," the woman said. She moved closer to get a better look. "*Very* well stitched. Did you buy it locally?"

Sarah looked at her in amazement. "No, I made it up from a pattern I bought in Dublin." She slid the paper bag across the counter, suddenly feeling self-conscious. "That's one and ninepence, please."

The woman handed her a florin. "You made it yourself? *Really*? Well, you're a very talented young girl . . ." She glanced around the shabby, untidy shop. "Do you work here full-time?"

"Yes," Sarah told her. "I actually only started today." Then, knowing that the woman was probably thinking that it wasn't much of a place to work in, she felt embarrassed. "It will look much better soon. They've been short-staffed and it's got a bit run-down. I've been busy cleaning and tidying the window and I'm going to start sorting things inside here now."

"You're obviously a hard worker," the woman said, "and very trustworthy to be left in charge on your first morning." She lifted her package and put it in her navy leather bag. "Do you mind me asking your name?"

"It's Sarah – Sarah Love."

"What a lovely, unusual name." She looked towards the door. The rain had stopped so she went over, picked her umbrella up and fastened it. "Well, Sarah, thank you for saving my bacon with the sequins. I tried Fenwick's haberdashery but they had no black sequins left, and a lady pointed me in the direction of your shop. If

I'm ever back up in Newcastle and need anything else, I'll know where to come."

The door had hardly closed when the bell went again and Lucy Harrison came in. She shut the door slowly behind her, then she turned towards Sarah with a deepened brow. "What have you done with the window?"

The look on her face made Sarah's heart lurch. "I gave it a bit of a clean . . ." Her eyes flickered over to the second window which was only half-done. "I haven't finished yet." She swallowed hard, trying to work out what she'd done wrong.

"But you've completely changed it . . ." The frown was still there and there was a little nerve working in one of her cheekbones. She shook her head and then walked straight past Sarah and into the kitchen.

Sarah stood for a few moments, then she followed her employer, asking herself what had she done wrong.

Lucy was sitting at the table with her head in her hands.

"I'm sorry," Sarah started explaining again, "but I thought you would want me to keep busy in between serving customers. I wouldn't have touched anything if I'd known you didn't want me to." It was then that she noticed the dark-haired woman's shoulders shuddering. "Lucy?" She moved towards her. "Are you all right?"

Lucy nodded her head. "Take . . . no . . . notice." Her voice was a half-sob. "It's me . . . it's not anything you've done. It's me . . ."

The shop bell went.

"I'll get it," Sarah said. "The kettle's boiled. I thought you might be ready for a cup of tea."

"That's kind of you."

A few minutes later, Sarah went back into the kitchen. Lucy Harrison was standing at the work-top with two filled mugs of tea.

"I'm sorry for my behaviour earlier." She cleared her throat. "And I'm sorry if it sounded as though I were criticising you. It was quite the contrary . . . I'm very, very grateful for the work you've done. It was the fact that I feel . . . I feel that you shouldn't have had to do it. I knew you were coming towards the end of last week,

91

and I should have made an effort to have the shop looking decent for you." She threw an agitated hand in the air. "But – as usual – I kept putting it off, and then, it was too late."

"It doesn't matter . . ."

"Oh, but it does. I procrastinate with everything and then make things doubly difficult for myself. I'd planned to ask you to help me to sort the windows when you had settled in. I had envisaged us taking turns, spending a few days getting things sorted out . . ." She halted again. "But I just didn't have the energy, and I convinced myself that it didn't look too bad."

"But it didn't," Sarah said quickly. She felt so bad for the poor woman that she wanted to say *anything* that might just make her feel better.

"It was unfair of me, it's your first day and you've worked so hard." Lucy's voice sounded crackly and upset again. "I don't know what comes over me at times. I knew in my head you were only helping but I just couldn't stop myself from feeling . . ."

"It really is okay," Sarah told her in a firm but kind voice.

"Thank you . . . thank you."

Sarah bit her lip, at a loss for what more she could say.

"I really should have been more understanding . . ." Lucy's voice tailed off. "My cousin told me you've just been through a difficult time back home – a *very* difficult time, and the last thing you need is some silly, highly strung woman telling you off."

Sarah caught her breath. Lucy Harrison obviously knew about the events that had caused her to leave home. She lowered her head, feeling waves of embarrassment and humiliation creeping over her. There was a silence again. When she eventually looked up and saw the anguish stamped on her employer's face her self-pity vanished to be replaced by a flood of compassion for this rather odd, dark-haired woman.

"Honestly, I'm grand." Sarah smiled warmly now. "Coming here will be the making of me. I enjoyed doing that bit of cleaning and tidying – it took my mind off all the trouble that happened recently." As she heard herself say the words, Sarah realised she was speaking the truth and not just placating her boss. She could see Lucy was listening now, so she continued. "It can't have been easy running the place on your own, trying to juggle the shop and orders and all that kind of thing. You'll find things much easier now there's the two of us."

The shopkeeper studied Sarah for a few moments and then she smiled. A proper kind of smile that reached her grey-green eyes. "You're right," she said. "Of course things will be different now there are two of us."

CHAPTER 12

When Sarah stepped out into Pilgrims Lane again, it was a much busier place than it had been earlier in the morning. She paused for a few moments observing the customers going in and out of the various shops, the bicycles and vans parked outside, and the odd car rattling down the cobbled stones. The smell of hops that had enveloped her earlier had evaporated, but she could still detect hot baking smells and the strong smell of coal smoke. She supposed that she would get used to the coal and begin to hardly notice it. The way she was with the turf back home. She often heard visitors in the hotel remark on the lovely peaty smoke that wafted over Tullamore, so she knew it was something you got used to.

Lucy had insisted that she take a full hour off now and have a walk around the surrounding streets to acquaint herself with the city. Remembering the book on crocheting she wanted to buy, Sarah crossed the cobbles to the bookshop, and then changed her mind. Instead of going in, she turned and walked towards the top of the lane, the part she had not seen yet. She had a feeling that if she went into the shop she would get stuck with David McGuire, and she did not want that.

She wanted to have a look around the shops and the streets on her own without having to talk to someone, or having to watch every word she said in case the subject came around to why she had come to Newcastle.

Within five minutes of browsing around, Sarah was fascinated by the variety of buildings and the different businesses within them. The city was now bustling with people and traffic and she had to be careful that she didn't walk into people or the tall lampposts or litter-bins that seemed to be placed every few yards.

When she wanted to cross a busy main road, she had to follow the crowds, watching carefully for cars and buses and trams. When the streets got wider and the buildings taller, she realised she was in the heart of the city. She looked along at the unusual curved, Regency-style stone buildings, and then glanced up at the place name – Grey Street – and she felt a small flutter in her chest. Only a few weeks ago she could never have imagined being in a place like this. She hardly knew Dublin and she'd lived only a train ride from it all her life.

Every time she caught the train from Tullamore to the city, she would have a knot of anxiety at the thought of negotiating her way through the crowds in Henry Street or Grafton Street, and the O'Connell Street Bridge which merged the two areas. Even catching the bus to and from the train station into the centre had seemed like a great adventure. And yet, here she was, in a city maybe bigger than Dublin, and knowing that she would be working only a few minutes away from all this every single day. Strangely, the thought of being part of such a big city seemed to comfort her.

In Tullamore almost every second person would acknowledge you, and she could guarantee that she would know someone to chat to on every single walk up the main streets. On her return from working in the hotel Martina had greeted her every night with, "Well, any news? Who did you see today?" And her sister-in-law would know almost everyone that Sarah mentioned. And if she didn't know them, she would make it her business to find out, ferreting around between Sarah and James until she pinned down the precise family and the townland that the person came from.

And while Martina was a particularly inquisitive person, Sarah knew that her friend Sheila's family would ask the same questions and so would Patricia Quinn's. A pang struck at her heart at the thought of her so-called friend, but she pushed it away and made herself concentrate on crossing roads and looking in shop windows.

As she went along, Sarah realised that all these strange people going about their business, taking no heed of her, made her feel the same as everyone else. She would bump into no one here who knew anything about her. No one who knew what Con Tierney and Patricia Quinn had done. She could walk around here with her head high and pretend that nothing bad had ever happened to her.

That knowledge gave her a warm comforting glow, and made her step all the lighter. She wandered around for another ten minutes, at one point wondering if she might have doubled back on herself. The smell of hot pastries drew her to stand outside a baker's shop. She deliberated whether or not to buy a warm sausage roll and maybe a cake to bring back to eat in the kitchen. Then, the familiar fragrance of frying fish wafted past and she noticed there was a café next door.

She walked up to the glass window, then halted to look in. It had dim, rose-tinted lighting, vinyl-covered seats in small booths, and a bar-type area with high stools. She could see several waitresses rushing up and down in their black dresses and white pinafores and hats taking or delivering orders. Most people were sitting in groups at the booths, but there were two girls around her own age sitting at the single seats in the bar area. They were both dressed in smart fashionable suits, with matching hats. One was flicking through a magazine while she smoked a cigarette, and the other looked as though she was reading a letter. There were three other unoccupied seats.

Sarah wondered if she had the nerve to go in on her own.

Then she heard the music – Elvis Presley singing "It's Now or Never" – and she made up her mind. She walked to the glass door, took a deep breath and walked in. She went over to one of the chairs, and then suddenly realised that the seat was several inches too high to just casually sit down on. She stepped back to check, and then realised there was a wooden bar on the legs which she presumably would have to hoist herself up on. She was working out how to negotiate it when she felt a hand on her arm. She turned around quickly.

"I thought I recognised that Rapunzel hair. Do you need a leg up?" David McGuire said, a wide grin on his face.

Sarah looked at him, then surprised herself by grinning back at him. She knew it was mad making so free with a stranger but there was something about his manner that made her feel she'd known him for years. "Yes, I was just trying to work out how to get up on this thing."

"Ah, there's a knack to it. Put your heel on the bar and then lean your hands on the counter and push up," he told her. Then, when she started to move, he reached a helping hand to hoist her up onto the stool. "Well done," he said, laughing. "You're obviously not used to sitting on the high bar-stool in pubs."

"Indeed I'm not," Sarah told him. "The only bar I've been in regularly is the one in the hotel back in Ireland where I used to work."

"A multi-talented woman." His eyes were bright with laughter. He sat up on the stool beside her now, then checked the crease in both legs of his perfectly pressed suit trousers. "And how are you getting on with Miss Harrison?" he asked. "Has she frightened you off yet?"

"No," Sarah said, "she's actually very nice."

David put his two forefingers in the shape of a cross. "D'you not think she looks a bit like a vampire with all that black hair and dark eyes and white face?"

Sarah lifted up the menu book. "I'm not even going to answer that." Then, without taking her eyes off the menu, she said, "Do you come in here regularly, or did you see me coming in?"

He turned his head to the side. "D'you mean you didn't even notice?"

Sarah looked at him now. "Notice what?"

He patted his head with one hand. "I was just coming out of the barber's when I saw you walking in here. He's practically scalped me. I won't need another haircut for about six months."

Sarah looked out of the window and spotted the red and white spiralling pole on the opposite side. "Ah . . ." She glanced at his tidy, glistening dark hair but couldn't see any difference from this morning.

He raised one eyebrow. "Did you think I'd actually followed you all the way from the shop, like?" He winked. "You did – didn't you?"

Her cheeks reddened. "Of course not! I just wondered," she hedged. "It's a bit strange bumping into you in a certain café which is quite a distance from our shops."

"But it's a well-known café, and the others are further away. Plus, it has a good juke-box."

"It's still a bit of a coincidence. It must be a twenty-minute walk."

"Are you sure about that?"

Sarah looked at him. "What do you mean?"

"We're only two or three streets away," he told her. "You go back out of here onto Grey Street, cross over and Pilgrims Lane is straight across. You can do it in two minutes. This is the nearest café to the shop." He started laughing again. "By the sounds of it, I'd say you've been wandering about in circles. It's lucky I came in or you mightn't find your way back to the shop. You could be wandering about for days."

She suddenly realised that he was serious, and that she had made an idiot of herself for suggesting he had followed her. "Oh, God!" she said, biting her lip. "I'm sorry . . . that was silly of me thinking we were so far from the shop. Imagine if I got lost and was late back for work on my first day!"

"It's all right," he said, laughing. "It's easy to get mixed up when everything is so new."

She checked her watch. She only had half an hour left, so she would have to order quickly or she would be late.

"I'll have fish and chips," she told the young waitress who came over to her.

"D'you want the fish tea?" the girl asked. "It comes with two slices of bread and a cup of tea. It's only sixpence more."

"Yes, she does," David answered. "And I'll have the same." When the waitress left he turned to her. "It's all right. I'm treating you – seeing as it's your first day."

"No, I won't let you."

"I insist," he told her. "You can treat me another time." He said it so matter-of-factly – the way any one of her friends might have done at home.

"Okay then," she finally said. "Thanks." But she didn't look straight at him because she didn't want to see the admiring look that she knew was in his eyes. She liked his banter, his good manners and his nice friendly ways – but that was it. She would waste no time in putting him straight if he crossed any lines.

An older man came to sit on the stool beside David and struck up a conversation about the changeable Newcastle weather, which somehow then led on to a discussion about how the whole country was going to the dogs. Sarah didn't mind. She was happy that she had company to sit with and took the time to glance around the busy café. She noticed the fancy, frilly little curtains on the windows and thought that the pelmet would work well in the shop window in a different pattern. Without making it obvious, she looked along the rows of diners, taking in the women's fashions. Most of them were dressed fairly ordinarily, but there were a few whose outfits stood out as being more fashionable and obviously expensive. The two girls beside her were too close to examine properly, and neither of them spoke to each other or to her – something that would never have happened in Dublin.

The fish and chips came. "Look at the size of it – I'll never eat all this!" she laughed.

"Don't worry," David told her. "I'll polish off anything you can't manage." Then he leaned in closer and lowered his voice. "And if I can't, I'm sure the fella beside me will. He's got the biggest mouth I've ever seen."

Sarah had to put her hand to her mouth to stop herself laughing.

They walked back to the shops together and as they crossed the busy road back to Pilgrims Lane, Sarah realised he had been telling the truth about the distance. Neither of them referred to it.

"I met someone who knows you this morning," Sarah said, as they walked towards the shop. "Harriet . . ." She couldn't remember her surname. "A young nurse."

"Oh, aye – I know Harriet," he said, nodding and smiling. "Lovely girl. She's often in your place, great pals with your Miss Harrison. I can't imagine what they have in common though."

Sarah thought about the conversation on medication she'd overheard, but she said nothing. She checked her watch when she reached the bookshop. "I've nearly ten minutes left. I might have a look for the book on crochet. I want to have a read up on it tonight."

"You're keen," he said. "I would have thought you'd be out and about or watching the telly."

"We don't have a telly at the house – it's a rented house."

He looked at her. "You could come out to our house and watch it any night. Me mam and dad like visitors, and they'd love to chat to you about Ireland. Me granny and granddad were from Dublin. Did I tell you that already?"

"No . . ." She had mixed feelings now. She would have loved to meet people from Dublin, but she knew that accepting his invitation would be a mistake. "Thanks for the offer, but I won't." She looked beyond him to the shops on either side of the cobble lane. "I've got things to do."

"Like what? Surely you're not going to be working in the evenings?"

"I need to get the local papers and start looking for a sewing machine to have back at the house."

"Okay, maybe another time. The craft books are down at the back of the shop on the right-hand side." He looked over at Harrison's shop. "Hey, she's got a new sign in your lovely clean window."

Sarah turned towards it now. There was a small, neatly written sign which said, *Alterations. Please See Inside*. Lucy must have

100

made the sign while she was out, using the templates she had bought. She had also finished cleaning the other window and had put the colourful lining paper in it, to match the one Sarah had finished. She hadn't put anything else, obviously waiting for her new employee to sort it.

"I'll definitely have to get the sewing machine now," she said, beaming at him.

A few minutes later as she was walking out of the shop with her wrapped book, David caught up with her again. "If you have time any night, and you fancy going to the pictures or something like that . . ."

Sarah could feel he wasn't going to give up easily.

* * *

The afternoon went by quicker than the morning. Sarah finished off the window display, using remnants of bright material pinned up on the board behind and posters displaying sewing patterns. Lucy actually went out to stand in the lane to get a proper look at it, and came back in and told her what an improvement it made.

Three people came in enquiring about alterations, and all said they would be back with the garments the following day.

"I don't suppose you could make me a pair of curtains, just small ones like, for the kitchen?" another woman asked. "I can bring in the measurements tomorrow."

Sarah said "yes" to everything. When she mentioned buying a sewing machine, Lucy waved away the idea. "You can use the treadle one in the back-shop when we're quiet, and I have an electric one at home that Mary used. It's just gathering dust. I'll drop it out to your house tonight."

One part of Sarah's mind went to work on ideas for items to fill the window, while the other part wondered how on earth someone with no interest in handicrafts came to own a sewing business.

"If it's okay with you," Sarah said, later in the afternoon when they were having a cup of tea, "I thought I might take some of the odd balls of wool and knit up a few scarves and maybe some gloves and socks for the window display? It's getting colder now and it might get people thinking about making their own. I could also do a few teddy bears and knitted clothes for dolls, the kind of thing that will catch children's eyes with Christmas coming up."

"You won't have time to catch your breath with all these plans."

"I know I must sound like a maniac going on about work all the time, but I need to keep busy or I'll end up looking at four walls every night."

"You're a young girl, you'll make friends and you'll want to go out."

Sarah lifted her eyebrows. "I've had enough of friends . . ."

Lucy looked at her. "Was it very bad?"

"It was one of my oldest friends."

Lucy bit her lip. "If you ever want to talk . . ."

"Thanks, but I've wasted enough time on it. I'm here to make a fresh start."

"Don't bottle things up, Sarah." The shop-keeper's voice was soft and low. "I've done that with things in my own life, and it's not good."

Sarah smiled at her. "I'm grand. I'm lucky to have got this chance, and I'm not going to waste it fretting over the past. What's done is done."

CHAPTER 13

When the door was locked on Harrison's shop, the two workers went their separate ways. Sarah went down towards the grocer's shop at the bottom of the lane with a list of things she needed for the house. She also had a brown package with three balls of red wool, knitting needles and a pattern for gloves and scarves, so she could get started on things for the shop that night.

There was a queue in the shop, and when it was her turn she went forward with her list. She read the first few items out quickly, and when the young girl behind the counter looked blankly at her, she remembered what Lucy Harrison had said. Before the girl had the chance to say anything, she repeated the items slowly and clearly.

She came out laden with more shopping than she had planned, and regretted getting carried away with the greater range of items than she was used to.

Lucy had loaned her a big shopping bag that was in the kitchen cupboard, and the lady in the shop had given her two brown-paper bags, one inside the other to reinforce it. She had bought potatoes, lamb chops, bacon and sausages, eggs and bread, butter and milk, plus basic toiletries like toothpaste, soap and shampoo. The shop surprisingly sold household items such as towels, so she bought two – a large and a small – to swap over with the two she had brought from home.

She stood for a few minute outside the shop, juggling items from one bag to another as she didn't want the paper bags to break, and she squeezed two of the balls of wool and the pattern into her handbag.

As she walked past the cathedral, she put the heavy bag in her right hand down on the ground to bless herself. After she did so, she found herself turning in towards the open door. The cathedral was silent, with only two people kneeling in pews up near the front. Sarah put her bags on the wooden bench and knelt down on the padded kneeler. She blessed herself and then she took a few minutes to look around the Gothic building. The unusual stencilling work around the arches and windows caught her eye, then she studied the beautiful stained-glass windows and the decorative tiles around the walls and the window sills. Sarah thought the window above the altar depicting the Blessed Sacrament was particularly beautiful and it reminded her of one of the windows in the church in Tullamore.

She prayed for her mother and father and her family and friends back home, and then, as she went to bless herself to go, she added another prayer that she would start to feel at home in Newcastle.

When she turned the key in the door of the house, she was pleased when she heard Jane's voice calling, "How was the first day?"

A surge of relief rose inside her at the friendly welcome, and she called back, "Grand," then kicked the door closed behind her and went along the hallway.

The kitchen windows were steamed up from boiling water and hot fat. Jane and Elizabeth introduced her to Anna – one of the medical students.

Anna was a large, well-made girl with a cheery face and a London accent. Like the other girls, she was dressed casually in jeans and a jumper. "I heard we had a nice, smart new lodger – pleased to meet you." She held her hand out.

Sarah dropped her shopping and shook the girl's hand. "Are you sure it was me they were talking about?"

"Well, just look at you – your nice smart suit and perfect hair. We're always flapping around in the mornings, trying to find something clean to wear."

"Give her time," Elizabeth laughed. "It's her first week and she needs to make a good impression."

"I'm doing chips and eggs and beans," Jane told her, "and I've enough for everyone. It'll save you cooking. You're probably tired going straight into work after all your travelling yesterday."

"That's very good of you. But I'll have it on one condition: if I can cook tomorrow's meal. I bought a few lamb chops and I was going to do them with potatoes."

"Lovely," Anna said. "Can you make that Wednesday."

"Fine." Sarah looked at the other two girls. "I can get another couple of chops, if you're brave enough to try my cooking."

"Thanks, but I'm on a late," Jane said.

Elizabeth rolled her eyes. "And so, unfortunately, am I."

"Vivienne is going home for a few days straight after work tomorrow," Anna said, "but I'll be more than happy to try your cooking," She pointed behind her. "The girl that previously had your room used the end cupboard, so it's empty if you want to put your shopping in it."

"Grand," Sarah said, lifting the bags across to unpack them.

"I love your Irish accent," Anna said. "It's different – it's really nice."

Sarah turned back. "Do you think so? I've been worrying all day that people might not understand me."

Anna wrinkled her nose. "Why on earth would you worry? You speak perfectly clearly. I had more trouble understanding the Geordie accent when I came here than I have understanding you."

Sarah opened the cupboard and started putting her things away, thinking that things didn't seem too strange here now. In ways they were a whole lot better. She could never remember Martina calling out to her in a friendly, welcoming manner when she returned from work. Not once. And even though her sister-in-law had been the stranger coming into Love's home-place Sarah could not remember a meal being made for her with good heart. And when she had cooked for her brother and his wife, the food had been eaten in silence and no remarks passed on it.

The only time Martina had been nice to her was when the news had come out about Con and Patricia Quinn. And James hadn't been much better. He had driven her up for the boat to England with hardly a word of affection or care as to how she would get on in her new life. She would keep all that to the front of her mind. When things were hard, she would remind herself that total strangers had been kinder to her than her own family.

* * *

By the time Lucy Harrison arrived with the sewing machine, Sarah had knitted a child's scarf with fringes and one glove. She was casting on the stitches for the second glove when the doorbell went. As she came down the staircase she could see her employer's blue Austin car through the stained-glass panel above the door.

"Here we are," Lucy said, lifting the sewing-machine case into the hallway.

Sarah thought she looked younger than before. She had her hair out loose and was wearing grey slacks with a grey cardigan and fine blue polo-neck sweater underneath. She looked less tense and worried too.

"That's very good of you," Sarah told her, taking the heavy cream case from her. "I really appreciate you bringing it out to me."

"Are you getting settled in okay?"

"Yes, the girls have all been very friendly, and my room is comfortable and warm." She didn't say how much warmer it was than her little room back in Tullamore. She paused. "Would you like to come up and see it?"

"Yes. Why not?"

They climbed the stairs and Sarah showed her into the room.

"It's not bad at all," Lucy commented as she glanced around.

"I'm going to make new curtains and a matching bedspread."

"Have you a table for the sewing machine?"

Sarah raised her eyebrows. "I never thought. I suppose I'll have to get one. It wouldn't be fair on the others to use the table downstairs. I need one I can leave the machine on all the time."

"I have a spare small table," Lucy said. She looked at her watch. "I can be back with it in ten minutes."

"There's no rush," Sarah said. "You've done enough tonight."

"Would you like to come on a run out to the house with me? It would give you a chance to see more of the city."

"Yes, I would," Sarah said.

She went over to the hook on the back of the door and lifted her suit jacket. As they walked downstairs and out to the car, Sarah looked down at herself and thought that she looked formal, and maybe a bit old-fashioned, compared to the other girls – and even Lucy. She decided that she would buy some slacks or jean to wear at home, and a pair of boots. It was bound to get colder over the next few weeks and a blouse and skirt wouldn't be warm enough.

They drove down onto the main street, then a short while later passed Clayton Street which was the turn for the shop, and then down past the station. Lucy then turned up Grainger Street and then they came up to Haymarket where the bus station was. They passed the Royal Infirmary – where Elizabeth and Jane were nursing – and finally Lucy pulled up outside a row of tall redbrick houses.

"This is it," she said.

"Do you walk to work from here every morning?" Sarah asked.

"Occasionally I go by car, but most of the time it's not worth it. It only takes me about ten minutes walking. It's about the same distance as your place, but on the opposite side of the city centre."

"Have you always lived here?" Sarah asked, looking up at the building.

"It was my parents' house, and I've lived in it on and off in the last twenty years, but when I was young I used to spend a lot of time in London. My mother was from London and she chose a school down there for me. I boarded during the week and went to my grandparents' house in Richmond at the weekends." She opened the car door and got out. "My mother used to travel down regularly to see both me and my grandparents. It's my father's side of the family who are related to Miss Reynolds – they are cousins."

"That's why you don't have a strong Newcastle accent," Sarah said as she joined her employer on the pavement. "Compared to Harriet and . . ." she almost said "and David McGuire" but stopped herself. She thought it might look as though she had boys on her mind instead of work, "and some of the customers."

Lucy gave a wry smile. "We weren't encouraged to have any kind of local accent in school – we all had to speak with the same received pronunciation. It made it a rather hard for me to mix with the local children when I came back home to Newcastle at the holidays."

Sarah didn't know exactly what "received pronunciation" meant, but she guessed that it explained her employer's careful but clear way of talking.

Lucy got out her keys and, opening the front door, ushered Sarah in.

Sarah caught her breath as they walked into the hallway, and when she followed Lucy into a large sitting-room she realised she had been expecting the same mess she first encountered in the shop. Instead, she found the opposite. A wine leather chesterfield sofa and matching deep-buttoned chairs were placed around a leather-topped coffee table with carved legs, holding a large crystal vase. The white marble fireplace had a gold carriage clock on top with matching Chinese vases on either side. There was another larger, tooled-leather-topped desk at the window. On top of it were about a dozen silver-framed family photographs. The wall opposite the fireplace held a bookcase with five doors in leaded glass. Each shelf was filled with books, all organised in matching jackets or size. Lucy Harrison obviously read at home as well as at work.

"This is a lovely room," Sarah said. "In fact it's a beautiful house altogether."

"Thank you. It's a bit big for one person, but I'm used to it. I don't know if Miss Reynolds told you, but my father hasn't been too well for some time and is in full-time residential care now."

Sarah vaguely remembered the teacher saying something about it, but so much had been going on when she was leaving that she didn't take it in. "That must be hard."

"I manage," Lucy said briskly, "I have a woman who comes in to clean every Friday, and it keeps things in order."

They went into the big airy kitchen and Lucy put a pan of milk on a ring of the gas cooker and then put a spoonful of Camp coffee into two mugs with two spoonfuls of sugar. When the milk was nearly boiled she poured it into the mugs, stirring quickly until there was a white froth on the top, and then she brought out some chocolate biscuits and a tin of Walker's shortbread.

Sarah took the mug of coffee, hoping that she would like it. She had only tried it a few times and couldn't imagine how people would prefer it to tea.

Lucy studied her for a few moments. "Are you finding things very different here from Ireland?"

"A little . . . I think it's because I'm used to living in the country. I would be the very same if I had moved to Dublin. In some ways I like the difference." Sarah sipped the coffee, and was surprised at how lovely and comforting it tasted.

"And how are you finding the other girls at the house?" Lucy held out the biscuits and Sarah took a piece of shortbread.

"They've been very welcoming – all very friendly."

After they had finished their coffee, Sarah followed her employer upstairs to get the table for sewing. When she saw the little polished, drop-leaf table she immediately said, "I can't take that! It's much too good."

"I don't need it. I have a table in each of the bedrooms and that particular one was actually in the way."

"Well, if you're sure. I'll take great care of it."

"There's some spare felt in the shop that you can have. If you put it over the table then it won't mark it."

As they carried the table down the stairs between them, Sarah thought back to when she had first met Lucy Harrison only a day and a half ago. The difference between how her employer seemed then and now was unimaginable. She was cheerier and more relaxed this evening, and her kindness was more in keeping with that of a friend than a boss. But then, Sarah thought, maybe there was a difference in the way she was looking at things herself.

* * *

They got the table upstairs in Victoria Place and, after Sarah saw her employer off, she went back to set up her new sewing machine. She put a towel under the machine to avoid marking the table and then had a good look at it. It had been left in good condition with the sewing box full of needles and threads, and when she plugged it in, it worked exactly as it should. She would be ready to start on alterations from tomorrow.

She sat in the old blue velvet armchair and knitted for an hour or so and then she looked over at the window and realised it was dark outside. She was closing the curtains when she remembered the house across the road and the ambulance from that morning. She paused to notice there were no lights on and wondered if they were all visiting whoever was sick at the hospital. Then she thought how long ago it seemed since she had last looked down on the street. The day had gone well and she had learned more and done more than she had envisaged.

She went downstairs and chatted to the three girls while the kettle boiled and a slice of bread toasted under the grill. She checked about the water for having a bath and was advised to put the immersion heater on for an hour. As she buttered the toast, she decided she would take the tea and toast back up to her room. It would be easy to sit at the kitchen table with them and drink her tea and join in with their chat, but she somehow felt it was too soon. There was also the chance that the conversation might turn to something personal she didn't want to talk about.

She went back to her room and finished off the second glove for the shop window and knitted a small child's hat. After that, she put her blonde hair in a thick plait and pinned it on top of her head. She then she went down for her bath.

She noticed some of the girls had a bottle of bubble bath and some nice shampoo, so she made a mental note to buy some when she was next shopping. She only washed her hair once or twice a week at most as it took so long to dry.

After her bath she got into bed and had a look at the book on crocheting. Within five minutes she was fast asleep and dreaming she was walking into the church in Tullamore on the arm of Con Tierney.

CHAPTER 14

She slept soundly and didn't wake until her alarm went off at quarter to eight. She lay for a while then got up and went over to the window. It was dry and bright with a clear sky. There was a milk float out in the street this morning, so she stood and watched the milkman move the vehicle every three or four gates. Then she saw the door of the house open and the dark-skinned teenage girl came out in her dressing-gown and lifted the two pints of milk from the step and go back in. Everything looked more ordinary than the day before. Then a young boy came along on a bicycle with a newspaper satchel over his shoulder, stopping at most of the houses to push a paper or a magazine through the letterbox.

She went downstairs and, as she washed and brushed her teeth, she thought that having milkmen and paperboys calling at your house was a good way to start the day off. Back home there were no deliveries; milk came from your own or your neighbour's cows or was bought in the shop along with your newspaper.

She stood in front of the wide walnut wardrobe for a few minutes deliberating what to wear, eventually deciding on a green short-sleeved linen dress with a wide, buttoned collar and a flared matching jacket. The weather was reasonable for the end of

September, so if it got warm in the shop she could always take the jacket off.

It was an outfit she had made for a First Communion two years ago, and had kept for special occasions or for Mass on a Sunday. She had made several outfits like this and thought she should get the wear out of them as they might go out of fashion, and dressing smart gave a good impression for the shop.

She tied her hair up in a long pony-tail, then walked down to the hill to the city centre, feeling much easier than she had the previous morning. She gave herself enough time to stop off at the cathedral for a few minutes and arrived at the shop just as Lucy was unlocking the door.

The first customers were the Bradley sisters, each carrying a bag of garments which needed altering. She had to take them through the back-shop to try on several of the garments, which prompted Lucy to say they would organise a proper changing area as soon as they got a quiet spell during the day.

The morning was busier than her first day and by lunchtime she had several other people in with alterations. Sarah noticed that while people were waiting to be served, they passed the time looking through knitting or sewing patterns and often ended up buying them or some other items such as sewing needles or elastic. She didn't mention this to Lucy as it might sound as though she was suggesting that her alteration service was bringing more custom to the shop, but she knew it had to be the case.

When her lunch break came, she left the shop quickly and without looking across to the bookshop in case she met David McGuire again. Whilst there was a part of her that wouldn't have minded spending an hour in his light, cheery company, there was a bigger part that was reluctant to give him an opening to be too friendly.

When she got onto Clayton Street she went left instead of crossing the road to the café she had been in the day before, and continued to walk along until she came to Grey's Monument. She looked at it for a minute or two, reading the inscription on the pedestal which gave historical information about the political career of Charles Earl Grey and said he was *'an advocate of peace and the fearless and consistent champion of civil and religious liberty'*.

She read the inscription a couple of times but it meant little to her, as did the figure of Charles Grey who seemed to be hundreds of feet in the air. She wandered onto Northumberland Street and there she found a large, impressive department store – Fenwick's.

As she walked through the ground floor, Sarah quickly realised that this was a more expensive store than she was used to. But as she glanced around at the other women, she could see that she was as well-dressed as any of them. She browsed around the perfume department and sprayed a little on her wrist. She might treat herself to a bottle when she had received a few pay packets and could work out where she was up to financially. She knew she had the money that James had given her plus her own savings, but she intended to put that into a post-office savings account for emergencies. She would start off working on her wages and stick to that.

There was a directory of all the different departments by the staircase so she went over to study it. The word 'Haberdashery' caught her eye, so she checked which floor it was on and headed for it.

Within a few minutes of browsing around the department, looking at patterns and feeling the weight and drape of the more unusual materials, Sarah knew that Fenwick's department store was catering to a very different type of customer to Harrison's. The people who came in here had a lot more money to spend, and could afford to pay for expensive materials and for alterations to new clothes. When one of the shop assistants came over to see if she needed help, Sarah discovered that they actually had a tailoring department where outfits were made to measure.

"We make every kind of outfits in the store," the young assistant told her. "People travel from all over to have things made for weddings and special occasions. We've even made dresses for famous film stars. A few years ago we had Anna Neagle getting fitted for a whole load of dresses for a film she was in. We had pictures of the dresses on display at the time, so people could see."

Sarah shook her head in wonder, although she did not admit that she wasn't exactly sure if she knew who Anna Neagle was.

"You're Irish, aren't you?" the girl said now. "My granny is from Ireland."

Sarah felt her body stiffen.

"She's from County Kerry."

Sarah's shoulders relaxed. Kerry was fine. It was a long way from Tullamore and no one was likely to have heard of her or Con Tierney. "I come from the Midlands," she told the girl, "but the town is so small you won't have heard of it."

As she walked away, Sarah suddenly felt silly for caring so much whether people knew Tullamore or not. If she stayed in Newcastle, the time would probably come where she would meet someone who might know her background, and she would just have to deal with it. Most people had things about themselves or their families they didn't want to talk about, and she would try to remind herself of that.

Fenwick's haberdashery had a much greater range of patterns than their own shop, so Sarah had a look through the patterns for soft toys and bought a bunch of them for a rag doll and some for a teddy bear, and while the assistant was wrapping them up and sorting out her change, Sarah noted down a few pattern makes and numbers to suggest them to her employer when the time was right.

When she left the store, Sarah walked around the outside of it, looking in at the window displays. Again, she picked up a few ideas that would help to improve both the interior and exterior of Harrison's shop.

* * *

There was a slump in business around four o'clock and Lucy suggested that they have a look at the space in the back of the shop for fitting clothes.

"I don't want to take too much space away from your sewing

area, but I definitely think we need to have a little area where people can try on the clothes that need altering." She gave a little sigh. "Some day I'll get around to sorting out the rooms upstairs, but there's so much to be done there that at the moment I can't face it."

A short while later Sarah was on the old treadle machine running up a pink rose-patterned curtain for the small changing-room they had fashioned in a corner. Lucy phoned a shop that had a long mirror on a stand, and they said that if she could wait until their own shop closed at half past five, then they would bring it down to Harrison's in the delivery van. Lucy then went down to a hardware shop to buy a few yards of curtain wire and some hooks for customers to hang their clothes on.

An old painted wooden chair was washed down and looked presentable with a flowery cushion which Sarah ran up on the machine with the leftover material. By the time they closed the door on Tuesday evening, the changing room was ready.

* * *

On Wednesday morning – a half-day in the shop along with Saturday – Harriet Scott called in at the shop again. She was her normal chatty self when all three were in the kitchen, but when Lucy went out to the rear of the shop to answer the phone at one point, she had whispered to Sarah, "What on earth have you done to the place? The window, the inside of the shop – everything. It's like a different place."

"Do you think it looks better?"

"Of course I do!" She rolled her eyes to the ceiling. "I love all the knitted things you have in the window. Did you do them yourself?"

Sarah nodded. "They're easy – they're only children's patterns."

"Do you sell them in the shop? I've a niece who's just started learning to knit at school. I bet she would love them."

"Have a look in the pattern book on the counter," Sarah told her. "The children's patterns are all at the back."

"I'll do that on my way out."

The shop bell rang and Sarah automatically got to her feet.

Harriet took a last mouthful of her tea and put her nurse's cap on. "I'd better get moving too."

When Sarah walked into the shop David McGuire was standing at the counter. "I got a second-hand book in on embroidery I thought you might fancy." He handed her the book. "It's only a tanner. No problem if you don't want it, like."

"Oh, thanks, that was good of you." Sarah looked at the cover and then turned the hard-backed book over to read the back.

"Good morning, Mr McGuire." Harriet's voice was light and warm.

"Ah, our friendly neighbourhood nurse!" He smiled at her. "Most people have the decency to wait until halfway through the day before having a skive off work. No wonder the National Health is in the state it is."

"You cheeky devil!" She laughed. "I don't start my rounds for another ten minutes. This very short stop-off is during my own time."

"Ah well," he said, shrugging. "That's what they all say."

Harriet tilted her head to the side. "Are you going to the dance in the town hall on Saturday?"

He shifted his gaze to the floor. "Not sure . . . I haven't really thought that far yet."

"You'll disappoint a few if you're not there." Harriet looked over at Sarah. "You wouldn't think it to look at him, but he's a great dancer."

David looked at Sarah now. "Why don't you come? It would be a good chance to get to know more people."

Sarah looked up from the embroidery book and caught the dark shadow that crossed the nurse's face. Immediately she knew that the attention David McGuire was giving her wasn't being received well.

"I don't think so," she said, "I've got a lot to do over the weekend, and dancing is the last thing on my mind."

"Ah, don't be such a stick-in-the mud!" he said. He looked at Harriet. "Tell her, that she needs to get out and about or she'll never meet people."

"No." Sarah's tone was definite. She had no intention of getting on the wrong side of the friendly nurse. If she did, she might not only alienate Harriet but Lucy Harrison as well. Besides, she didn't want to encourage any further interest from the bookshop manager. "I've no notion of going to a dance this weekend. I've loads of sewing to keep me busy."

He winked at her. "You could maybe meet the man of your dreams."

Sarah knew she had to nail the situation down, even if it meant some embarrassment for her. "As I already told Harriet, I had enough of men back in Ireland, thank you," she said. "And the last thing I'm looking for is the man of my dreams."

Harriet's shoulders instantly relaxed. "Oh, leave the poor girl alone," she said. "When she's ready she'll come with us – won't you, Sarah?" She put her arm through Sarah's arm as though they were life-long friends.

David looked exaggeratedly dejected now, as though his attention had all been in jest. "Ah well . . ."

"I'm sure Harriet's a good dancer," Sarah's voice was deliberately light, as though she hadn't noticed his disappointment. She went to open the book then she suddenly remembered. "I'll get that sixpence for you now."

Lucy was still on the phone in the back-shop as Sarah went past her into the kitchen to get the money from her handbag. She loitered about for a few minutes, putting the mugs into the sink, giving David and Harriet time to talk on their own. Instinctively, she was sorry for Harriet – it seemed obvious that David had no interest in a romance with her. But Sarah knew that he liked her. She'd had enough lads after her back home to know when someone had his eye on her. Also, she didn't know how serious Harriet's feelings were for him, and she would hate her to feel there was any competition when there most certainly wasn't.

The shop-bell rang and Sarah took the sixpence and went back into the shop, knowing that both Harriet and David would go now that a customer had appeared.

* * *

The morning was busy with customers collecting their alterations and others depositing items to be altered. When they were having a cup of tea around eleven o'clock, Lucy commented that the takings were up on previous Wednesdays.

"We've also sold a lot more knitting patterns for gloves and scarves," she told Sarah, "and we're completely sold out of the pattern for the rag-doll you have in the window."

"That's great, isn't it?" Sarah checked.

"Of course, because we've also sold all the things needed for the doll like embroidery thread and stuffing. We haven't sold much more material because people use the odds and ends they have at home, but it's still extra sales." She paused, thinking. "Will you be okay tomorrow on your own?"

Sarah looked at her quizzically.

"I usually have a Thursday off . . ." She cleared her throat. "But I can cancel it if you feel it's too soon to leave you on your own."

Sarah thought quickly. "I'll be grand. You have your day off." She sounded confident but inside she wondered whether she would manage if a crowd of customers came in all at once. What if someone wanted to order something they didn't have? She hadn't learned about the ordering system with the wholesalers yet.

"Are you sure?" the shop-owner checked.

"I'll be fine." She would ask about the ordering system later, and if the worst came to the worst, she would wait until her employer returned on Friday. "I'll just do everything the way you've shown me."

Lucy raised her eyebrows. "I think you would actually be much better just doing things your own way, Sarah." She smiled. "Anything you've done has been an improvement, so just continue."

On her way home from work, Sarah stopped at the grocer's shop again and bought another chop for Anna, some carrots, a tin of peas and a packet of Bisto to make gravy. When she got back to the house in Victoria Street, she changed into a comfortable sweater and skirt. She had a cup of tea and then she started peeling the potatoes and carrots for the meal she had promised to cook.

"Well, this is a lovely meal to come home to," Anna said, when she sat down at the table. "I'm absolutely starving." She immediately started cutting into her chop.

"It's a pity the others were working," Sarah said. "I'd have been happy to cook for them as well."

Anna grinned at her. "Don't worry, when they hear how good a cook you are, you'll have plenty of opportunities!"

Sarah beamed back at her. It had been a good day

* * *

Thursday went by even quicker than the previous days. The window-cleaner came in the morning, and Sarah noticed the sparkling glass made a real difference in the shop window. Every day she added something she had made the night before at home to the display – a mixture of bright knitted items and things she had sewed. The latest items were peg-bags and tea-cosies. She didn't have a pattern for the peg-bag, it was just something she had made up herself, and she was delighted when several customers asked if she would make one for them.

"I'll have to check with Miss Harrison," she told them. "But if it's okay with her I'll make a few up to sell in the shop."

As the day progressed, instead of being anxious at coping with the shop on her own, she found she was actually more relaxed and confident. She managed the customers easily, working quickly and asking anyone who needed more detailed advice on knitting and sewing patterns if they would wait a few minutes longer until she'd served the others first.

At lunchtime Sarah slipped out for a few minutes to buy a pie and a cake and after taking a break to eat them, she went to work on her alterations on the shop sewing machine. Apart from saving time, it meant she wouldn't bump into David McGuire. He had dropped into the shop in the afternoon, but when Sarah made it plain that she was too busy to chat, he left quickly.

The day flew in and by the time she closed the door at half-past five, she knew that the shop takings were up again on the previous days. She also had a feeling of satisfaction knowing that in less than a week she could run Harrison's on her own.

CHAPTER 15

When Sarah came home from work on Saturday afternoon, her mind was full of all the things that would keep her busy over the weekend. She had two bags of alterations and a skirt to make for a customer. If she got through everything for the customers, she had plenty of sewing she wanted to do for herself.

She dropped the bags upstairs in her bedroom, and then came down to the kitchen to make a sandwich. After that, she planned to walk back into the city to have a look at the shops. Her wage packet had held more than double the amount of money that she'd got from the hotel. She had checked the amount of rent she had to pay for her room with Lucy Harrison, and she would ask the girls how much she owed for the heating and lighting, and for the communal foods they bought.

She calculated that she would be able to save a bit of her wages every week, and she would add the money she made from the alterations to that as well. The shopkeeper had told her that anything she did outside of her working hours was her own business.

She was sitting eating her sandwich when she heard the front door opening. She looked up expectantly to see a medium-built girl with long hair who she didn't know.

The girl did a double-take. "Ah . . . you're the new one," she said. "Someone mentioned we had a new one."

Sarah realised it was the trainee doctor she hadn't yet met. She smiled and put out her hand. "I'm Sarah – Sarah Love."

"Vivienne Taylor-Smith." Her face remained serious. "Are you *Irish*?"

Sarah smiled. "I am, for my sins." As she looked at her, she noticed that the girl's face was badly marked with small acne scars.

Vivienne raised her eyebrows. "We have lots of your kind working in the hospital." Her words were short and clipped. "Nurses mainly. In fact, we're inundated with them. Don't you have hospitals back in Ireland?"

Sarah felt a sudden jolt at the trainee doctor's abrupt manner, then she caught herself. She still wasn't used to the different English accents and their way of going on. She shouldn't take offence. "We don't have the number of hospitals at home that you have here. I think it's hard for nurses to find work there."

"You would wonder at so many Irish girls training to be nurses, if they know they won't find work back home. They are obviously planning on staying here long-term."

She walked over to the kettle.

"It's just boiled," Sarah told her.

Vivienne switched the kettle back on. She moved across the room to stare out of the window, which looked out on the wall from the house next door. "Are the others out? The house seems very quiet."

"They must be . . . I've not seen anyone since I came in. I do half-days Saturdays." She paused. "I think Jane said she was on day-shift today, so she probably won't be in until later."

"And what are *you* doing over here?" Vivienne asked. "What do you work at?"

"I'm in a sewing shop in town."

"A *shop*?" Her voice was high with surprise.

The front door went again and then shouts of greeting were heard as Elizabeth and Anna came bustling into the kitchen carrying bags of shopping.

Anna's round face was red and damp. "I'd swear that hill gets higher every day." She dropped the bags and threw herself down into one of the chairs in an ungainly heap.

Vivienne raised her eyebrows. "You need to get fitter."

Sarah caught her breath, wondering if her colleague was going to be offended at the pointed remark.

"No, I'm fit enough," Anna said, not sounding in the least offended. "We just need to buy less shopping!"

They all laughed now, and it made Sarah feel that she was out of step with them. Vivienne's remark had obviously been a joke and she was too sensitive. She sat there for a while longer, sipping her lukewarm tea while the others made drinks and sandwiches and came to sit at the table beside her.

"We bought new dresses for the dance tonight," Anna said. "The same style of dress but in different colours."

Vivienne gave a little snort of laughter. "You'd look like the Teaser Twins except funnier because you're totally different shapes." She walked over to sit at the table. She kicked one of the shop carrier bags. "Come on then, let's see what you bought."

Anna reached down the side of her chair and lifted up a Fenwick bag. She brought out a sleeveless pale green dress with broad shoulder straps and a large bow at the waist.

"Very nice," Vivienne said. "Hold it up in front of you and let me see how it looks."

Anna did as she was told.

"The colour definitely suits you . . ."

Anna smiled. "Thanks."

Vivienne hadn't finished. "I'm just not sure if that bow is best placed for your stomach." She bit her lip. "I don't want to throw cold water on things . . . it's just that I know you're conscious of it and wouldn't want to draw attention to your worst feature."

"It looks lovely on her," Elizabeth said quickly. "The bow – everything about it is nice."

Vivienne shrugged. "Well, if you're both happy with it, that's terrific."

"I'll have to try the dress on again, and see how it looks," Anna said, folding it over and putting it back into the carrier bag. "You can't always tell with shop mirrors."

Vivienne clapped her on the back. "I'm sure it will be just fine . . ."

Sarah noticed that the heavier girl's neck was flushed and she now looked uncertain about the new dress. She could feel the tension in the room and was amazed that neither of the girls had tackled Vivienne about her rudeness. Then, she was suddenly reminded of her brother's wife, Martina, back home, and all the nasty, personal comments she used to make. She had often had to bite her own tongue and rush to the solitude of her bedroom to avoid a major row. Anna was obviously doing the same thing.

Sarah noticed that Vivienne didn't ask to see Elizabeth's dress. The nurse had the slim type of figure that any dress would look well on.

Sarah finished eating her sandwich in silence, then she said, "I'm going down to the shops for few things, so if anyone wants anything . . ."

"I think we have everything we need," Elizabeth said, smiling appreciatively.

She wanted to say to Anna that if she needed the bow moving or altering, she would be happy to do it, but she didn't want to look as though she were making an issue of it in front of the others. She would wait until she came back, and speak to her alone.

She washed her plate and cup and went back to her room.

A short while later as she was coming downstairs with her coat and handbag, Sarah heard Vivienne's raised voice coming from the kitchen. Something in the trainee doctor's tone made her halt in her tracks.

"I'm not at all happy," Vivienne stated. "I think we should have been consulted about this before she came. It's us who have to live here and we must have some rights. Mr Spencer had no business sending her here without talking it over with us."

"The landlord decides who lives in this house," Elizabeth stated.

"Nobody asked me or Jane if it was okay when you and Anna came. We were just asked if we would be in when you arrived. There was no discussion about it, and it's no different with Sarah."

"But it's entirely different," Vivienne argued. "I'm sure he knew you wouldn't have any problem living with two educated English girls." She paused. "This is a matter he should have consulted us over."

Sarah stood listening, her feet rooted to the stairs. Then, as the conversation continued, she began to feel a sickness in the pit of her stomach.

"I think she seems a nice, quiet girl," Anna said. "I don't see what the problem is."

"The problem is she's *different*." Vivienne's voice was shriller now as she enunciated each word clearly. "This is supposed to be a house for professional women. She's not professional – she works in a shop *and* she's Irish. Our landlord didn't ask us if we wanted to share with someone like that. If I wasn't working tonight I would go straight down to his house and demand an explanation."

"It's too late," Anna said. "We can't possibly ask her to leave now."

"The woman she works for is a friend of theirs," Elizabeth added. "She brought Sarah here when she arrived, and she seemed a perfectly nice Englishwoman."

"I'm sure that Sarah is from perfectly decent people," Anna chipped in again. "I don't think we should be judging anyone just because they're not English."

"Well, maybe some of us have higher standards," Vivienne snapped back. "And I for one would like to have been consulted about whether we brought a foreigner into this house or not. It's bad enough we have to live across the road from coloureds, but having to share a house – share a bathroom – with a common Irish worker is just a bit too close for comfort."

"Shhhh!" Elizabeth's voice was urgent. "She's just upstairs – she'll hear you."

Sarah put her hand over her mouth. She was afraid to move now

126

in case the old wooden stairs creaked and they realised she was outside listening.

"Surely you've heard the terrible reputation the Irish have – haven't you, Anna? Drunken and dirty. Some of them have never even seen a proper bath until they came to England."

"I really don't agree with you," Elizabeth stated. "Sarah seems a very clean and tidy person to me, and her clothes are smarter and more professional-looking than most of mine. I can tell she's not the sort to get drunk – and she didn't look surprised when we showed her the bathroom, so I think you're wrong about that too."

Sarah felt the smallest flicker of comfort when she heard the nurse defending her.

"You hardly know her," Vivienne went on. "Wait until she's been living here for a while. And even if she is nice she's still only a shop assistant. She's only a step up from the Irish skivvies in the hospital and she's not the sort who should be living with professional women. Just give her a while and her true colours will come out. Wait and see." She gave a snort of laughter. "We should have had one of those signs put up outside saying, '*No blacks, No Irish, No dogs*'."

Sarah could hardly breathe now.

"Enough, enough!" she heard Anna say now. "Enough of the arguing. Who wants a cup of coffee?"

Sarah closed her eyes. *My God!* she thought. Vivienne really didn't want her in the house, and all those awful things she'd said about the Irish. She obviously thought they were backwards and ignorant. Even Elizabeth, who had defended her, would be shocked if she knew she had grown up in a small cottage with a makeshift toilet and a tin bath. Sarah had never imagined that any of this would matter.

Her mind had been so taken up by what she had left behind – the loss of everything that was familiar – that she had never considered what might lie ahead. She had just presumed it would be like living in a bigger part of Ireland – somewhere like Dublin. Somewhere with decent people – friendly people. She didn't think people would look down on her and would be so horrible about her being Irish.

Her heart was thudding now – so hard she could feel it against her ribs. What on earth had she done coming to live with people like this? And if things didn't get better – where would she go now?

She stood a few moments longer, and then eventually she moved herself and went down the stairs and out of the house. When she got to the gate she stopped, and took in great gulps of air. Tears started to sting her eyes, but she blinked hard to force them back.

Then, a feeling of determination rose up in her. The same determination that had given her the strength to walk away from Con Tierney and Patricia Quinn.

She had been wronged once and survived, and she would do it again. She would not lie down and let people walk all over her. She would show that stuck-up bitch of a medical student and her cowering friends that she was as good as them in every way. She would use the bath so often that they would be sick of knocking on the door to use it themselves. Her instincts were always to be clean around the house, but she would make sure that everything she used would be scoured and cleaned to the last. They would be sick of the smell of bleach and disinfectant.

And she would make that horrible Vivienne eat her words. She didn't know how she was going to do it yet – but she would find a way.

* * *

Sarah was closing the gate behind her when the door opposite opened and the young dark-skinned girl came out and onto the street. She glanced across at Sarah and then she looked away and started to walk down the street

For a moment Sarah was relieved she hadn't spoken. She was in no frame of mind to chat to anyone now. She started to walk, then something made her call out, "Excuse me!"

The girl turned around to look at her.

Sarah hurried across the street towards her. "I hope you don't mind me asking – I don't mean to be nosey – but I saw the ambulance at your door earlier in the week. I hope it wasn't anything serious?"

The girl's face softened. "It was my father, and he's all right now, thanks. He has a problem with his heart and he gets these turns. He should be getting home on Monday. I'm going to see him now."

Sarah was surprised that the girl had a Newcastle accent – similar to Harriet's. She had expected her to have a strange, foreign accent. "I wasn't sure what to do when I saw the ambulance," she told her. "I've just moved here – I'd only arrived in England the night before. I didn't like to come over to your house in case you thought I was interfering."

"It's nice that you thought about us. Where are you from?"

They started walking along together. "Ireland," Sarah told her. "From a town down the country." She was trying to concentrate on the conversation, and not think of the awful things she had overheard back at the house.

"You lived in the country? You must find it very different here."

"Yes, I do." She thought for a moment. "I should have said earlier, my name's Sarah Love."

"And mine is Lisha Williams."

"Lisha is a lovely, unusual name." Sarah felt as though half of her mind was normal and trying to keep up with a normal conversation, while the other half was falling to bits inside her head.

The girl looked at her for a moment then suddenly blurted out: "It's a Nigerian name. My real father was from Nigeria." She glanced sideways at Sarah. "My mother, Fiona, is English though, and so is my stepfather. Williams is his name and I got his name when they got married."

"And your brother's name is?"

"Mark. He's my half-brother."

Sarah had never really spoken to anyone from a foreign country before. She had served tourists in the hotel, but that wasn't the same as a proper conversation. The quiet, calm side of her mind told her to ask polite, safe questions. The kind of questions she would ask a young girl back home. She couldn't bear to say the wrong thing and feel even more of an outsider than she already was. "Are you still at school, Lisha?"

"Yes, unfortunately." The girl smiled. "I suppose it's not that bad. I like some of the subjects."

"How old are you?"

"I just turned sixteen."

"What subjects do you like?"

"I like English," She shrugged. "I love reading so that's a big help with English Literature, and I like history and every kind of sport."

"What do you hope to do when you leave school?" Sarah wondered at herself asking such mundane questions. Would she be able to keep on like this all weekend, all next week? Would she always be able to pretend that she was a different person outside and another one inside?

Lisha shrugged. "I don't know . . . maybe teaching if I get the qualifications. That's what my mother would like me to do." She looked at Sarah again. "Do you work?"

"Yes, I work in a sewing shop and I make and alter clothes as well."

"That's one of my favourite subjects too – domestic science. We do cookery and sewing and that kind of thing." She rolled her eyes. "I'm not exactly brilliant at it, like – I made a pair of pyjamas for my exam last summer but the machine I had was an old one and it kept dragging the material so they didn't turn out exactly as they should."

"That can easily happen."

They walked down the hill to the station chatting in the same vein. It was neither an easy nor an uneasy conversation. Lisha said she would walk up by Harrison's shop to see where Sarah worked, since it was just as easy to take that route to the hospital as any other.

"I like all the things in the window," the young girl said when they got there. "Did you make them?"

130

Sarah told her she did.

"I think my mother would like one of the peg-bags," said Lisha. "I'll come into the shop next week."

"I'll be making more over the weekend," Sarah told her. "And you can have one as a present."

"No, no – I'll buy it."

"I'd be happy to giving you one, especially after all the worry your mother has had this week. It might cheer her up."

"That's very good of you. When will I come over for it?"

Sarah thought for a moment. She didn't want the girl to get a cold reception from the awful Vivienne. "I'll watch out for you, or I'll bring it over."

Sarah spent a few hours looking around the shops. She went into a newsagent's and bought a blue Basildon Bond airmail writing pad and envelopes and a *Woman's Own* magazine, and then she wandered around the haberdashery department in Fenwick's. Although she was drawn to the rolls of lovely material and the racks of trimmings, her heart wasn't in it, the way it had been on her first visit to the shop.

As she walked around she felt a slight nagging feeling in her lower stomach. It was familiar enough to make her calculate her monthly cycle. She usually got this warning a few days before her period started, so she looked for a chemist's shop and went in. There was a man behind the counter and woman behind the glass partition, so she browsed around the shop with a basket until the female assistant was free. By that time she had picked up two bars of Cameo soup, a deodorant stick, bath cubes, Vosene shampoo and a bottle of bubble bath. She asked the woman in a low voice for the sanitary towels and some aspirin and then paid for the items in the basket.

When she came out from the chemist's shop there was a shower of rain, and since she found herself near the café with the juke-box, she went in and ordered a coffee made with hot milk. She looked at the cakes, but her stomach still had a knot in it from the episode back in the house, so she ate nothing. She sat alone in one of the booths, either stirring her coffee with a spoon and staring out of the window, or sipping it slowly. The waitress came and took away her empty cup and since she felt awkward just sitting, she ordered another coffee and took just as long drinking that.

The sky started to darken and Sarah suddenly realised that the shops were all closing around her, but she still didn't move. The longer she was away from the house and the other girls in Victoria Street the more she dreaded going back. Whilst she knew the other girls had been nice enough to her, she didn't know if she could force herself to speak again to the medical student who hated the Irish so much.

There was a sign in the café saying that it stayed open until ten o'clock on a Saturday night, and Sarah felt comforted by the knowledge that she had somewhere warm that she could stay in if she wanted to stay out until bedtime. She knew it might look strange to the waitresses, but she didn't care.

It must have been after six o'clock when a group of seven or eight girls and lads came in the door, all laughing and chatting. They looked like people who had just finished work for the day.

The café was now crowded and Sarah wondered if she might need to move into the corner of the booth to let someone sit beside her. She dreaded the thought of sitting so close to strangers, but the thought of going back to the house was worse.

She glanced up from her magazine and saw David McGuire in the middle of the group, talking and laughing. Her heart sank. This was all she needed. She lowered her head, hoping he wouldn't see her. From the corner of her eyes she could see he was busy chatting and gesturing to the others – the main focus of attention. Sarah wasn't surprised.

The group hovered at the counter, and then one of the girls leaned over to David and said something. He nodded and the three girls moved towards the top part of the café where there were more seats. The lads stood for a few minutes debating the menu, and then David turned to scan the tables.

Sarah dropped her head but, after a few moments, couldn't resist glancing up again and that was when he spotted her. He said something to the lads and then came straight towards her.

"Are you all by yourself?" he asked.

"I am now." She was trying to sound casual. "I was with a friend earlier." She knew it was bending the truth, but she had been in the city earlier with Lisha, and she hadn't said she was actually in the café with a friend.

He slid into the vinyl-covered bench across from her. "Are you okay? You look very pale or something."

"I'm grand," she said automatically. "Apart from being a bit tired. That's why I said I wouldn't go to the dance tonight."

"I'm not going either. It's the same old faces week after week." He smiled at her. "I would have made an exception for you – you're a new face." He looked straight into her eyes but she looked away.

The waitress came to the table for their order.

"Will you have a Coca-Cola?" David asked her.

Sarah looked at her cup of lukewarm tea, then she looked at her watch. A drink would kill another while. She knew that earlier in the day she had promised herself not to get too friendly with him on account of Harriet, so she would be careful.

"Don't you want to join your friends?" she said.

"They won't miss me – there's enough of them there." He turned to the waitress. "Two Cokes, please." When she left he looked at Sarah again. "Are you sure you're all right? You don't look as bright as you usually do."

"It's nothing really . . ." Then, she looked at him and when their eyes met hers suddenly filled up. Just the way they had that morning with Harriet. She quickly picked up a paper napkin, held it to her face and gave a light cough. "Excuse me . . ."

"Sarah," he said quietly, "has something upset you? You can tell me, you know."

She took a deep, shuddering breath and composed herself again. "I'm sorry, I'm just being stupid."

"Are you still thinking about Ireland?"

She felt her stomach clench. Harriet had obviously been talking about her. When they both left the shop together the other morning, she must have told him that she had got upset. But she now had to guess what he knew. Had Harriet told him how she had been betrayed by her fiancé and her best friend? She couldn't bear to discuss any of that. She would go. She would walk the darkening streets in the city now rather than talk about it with him. She reached down for her bag but when she picked it up and went to move, the waitress appeared at the table with their drinks.

While David McGuire sorted the bottles and straws and gave the waitress the money, Sarah fought back the urge to run out of the café. The more rational side of her knew that it wasn't the answer. She had already run out of the house that afternoon. She had already run away from Ireland. At some stage she needed to stay and face things.

He handed her the Coke bottle and a straw now. "Okay?" His eyebrows were raised in concern.

"I'm okay, thanks." She took a sip through the straw. "Actually . . . I was a bit upset this afternoon. Something happened up at the house."

"What, like?"

"It's one of the other girls . . ." Her throat went dry. She gave another little cough. "She doesn't like me living in the house. She doesn't like Irish people at all."

He leaned across the table towards her. "How do you know?"

"I heard her. I was coming down the stairs and she was in the kitchen. She was talking loudly . . ." She broke off. She composed herself again. "She said some terrible things . . . all about people coming over to England looking for work, when they should be staying in their own country. She said we were uneducated and dirty."

"Blidey hell! I thought that kind of carry-on had all finished."

She looked up at him through tear-rimmed eyes.

"My mother talks about the rows out in the street when she was younger, the name-calling they got because my granny and granddad were Irish, but that was years ago." He rubbed his chin. "You wouldn't expect educated people to be talking like that. There's all kinds in Newcastle, especially working in the hospitals."

"This *was* serious – really nasty. She was arguing with the other girls, saying that the landlord had no right to allow me in the house without talking it over with them. When the other girls pointed out that he had never asked anyone's permission about who he gave rooms to, she said it was different because I was Irish."

"Did you tackle her about it?"

"No . . ." Her voice sounded hoarse. "I was just coming down the stairs, on my way out, when I heard her giving out to the others about me. I got such a shock I didn't know what to do."

His brow deepened. "What's this girl like? Is she a Newcastle lass?"

"She's from London. She's training to be a doctor."

"Well, she won't be very popular with her patients with an attitude like that. She probably doesn't like Geordies either. Her type only like people like themselves – stuck-up snobs."

"I feel terrible." She was unable to stop herself now. All her earlier determination draining away. "I feel like going back to Ireland – maybe to Dublin or Galway or one of the bigger cities."

"Ah, Sarah – don't let one horrible person put you off."

"But I feel as though the other girls didn't stick up for me either." A sick feeling came into her stomach as she remembered Elizabeth saying she couldn't imagine her not having a bath at home. "They might prefer to have only English girls living in the house too."

"You haven't spoken to any of them yet – you don't know how they feel."

"I know how *I* feel."

"Don't jump the gun. Give yourself more time," he told her. "You've started to make friends already, it's obvious that your boss is happy with you and Harriet was singing your praises the other day. She was saying you could really feel a difference in the shop, how it's far more professional since you've arrived, and Lucy said all the customers really liked you." He touched her hand. "Most people are nice, Sarah. Don't let one rotten apple spoil it for you."

Sarah began to feel a little lighter. "Thanks," she said. "I feel better now that I've talked to you."

"Good, because –" He suddenly stopped as a hand touched his shoulder. It was one of the girls he'd come in with.

"Excuse me for interrupting, but we wondered if you were going to join us?"

"Oh, I'm sorry, Joyce," he said, smiling at her. "But I've had a change of plans."

"Well, thanks for letting us know," she said. "We were all waiting until you came back to the table to order. I don't suppose you're going to the dance either?"

"No," he said, "but I wasn't going anyway. I told some of the others."

"That's fine." Her injured tone didn't sound fine at all. "I'll tell them we don't need to wait any longer, and we can order our chips now."

David looked at Sarah now and gave an embarrassed grin. "I think I'm in trouble."

"Oh, no . . ." Sarah reached for her bag, flustered now. It was obvious that she had spoiled his plans. "I need to go now."

"Look, they're not even close friends. I just meet up with them after work now and again." David stood up now. "I'll walk you back."

"No, no . . ." she said, sliding out of the booth. "I'm happy to walk back on my own." She caught a glimpse of the crowd at the table and she could see they were all looking down at her and David. She kept her gaze fixed on the floor as she walked out.

"There's no point in arguing," he said, as he held the door open for her. "I've nothing else to do and I'm not letting you walk back to that miserable house on your own. We might even stop for a drink on the way back. There's a few decent pubs on the way down to the station."

"But you need to get home."

"To sit and watch the telly with me mam and dad? Because that's all I'm going to do. My brother will be out dancing and my sister is staying at her fiancé's house."

There was nothing she could really say to that, and she didn't want to have a disagreement in the middle of the street. They walked across the main road and a few minutes later they were walking down the cobbles in Pilgrims Lane.

"It's different when all the shops are closed," David said. "Isn't it? Most people keep to the main streets, because they're better lit up. But there are a few lampposts down here, and when you know a place well you don't think about it."

"I'm used to everything being dark in Ireland," Sarah said. "We only have street lamps in the middle of the town."

"Do you miss it a lot?" he asked.

"A bit." She hoped he wasn't going to start prying into her background. "But if things settle down at the house, I'm happy enough here." Her words were braver than her feelings about staying, because she knew for the time being she had no option.

David slowed to a stop under a lamppost to examine his watch. "Neither of us is in a rush home – why don't we go to the pictures?"

"No. Thanks for asking but I've work to do."

"You'll need to have a break, a bit of a laugh at some point. You know what they say about all work and no play."

"I'm only here a week, there's time enough for that."

The bookshop manager kept up the chat all the way to Victoria Place.

"It's just up here," she said, when they turned the corner and the tall grey-stone buildings came in view. She came to a halt. "Thanks for seeing me back, it was good of you."

"Right to the door." He continued to walk. "And I wouldn't say no to a cup of tea if you want to invite me in. I could have a word in that snooty doctor's ear."

"Definitely not," she said. "Anyway, I'm going straight to my room." She opened the gate and walked towards the front door. She felt as though she was running away from one awkward situation and heading towards one she dreaded even more.

"Are you going to ten o'clock Mass in the cathedral in the morning?" he asked.

"I haven't really thought about it. There are three Masses on so I'll see which one I'm ready for."

"I might see you there."

For a moment she considered telling him that Harriet would be upset if she was to become too friendly with him, but she decided against it as it might seem like she was betraying her friend. Besides, David would probably say he didn't care what Harriet thought. Then she would have to explain she had no interest in courting. On the other hand, he could easily laugh and tease her that he was only being friendly and she would feel a fool. She didn't know him well enough to gauge his reaction – so she said nothing.

She took her key out. "I thought you would have gone to a church nearer your home."

"It depends," he said. "Sometimes I fancy the change."

She stood on the doorstep. "Thanks for the Coke and for walking me back. It was good of you." She put her key in the door. "I'll probably see you Monday."

The house was silent when she went in. She went upstairs to her room and closed the door behind her. The girls would be out for the night and she would have the house to herself. She heaved a sigh of relief.

She sewed for a few hours – making six peg-bags – then she went down to make a cup of tea and a slice of toast. She worked on until almost eleven o'clock and then she changed into her dressing-gown and went to the bathroom, taking her toiletries with her and her towels.

The water went lukewarm after a while, so when the bath was just half-full she poured in a capful of her rose-scented bubble bath and got in. She washed her hair in the bath with the shampoo and then knelt to rinse it off under the now-cold water from the tap. She wrapped the smaller towel around her head and dried herself with the larger one, then put her dressing gown back on. She put the tops back on her bubble bath and shampoo bottles and put them in a corner along with her blue facecloth and soap. She carefully washed the bath out and rubbed any splashes on the sides and the floor with a piece of toilet tissue.

Back up in her room she rubbed her hair as dry as she could and then brushed it all out. The length and weight meant it took ages to dry properly, but it wasn't a problem tonight as she knew she wasn't going straight to sleep.

She returned to her sewing. Some time later she heard the girls coming back in. They went into the kitchen and a few minutes later she heard footsteps coming up the stairs. They stopped outside her room and then a light knock came on the door.

"Sarah?" she heard Elizabeth call. "I'm making toast if you'd like some."

Sarah held her breath. "No thanks!" she called back. "I had some earlier and I'm in bed already."

There was a little pause and for a moment she thought the nurse might come into the room and see she wasn't in bed at all.

"Okay," Elizabeth called. "See you tomorrow."

She felt a small wave of relief. "See you tomorrow," she echoed.

It was one o'clock when she went to bed. It was nearer three o'clock by the time the anxious thoughts died away and she eventually fell asleep.

CHAPTER 16

On Sunday morning Sarah woke just on half past seven and before she had time to doze back to sleep again, she put her lamp on and then moved out of bed. She would have preferred to go to a later Mass as she felt so tired now, but she knew there was a chance she would run into David and maybe some of his family – and she didn't want to risk it.

She went downstairs to the bathroom and after washing and brushing her teeth she padded into the kitchen to drink half a glass of water. She couldn't eat before Mass and Holy Communion so she hurried back upstairs, gave a quick glance out of the window and then went to her wardrobe.

Even though it was first Mass and nobody was likely to be dressed up, she lifted out her best red and black suit and black velvet hat. If anyone thought she was too done up, she didn't care. It wasn't Tullamore where people would comment and talk about her. She needed something to make her feel she was as good as the other girls in the house.

The cathedral was half-full. She went into a pew on a side aisle at the back. As she glanced around during Mass she reckoned the congregation was mainly made up of young and middle-aged mothers who would go back home and cook breakfast and then a Sunday dinner for their family. Most of the women were in plain, sensible clothes, but there were several dressed in their Sunday best like herself.

When a couple of men tried to catch her eye, she kept her gaze straight ahead.

On her way to Communion she could feel someone in one of the front pews looking at her and on her way back she felt it again. Her eyes flickered in the direction and she realised it was the dark-haired sophisticated woman who had come into the shop looking for sequins. The woman smiled and winked at Sarah which disconcerted her, as only lads would dare to do such a thing in church in Ireland. In fact, Sarah was surprised to see her in Mass as she seemed more like the well-off Protestants from back home.

As soon as the priest left the altar, Sarah moved out of her pew quickly and straight out of the cathedral. It was dry so she took a walk up to a newsagent's in Pilgrims Lane and bought a paper to kill time. They also sold rolls which she was told had been baked overnight, so she bought four – two for today and two for lunch tomorrow. Then she walked slowly back to the house.

There was no movement from any of the rooms, so she went into the kitchen and boiled two eggs and ate them at the table with a roll and tea. Anna came down at one point to use the bathroom and stuck her head in when she was passing the kitchen . She was wearing a quilted dressing gown with the belt tied around her thick middle.

"Morning," she said, rubbing her eyes. "You're surely up bright and early." She paused. "And looking very elegant in your nice suit."

"I've been to church," Sarah told her.

"I'm shattered," the girl said. "I couldn't face church this morning. I'm going back to bed. See you later."

Sarah finished her breakfast, then she went back up to her room and stayed there until the afternoon. Since it was a Sunday – the day the Church said people shouldn't be working – she felt she couldn't do any of the things for the shop. Instead, she altered the cuffs on one of her blouses and hemmed a skirt. She read for a while and when she got fed up she started knitting a pink jumper she was working on.

There had been movement upstairs and downstairs some time after eleven o'clock, then around twelve o'clock she heard someone going out the front door.

She went to the corner of the window and saw Anna and Elizabeth going down the street. That left only Vivienne in the house. Her throat tightened.

She had no intention of speaking to the nasty, prejudiced student. No matter how long she had to go without tea or something to eat, she was determined she would stay in her room until the others came back.

The girls were back just after two, and Anna came straight upstairs to knock on Sarah's door. "Can I come in?"

"Yes . . ."

"My God! Are you working again today?"

"It's only a jumper I'm knitting for myself . . ." Sarah couldn't summon up any false warmth in her voice.

"You're a glutton for punishment working on a Sunday." Anna paused. "If you haven't cooked anything yet, I've got a chicken in the oven and enough roast potatoes for everyone."

A picture of Vivienne came into her mind. "Thanks, but I'm not very hungry."

"It won't be ready for about an hour. You might fancy it then."

"I'm grand . . . I couldn't eat it." Sarah turned back to her knitting.

Anna hesitated at the door. "Is everything all right?"

Sarah looked straight at her. How could she pretend to be so friendly now? She had said not a word in defence when Vivienne had said all those awful things about Irish people. "I'm perfectly all right, thank you."

Apart from going down to use the bathroom, she stayed upstairs all afternoon sewing, knitting or reading.

She made the peg-bag for Lisha and toyed with the idea of

taking it over to the house. Several times she picked up the bag and then changed her mind for fear of bumping into any of the girls as she was going out of the house. She also felt a bit shy about calling over because she hadn't met either of Lisha's parents.

At one point she got to her feet to change the thread on the sewing machine when she heard the ice-cream jingle and heard the van pull up outside. She watched and then saw Lisha come out with a dish in her hand, which Sarah knew was for ice-cream, as she had seen other people doing it.

She went to lift the window to call out to the girl, then she stopped herself. The natural thing would be to bring the peg bag down to her or have Lisha come across to the house for it. She wasn't prepared to do either. She wasn't ready to face Vivienne after hearing her vicious ranting, and she couldn't risk Lisha coming over to the house in case she said something to the girl or even ordered her out of the house.

She would wait and catch her on another occasion when Vivienne wasn't around.

When the noises around the house told her that the Sunday dinner had been eaten and everything cleared away, she went down into the empty kitchen and heated up a tin of chicken soup. She then put the bowl on a tray with bread and a glass of water and took it back upstairs where she remained for the rest of the evening.

CHAPTER 17

The following week went by just as quickly. There was little spare time in the shop between serving and doing alterations. Often she was only settled at the sewing machine when the doorbell would ring several times in a row, and she would leave her sewing to go through to help Lucy with the queue of customers.

When the next Thursday came around and she was in charge of the shop again she didn't even try to sew during the day, as she was kept busy with serving and tidying and re-organising the window to show off her latest craftwork. David McGuire called in most days and was now flagging in his efforts to get her to go out with him. He was beginning to accept that work was her priority and she didn't have time to go dancing with him or to visit his family.

She came close to telling him that she wasn't interested in any romantic friendships because she had just broken off an engagement but she thought, instead of putting him off, it might only encourage him to wait until he thought she had got over it. She wished he would ask Harriet out, but she could tell he had no interest in the nurse. Poor Harriet had used every excuse she could think of to get him to go out with her. She asked him to a wedding where she needed a partner and to a concert saying she had a spare ticket, but he had made excuses. Sarah didn't tell her that David had asked her out, and changed the subject every time his name came up.

She was more relaxed in the house as she had got to know Vivienne's work rota at the hospital, and kept to her bedroom when the trainee doctor was around. The other girls were friendly and nice to her any time she was in the kitchen making her meals or sitting at the table with them. They had given her no cause to think they didn't like her, and she had pushed the memory of the discussion she had overheard to the back of her mind.

She had got into the habit of having a bath most nights, and the other girls often joked about her being so clean that she would wash herself away. She noticed that most of them only bathed once or twice a week. It gave her some small satisfaction to feel that their standards were even lower than hers had been back home when all she had was a tin bath. She also noticed that Vivienne never cleaned the bath, and had heard the other girls grumbling about having to clean it before using it.

Jane, who had been working on the day of the row, had grown friendlier towards her. She often brought two cups of tea upstairs to Sarah's room and sat chatting with her. They had even gone to the cinema together one evening to see *Some Like It Hot* when the others were working. Afterwards they had gone to the café with the juke-box for a Coke and chips and a discussion about the film and Marilyn Monroe's lovely clothes.

Sarah wondered if Vivienne had voiced her feelings about the Irish to Jane, or whether the other girls had mentioned it. A few times she thought of bringing the subject up, but she had held back at the last minute. For all she knew, Jane might be great friends with the medical student and she didn't want to find herself living in a house where no one spoke to her at all. All in all, it had now become a dismal situation and she felt deflated after the high hopes she'd had for her new life.

She received several letters from home. Father Kelly had written to say he hoped she had settled and that he and Miss Reynolds hoped to make a trip over in the summer. Martina's letter was short, telling her how they had painted her bedroom yellow for the baby coming, but had still kept her bed in case she ever wanted a holiday back home. Sarah had held the letter in her lap for a few minutes, digesting the fact that from now on she would only be an occasional visitor in the house she grew up in. Sheila's letter was longer and full of news about people they knew from school and church. She said she didn't know where Patricia Quinn was hiding as she had not seen her since Sarah had left. She asked what the dances and the boys were like over in Newcastle, and if she was planning on coming home for Christmas.

Sarah felt strange after each letter, and had taken a few days to reply. She told each one that she was living in a nice house with nurses and trainee doctors and that she loved her job. She told them about her visit to the cinema and the nice café she often went to. She didn't reply to the bits about dances and boys, and instead told them all the details of the alterations she did and all the lovely shops in Newcastle.

It surprised her that she felt nothing when she read Patricia Quinn's name written in the letter. She was glad, because she thought she might have felt upset and started brooding all about her wedding again.

Ireland was beginning to seem like a dim and distant place to her.

One week ran into the next. She had got used to life in the house and working in the shop and going around the busy city centre. She now knew her way around the streets and had visited most of the shops. She knew most of the shop-keepers in Pilgrims Lane and they all called out to her as she walked past. A lad in the butcher's shop had asked her on a date and so had one of the tellers in the bank that Harrison's used.

Sarah had declined them both with a smile, and given the impression that she already had a boyfriend so they wouldn't bother her again.

She had been in the shop nearly a month when Lucy arrived on a Tuesday morning to say she wasn't feeling well. Her eyes were heavy and her throat was sore. Sarah told her she should go home but she said she would see how she felt in an hour or two. When Harriet called in around lunchtime, she insisted that Lucy go home to bed.

"It looks like tonsillitis," Harriet said, "so you'll need an antibiotic and a couple of days in bed."

By that time Lucy wasn't fit to argue. They even had to call a taxi to take her home as she wasn't fit to walk.

"I hope she's all right," Sarah said, when she and Harriet were on their own.

"She needs to take things easier," the nurse said. "She's so busy looking after the others that she neglects herself, and that drive to Durham every Thursday must wear her out."

"Is that where her father is?"

"No, he's in a home in Newcastle." A flush came on Harriet's face. "I'm not sure why she goes there . . . Sometimes she plays golf – it might be where one of the clubs is. Lucy is a very private person – it's sometimes hard to figure her out." She lifted her bag and hat. "I must go or I'll be late for my next patients."

Sarah was worried about her employer, but decided that she was best left alone for the first night. Then she called up at the house on the Wednesday, taking grapes, a box of chocolates and a bottle of *Lucozade*. She felt guilty when a white-faced Lucy opened the door wrapped in a dressing-gown.

"I'm sorry for disturbing you and I won't come in. You need to get straight back into bed." She halted. "Unless you'd like me to make you something to eat?"

"Thank you, but I can't swallow very well," Lucy croaked. "And I don't feel like eating."

"Could you manage something like soup?"

Lucy shrugged.

"It might help you to eat something."

"I think there are tins in the kitchen cupboard somewhere." She held the door open. "I really don't want to put you to any trouble."

Sarah watched while her employer climbed the stairs and then she went into the kitchen and, after checking a few cupboards, she found several tins. She decided that tomato soup would be easier to swallow than one with vegetables. She heated it on the gas cooker and then brought it upstairs with a glass of fresh water.

Lucy managed about two-thirds of the bowl. She stopped every so often to touch her hand to her throat when she swallowed. When she finished, she lay back on her pillows looking exhausted.

"Is there anything else I can do for you?" Sarah asked.

Lucy shook her head. "Is everything okay at the shop?"

"Grand, it's ticking over just fine. I banked yesterday's money at lunchtime and it's all entered in the book."

"I hope you're not finding it too much?"

"I'm enjoying it, and it's keeping me busy."

"You're great," Lucy said, giving a weak smile. "I don't have to worry about the shop since you arrived. It's all the other things I can't manage that are concerning me. I hate letting people down."

"Do you mean visiting your father and your golf outings? Do you want me to phone anyone and explain you are ill?"

Lucy's brow furrowed. "I haven't been playing golf recently, not since Mary left the shop." She suddenly caught her breath and then went into a fit of coughing.

Sarah gave her a glass of water and waited until the coughing eased. "Harriet mentioned that you went to Durham every Thursday. Is there anyone there I could phone?"

Lucy's whole body stiffened and her face was like chalk. "Harriet told you *what* about Durham?" she rasped.

Sarah was suddenly reminded of her boss's reaction the first day when she had changed the window. She had obviously said something now that had touched the same nerve, although she couldn't imagine what could be so secret about her visits to Durham.

"She didn't actually tell me anything," she said in a calm and level voice. "She just said you wouldn't be fit to travel to Durham and I thought you might have to let the people know you weren't up to going."

Lucy closed her eyes and seemed to be struggling to get her breath under control. "It's okay . . ." she eventually said. "I'll ring them myself tomorrow."

Sarah took the used dishes and glasses back downstairs and washed them. Then she brought a fresh glass of water and checked if there was anything else Lucy needed before she left.

"I will probably just sleep now," Lucy said, her throat sounding tight and tender. "Hopefully the antibiotics will work well overnight."

"Is it okay if I ring you tomorrow to check you are all right?" Sarah asked.

"Yes . . . thank you." Lucy's eyes seemed to fill up.

Sarah couldn't tell whether it was her illness or whether she was upset.

She decided she would say nothing for fear of saying the wrong thing again.

CHAPTER 18

Lucy woke around seven o'clock on Thursday morning, feeling not a great deal better. She took a few sips of water, then she went back into a fitful sleep. At one point she dreamt she was being chased down a dark tunnel by men dressed in long, strange robes. She woke out of the dream panicking and sweating around ten o'clock. She lay for a few minutes, letting her heart settle to a normal pace, and then she pulled her dressing-gown on and made her painful way to the bathroom. Her throat still ached along with all the muscles in her back and legs. When she finished, she went downstairs – taking it a step at a time – to make two calls.

She dialled the first number.

"St Lomand's Nursing Home."

She recognised the staff sister's voice. "It's Lucy Harrison." Her voice was so croaky she had to immediately repeat it.

"Miss Harrison, you don't sound at all well . . ."

"Tonsillitis – I didn't make it in for visiting last night and I won't make it tonight."

"You would be best to stay at home and rest," the sister advised. She paused. "We thought that you were having a break from visiting . . . after the last episode."

150

"Bitch . . . whore . . . trollop! No daughter of mine!" Her father had screamed the words at her. All conversation in the ward had come to a halt, as everyone listened in a mesmerised silence. Most of the patients were unable to hold a coherent conversation, and their visitors welcomed any diversion that helped the clock hand tick closer to the end of the long hour.

Lucy swallowed, feeling as though a razor blade was stuck in her throat. "No," she said. "I had hoped to come in . . ."

"Prostitute . . . murderer . . . good-time-girl! The words ricocheted around the walls of the ward like bullets. His vocabulary had always been extensive, but these outbursts had been said in private before – and in a hushed tone.

"Miss Harrison, we understand if you want to take a break. No one is judging you. It's very hard taking that kind of behaviour, and we want you to know that we don't take any notice of the things that patients say. We get it all the time."

"You're a sham! You're not fit to be a businesswoman – they should run you out of town. You should be made to wear a badge on your arm to show your true colours. Like they did with the poor Jews – only they did nothing wrong!"

Lucy closed her eyes, trying to block out the memories of the last time she had seen her father. Blocking things out was the only way she coped.

"How is he?" she asked, pulling her dressing-gown tighter around her. "Is he eating better?"

He had thrown the remnants of a bowl of cold soup over her. Then a nurse had been summoned into the office to explain why it hadn't been removed from his locker earlier, and why it hadn't been noted down that he hadn't been finishing his meals.

There was a silence.

"He's asleep at the moment but he has had some breakfast. He wasn't too good last night. He was difficult with one of the younger nurses – similar to the way he was with you. He actually hit her."

"Oh, I'm so sorry . . ."

"Don't worry – we'll talk about it when you feel better."

151

Lucy rang off then sat for a few minutes staring down the hallway, before dialling the second number.

"It's Lucy Harrison," she said when the phone was answered. Her throat and voice had warmed up a little. "I'm afraid I'm ill, so I won't make it in for my usual Thursday visit today."

"Thank you for calling, I'll pass that message on."

"Please tell the group I'll be there next week."

She sat for a few more moments and then stood to tie the belt of her dressing-gown when she was startled by the shrill ring of the phone. Her hand flew to cover her heart and when she had caught her breath she picked it up.

"Miss Harrison?" a male voice said.

"Yes?"

"It's Peter Spencer – from Spencer and Brown Solicitors here in Newcastle."

"Hello, Mr Spencer." She relaxed a little. He was always a pleasant, courteous man to deal with.

"I must apologise for not getting back to you sooner. I'm afraid there's been a bereavement in the family and I'm just back in the office today."

"Oh, I'm sorry to hear that . . ." She cleared her throat. "I hope it wasn't anyone close?"

There was a silence. "Actually," he said. "It was my wife."

Lucy's face flushed. She wished she had said nothing. "I'm so sorry . . ."

"She had been quite ill for several months," he said, as though sensing her discomfiture. "In many ways it was a relief at the end, although I shall miss her terribly."

"Of course," she said. "I hope things get easier for you."

"Thank you. Now, a date for our meeting."

She thought quickly. She didn't want to explain about being ill – it would sound trite given that he had just nursed a seriously ill woman. "Can I make it some time next week?"

"How about Wednesday? Say, three o'clock?" Then he paused. "How did the young Irish girl get on in the house in Victoria Street?

152

Has she settled in all right? I haven't had a chance to go around there with everything that has happened recently."

Peter Spencer owned several houses in Victoria Street. When Lucy had been looking for a room for Sarah, she had been advised to go to him. He had a good reputation as a landlord as he was fair with his tenants and kept the buildings well maintained.

"Yes," she said. "I think so . . ." It dawned on her that she hadn't asked Sarah for weeks how things were. She seemed so competent and organised that she was sure everything was fine. She must ask when she saw her next.

She went back upstairs – back to the comfort of her bed. To hide under the warm sheets and blankets. But it would only be for as long as the tonsillitis lasted. She had been down this route before and knew she had to break the cycle sooner rather than later. Each time she had hidden away, it had got harder to face the world and all her responsibilities. Harriet had helped her wake up to that. Amazing that a younger woman could see the patterns in her life that she couldn't see herself.

Things had improved beyond measure now, thanks to Sarah Love. Her arrival had brightened up the dark and dismal shop with her coloured handicrafts and her cheery welcoming smile. And she seemed to sense the days that were difficult for her employer. The days when she wasn't firing on all four cylinders. Days when she hadn't slept and didn't have the energy for work, or when her medication left her dull and lethargic. She cringed with embarrassment when she remembered falling asleep in the kitchen on Sarah's first day, and was grateful that the girl had been kind enough not to make an issue of it.

Since Sarah had started work in Harrison's, Lucy no longer dreaded getting up every morning. The shop owner could relax knowing that everything would be all right whether she was there or not, that the young Irish girl could cope on her own. In many ways she envied her. She was young, bright and beautiful and her whole life was in front of her. Of course she had problems like everyone else – her shattered wedding plans for one thing – and had probably made her own mistakes. But it was within the normal realm of things. There was nothing major to hold her back from achieving anything she set her mind to.

Lucy pulled the blankets up around her neck. What she would give to be in Sarah's shoes! To be back in her twenties when life was simple and straightforward. Back when she had hopes and dreams.

Any dreams she had these days were the nightmares she woke from.

And all the hope was ground to dust amongst the debris of all the mistakes she had made.

CHAPTER 19

When Sarah arrived back at the house, tired after her long walk, she went straight to the kitchen to put the kettle on. It was only when she was at the tap filling it that she saw Vivienne sitting at the table eating on her own.

The student doctor glanced over and then gave a cool, slow "Hi . . ."

Sarah held her gaze for a few moments and then turned on her heel and walked back out without saying a word. Thirsty and hungry as she was, she knew she couldn't stand to be in the same room with Vivienne.

She was making for the stairs when she realised she had left her handbag in the kitchen. A feeling of dread washed over her. She couldn't bear the thought of having to walk back into the room. She closed her eyes and whispered, 'Oh no . . .'

She stood in the hall trying to decide what to do, then she realised she was breathless and shaking. She took several deep breaths and tried to hold her body still. Then, a feeling of indignation rose up inside her. For a whole month she had avoided this girl and had stayed confined to the four walls of one room. After a day's work she should feel free to come downstairs and listen to the radiogram or relax in one of the comfortable armchairs by the fireside or sit every night at the large table. She paid the same rent as the others and paid her share of the bills. She was clean and tidy and did more than her share of the housework.

She was entitled to live in a relaxed manner in this big old house that was now her home.

She had endured long months of feeling like an outsider in her own home back in Ireland because of Martina, and now this girl was doing the same thing to her in Newcastle. She wondered why people thought she deserved such treatment and how much longer she could take it.

And then it struck her. She didn't need to feel like this. She had a choice. She could just walk away. She had the money James had given her – plus her own savings – and she had a decent wage. She could afford to rent a room anywhere in Newcastle. She could even afford to book into a nice hotel for a few weeks or even months.

Why hadn't she thought of it before?

She didn't need to stay in a house where she wasn't wanted, where she was regarded as a second-class citizen. She wouldn't take that treatment any more. As the realisation hit her, she suddenly started to smile. She was free! She could say and do anything she wanted. She had nothing at all to lose.

The sudden clarity in her thinking propelled her straight back into the kitchen.

"Vivienne," she said, in a firm, confident tone, "I'd like to speak to you."

The student raised her brows. "Yes?"

"I should have said this to you weeks ago."

Vivienne's eyes narrowed.

"I overheard the nasty things you said about me personally and about the Irish in general. I heard you say that you didn't want me living here and that I wasn't a professional woman. I want to tell you now that I don't want to live with someone like *you*. You may be more educated than me but your behaviour is that of an ignorant, mannerless person."

Vivienne's eyes widened in shock. "Just hold on now –" she started.

Sarah's hand flew up to halt her and her deep-blue eyes glinted. "I am not *finished* yet!" She was almost shocked by the ferocity in her own voice and could see the stunning effect it was having on her housemate. "In my opinion, someone with your views is unfit to work as a doctor, where you'll be treating people from all sorts of backgrounds. I think the Medical Board should know that they are employing someone who is prejudiced against Irish and coloured people, and probably anyone else who isn't the same as herself."

The medical student's face paled. "Good Lord . . ." She swallowed hard, taking in Sarah's threat. "It really wasn't meant that way . . ."

"Then how was it meant?"

The door opened slowly and the other three girls stood in an awed silence at the door. They had obviously heard Sarah's raised tones. Their presence didn't daunt her one little bit. In fact, it only fuelled her temper further. She didn't care what they thought. She was going from this house now and it didn't matter a damn whether they chose to speak to her again or not. Elizabeth and Anna had listened to Vivienne with hardly a word of protest when she had spouted all those awful things about foreign nurses and Irish people being dirty. Their opinion didn't matter to her now.

Sarah turned back to the ashen-faced Vivienne. "Well?" she demanded. "I'm waiting to hear exactly what you meant when you said that I wasn't fit to share a house with you all – that my job wasn't good enough and that the Irish should be banned along with blacks and dogs."

"Did she actually say that to you?" Jane asked in a shocked voice.

"Of course she didn't say it to my face," Sarah told her, "but I overheard her saying it to Anna and Elizabeth. It was a Saturday afternoon when you were working – when I had just arrived."

"There must be a mistake!" Jane turned to the other girls. "Surely Vivienne didn't say anything like that?"

"She bloody well did!" Sarah snapped. "I might be Irish but I'm neither deaf nor stupid."

The two girls looked at each other now, then Anna's gaze moved to the floor and a deep flush came on Elizabeth's face and neck.

Sarah could see the girls squirming but she was determined to do nothing to ease their discomfort. She felt they deserved it because they had not stuck up for her when Vivienne was so nasty.

Jane held her hands out. "But we would never allow anyone to say –"

Sarah cut across her. "But they *did* allow her to say it. I heard it with my own ears. And they didn't correct her – they only tried to get her to change the subject."

"I spoke up for you," Elizabeth protested in a strained voice. "I told her you were a lovely, beautifully dressed girl – smarter than the rest of us. And I said you were spotlessly clean and tidy in the house."

"You didn't tell Vivienne how wrong she was when she said there should be a notice up banning Irish, blacks and dogs!" Sarah was surprised at the viciousness in her own voice. The last time she had felt so angry was when she slapped Con Tierney.

Elizabeth started to cry, but Sarah ignored her and whirled around to Anna now. "And you just told her to stop arguing – you didn't tell her what she said was wrong and prejudiced."

"I'm sorry," Anna said. "I really am. But she has said nasty things to me. She's always making little digs about my clothes and my weight."

"You should have spoken up for yourself before and it might have made her think twice before doing it to someone else." She looked over at the three girls. "I've been here nearly a month now and I've spent practically every day locked in my room because of what happened. I don't know what kind of people I've landed amongst."

"That's not fair," Jane told her. "I would have spoken up if I'd been here. I don't agree with people being nasty towards others because of their colour or religion."

"And neither do I," Anna said. "I just didn't want to get into a big row over it." She looked sorrowfully at Sarah and shook her head. "I didn't know you overheard and I just wanted it forgotten."

"Avoiding things doesn't help," Sarah snapped. "It would eventually have come to this. I would have sensed that I wasn't wanted."

"I can't speak for Vivienne, but the three of us like having you here," Elizabeth said. "We all said how nice you were. We just thought you liked your own company and we didn't want to distract you from your work."

Sarah softened a little. "You have all been nice to me in other ways. I don't want you to think I wasn't grateful for the cooking and the cups of tea you've brought up to my room . . ."

"Look," Vivienne said, her voice trembling now. "You've got me all wrong. It wasn't meant like that. Sometimes – when it's the time of month – I say things I don't mean. I even do it with my own family." She looked at Sarah. "It was just the mood I was in – I'd been working for twenty-four hours with only a short break."

Sarah looked at her scornfully now. "Your work hours are not an excuse for bad behaviour and, if I recall correctly, you had actually just come back from a break at home."

"Well, I definitely had my period . . ." Tears suddenly came into her eyes. "I'm very sorry . . . I didn't mean it. I lash out at everyone when I feel like that."

Anna turned to her medical colleague now. "I agree with Sarah. It's no excuse for the things you said about her being Irish and about her job." Her voice was strained and shaky. "And I'm sorry that I didn't speak up and tell you what I really thought. I'm actually ashamed of myself."

Elizabeth nodded her head. "I am, too . . ." She looked at Vivienne. "You're a dreadful bully. You've said terrible things to us all. That very day you were so vicious about Sarah, you made a mockery of Anna's new dress. She was so upset she was going to take it back to the shop."

Vivienne stared down at the floor and shook her head. "I am so sorry, I only meant it in a joking kind of way . . ." She took a deep breath and then somehow seemed to find it hard to breathe normally. "It seems I've got everything very wrong. I feel like the worst person in the world now." Her voice sounded high and almost hysterical now.

Sarah suddenly felt exhausted with the whole thing. She went across to the table and lifted her handbag. "I'm going upstairs now, and I'll be organising new lodgings for myself over the next few days."

Jane looked horrified. "Oh Sarah, don't! Please don't go!"

Vivienne stood up. "If anyone should go, it should be me. I'm sure I'm not very welcome after all that's been said."

"If you will stay, Sarah," Elizabeth said, "then it's up to you about Vivienne."

There was a silence now and then Sarah said. "I would have to be sure . . . things would have to be very different."

"Believe me – they will be," Vivienne said. "I promise."

Sarah turned away. "We'll see . . ."

Quarter of an hour later there was a knock on Sarah's door. She was lying on the bed with her coat still on and staring up at the ceiling. She quickly moved into a sitting position, then called, "Come in!"

Jane came in with a cup of tea and two digestive biscuits. "If you haven't anything planned for dinner, we thought we would all get dressed and go down to the nice restaurant at the railway station." Then, before Sarah could say anything, she said. "We *all* want to treat you to a meal . . . to say we're sorry about what happened and that we want you to stay."

There was a pause. Sarah wasn't sure what to do. Then, she decided that it didn't really matter. If things didn't suit her, she could leave any time she wanted. In the meantime, if things improved then that was grand.

It was a far better position than she'd been in back home with Martina and James.

She now had options.

"Okay," she said, "That sounds very nice."

CHAPTER 20

It was the following Monday before Lucy returned to work, looking paler and thinner than before.

She stood in the middle of the shop and looked around her. "After being away for a while, it's like coming back to a completely different place. I can't believe all the changes you've made."

Sarah insisted on her taking it easy, and said she should put her feet up in the kitchen and sit with a book unless it got really busy.

"All I've been doing is taking it easy, while you've obviously been working like a Trojan." She lifted up a navy velvet cushion which was trimmed with a twisted golden cord. "This is beautiful!"

"I made four of them from a remnant I found in the stock cupboard," Sarah said, "and I sold three of them the morning I brought them in. I have an order for five more in red velvet."

Lucy shook her head. "I don't know where you get all the ideas from."

"I enjoy it," Sarah told her. "I get a great feeling from seeing something I've made, and I like trying new things." She pushed the picture of her most ambitious creation – her own wedding dress – out of her mind. "And anyway, it passes the time now the evenings are getting dark earlier."

"Don't you go out with the girls in the house after work?" Lucy thought back to all the evenings she spent in golf clubs, cinemas and dance halls when she was younger. It seemed a long time ago.

Sarah's gaze moved to the door where a customer was standing, looking at the window display. "No," she said. "They do ask me, but I don't have any great interest in going out."

Lucy suddenly remembered Peter Spencer's phone call. "Are things okay up at the house? Are you getting on with the others?"

"Yes, it's fine." For a moment Sarah toyed with telling her about the difficult start she'd had with Vivienne, but something stopped her. Lucy had enough on her plate recovering from her illness and dealing with an elderly father. She didn't need a complaining employee. Besides, things had improved back at the house and there was no point in raking over old wounds.

"You should have some leisure time," Lucy said. "Get out and meet other younger people. Maybe meet a nice young man?"

Sarah shook her head, her eyes still on the customer at the door. "I have no interest," she repeated.

The doorbell rang as the woman opened the door. "You have some lovely velvet material in the window. If I get the measurements, could you make me a pair of curtains and some cushions, please?"

Lucy looked at Sarah and raised her eyebrows. There would be a lot of work involved. Would it be too much with the bags of alterations she had waiting?

Sarah smiled. "Of course. Have you decided on a colour yet?"

* * *

The weeks went by quickly with Sarah's routine of working in the shop and sewing in the dark nights and weekend. It was only when she received a letter from her friend Sheila that she realised Christmas was just around the corner.

Sheila was checking if she had plans to come home for the festive period. Without having to think about it, Sarah knew she would stay in England. She had several good reasons for this. She had no intention of going back to Tullamore where she would inevitably run into Con Tierney or Patricia Quinn. Neither did she want to be a source of entertainment for all the gossips. And the hardest thing to face was the fact that she knew Martina and James would not want her in the house. Martina had written on several occasions, giving updates of her pregnancy symptoms and telling her any bits of news – usually bad news about other people. At no time had she mentioned Sarah coming home for Christmas, which Sarah took as a clear message.

Whilst she knew what she *wasn't* going to do for Christmas, Sarah had no idea what she would actually do. She had heard the girls in the house discussing who was going home and who was working. It sounded as though the ones working would be having Christmas dinner in the hospital, so she wasn't likely to have any company at the house. When they asked about her plans, she avoided giving a straight answer, saying that she wasn't sure what she was doing yet.

"Knowing you," Vivienne had said, "you will probably end up at that blasted sewing machine even on Christmas Day."

Sarah had laughed along with the others, steadfastly refusing to take offence at the medical student's comment. She had already stood her corner and she knew Vivienne wouldn't dare purposely to offend her again. While Sarah would never consider her as a real friend – knowing that the student was capable of such prejudice and nastiness – there was a kind of truce between them which allowed Sarah to live in the same house with her.

David McGuire had come into the shop one afternoon when Lucy had a meeting with her solicitor, to enquire what Sarah was doing at Christmas. He had a knack for knowing when the coast was clear and he could grab a few minutes with Sarah when her boss was out.

"I'll probably be spending it at the house with the other girls who aren't going home," she had told him.

"Why don't you come down to our house for your Christmas dinner?" he asked. "My granny and granddad keep asking when they're going to meet this Irish girl from the sewing shop."

"That's nice of you asking . . ." Sarah was both touched and awkward at the offer. "But Christmas is for families, and I wouldn't feel comfortable intruding on you all."

"But that's daft, man! Our house always has people coming and going. They love having visitors and they would hate to think of you feeling homesick when you could be amongst Irish people. You can't spend Christmas and Boxing Day without a family."

There was a small part of her that was tempted. She could tell that David's family would be every bit as friendly as he was and she knew she would probably have a lovely time with him, but she couldn't take the chance of making him – or his family – feel that she was interested in him.

"Thanks again for asking," she said, "but, no . . ."

It didn't make her feel any better when an upset Harriet came into the shop one morning that same week to say that she had asked David to come to her clinic staff's Christmas party with her.

"He didn't even give me an excuse," she told Sarah. "He just said he didn't fancy it." She shook her red curly head and shrugged. "Who doesn't fancy a party at Christmas? Especially when it's free – I was going to pay for his meal. I think it's more like he doesn't fancy *me*." She looked at Sarah. "I think he might have a girlfriend. Have you heard him mention anyone?"

No," she said, "He's never mentioned any girlfriend to me, but I don't suppose he would. I don't talk about personal things to him."

"You're so lucky," Harriet sighed. "I'd give anything to work across the lane from him and see him every day."

"He is a nice enough," Sarah was deliberately casual, "but I'm sure there are plenty of others around like him."

"No," Harriet said. "He's different. He's a decent, genuine fellow and I really thought he liked me." She calculated. "All over the summer and up until the last few months he seemed quite keen. He always asked me to dance, and a couple of nights he walked me home. We weren't officially courting or anything, but I got the impression it would eventually lead there." She shrugged. "He

164

seems to have cooled off recently. I suppose I'll just have to keep hoping. You'll let me know if you hear anything about him and other girls?"

"I don't really get into personal chats with him," said Sarah. "But if I hear anything I'll tell you."

How could she tell Harriet that the bookseller's attentions were directed towards her? She couldn't. It would spoil their friendship and possibly stop Harriet from calling into the shop, which wouldn't be fair on Lucy. It made things complicated and she wished David McGuire would just leave her alone. She'd had enough of awkward relationships back at the house and felt she needed a spell where things were quiet and easy. She thought back to how simple life had seemed only a few months ago. She'd had the same friends since she started school and she'd never had any major rows with them. Even though Sheila and Patricia had always made little digs about each other to Sarah, they had always been nice to her. But that had all changed with the events that happened leading up to the wedding.

She gave a deep sigh. Looking back didn't help. She had to keep looking forward, and be grateful for the one dependable thing in her life – her work.

CHAPTER 21

On a cold afternoon in early December, just as Sarah had finished putting the lights on the Christmas tree in the window, Lisha Williams and her mother came into the shop. They were looking for material for a dress for the sixteen year-old girl's school party. Sarah was struck again by how good-looking they both were and how much they looked like each other apart from their hair and skin colour.

"I don't want anything old-fashioned," Lisha had explained, her eyes flitting anxiously towards her mother. "We've been to the shops and I haven't seen anything that suits me."

Fiona Williams looked at Sarah, smiled and then lifted her eyes to the ceiling.

Sarah understood that there had obviously been some disagreement between then. "I think we'll be able to find you something here that you like," she said. "And if you're not sure, you can always adapt it." She got out the pattern books and they spent some time poring over them.

Eventually, Lisha pointed to a jade-green, silk cocktail dress with a low neck and a matching stole. "I like that one," she said. "That's exactly the sort I'm looking for."

Fiona Williams looked alarmed. "I think that's a bit grown-up for you, Lisha," she said. She pointed to a pink lace evening gown with a high neck. "I think that would be more suitable."

"But, Mum, I don't like it!" Lisha said. "The other girls are wearing shorter dresses and I don't want to be different."

"But the neckline isn't for a young girl . . ."

Sarah could immediately see her mother's concerns. "It's easy enough to bring the neckline up a big higher," she said quickly. "It's just a case of measuring it carefully."

Fiona looked doubtful. "I wasn't really planning on making something so complicated. I'd hoped to actually buy a dress for her, but there was nothing she liked."

"But you're good at making things," Lisha said, smiling at her mum.

Fiona looked at Sarah. "I make a lot of my own skirts for work and plain things like that. I'm not confident about doing something as complicated as this."

Sarah went over to the drawer to where the patterns were and found the one they were looking at. She brought it back to the counter and opened it up. "I don't think it's too difficult."

"Do you have the same green material?" Lisha asked. "I really like that colour."

Sarah left them studying the pattern and went to check the rolls of material. A few minutes later she came back with a roll of dark green satin.

Lisha's eyes lit up when she saw the fabric. "Oh, that's gorgeous! It's exactly the colour I want."

"It is lovely," her mother agreed. She looked at Lisha and then shook her head and laughed. "Oh, go on. You're not going to be happy with anything else."

"Oh, thanks, Mum," the young girl said, putting her arm through her mother's.

"See how you get on with it," Sarah said, rolling the material out onto the counter to measure it. "And if you get stuck at it, I'll give you a hand."

"Oh, we couldn't put you to the trouble," Fiona said.

"It's no trouble," Sarah told her. "You know where I live – I'm only across the road from you."

Fiona smiled. "Thanks, it's very good of you."

It was only later that Sarah thought of Vivienne and suddenly wondered if she would have anything to say about Lisha calling to the house and maybe even be abusive to her. Then she realised that Vivienne wouldn't dare. She knew that Sarah would carry out her threats of reporting her to the hospital authorities. Whether it was something they could, or would, do anything about, didn't matter. Any kind of complaint would still make trouble for her.

* * *

The following frosty Sunday morning David McGuire introduced Sarah to his mother as they were coming out from Mass in the cathedral. Sarah cursed herself for having a long lie in bed and missing the earlier Mass – and for also forgetting that this might happen.

"Mam," David said, guiding a slim, dark-haired, well-groomed woman by the arm, "this is Sarah, the Irish girl I was telling you about."

Mrs McGuire's face broke into a smile and she had the same bright, cheery look in her eyes that her son had. "So this is the great worker from the sewing shop?" She stretched her hand out. "And don't you have the loveliest blonde hair? It's so long you must be able to sit on it. Isn't it lovely, David?"

"It is beautiful – she's a beautiful girl," he said, looking directly at her.

Sarah felt her cheeks burning as she shook hands with the cheery woman. "It's very nice to meet you."

Mrs McGuire stepped back. "And the lovely suit you're wearing! Did you make it yourself?"

"I did," Sarah said, looking down at the deep blue three-quarter swing coat with the fur collar and matching skirt. "It's a fairly easy style."

"David was telling me that you're great at making and altering things. I've a few things I was going to drop into the shop. Would you be able to put a new zip in a skirt for me?"

"Of course I would," Sarah said. She avoided looking directly at David but she could see there was a beaming smile on his face.

"You must come out to our house when you're not so busy," Mrs McGuire said. "David was telling his granny and granddad all about you and they're dying to meet you." She raised her eyebrows and smiled. "For some reason they always think young Irish lads and girls get very homesick when they leave Ireland. I think it says more about themselves. I'm sure a lovely girl like you has made loads of friends already?"

"She's too busy working – aren't you, Sarah?" There was a note of criticism in his voice. "She never takes a weekend off to go to the dancing or anything. I've asked her out to the house loads of times."

Sarah felt a wave of embarrassment wash over her. "I'm sorry . . . I'm just so busy. I've got a lot of alterations to do and quite a few orders for things to make before Christmas. As David probably told you, the business needed a lot of work to get it back on its feet."

"Surely you'll have a bit of time off over Christmas?" Mrs McGuire asked. "You must have an afternoon or evening when you can drop up to the house to see the old couple? They would just love talking to you about Dublin and Galway and all those places they remember."

"It's very good of you," Sarah said, "and I really appreciate you inviting me. I'll see what time I have over the next few weeks." She put her collar up. "It's getting very cold now, isn't it? Again, thanks for the invitation – and it was lovely to meet you."

As she turned away, Sarah saw the friendly woman give her son an apologetic look. A look that that said she'd done her best to encourage the girl he liked to come to their house. Sarah felt very bad about turning down the invitation, especially the thought that she had snubbed his elderly grandparents. She knew how friendly Irish people were, and how strange they would think she was, not wanting to meet some of her own kind.

Sarah wished she could explain the situation to Mrs McGuire – tell her that she couldn't risk hurting Harriet Scott by getting involved with the boy she had set her heart on. Tell her that even though she liked David very much, after her own experience of betrayal she wasn't sure if she could ever risk a close relationship again.

As she walked briskly back to Victoria Street, she mulled the situation over in her mind. By the time she had reached the house, Sarah had come up with a solution. A solution, she hoped, that would keep everyone happy.

CHAPTER 22

The week before Christmas – her cards and presents all sent to Ireland – Sarah's thoughts turned to organising food for Christmas Day. There was only going to be herself and Jane in the house, but they had decided they would still put in the effort and have the meal with all the traditional trimmings. Sarah was actually going to do the cooking, as Jane would be working on the early shift and would be home around four o'clock.

As she sat at the table writing out a shopping list, Sarah thought that a chicken would be big enough for the two of them. She wasn't sure if Jane was working Stephen's Day – or Boxing Day as it was known in England, she had to remind herself. If the nurse wasn't working, she thought they might be as well to get a small turkey to last a few days.

Then, Jane dropped the bombshell when she came in from work, her navy hat and coat covered in snow.

"Oh, Sarah," she said, shaking the snowflakes off her hat, "I just discovered this morning that most of our patients will be gone over Christmas, and the sister says they can manage without me."

Sarah stared at her blankly.

"That means I can go home for Christmas dinner. I'm really sorry, Sarah." She paused, twirling the hat between her hands. "In fact, why don't you come with me? My family would love to meet you."

Although she was hugely disappointed, Sarah's expression remained deadpan. "I couldn't," she said quickly. "Thanks for asking but I wouldn't feel right. It would be intruding." She forced a smile on her face. "I'll be absolutely fine on my own."

"Please think about it," Jane said. "I feel awful telling you at the last minute, but I really want to go home."

"Honestly, I understand. I'll be grand."

Then the doorbell rang and Sarah was relieved when Jane rushed out to answer it. She didn't know if she could pretend much longer. The thought of spending Christmas alone in the house was devastating.

She moved from the table to put the kettle on, to try to take her mind off the situation. To try and be normal when her house-mate came back in.

Jane was chatting at the door for a few minutes, then Sarah heard voices coming along the hall. The nurse came into the kitchen followed by Lucy Harrison, who was carrying a tailor's dummy. She stood it in the middle of the floor.

"I was looking for the Christmas tree up in the attic when I came across this," she told Sarah. "I know you were thinking of buying one, so it will save you the money."

Sarah felt her heart lift as she looked at the dummy. "That is so good of you! It will make all the difference when I'm working." Suddenly her dashed Christmas plans didn't seem quite so bad. She would pass the time away easily making some new outfits.

"And I'm delighted I called when I did, because Jane has just solved a problem for me."

Sarah looked at her. "What was wrong?"

Jane cut in. "And I'm relieved too. It solves everything." She looked at her watch, then stuck her damp hat back on and tied her scarf tighter. "I've got to run out to the phone box and ring home. See you both in a bit."

When the door closed Lucy turned to Sarah. "If you've no major objections, you'll be having Christmas dinner with me. You'll actually be doing me a big favour."

Sarah's brows shot up. "But you have your own plans!"

172

"Two old aunts who have their own families and my father in the nursing home," She gave a wry smile. "Not exactly uplifting company."

"Are you sure?"

Lucy nodded. "I never thought of asking you because I thought you'd prefer the company of the younger girls in the house. When Jane mentioned that her plans had changed I thought we might as well be company for each other."

Sarah suddenly felt lighter – as if a huge weight had been lifted off her. "That sounds lovely, and you needn't put yourself under any pressure. I'll help you with the cooking of course."

"To be honest, I don't feel at all pressurised. I feel more relaxed around you than I do with anyone else. And you do much more for me than anyone else I've worked with."

"That's very nice of you but –"

"It's true," Lucy told her. "I thought you might like to come and stay Christmas Eve? We could have supper together watching television or listening to the radio. The only thing is that I have to pay a visit to Durham to my friends early on Christmas Day." She lowered her gaze. "It's really just a morning visit and I should be back around lunch-time."

"I'll be at ten o'clock Mass in the morning, anyway," Sarah told her, "and I can help by getting things ready for you."

"That sounds great. I can drop you down at the cathedral when I'm going off. I thought I'd cook the turkey overnight and reheat it – so we don't have that to worry about – and we can have the vegetables all prepared and ready to go on." She held her head to the side, calculating. "We will probably be ready to eat about three o'clock – or maybe just after the Queen's Speech."

Sarah thought for a moment. "Are you sure you don't want to spend the day with your friends in Durham?"

"Not at all," Lucy said, putting her gloves back on. "It's not that kind of place and they're not that sort of people." Then, before Sarah could quiz her any further, she went over and patted the dummy on the head. "I'm glad to see old Edna getting a new lease of life." She smiled. "That's what my father used to call her. He used to have quite a sense of humour at one time. It's sadly gone now."

Sarah wondered at her changing the subject away from Durham again. It was obviously a private area of her life. "Will you be visiting your father on Christmas Day?"

"I doubt it." There was a hint of a sigh in the shopkeeper's voice. "The nurses have said there will be enough activity going on there to keep him occupied, so he won't miss me." She moved towards the door. "I'm glad we've sorted that all out." She looked at Sarah, lightness in her eyes. "We'll make it as good a time as possible. We'll spoil ourselves. I have Christmas pudding and a Christmas cake and chocolates and wine – everything we need."

Sarah told herself to get over the disappointment of Jane letting her down. To get over the feeling that she was already following her employer down the lonely road of spinsterhood. "It sounds lovely!"

Lucy looked her as though she had read her thoughts. "It *will* be lovely," she said, "if we both make the effort."

* * *

Sarah got the chance to use Lucy's dummy the following evening when Lisha and her mother came across to the house with grim faces.

"I can't get the neck of the dress right," Fiona Williams told her. "No matter what I do the material is bunching together and I've ripped it out so many times it's beginning to fray and pucker."

Sarah examined it closely. "I think it looks as though you might have used the wrong stitch size. When it's too tight it makes it bunch up."

"I'm sorry to be a nuisance, especially being so close to Christmas," she said in a low voice, "but I'm at my wit's end with it and Lisha needs it for tomorrow night."

"Don't worry – I'm sure it will be easily fixed." Sarah brought them into the hallway and was just showing them up to her bedroom when Vivienne came out of the kitchen.

She looked startled. "Oh, sorry," she said. "I didn't realise you had visitors." Then she took a deep breath. "Would you like me to bring some tea up?"

174

Sarah felt a little glow. Vivienne usually got the others to make it for her. "That's good of you," she said, smiling warmly at her. She looked at Lisha's mother. "Have you time for tea?"

"Thanks, but we're not going to be here long," Fiona said quickly. "Lisha has a friend calling to the house at seven o'clock."

Sarah noticed the wary look the young girl gave Vivienne as she thanked her, and wondered if they had sensed her earlier hostility towards them.

When they got up to the room, Sarah asked Lisha to slip the dress on to let her see how it looked. She turned away as Lisha stripped off to her petticoat and then pulled the dress on. When she turned towards her again she was amazed at the transformation.

"Lisha! You look beautiful!" The girl's figure was slim, her bust high and firm and her skin flawless. "You look like a model. The colour and cut of the dress is absolutely perfect on you. Turn around and let me have a look at the back." The back was equally flattering on her. Sarah went back to look at the neckline and thought for a few moments. "What do you think if I make some small roses in the green material to put around the neckline? It would hide the stitch marks and would bring the neck up a little."

Lisha's eyes lit up. "It sounds lovely, but wouldn't it be a lot of work?"

"Let me worry about that," Sarah told her.

As she showed them out, Lisha ran on ahead to be home for her friend while her mother lingered to have a few words. "I'm really grateful, and relieved you can sort the neck. The idea of putting the flowers is brilliant. She's too young to have it so low. She looks too old for her age as it is, and I don't want her looking . . . I don't want her giving people the wrong impression."

* * *

At ten o'clock that same night Sarah took the finished dress across to the Williams' house. She knocked on the door and a tall, frail-looking man answered.

Sarah caught her breath. His pallor, his prematurely hunched

175

shoulders and his dark eyes told she was looking at a man who was probably dying.

He looked unsure as to who she was for a moment, and then he recognised the bag she was holding. "Come in," he said, his pale, thin face lighting up. "I'm Tony Williams; I take it you're the talented lady who has been sorting out the problem with the dress?" He held his hand out to her.

Sarah took his hand, and was surprised at the firmness of his handshake which gave the impression of a strength his body obviously did not possess. "Fingers crossed I have it sorted," she said laughing.

"They're in the sitting-room deciding on handbags, I think." He gave her a wry smile, his eyes seeming large compared to his drawn, pale face.

Sarah followed him down the carpeted hallway into a warm room that smelled of pine and oranges. A coloured Christmas tree full of baubles and tinsel with a pile of parcels underneath stood to one side of the fireplace, and a television and radiogram stood at the other side. Festive decorations stretched from the corners of the ceiling and a bright picture of Santa Clause and his reindeers filled the top half of one wall.

It struck Sarah that this was the first time she had been in a real family home since leaving Ireland.

There were screeches of delight when Sarah showed them the work she had done on the dress, and when Lisha put it on it looked exactly as Sarah had envisaged.

"I love it!" Lisha said. She turned to preen at herself in the mirror. "I can't believe it's me. I look so grown up!"

"You do," her mother said. "So you will have to start acting it now – no more sulks if things don't suit you."

"Aw, Mum!" Lisha came over to put her arms around her mother's neck. "Thanks, I really love it."

"Well, that's what matters."

Sarah thought how close they looked and wondered if it would have been like that for her, had her mother still been alive.

Fiona Williams playfully patted her daughter on the bottom

and then went to get her purse. "We must pay you for all that work."

Sarah held her hand up. "No, honestly."

"But you hardly know us!"

"I'm happy to do it for you."

"Well, if there's something in the future that Lisha and I could help you with . . ." She spread her hands out. "Anything – anything at all."

* * *

The weekend before Christmas was the only time all the girls at the house in Victoria Street would be together, so they went out for a meal in the city centre and exchanged the gifts they had bought each other.

Sarah had toyed with the idea of knitting the girls scarves and gloves, but was afraid that it might look mean – that they might assume she had got the wool for nothing. Then Sarah had admired a lovely brooch of Anna's, and the medical student told her that Vivienne had bought it for her the previous Christmas. That had made her mind up about the sort of gifts she should buy.

Money wasn't an issue as she had saved quite a bit since starting work. After looking around for ideas, she settled on earrings. They all had pierced ears so she picked the same style – three graduated gemstones in a nine-carat gold setting – so it wouldn't look as though she was favouring one over the others. She chose different-coloured stones in blue, pink, green and purple which she matched to their eyes or birthstones. The assistant put them in velvet boxes and wrapped them up in Christmas paper, then put them in individual tiny bags with the shop's name on them.

The girls' delight with the earrings was obvious, and Sarah didn't mind when Elizabeth and Jane swapped with each other, as the green matched Elizabeth's new dress. Anna and Vivienne had clubbed together to get Sarah, Jane and Elizabeth a silver charm bracelet each and Sarah was touched when she saw the thimble charm they had bought her to start her collection of charms off.

Elizabeth bought them all a bubble bath set each and a purse.

Jane gave the others bottles of Avon perfume and Sarah was surprised when she gave her a long slim box, wrapped in gold paper with a green bow on top.

All the girls watched Sarah's face as she carefully unwrapped the box to reveal a gold envelope. She opened it and slid out a card embossed with silver bells and ribbons – a ticket to the hospital New Year's Ball in the Station Hotel. Sarah gasped when she saw the price on it.

"Oh, that's too much!" she said, looking at Jane with wide, shocked eyes. Her stomach flipped at the thought of the dance.

"No, it's not," Jane told her. "It's to make up for leaving you in the lurch over Christmas. I know your boss is a bit on the quiet side and older, so I thought it would give you something exciting to look forward to." She looked at the others now. "And we're not taking any excuses from you, because you've been here for months now and you've never been to a dance. Besides, we're all going! It must be a miracle – somehow we've all managed to get the night off from work. The older staff with families said if we worked some of the shifts over the Christmas period so they could be with their children, then they'd work New Year's Night."

"You'll have to dig out an evening dress," Anna told her. "It's a really fancy do."

"I didn't bring one with me," Sarah said, half-hoping that it might get her out of going. For some reason she felt almost fearful of the dance now.

"The shops are full of dresses," Vivienne said, "and with the size you are, you won't have any trouble finding one to fit."

"With the speed you work at," Jane said, "you could even make a dress for it."

Vivienne pulled a face. "I think that's asking just a little too much. The Christmas holidays are for rest and play – even for someone who lives for work like Sarah Love."

Sarah laughed along with the others. She had no choice. It would look ungrateful and miserable to refuse to go. Like Cinderella, she would go to the ball.

CHAPTER 23

Since Christmas was on a Friday, Lucy decided that they would work the full day on the Wednesday and then lock up for the holidays.

"We've often worked a half-day on Christmas Eve," she told Sarah, "but I really don't think it's worth it. Thanks to all your hard work, our takings have been higher this year than any other Christmas, so I think we can have a full day off."

"I think we've both worked very hard," Sarah said, smiling.

She was pleased with the extra day off as it would give her time to pick up a few things to take out to Lucy's house before she went to stay.

"One of the girls gave me a ticket for a New Year's Eve dance at the hospital," Sarah told Lucy when they were having their mid-morning cup of tea. "So I think I might go."

"Wasn't that a lovely gift?" Lucy said. "It will do you good to get out."

Sarah found herself nodding. There was no point in saying she didn't want to go.

At lunch-time on the Wednesday she took a walk around the dress shops to see if anything caught her eye. She tried on a few dresses but there was always something about the fit or the detail that she didn't like. She wondered if she had time to make a dress before it. She had the whole week off between Christmas and New Year. Surely that would be time enough? She thought about the patterns back in the shop, and reckoned that there wasn't anything special enough amongst them. Then she checked her watch. If she hurried, she could make it to Fenwick's sewing department to look at their more expensive range.

A short while later she came out of Fenwick's smiling to herself. She had found a pattern for the most amazing dress and stole. In fact, she would have been grinning with delight if the dress hadn't been for the dance. She told herself to stop being such a misery and go and enjoy the dance like any normal young woman. What was the worst that could happen? Some fellow she didn't like might ask to her to dance. It wasn't something to get worked up about and she had survived it many times before. The dance would mark the start of a new year for her and she had to find a way of mixing better without being suspicious of men all the time.

When she showed Lucy the pattern, she shook her head. "I don't think satin will work. I think you need a special type of taffeta to make the best of the pattern, and we don't have it here." She thought for a moment. "The wholesaler is bringing a delivery later this afternoon. Why don't you give him a ring and ask him to bring a selection of taffetas?"

Around four o'clock the delivery came and after the man carried the boxes and parcels into the stockroom, Sarah and Lucy examined the rolls of taffeta he had brought.

"I think you're right about the materials," Sarah said as she compared a roll of satin to a roll of taffeta. "The taffeta will definitely work better with the pattern, especially around the neckline."

"Which colour are you going to have?"

Sarah had narrowed it down to two. A gold colour with a black sheen and a dark grey with navy. "I really can't decide . . ."

"Hold them up to your shoulders," Lucy instructed. She stood back as Sarah held the end of one roll up and then the other.

She smiled. "I can't decide either. Both colours are beautiful on you."

"They would be beautiful on anyone," Sarah said, staring at her reflection.

"I thought I was the world's worst at taking a compliment," Lucy laughed. "but you're every bit as bad!"

Sarah looked at her and started to laugh as well, and it struck her how much younger Lucy looked when she was in a light mood.

The shop bell rang and David McGuire came in.

"You asked me to call in to collect the things for my mother."

"They're all ready," Sarah said, turning towards the back-shop. "I'll just get them for you."

"Has business been good for you this Christmas so far?" Lucy asked him.

"Very good," he said. "Our sales are well up on last year."

"That's always good to hear."

"And I can see your own business has done well – every time I look over you have a queue of people."

"A certain person is responsible for that."

Sarah came back with the carrier bag containing Mrs McGuire's skirt with a new zip and a blouse which had new cuffs. "I hope they're okay for her," she said.

"Oh, I'm sure they will be," he said, rolling his eyes to the ceiling.

"Actually," Lucy suddenly thought, "maybe we need a man's opinion, Sarah. The material," she said, holding up the gold and grey rolls. She looked at David. "Which one do you think is the nicest?"

David's hand came up to hold his chin as he studied the material. "Who's it for?" he asked.

"Sarah," Lucy told him. "She's making a dress for a New Year's Ball."

He looked at Sarah. "Where's it being held?"

"It's in some hotel . . ." Sarah felt herself flush. She wished Lucy had kept quiet about it. She knew he would be upset that she had turned down his offers of going to dances so many times before.

"It's for the hospital staff . . . the girls at the house bought me a ticket." She felt annoyed at having to explain herself to him.

He looked at the fabric again. "The grey with the blue," he said. "I think it matches the deep blue of your eyes."

Lucy nodded. "It does actually match her eyes. Well spotted . . ."

David paid Sarah for his mother's alterations, while Lucy went through to the stockroom to check on the new delivery. He put a card on the counter with his name, address and phone number on it. "I'm hoping you'll still call out to visit us some time around Christmas."

"Hopefully I'll get time." Sarah did not to look directly at him.

"Just give a ring and I'll come and meet you off the bus." He turned the card over. "I've written down the number of bus you catch from the station and the name of the road you should get off at."

"Would it be okay if I brought one of the girls with me?" She made it sound casual.

"Yeah, no problem." He just looked pleased that her visit seemed more definite.

"My granny and granddad live a few houses down from us, so we can either go down to them or they'll come up to our house."

"It's really nice of them to invite me, and I'm looking forward to meeting them." She hoped he got the point that she was coming to meet his Irish relations rather than going to see him.

Just as he was leaving he said, "Will you call over to the bookshop when you've finished work? There's something that I want to give you." Then, anticipating her reaction, he said. "It's only something small . . . but I want you to have it to open on Christmas Day."

Sarah's heart sank. She hadn't even written a Christmas card for him, so wary was she of encouraging him. "You shouldn't have. I haven't got anything for you."

"I wasn't expecting anything and I wasn't planning on buying you a present, but then I saw this thing and I knew you would like it."

There was a small silence.

"Okay," she said. "I'll call over and collect it when the shop is closed."

As she watched him cross the road back to the bookshop, Sarah though how bad she felt being so stand-offish and cool with him, because he was such a nice, decent fellow. She wished she could be normal and go on dates with somebody like David McGuire who was intelligent and could talk about anything – and who could make her laugh. Someone who was so similar to herself in many ways, even though he was English. She wished that Harriet hadn't set her cap at him which made things more awkward. But most of all, she wished she hadn't the deadness inside that Con Tierney and Patricia Quinn had caused.

* * *

Harriet came rushing into Harrison's just before five o'clock.

"Here you are," she said, giving Sarah and Lucy a Christmas card. "I've been so busy today that I didn't get a chance to call in before now."

Sarah gave her the Victorian-style card with sparkly snow on it she had under the counter, and they chatted for a while about their plans for Christmas and then Lucy came out from the kitchen with a parcel and a card for Harriet.

"You shouldn't have!" Harriet said, shaking her head.

"It's just a little thanks for everything you've done," Lucy said quietly.

There was a slight awkwardness and then it dawned on Sarah that Lucy wanted to speak to the nurse in private, and she found an excuse to go into the kitchen. Over the months since being in the shop, she realised that Harriet knew a side to Lucy that she didn't, and one that Lucy didn't want to reveal to her.

She came back into the shop when Harriet called goodbye in to her.

"I'm just going over to drop a card into the bookshop for Mr McGuire," Harriet said. "I was hoping I might see him over Christmas but it's not looking very likely."

Sarah walked her to the door. "Are you free any day between Christmas and New Year?"

"Why?" Harriet asked. "What have you in mind?"

"Something you'll find more interesting than me – a visit to David's family."

"You're joking!" Harriet's hands came to cover her face. "Why are you going there?"

"It's got nothing to do with David," Sarah said quickly. "His grandparents are from Ireland – from a county next to the one I'm from – and his mother invited me to meet them. I've bumped into her and David at Mass in the cathedral a few times."

"Catholics – of course." Harriet paused. "Does he know you were going to ask me?"

Sarah shrugged. "I said I was bringing a friend. I didn't want to say it was you until I'd asked you."

Harriet looked across to the shop. "Do you think I should say anything about it when I'm dropping off the card?"

"It's up to you . . ."

"I'll see if it comes up in the conversation." She suddenly stopped and gestured towards the window. "Oh, there he is coming out of the bookshop now! I'll run out and catch him with the card."

She was gone less than a minute and Sarah noticed the light in her eyes when she returned all breathless.

"He was rushing to collect something from one of the shops before it closed but he seemed pleased with the card and he said we'd no doubt bump into each other over Christmas." She halted. "Do you think that sounds hopeful?"

"Yes," Sarah said, "and any time I've seen you both chatting, he's seems very relaxed with you."

"I really feel if we got the chance to spend more time together that he'd see we had such a lot in common." She glanced up at the ceiling. "But maybe I'm only deluding myself . . ."

Sarah touched her arm. "Sometimes these things take time."

"There wasn't time to mention anything about going out to his house with you. But it might be best to surprise him." Harriet shrugged. "Christmas is a time when everyone is relaxed and nice to each other, so it might be a good opportunity. When should we go?"

"Are you off the day after St Stephen's Day?"

Harriet wrinkled her brow. "*St Stephen's Day?*"

Sarah looked at her and then laughed. "I said it without thinking – you call it Boxing Day."

Harriet smiled and nodded. "I'm off the week between Christmas and New Year, so the twenty-seventh is fine by me."

"David has given me the house phone number, so I'll phone them in the next few days and check the time, and then I'll phone you and let you know when we'll meet up."

"Lucy has my phone number," Harriet said. She pulled on her woollen gloves then clapped her hands together. "Thanks, Sarah, that's given me something to look forward to!"

After work, Sarah was almost half-way down the lane and heading for home when she remembered the present that David had asked her to collect. She stopped for a few minutes, deciding whether or not to go back for it. The thought of taking a gift from her made her feel very awkward, but David was so nice she really couldn't bring herself to be rude enough to ignore him.

She turned and slowly walked back up to the shop.

He was standing by the till counter chatting to Mrs Price, his oldest assistant, when Sarah walked in. He smiled when he saw her and winked. Mrs Price moved towards the back of the bookshop and David went around the counter to retrieve the gift.

As he came towards her Sarah noticed his face and neck starting to turn red and she could tell he was feeling anxious. She wondered why, because he always seemed so cocksure about things.

"It's nothing big," he said, handing it to her. It was carefully wrapped in black and gold paper with a gold bow on it.

"It looks lovely . . ." Sarah said, her own face hot now. "But you really shouldn't have." She could tell by the size and feel of the present that it was obviously a book.

"I just thought it was something you would like."

"Thank you," Sarah said. "I'll look forward to opening it on Christmas Day."

CHAPTER 24

On Christmas Eve Sarah stood in a queue in the off-licence department of one of the local stores waiting to pay for a bottle of sherry for Lucy. As she held the dark blue bottle, her thoughts turned towards Ireland – to the previous Christmas – when she had brought a bottle of sherry to Sheila's house. A heaviness came into her chest as her mind went back to previous, happy Christmases when her father was alive, and further back to when her mother was alive. Back to Christmases when she felt she belonged in the house she was born in. Bitterness then started to creep in as she imagined James and Martina all cosy together back in the cottage, delighted with the new yellow room. The room that should still be hers. The room where the perfectly stitched wedding dress had hung.

She dragged her mind away to pay for the sherry, and then as she walked back to the house she made herself repeat the words of the new Beatles song, "I Want To Hold Your Hand", over and over in her head to drown out the thoughts of Ireland.

Lucy called to Victoria Street at half past seven to collect her as planned, and when Sarah opened the door she was surprised to see her dressed in light tan slim-fitting trousers with a black ribbed polo-neck sweater and pearls. Her dark thick hair was loose and flowing.

"Lucy, you look really lovely!" Sarah blurted before she had time to think about it. "I don't know whether it's the very fashionable clothes or what, but you look much younger."

Lucy looked startled for a moment, and then she blushed and smiled. "Well, thank you . . . that's very kind of you to say." She looked down at the trousers. "I wasn't too sure about them, but the saleslady said they looked fine. I'm not terribly adventurous about new styles, but I must say they are very comfortable."

"Where did you get them?"

"I bought them in a new shop up near the bus station. Everything is well-priced in it. They had the trousers in black as well, so if they look so nice I might treat myself to another pair after Christmas."

"I wouldn't mind a pair myself," Sarah told her. "You could wear them with anything."

"I'm sure you could probably make them quite easily."

"Yes, but it's nice to just walk in and buy something now and again." She looked down at her blue wool costume and pale-blue buttoned blouse. "I feel quite old-fashioned beside you."

Lucy laughed. "You look perfectly elegant as always, and if it's any consolation, I spend most of the time feeling old-fashioned compared to you!"

"Well, we're a pair together then," Sarah said, laughing too. It was strange, she thought, how different she viewed Lucy now to the way she did when they first met.

When they arrived at the seasonally decorated house, Sarah gave her host a big purple ribboned box of Cadbury's Milk Tray and the bottle of sherry. She had also brought two plum tasselled velvet cushion covers, as Lucy had admired similar ones she had made for a customer.

"These are gorgeous!" Lucy said, holding one of the cushion covers up to the light. I love the piping along the edges and they are just perfect for the armchairs."

"I thought you could see how they looked," Sarah said, "and if you like them I can make another few for the sofa."

"I love them, but you've been much too generous."

Sarah felt a little glow knowing that she had got things right with her choice of gifts. And the best one was still to come: she had carefully wrapped a pair of fine black leather gloves from Fenwick's for Lucy to open on Christmas morning.

Although she spent almost every day with Lucy in the shop, she had been slightly nervous about spending two nights as a guest in such a fine house. While they had the same attitudes to work, she was aware that her employer was from a wealthier and more sophisticated class than her own family, and she had wondered if their differences would be more obvious in this setting.

She had brought her newest pyjamas and dressing-gown and slippers, and carried them all in a smart olive-green weekend case which she had bought this afternoon especially for her visit. The suitcase she had brought all her belongings in when she came over to Newcastle was much too big, and she didn't want to arrive at Lucy's with a shopping bag, so she went into The Saddle Shop at the top of Pilgrims Lane where she had seen smaller bags and cases in the window. The serious-looking man in the shop enquired as to whether a small overnight case would do for Madam, or whether she might need something bigger like a weekend case. Then, he had brought her a sample of both cases so she might see the difference.

"It all depends on whether you are planning to travel much," the man said. "An overnight is fine for just that – one night – whereas the weekend one will take you anywhere."

She had never had the occasion to use a weekend case before, and felt quite sophisticated when she came out of the department store, thinking that she must start to visit some of the popular places like Whitley Bay, Scarborough and Blackpool that she had heard people talking about.

After Sarah took her case and handbag up to the big bedroom with the dark mahogany furniture where she would sleep for the night, the two women sat in armchairs at either side of a log fire drinking sherry and eating sandwiches and mince pies.

They listened to a music show on the radio, and afterwards, Lucy brought them out a tumbler each of Snowball, a yellowish sweet drink which Sarah loved.

"It's not a strong drink," Lucy told her, "but it's nice for Christmas."

Later, they ate some of the chocolates and sipped Babycham from the flat, gold-rimmed glasses with the perky little deer on the on the side, while watching a silly comedy film.

Sarah was relieved that, instead of feeling that them spending Christmas together was a last resort, Lucy was openly delighted to have her company. Sarah thought that she had never seen her so relaxed and chatty. As she sat sank in the deep armchair, full of lovely food and drink, she thought how cosy and relaxed she felt in this house. If she worked hard enough, she thought, one day she might have a house like this.

At the last advertisement break in the film, Lucy went into the kitchen and came back with two mugs of cocoa and they sipped it through the remainder of the film.

"Are you looking forward to going to the New Year's Ball?" Lucy said as she switched the television off.

"Not really, I've no great interest in things like that . . . but it was very nice of Jane to buy me the ticket."

"I bet you'll enjoy it more than you think."

"Well, hopefully I will. The girls said it's always a lovely meal and they have a good band playing."

"The ballroom in The Station Hotel is very big, so presumably there will be a good crowd at it." Lucy paused, thinking. "There will be a lot of doctors at it as well."

Sarah gave a little sigh. "I hope I don't feel too out of it. The other girls all work in the local hospitals so they'll know lots of people."

"Yes, but there's a huge staff – hundreds of people working in all the different departments – and they can't possibly all know each other." She smiled. "You never know, you might meet a handsome doctor who'll make all your dreams come true."

"I really have no interest in meeting anyone," Sarah repeated.

"I understand, after what you've been through," Lucy said, "but I think you should be open to meeting someone if the right person comes along. You don't want to look back in years to come and regret turning someone very suitable down."

"I don't care," Sarah said. "I'd be quite happy on my own. I don't think you have to be married to be happy."

Lucy raised her eyebrows. "I thought that once, and by the time I thought I was ready to settle for a nice, decent man I discovered that I'd left it too late. I'd missed the boat – and all those clichés."

"But you're happy enough," Sarah told her. "You have a good business, a beautiful home and you have a good social life playing golf and going to concerts and all that."

"It's not the same as having someone to share things with. Someone to eat with every night, someone to talk things over with. Somebody to look after and worry about you." She paused. "Somebody to share a bed with."

Sarah looked at her now, not knowing which way to go. Surely, she thought, Lucy was referring to having someone for company. Surely a woman her age – who was a spinster – wasn't referring to sex? She waited.

"Well?" Lucy said. "Don't you agree that it's silly to be lonely when you could have someone who could meet all those needs?" She paused. "You might not think it's important now, Sarah, but women have needs too. Physical needs . . ."

Sarah wondered if perhaps the sherry and the Babycham had gone to her employer's head. She herself didn't feel anything untoward from the drink apart from a nice relaxed feeling that, due to the uncomfortable conversation, was now gone.

There was an awkward silence which Sarah was compelled to fill. "I don't have any of those feelings." She smiled to lighten things. "I'm happy with my work and the odd night at the pictures with the girls. I don't need anything else."

"You're a lucky person then. I'm afraid my life is full of regrets."

Sarah now felt a flicker of curiosity. "But why?' she asked. "When you have so much?"

Lucy reached her hand up to her thick hair to tuck it behind her ear. Her gaze seemed far away. "Because I remember the feeling of being with someone who understood me, who accepted me and who . . ." She halted. "Someone who loved me."

"Do you mind me asking what happened?"

"I was still silly and immature into my twenties," Lucy said. "I thought he wasn't exciting enough, that there should be . . ." She motioned with her hand as though trying to catch the words. "That there should be *more*. I thought anyone my parents liked must be boring. I was determined to go my own way and make my own choices." She gave a bitter little laugh. "But I learned my lesson about exciting men and I paid a high price for my stupidity. I certainly did." She looked directly at Sarah now. "But unfortunately I've made other people pay as well, and I'm reminded of it every single day. My father makes sure of that." She suddenly sat up straight and then looked at Sarah in a startled way, as though she had suddenly woken up and found herself in a strange place. "Goodness! I think I'm being boring now." She was awkward, flustered. "It's Christmas Eve and I shouldn't really be talking to you like this. I'm terribly sorry . . ."

Sarah realised that the person she worked with every day had suddenly disappeared, and she was now in the presence of the anxious, distant woman who had collected her at the station on her first day in Newcastle.

"I enjoy talking to you." Sarah thought her words sounded feeble, that she needed to say something more to reassure Lucy that she hadn't said anything untoward. "It's nice to be with someone who can speak in such an honest way."

Lucy didn't seem to hear her. "I meant to put the electric blankets on earlier." She jumped to her feet. "It's a cold night, we'll need them on."

When she came back down, it was as if the conversation had

never taken place. Lucy wore a smile which Sarah thought looked as though it was paining her. They worked together bringing the glasses and plates out to the kitchen and washing and drying them and putting them away. Their conversation was now about things like where the clean cutlery went and what time they would have to be up in the morning.

They went into the sitting room and talked about the programmes that were on television on Christmas Day while they straightened the cushions, switched off lamps and put the fireguard in.

"I'll set my alarm for eight o'clock," Lucy said, "and that will give us plenty of time to get you to the cathedral for ten."

* * *

In the morning things were back to normal between them. Sarah gave Lucy the gloves which she was delighted with, and which fitted perfectly, and Lucy gave her a pale grey, cashmere sweater with a turtle-neck.

"I know you can knit beautiful sweaters," she said. "But something like this is hard to make and I thought the colour would suit you. I bought it from Fenwick's, and I still have the receipt so if you don't like it, or it's the wrong size, you can take it back."

"I love it," Sarah said. "And it will go with my skirts and suits – and it will look lovely with trousers, because I'm definitely going to buy a pair like yours. I'll try it on when I've had my bath." She was thrilled with the gift as she had seen the shelves of Ballantyne Cashmere sweaters in the department store and, apart from being soft and beautiful, she knew they were expensive.

Lucy put the small prepared turkey into the oven on a low light and then they sat together at the kitchen table while Lucy ate a boiled egg and toast with a cup of tea. Sarah had nothing as she was fasting before Communion.

"I don't know how you can go out in the morning without eating," Lucy said, "I have to have a cup of tea before I begin to feel normal."

"I'm used to it," Sarah said. "I've done it ever since I made my First Holy Communion."

Lucy turned as though she was looking out of the kitchen window and Sarah noticed she put some pills into her mouth.

"I should have made the effort to go to church over Christmas," Lucy said, "but time has just run away." She looked at the clock. "I must watch the time. I don't want us to be late."

Sarah wondered why she was going all the way to Durham on Christmas morning, but she said nothing. "I'll go and have my bath now," she told her host. "I washed my hair yesterday to save time, so I should be ready for half past nine."

"I had mine earlier," Lucy said, "so I'm going to light the fire in the sitting-room now, and it should be fine by the time you get back from church."

Sarah came back downstairs at twenty past nine wearing her new sweater with a red skirt and long black leather boots. She carried a three-quarter-length matching red coat and a black scarf, gloves and beret.

"It fits perfectly," Lucy said, "and it's lovely with that outfit. Did you buy it here?"

"No, I made it at home last Christmas."

"The coat as well?"

"Yes. It was fairly straightforward."

"You amaze me," Lucy said. "The more things I see you've made, the more I'm beginning to think your talent is wasted working in my shop."

"I love it," Sarah told her. "And there's nothing better than loving your work."

"Well, it's lucky for me that you feel like that, but I hope one day you'll find something better to love."

Sarah decided to take a chance. "We'd better stop," she said, grinning, "Or we'll be back in the exact same conversation as last night."

Lucy hesitated, and then she smiled.

* * *

193

When Sarah was getting out of the car at the cathedral, the cold wind whipped her beret off and onto the roof. As she stretched to retrieve it, she noticed the pile of Christmas presents on the back seat all wrapped up in Santa Claus and snowman paper. Beside them were a dozen or so Cadbury's selection boxes.

Lucy was obviously going to see a family in Durham and Sarah wondered why, when she had been so open about very personal things last night, she was being so secretive about the visit.

Although she was early, the cathedral was already quite full. She picked a back pew over at the far wall where she thought she would not be noticed, and where she could slip out easily just as the Mass was ending. She did not want to run into David McGuire or his family today.

When she came back from Mass Sarah checked on the turkey, filled the basin in the sink with hot water and began peeling the vegetables that were laid out on the worktop. She put the carrots into the basin first and then lifted the paring knife. She put her hands into the comforting water to take out a carrot, and then stood still, staring out of the window into the cold wintry garden.

It hadn't been a bad winter in Newcastle so far, she thought, not compared to last year when they had been snowed in at the farm in Tullamore. The newspapers and radio all said it had been the coldest winter for years. It had started in earnest just after Christmas, causing everything to grind to a halt. At the farm things had been chaotic and they all had to pitch in. James had brought two newborn lambs into the kitchen and she and Martina had fed them with a bottle. Then a picture of Con came into her mind when he appeared at the cottage door like a snowman, wearing long Wellington boots and carrying a bottle of whiskey and a porter cake his mother had made.

Sarah then thought of the letter she had received last week from Sheila Brady with her Christmas card, saying that she had heard that Con was working for a decorating firm out in Bray. Seemingly the company got contracts for all the big houses and hotels out in the sea town. She heard he was coming home for Christmas and that she would keep Sarah informed of any news and whether she saw Patricia Quinn or not.

Sarah intended to write back in the New Year and tell her friend that she didn't want any more news about him or Patricia Quinn. Now she suddenly thought that she didn't want to hear anything from Sheila. Her letters, full of news and gossip about people they had gone to school with or knew from church, only unsettled her.

Maybe it would be best to take her time replying, and that would mean it would be longer before she heard from Sheila again. And when she did reply, she would only refer to the more chatty news about Sheila's new boyfriend and that kind of thing, ignoring any references to Con Tierney.

She lifted a large carrot now and made herself concentrate on peeling it. She watched the thin curls of orange skin slide into the basin. She tried to make each curl longer than the previous one. When she had peeled enough, she chopped the carrots and put them into a pan of cold water, then, before starting on the brussel sprouts, she went over and switched the radio on to provide distraction from any further thoughts. After she finished the vegetables she would set the table and then she would go into the sitting-room, where the fire was now blazing, and read one of the magazines that Lucy had left for her.

* * *

Lucy came back at half-past two, looking thoughtful, and offering no details of her visit. At one point when Sarah went into the kitchen to check if the roast potatoes were nearly ready, she saw her employer studying a calendar that looked as though it had been made by a child – the sort clumsily made in school from an old Christmas card. Lucy silently slipped it into a drawer and then they both turned their attention to the finishing touches of the meal.

The afternoon and evening went in the same pleasant way as the previous one, as they ate and drank of the best, watched television and listened to the radio. Sarah only had one glass of wine with her meal as it was something she had not yet acquired a taste for.

She drank lemonade and more of the little sweet bottles of Snowball.

It was getting on for ten o'clock and Sarah was thinking of bed when Lucy asked her if she had plans for the next few days.

"My dress for the New Year's Ball. It will take me a few days' work to get that done." Then, she hesitated before adding. "And I've been invited out to meet David McGuire's grandparents. I'm going on Sunday and Harriet is coming with me."

"Really?" Lucy's voice was high with surprise.

Sarah reeled off the story about the grandparents being Irish. "I don't want to snub them," she explained, "but I don't want to give the impression that I fancy David or anything like that to him or his family. That's why I'm taking Harriet. She does actually like him and it might give him the chance to get to know her better."

"It's unlikely that he's going to suddenly develop feelings for her," Lucy sighed. "David has known Harriet for the last number of years, and if he had any notions about her I think their friendship would have progressed further by now." She looked at Sarah. "He's a very nice fellow. He's intelligent and more than presentable-looking . . . and from what I've seen, I think he has strong feelings for you."

Sarah closed her eyes and shook her head. "I can't seem to put him off – he started asking me out to the pictures the very first week I was here."

"Would it do any harm to go? You might find you like him."

"I do like him," Sarah admitted, "but only as a friend."

"You have a lot in common," Lucy said. "You're both the same religion which is always a big help, he's from an Irish background and you are both passionate about the work you do." She smiled. "And you both have a similar sense of humour. It's very important to be able to laugh with someone."

"I'm okay as I am," Sarah said, not wanting her employer to go back down the same road again as last night. "You really don't need to worry about me. I'm getting on fine with the girls in the house –"

Lucy cut in, sensing her defensiveness. "I just don't want you to cut yourself off from a nice, decent fellow because of what

196

happened to you back in Ireland. You can't live your life totally alone, and in the future you might find you've thrown yourself in desperation at the wrong type."

"But," Sarah said, "I have no intentions of doing that. I'm not that stupid."

"I was exactly like you," Lucy told her in a voice shaking with emotion. "I thought I was fine on my own and then something happened which made me realise how lonely I was and I ended up making the biggest mistake of my life."

Sarah wanted to know what Lucy's mistake was. Since Lucy was the one who had pushed the subject to such an uncomfortable level, she felt she had the right to press her now. "What happened?" she asked in a gentle voice. "What mistake did you make that you feel is so bad?"

Lucy put her head in her hands. She was silent for almost a minute and then she said, "I had an affair with a married man."

Sarah felt her heart speeding up. This was not the sort of thing she expected to hear from an employer she should be looking up to. What would Miss Reynolds and the priest back home think if they heard this?

"I'm not proud of it. I was a foolish, foolish girl who believed she had met the love of her life and I was lured into situations I would never have believed possible." She looked up at Sarah. "I can't tell you the worst things that happened, but I can tell you that it has left me with feelings of worthlessness and despair. And it ruined my relationship with my parents . . . my father blames me for my mother's death. He said she made herself ill worrying about me . . ." Her hands came up to cover her face and she suddenly started to cry.

Sarah looked at her in stunned silence and when she heard the wracking sobs she moved across the floor to put her arms around the older woman to comfort her. Whether what Lucy had done was right or wrong she didn't know – and more surprisingly – didn't care. The only thing Sarah knew for sure was that Lucy Harrison was a kind and decent person.

And Sarah was beginning to realise that sometimes good people do bad things.

CHAPTER 25

Lucy woke with a start just after nine o'clock on Boxing Day and immediately the vivid dream came flooding back. Another of the recurring ones – the one in the courtroom. The one where everyone screamed that it was all her fault. She closed her eyes and willed it away.

Then, the hangover from the dream was replaced by a feeling of regret when she remembered the things she had told Sarah last night. Why, oh why did she feel so compelled to tell the young girl things? There was no need to allow Sarah so close to her. There was no need to reveal the dark side of her past.

Lucy wondered if she had frightened Sarah off. If she had made her wonder what type of woman she was working for. If she said anything more, she might lose her and she couldn't risk that. And if she lost Sarah she would go back to the disorganised, disinterested spinster that she had been for the last number of years. She would lose all the light and optimism and faith in the future that the talented young woman had so generously shared. And all the more generous of her, since Sarah was still nursing a recent raw wound herself. But she was a survivor. She had picked herself up and moved to begin a new life in a new country. She had already made a brilliant start in a few short months and Lucy knew the Irish girl would continue determinedly along the same vein. But, Lucy now worried that if she revealed any more of her darker side, Sarah might well decide to move to a more uplifting working environment than Harrison's shop.

Lucy sat up now. She needed to talk to Harriet. She needed to explain that having lifted the lid on these past episodes in her life – having discussed them in a clinical way – they were now appearing in normal conversations in a most inappropriate way.

She also needed advice on her medication. Maybe one tablet more or one less might make a difference to the way she was feeling. It had happened before. She leaned across to the phone by the bedside cabinet and dialled the District Nurse's number.

"Lucy!" Harriet said, when she heard her voice. "How did Christmas go with you and Sarah?"

"It went very well, thank you."

"Are you all right?"

"I think so." Her throat tightened. "I'm just a little concerned that my medication might not be . . . might not be controlling things as rigidly as before."

"Has something happened? Has there been another incident with your father?"

"No, thank God. I haven't been to see him. The unit said it would be best to let him get Christmas over." She swallowed, trying to moisten her throat. "It's me. I feel I'm talking too much."

There was a pause. "To yourself?"

"No . . . but knowing me, that's probably just around the corner."

Harriet started to laugh. "I'm glad you've got a sense of humour about it."

Lucy found herself smiling in spite of the seriousness. "Hopefully I won't start talking to myself until my dotage, like my father."

"Well, go on," Harriet said, "I'm listening."

"Basically," Lucy said, "I feel I'm talking too much to Sarah – I feel I'm confiding in her too much. Letting my guard down."

"Well, it's good to have someone you can talk to, and Sarah is a lovely, trustworthy girl. What exactly have you told her so far?"

"Just about the trouble I got myself into over men."

There was a silence. "Did you tell her *everything*? Did you tell her about Durham?"

"No – no! Of course not . . ."

"It wouldn't be the end of the world if you did." Harriet's voice was gentle.

"I couldn't." Lucy was struggling to breathe deeply now. "What would she think of me?"

"I know about it," the nurse said. "I don't think any less of you."

"But our relationship is different. There's a professional confidentiality there." She closed her eyes. "You're used to seeing and hearing the worst of people and your job means you have to do it without judgement."

"But I'm not working with you any longer, Lucy. You're up and about and functioning fine. I come to see you as a friend – a concerned friend – I don't *need* to do it. I do it because I like coming into the shop to chat with you and Sarah. I enjoy it."

"You're very kind . . ."

"You're not the first person to have made mistakes, Lucy."

"I know that, but there aren't many women who have made such a serious mess of their lives as I have."

"You've improved over the last few years," Harriet reminded her. "And I've seen the biggest improvement in you since Sarah came to work in the shop. I think you and she are becoming very good friends, and people naturally reveal more about themselves when there is an element of trust in the friendship."

Lucy finally managed to take a deep, restorative breath. "So you don't think I've done or said anything terribly wrong?"

"I'm sure you haven't. But it might make you feel better if you stick to chatting about more ordinary things for a while." She thought for a moment. "Were you drinking by any chance?"

Lucy felt her face flush. "Yes, but not that much. A small glass of sherry before dinner, a glass or two of wine with the meal . . . nothing outrageous. I've drunk more when I've been on golf outings and felt fine."

"It may have mixed with your medication," Harriet said, "but I'd guess it's more to do with you feeling relaxed with Sarah and feeling you want her to know the real you."

"Do you think so?" Lucy wondered now. It was so long since she'd had a proper female friend that she had forgotten how deep any confidential exchanges had been with other friends in the past.

"I do . . . I really do." Her voice brightened. "So, what have you planned for the next few days?"

"I'm going into see my father tomorrow afternoon and then I have a golf tournament on Saturday." Lucy realised she felt much better already.

"Good," Harriet said. "Has Sarah told you I'm meeting her tomorrow?"

"Yes, she has." Lucy's voice was lighter. "That's lovely."

"We're going out to David McGuire's house. Sarah was invited to meet his grandparents and they've invited me. I really like him, so keep your fingers crossed for me, will you?"

"They're crossed already."

"Before I go," Harriet said. "I want to point out to you that I've just confided in you about liking David, and I know that Sarah has confided in us both about some of the things that happened to make her leave Ireland." She paused. "That's what friends do. Do you get the point I'm making?"

"I do, Harriet," Lucy said. "And thank you." She put the phone in its cradle now and lay back in the bed, feeling much lighter than she'd felt in a long time.

* * *

Sarah heard Lucy going downstairs and went into the bathroom for a quick wash and to brush her teeth. She went into the kitchen in her dressing-gown, carrying a Christmas present she had only remembered that morning. It was the one that David McGuire had given her. She had tucked it into a corner of her case and only found it this morning when she was looking for her face cream. She brought it down to breakfast as she didn't know how her employer would be this morning, and it would give them a safe subject to talk about. Sarah felt very confused about all the things Lucy had confided in her. She also thought it would show Lucy that she valued her opinion, as she was afraid she had come across as defensive last night.

"Did you sleep well?" Lucy asked, smiling brightly at her.

"I did, thanks." Sarah was relieved to see her back to her normal self. "How about you?" When their eyes met, she felt awkward and looked down to fiddle with her dressing-gown belt.

"Not bad," Lucy said, turning towards the cooker. "I have a pot of tea made and I thought we'd have some toasted crumpets for breakfast if that's okay with you?"

"Lovely," Sarah said, going over to look out of the window at the weather.

There was a small pause.

"I'm sorry about last night," Lucy said. "I got rather emotional. I said things I shouldn't have, and tried to tell you how you should live your life – which was wrong of me." She took a deep breath. "I'm afraid I've been inclined to keep things bottled up. I don't know what happened when we were chatting, but it all just seemed to spill out. I really am very sorry if I offended or embarrassed you."

Sarah turned towards her. "You didn't," she said. "You were just trying to advise me and I appreciate it." Two hot red circles came on her cheeks. "I've had the loveliest Christmas I've had for a few years here with you. I've really, really enjoyed it – and that's the important thing." Then, when she saw the obvious relief on Lucy's face, she felt a sudden rush of compassion. "You have been more generous and kinder to me than my relatives back in Ireland, and I know anything you say to me is to help me avoid any pitfalls that I might not be aware of, and I do appreciate it."

There was a moment when both of the women thought of

rushing over to hug the other, but each knew that it would break down the last of the barrier that was needed to keep the working relationship in its proper place.

They both moved at the same time, Lucy to find the packet of crumpets and Sarah to show her David McGuire's present.

"What do you think?" she said, holding out the book.

Lucy took it from her "'*Danta*' . . ." She halted, trying to pronounce the next word. "'*Grad – ha*'?"

"It's Irish – the Gaelic language – it means 'love poems' and you say it '*dawnta graw-ya*'."

Lucy raised her eyebrows and smiled. "Do you think he's trying to tell you something?"

Sarah sucked her breath in. "Oh, don't! I'm trying to believe what he said when he gave it to me."

"What did he say?" Lucy was still smiling. She opened the book and started leafing through it.

"He said that it came into the shop in a box of second-hand books, and since it was written in the Irish language he immediately thought of me." She looked at Lucy. "One of the times I bumped into him, we were talking about school and I told him that we used to speak in Irish in school. Where we live very few people speak it now, so my Irish is a bit rusty."

Lucy held out the open book. "I wouldn't know how to pronounce one word in it. I wouldn't even have known that it was in the Irish language if you hadn't told me."

Sarah looked down at the book. "But David would know how to recognise written Irish from his grandparents." She bit her lip. "I can't let Harriet see this . . . she might take it the wrong way. I'm sure he only bought it because it was Irish, not because of the love poetry thing."

"Well . . ." Lucy looked thoughtful, "I think you're right not to mention it to her. He may have meant nothing by it, and you can thank him quietly when you're on your own. Just keep it light and friendly."

"I'll tell him I like poetry, which is true," Sarah said, "and leave it at that. And I'll make sure Harriet isn't there."

CHAPTER 26

Sarah stood waiting at the empty bus stop outside the station where she had arranged to meet Harriet at two o'clock. It was a cold but dry day, but she was wrapped up well. She was wearing a fine, plum-coloured jersey suit under her camel-hair coat, with her long black leather boots, black gloves and scarf. Her hair was in a French plait and she carried a large crocodile, square handbag which held two boxes of chocolates for David's mother and grandmother. She had a bit of discreet make-up on, but nothing too obvious.

She walked up and down at the stop to keep warm, and thought how quiet it was, and how most people were probably lying low after the Christmas period, having overspent and overeaten.

When Harriet came cycling down to meet her, Sarah thought she looked particularly lovely in a bright green coat and with her long curly hair caught back in a clasp and make-up on. Harriet never wore make-up for work, but today she had made a big effort with some eye-shadow, mascara and lipstick. Sarah hoped the effort Harriet had made might give David a jolt and make him realise how lucky he was to have such a fine-looking girl interested in him.

Harriet dismounted and lifted her handbag out of the basket at the front of the bicycle along with a Marks and Spencer carrier bag and dropped them at Sarah's feet. "I'll just leave the bike chained up here," she said, indicating the office at the side of the building. "We've ten minutes until the bus comes so we're in plenty of time."

The bus to Jesmond had plenty of empty seats but they climbed upstairs to get a good view of the passing scenery.

"Did you speak to David?" Harriet asked.

"Yes, I told him we'd be there around half past two."

"Did you say I was coming with you?"

"No, it was a quick call and I didn't get a chance to elaborate," Sarah said. "I just said it was a friend."

"You got chocolates for them, didn't you?" Harriet dug into her handbag. "I brought two boxes of Marks and Spencer's biscuits. I hope they're all right, my mother said you can't go wrong with them . . ." She bent down to the carrier bag at her feet and brought out one of the boxes.

"They look lovely," Sarah said.

The bus conductress came up and Sarah paid the fares. "I invited you, it's my treat," she told Harriet when she tried to give her the money.

They chatted as they went along, with Sarah glancing every so often at the route directions David had given her, so they would know when to get off. Harriet knew the main areas in Jesmond, but she wasn't sure exactly where the McGuire family lived.

"I'm getting nervous now," Harriet said, when Sarah said she was sure there were only three more stops to go.

"Don't be," Sarah told her, beginning to feel nervous herself. What if David was annoyed she had brought Harriet? What if he was rude to them? "It's only a visit," she said, smiling. "What can go wrong?"

They came into Jesmond and Sarah spotted the road name they were looking for, high on the side of a wall.

"The next stop is ours," she said.

"Oh God . . ." Harriet said, and they both lifted their bags and headed for the stairs.

There were several other people getting off, so they stood at the bottom of the stairs. "There he is," she said, when the bus-stop came in sight. "You go first, Sarah, or he might get a fright and think you haven't come."

As the bus started to slow down, Sarah steadied herself by gripping onto the silver pole. "Relax," she whispered to her friend. "It's not as if he's a stranger."

David was waiting in the bus shelter and as the bus drew in, he stood back to let the passengers off. When he saw Sarah, his whole face lit up. "You found it all right?"

His dark brown eyes were fixed on her, seeing nobody else.

"Yes, we did," She emphasised the "*we*". She glanced behind her. "As I said I might, I brought a friend – Harriet came with me." When she turned back towards him she could see he looked thrown off his guard.

"I hope you don't mind another guest," Harriet said, smiling anxiously.

David caught himself. "Harriet!" he said, smiling back. "What a lovely surprise. I'd no idea you were off today. I knew most of the shops would be closed, but I imagined you were flying around on your bike, visiting patients."

"We're entitled to the odd day off, you know," she laughed.

"And it's nice to see you wearing clothes for a change," he said, winking at her.

"You cheeky thing!" Harriet made a pretence of slapping him. "If anyone heard you saying that, God knows what they would think!"

Sarah felt herself relax. It was going to be all right. David was being his old cheery, chatty self.

They walked along the road for a few hundred yards past rows and rows of tall, Victorian redbrick houses, talking about what they had done over Christmas and things like what they had seen on television.

"And how did you find it spending two whole nights with Miss Harrison?" David asked.

206

"Very, very nice," Sarah told him. "She really spoiled me with lovely food and drink and chocolates."

"I couldn't imagine her letting her hair down somehow."

Sarah silenced him with a warning eye as she didn't want Harriet thinking she discussed her boss outside of work. "You can have a good time doing quiet things, can't you, Harriet?" she said, drawing her friend in.

"Yes," Harriet said, "but it's nice to get out and about too."

They turned down a quiet residential street with the same tall buildings. "It's just near the bottom of the road here," David said. "We have a house on one side and my grandparents further down on the other side."

Sarah was taken aback. These were substantial, quite imposing houses – almost as big as the house in Victoria Street. For some reason she had presumed David would live in a small terraced house. He had never given her the impression that his family were well off, and she had thought they were just ordinary Irish people like her own family.

"This is a lovely area," Harriet said. "Have you lived here long?"

"My grandparents moved here first," David said, "and then we bought one about ten years ago. We've always lived in Jesmond though – our old house is only a few streets away."

Mrs McGuire was waiting for them in the large, modern kitchen, and after she thanked them for the chocolates and biscuits, she took them into the sitting room which had a dining area at the back with a table set with cold meats and salad.

She shook Harriet's hand and said, "I'm delighted this girl took a day off her work – from what David tells me she's at the sewing machine night and day!"

"She is," Harriet agreed. "She's never stopped since she arrived in Newcastle. I met her the first week she was in the shop, and every morning I came in she had done something different to the place. There were times I had to look around to check I was in the right place."

Sarah just laughed along with them and said, "It was kind of you to invite us."

"Oh, I had an ulterior motive, didn't I, David? I've a few jobs I want you to do for me, and I thought if I got you out to the house I would be able to hog your attention rather than queuing in the shop."

"I'd be delighted to do any sewing you need," Sarah said with a smile.

She looked around at the pale green walls with the gilt-framed paintings and family portraits, some old and some that looked fairly recent. She saw Harriet looking at one with Mrs McGuire and presumably her husband, with two boys who looked to be in their twenties and a girl perhaps older. The boy seated in the middle of the photo had David's unmistakable grin.

"That one was taken at David's eighteenth birthday," Mrs McGuire said.

"I knew it!" Harriet exclaimed, "I recognised him straight away." She picked up a small silver-framed picture taken around ten years previously with all four children in school uniform. "Ah," she said, looking over at David, "don't you look cute in your little blazer and cap?"

"Aw, Mam!" David said, rolling his eyes and laughing. "Why do you have these out on show where everyone can see them and take the mickey out me?"

"You're lucky we're not hiding them with the faces you pulled in some of the photos," she retorted.

They all laughed and, as the others studied more of the photographs, Sarah's professional eye was drawn to the dark-green velvet curtains with the wine and green tasselled pelmet and ropes that tied them back. The windows were huge – similar to Lucy's – and she knew that these particular curtains had been made by a long-established, professional company.

"Nora and Jim, my mother and father-in-law, will be here in a few minutes," Mrs McGuire said. She looked at Sarah. "They can't wait to meet you and hear your lovely Irish accent. David's sister,

Pat, is coming too, with her little girl Jessica." She glanced towards the window. "They should be here any minute. They live out in Gosforth. Mike, my husband, had to go into the office for a few hours but he's hoping to get away this afternoon."

"What does he do?" Harriet asked.

"He's a building supplier. It's a family business – McGuire's Concrete – his father started it when he came over from Dublin years ago. They have an office in Newcastle and another in Manchester that David's eldest brother runs." She looked over at David and smiled. "David took after the Frasers – my side of the family – they're the ones who are all about books, especially my brother Brian. This fellow is the very same as him. When he was young, the house could have fallen down and you'd find David under the rubble still reading a book."

"Enough!" David said. "The next thing you'll be bringing out pictures of me lying on a cushion with no clothes." He looked at the girls solemnly. "I was only six months old and didn't know what I was getting into."

His mother put her arm around him and kissed him on the cheek. "And you're still my little baby!"

"Girls," David said, laughing and struggling out of her embrace, "what can I get you?" He gestured towards a dark wood drinks trolley. "Have a look and see what takes your fancy."

"There's some white wine in the fridge as well if the girls would like that," his mother said.

"That would be lovely," Harriet said.

Sarah smiled in agreement.

"I'll go and open it now along with a bottle of red for my granddad," David said.

Sarah looked over at Harriet now. Her eyes were shining – she was obviously enjoying herself – and Sarah was glad she had thought of bringing her. If she had come on her own, David's family might have assumed they were more than just friends, and she was delighted to see how well he and Harriet were getting on.

The talk turned to Christmas and all the presents the children in the family had received, which made Sarah think of the gift David had given her. She asked where the ladies' was and was told there was one down at the bottom of the hallway, so she excused herself. She went straight to the kitchen.

"David," she said, coming in and closing the door behind her, "I wanted to thank you for the book."

He turned towards her. "Did you like it?"

"It's lovely," she said. "It was thoughtful of you – the fact that it was in Gaelic. My Irish is a bit rusty, so I must get my brother to post over my Irish into English dictionary so I can read it properly."

He looked pleased now. "Obviously I couldn't understand a word of it. But I just thought it was the sort of thing you would like to remind you of home."

"I was just thinking," she said, directing her gaze towards the window, "that it might be best not to say anything to Harriet about it. She might get the wrong idea . . ."

His brow furrowed. "What do you mean?"

"It's a book of love poems."

"Is it?"

Sarah couldn't tell if he genuinely didn't know. "Well, yes . . ." She looked at him now and raised her eyebrows and smiled. "I wasn't suggesting that you were giving it to me because of anything like that – I know we're just friends. It's just that Harriet might ask to see it, and I would feel awkward. She didn't say anything about you giving her a Christmas present, and you've known her far longer than you've known me."

Sarah noticed that his face was flushing. It was the first time she had ever seen him anything but cocky and confident.

"I've only ever known Harriet to speak to in passing," he said quietly, "and it would have looked odd to give her a present out of the blue. I see you every day because we work across the lane from each other. I wasn't planning on buying you anything and then I happened to see the book in the shop."

Sarah nodded. "Well . . . it was very nice of you, but we'll just keep it between ourselves."

He looked at her and she could see comprehension dawning in his eyes. "Is this what it's all about – Harriet? Is she the reason you won't come out with me to the cinema or go to a dance?"

"David," Sarah said, "I don't want to go out with you or anyone. My work is more than enough for me." She stopped then as she heard the front doorbell ring and then heard it opening.

"Okay," he said. He turned away to concentrate on the bottle of wine he was pouring.

She hesitated. "I don't want this to cause awkwardness between us. I'd like us still to be friends."

He gave her a wink. "Of course we will."

Pat Wood – David's sister arrived with her five-year-old daughter, Jessica – and the noise level in the house increased as everyone chatted. David brought around glasses of sherry and wine for the girls and Mrs McGuire had a whiskey with dry ginger. When David's grandparent's arrived, the noise increased further as the girls were introduced to the very fine-looking, white-haired couple who both still had strong Dublin accents.

They immediately launched into a series of questions asking Sarah exactly where she was from and if she knew this one or that one from Tullamore. Sarah had to tell them – with some relief – that she didn't know any of the names they mentioned.

"Ah, they're probably all dead and gone now anyway," Jim McGuire said shrugging. He turned to Harriet. "And are you a seamstress as well?"

"No, no, I'm a nurse – a District Nurse," she told him.

Sarah felt her heart sink a little as she realised David had obviously never mentioned Harriet to any of his family, and she wondered if the nurse had noticed.

David's grandmother, Nora, took Sarah's hand and brought her over to sit on the sofa over by the window.

"I don't hear too well when there's a crowd," she said, "and we can chat here easier away from the noise." She went on to tell Sarah about a special job she would like doing. "It's for Pat, you see," she explained. "I don't know if David's told you but she's expecting another little one in the summer. Well, we use the same christening gown that we've had in the family for years, but unfortunately . . ." She looked around to check no one else could hear. "Poor Amanda – David's sister-in-law – was the last one to use it last year when little Charlotte was christened – and unfortunately she had an accident with it. She wanted to give it back to me in perfect condition and went to the trouble of hand-washing it." She sighed and shook her head. "Then she thought she would press it all neat for me and that's when she caught it with the point of the iron and some of the fine lace got stuck to the bottom of it."

"Oh, no!" Sarah said. "That's so easily done with lace."

"You can imagine how the poor girl felt."

"Do you have it with you?" Sarah asked.

"No, because I haven't told anyone. You know how families can be, and I don't want poor Amanda feeling bad about it." She leaned in closer. "I'll give it to David and he'll bring it in to you in the shop. He won't say a word – you can trust David with anything." She tilted her head to the side. "Did you like your book?"

Sarah looked at her. "My book?"

"The Irish poetry book he gave you."

Sarah's face flushed. "Oh, yes," she said, "it was lovely."

"He really likes you, you know."

There was a sound at the door and Sarah whirled around to see little Jessica come running in after a ball. She turned back. "But we're only friends," she said. Someone else came in to get the child, so she kept her voice low until they went back out.

Nora McGuire raised her brows. "Well, he thinks more of you than a friend. He's a good lad – and a decent lad." She leaned forward, and tapped her finger on the coffee table. "Now, I'm speaking plainly to you as one Irishwoman to another – and because I like you. A hard-working girl like you would be very silly to pass up a fellow like that. There are plenty of girls who would jump at the chance of him." She thumbed out in the direction of the hall. "Your friend, the nurse, wouldn't be so slow. She can see he'd make a fine husband."

Sarah could now feel the resentment she had felt with Lucy the other night begin to simmer. Did she really come across as some timid little mouse in desperate need of a husband? She swallowed the feelings back because the elderly woman meant well and she didn't want to offend her. "David hardly knows me. I've only been in Newcastle a few months and I'm still finding my feet."

"Well, don't go missing the boat," Nora McGuire warned. "Because he's been offered the chance of a big job down in London and he's turned it down because of you."

Sarah's face blanched at the news. "Because of me?" She shook her head. "That's madness! I've never given him any encouragement. Surely he can't turn down a job because of me!"

"Well, I think he's hanging on for a while longer. He knows if he goes to London then that will be the end of it."

Sarah bit her lip. "Has he actually said all this to you?"

"Well, not as such, pet, but you'd know by the look on his face when he's talking about you."

There was a pause and Sarah took the chance to stand up. "I should get back in . . ."

"Hold your horses! Sit yourself back down," Nora said, putting a hand on Sarah's arm. "I've one more thing to say – just so you know the kind of man you're snubbing. You know the book he gave you?"

Sarah nodded.

"Well, I have the exact same one at home that his grandfather gave me as an anniversary present years ago. And since he was a young lad, David used to listen to him reading the poetry out in Irish." She smiled. "Jim still reads the book regularly to keep his hand in."

"But David told me that he came across it by chance amongst the second-hand books in the shop – he even pretended he didn't know they were love poems."

"Oh, he told me it turned up by chance too," Nora said. "But my guess is he went looking for it. It's not a book you'd pick up too handy. One of his uncles on his mother's side has several bookshops down in London, and he told me at a wedding recently that he's never come across that book." She looked at Sarah. "A lad doesn't give you books of love poetry without it meaning something."

The door creaked again and when Sarah turned around she saw Harriet framed in the doorway. Her face told Sarah that she had overheard them.

* * *

For the rest of the visit, Sarah kept trying to get Harriet on her own to explain the situation, but any time the opportunity arose Harriet seemed to slide away to another part of the room to talk to someone else. She was laughing and chatting and acting normally, so Sarah couldn't tell if she was still upset or even angry.

Sarah used every excuse to pass the time like taking Jessica for a walk out into the garden and going upstairs with Mrs McGuire to look at items that she wanted Sarah to alter for her. Sarah was grateful that she never referred to anything about her and David, and talked about ordinary things.

When she came back downstairs, Jim McGuire was waiting with a map of Dublin city to pin-point exactly where they came from. Then, Nora told them about her sister who had been quite a famous singer in Ireland, but who had sadly died a few years previously. There was general chat about the shops and places in Dublin that they knew, and how they loved their rare visits back.

"Unfortunately," Jim said, "when you get to our age, the trips are mainly to funerals."

"And have you been back home to Ireland since you arrived?" Nora asked.

Sarah smiled and hoped it looked genuine. "No, I've only been here a few months. Maybe next year."

When the time came for them to leave, Pat said she would run them back to the city centre in the car. "I'm in no rush today," she said, "and it will keep Jessica occupied having more company in the car."

David walked out to the car with them. Sarah thought he was slightly subdued, but he was still friendly and pleasant.

"Thanks for coming, girls," he said as they got into the car. "My grandparents were really pleased to meet you both."

"It was lovely," Harriet said, "for them to meet a nice young girl from the same part of the world as themselves."

"Thanks, David," Sarah said and got into the car.

When Pat dropped them off at the station, the two girls stood for a moment waving the car off and then Harriet turned to Sarah, all smiles gone.

"Did you bring me out to David's house today to humiliate me, Sarah?"

Her tone made Sarah feel she had been punched. "What do you mean?"

"All the things his grandmother said – I heard – I was at the door with David's niece," her voice rose higher, "I heard *everything* she said – all that stuff about how the young nurse wouldn't be so slow – how I could see that he would make a fine husband. God! She made me sound absolutely desperate."

Sarah moved forward to touch her friend's arm. "I'm really sorry. I had no idea what she was going to say."

Harriet pulled away. "I shouldn't have been so stupid as to go there with you. I've been totally blind – it's obvious that David's mad about you and you used me to try to put him off you."

"It wasn't like that at all! Honestly!"

"No? Did I hear wrong or has he asked you out on a date?" Harriet quizzed. "Did I imagine that his grandmother said he'd bought you a poetry book?"

Sarah dropped her gaze. "He did give me a book . . . but I thought it was all harmless stuff. A bit of a crush. I didn't think it was serious. I know you like him and I thought it was a chance to let you meet up with him and his family. I really thought that when he saw us all together he would realise he and you were far more suited. I think you would make a lovely couple and I thought I was doing the right thing."

"Well, that's very kind of you." Harriet's tone was brittle. "You obviously have plenty of experience in palming unwanted men onto other people."

Sarah flinched at her hard words. "I told you everything that happened to me in Ireland. You know I was supposed to have been married and you know I had no choice in what happened."

Harriet looked away, too wrapped up in her own embarrassment to care. "You've put me in a really humiliating situation. To hear his grandmother saying he had turned down a job in London so he could stay close to you! To hear that he'd bought you a book of love poetry for Christmas!" She shook her head. "You should have known that I wouldn't have gone to meet his family if I thought they all knew he had feelings for you."

"I'm sorry, Harriet, but I really didn't place any importance on the book. I thought it was because it was in the Irish language." Sarah knew her words rang hollow.

"Well, *he* obviously placed importance on it, especially since his grandfather had given the same book to his grandmother." There was a raggedness to the nurse's voice now. She suddenly halted. "Does Lucy know about the book?"

Sarah's face coloured instantly. "I was at her house on Christmas morning when I opened it."

"Does she know I was going out to David's house with you?"

"Yes, I mentioned it."

Harriet threw her hands up. "Lovely – so now I have a double humiliation!"

"What do you mean?"

"Lucy Harrison was a patient of mine, she looks up to me. Or at least she *did* look up to me. Now she'll only pity me." Her eyes blazed as she took in the implications. "Do you realise what you've done, Sarah? I spent two years helping Lucy Harrison get over a nervous breakdown because she made a fool of herself over a man. We became friends because she could confide in me – tell me things she'd never told anyone else – not even the psychiatrist at the hospital. She said I was mature beyond my years and she could always come to me for advice. How can she ever look up to me again, when she knows that I've now made an idiot of myself chasing a fellow who was blatantly in love with *you*?"

216

Sarah felt dizzy, confused – couldn't digest all the things that Harriet had said. The things she had accused her of. "My God . . . I am so sorry," she said. "I didn't mean any of this to happen. I know that Lucy thinks the world of you and I wouldn't dream of causing any awkwardness between you." Tears came into her eyes now. "I like you very much too, Harriet. I look forward to your visits to the shop. I can't believe I've made such a mistake. I truly did not mean it the way you are taking it. Please believe me. I really hoped you and David would get together."

Harriet's face was white and stiff. "Okay . . . I believe you didn't do it on purpose," she eventually said, "but it was a mistake I'll find hard to forget." She looked over to the office. "I'm going to get my bike now."

"If I don't see you," Sarah said, "I hope you have a good New Year."

"Well," Harriet said, walking away, "It can't be any worse than the end of this one." Then she suddenly halted and turned back. "Can I ask you to do one thing to make sure it definitely isn't worse?"

"Yes? I'll do anything . . ."

"Forget all the things I said about Lucy. I was upset and it just came out. It's confidential information, and if she knew I told you she might just report me and I could be sacked." She looked Sarah in the eye now. "I've already lost one friend today in David and I don't want to lose another friend or even my job."

Sarah's eyes filled with tears and her body was trembling. "I wouldn't dream of saying anything. You have my word I will never mention it. I know you have a very low opinion of me after today, but I'm really not a bad person." Tears started to spill down her cheeks and she lifted her handbag to search for a hanky.

"I know you're not bad." Harriet's voice softened. "But I'm afraid I can't get over what happened today just as quickly as you would like."

* * *

The house in Victoria Street was quiet – empty apart from Jane who was in bed after doing a night shift – so Sarah was thankful that she didn't have to appear bright and chatty. She went up to her room and tried to read, but couldn't concentrate. She took out the pattern for the evening dress, but couldn't focus enough to do it properly.

The row with Harriet overshadowed everything.

She went downstairs and made tea and toast, then brought it back upstairs. When she was exhausted with thinking she put a radio programme on and eventually the music seemed to relax her. She went back to the pattern and several hours passed as she worked out the exact measurements and then cut out each piece and started work tacking together the basic seams. She heard Jane coming out of her room around seven o'clock and went out to meet her in the hallway. Then they went downstairs together to have supper.

Sarah went over and switched on the gas fire. "You've been on your feet all night, so sit there and I'll do us beans on toast."

She busied herself sorting the food and then came back to eat at the table. Jane told her all about how Christmas had gone back home and Sarah told her all about the lovely time she had with Lucy.

"I'd like your advice," Sarah said, putting her fork on the barely touched beans. "I've upset a friend and I don't know what to do about it." She went on to explain the situation about Harriet.

Jane sat in silence for a few minutes, eating her supper and contemplating the facts. "I can see how she feels," she said, digging into her beans, "but at the end of the day, you were actually trying to do her a favour. You were trying to set her up with a fellow she really likes. It wasn't your fault that it didn't work. It wasn't your fault that his grandmother said all those things about the poetry book – it was stuff you didn't know anything about." She shrugged and put the forkful of beans in her mouth.

"But she heard his grandmother saying that she wasn't so slow and that she knew David would make a fine husband."

Jane swallowed. "Well, the fact is he already knew she liked him, and I know it's uncomfortable for her to know that he doesn't fancy her the same way, but we've all had to put up with rejection. I hear things like that in the hospital day in day out – people always fancy other people who don't fancy them. It's not the end of the world, and she just has to get over it." She raised her eyebrows. "You didn't do anything nasty and she can't blame you for what his grandmother said. End of story."

Sarah was washing up the dishes when Jane left to have a bath.

The nurse stopped at the doorway. "Your friend will get over it, Sarah. Look at the big row you and Vivienne had. Even though it was pure ignorance and nastiness on her part, you still managed to forgive and forget, and you're both getting on fine now. You did nothing deliberately and Harriet will eventually realise that."

Sarah felt much better after that and went back upstairs and put her mind on the dress. She worked until midnight and fell asleep exhausted. Then she woke again around three o'clock and lay awake for hours wondering how she had made such a monumental mistake.

Now and then she allowed herself to wonder why Harriet had set her cap so firmly on a lad who had made it plain he had no interest in her. It was easy enough to know when someone liked you, she thought. Most males were so obvious when they did fancy someone. Surely Harriet should have taken the hint long ago and moved her attentions elsewhere?

Be that as it may, Sarah felt guilty for being part of poor Harriet's humiliation and she went over the whole situation again and again, blaming herself.

By the time she had eventually fallen asleep, she had convinced herself that neither Harriet nor Lucy would ever speak to her again.

* * *

The following morning she decided to take one of the bulls by the horns and went out to the phone box to ring Lucy. She repeated the same story she had told Jane the previous night and then listened to the response. It was the exact same as the nurse's.

"Harriet will just have to get over it," Lucy said. "It's not your fault that David only sees her as a friend." She paused. "Although I must say I agree with his grandmother."

"About what?" Sarah asked.

"About your passing up the chance of a nice fellow like David McGuire. I told you that the other night. You can't let him go to London without giving things a chance with him. You wouldn't do that just because of what happened to you back in Ireland, would you?"

"But I've no feelings for him," Sarah said. "And after what has happened with Harriet, I'll be giving all lads a wide berth."

"Well, let's hope that's not something you might live to regret."

Sarah walked back from the phone box with a lightness in her step. She felt much better having got the same response from both women. She would give Harriet the time she needed to come around, and she would put the incident out of her mind now and get on with making her dress.

CHAPTER 27

The house in Victoria Street buzzed with activity on New Year's Eve as the girls prepared for the dance. The two nurses, Jane and Elizabeth, were working the late shift on the ward until eight o'clock, and had taken their outfits to the hospital with them to change into when they finished. They had a taxi booked to take them down to the Palace Hotel where they would meet the others.

Sarah, Anna and Vivienne took turns bathing and drying their hair. Sarah had toyed with the idea of going to the hairdresser's to have her hair put up, but the other girls talked her out of it.

"If I had lovely long blonde hair like yours," Anna said, as they all sat in the kitchen in their dressing-gowns drinking tea, "I would wear it loose all the time. You always have it tied up or plaited, and we only get to see it out when you're letting it dry."

"I have to tie it up for work," Sarah sighed. "It's such a nuisance if I don't – it gets in the way of everything. And it's so heavy when it's in a bun that sometimes I get headaches from the weight of it."

"Then leave it loose," Anna said. "It's absolutely striking. Have you decided what you're wearing tonight?"

"I've made a new dress. I saw one I loved in Fenwick's with a nice beaded neck and I made a copy of it."

"What colour is it?"

"It's quite unusual – a dark grey taffeta with a navy sheen to it."

Vivienne's eyebrows shot up. "Wow!" she said. "It sounds amazing. Can we come up and have a look?"

"Yes, if you want to." Sarah hid her surprise, as Vivienne had never shown much interest in her work before. The other girls had asked her to do the odd alteration for them, and Sarah had made cushions for the sofa downstairs and a nice pair of lined curtains for the bathroom.

All three went upstairs and, when Sarah opened the door, they had a full view of the dress and matching stole hanging on the wardrobe door.

"You actually *made* that?" Vivienne gasped. She went over to the wardrobe and carefully examined the dress. "It looks like something you would buy in Harrods!"

"Harrods often sell the same designs as Fenwick's," Sarah told her. "And it's a *Vogue* pattern."

Vivienne raised her eyebrows. "You can tell."

"It's gorgeous," Anna said. "Did it cost you a fortune to make?"

"The material is expensive," Sarah admitted. "I had to order it in, but Lucy was good enough to let me have it at cost price."

"Can I hold it up and look at it in the mirror?" Vivienne asked. "I'll be really careful."

"Of course you can," Sarah said. "It's tough material."

The student doctor lifted the dress down and then moved back to get a good view in the mirror, holding the dress in front of her. "That is truly beautiful," she said. "It's a work of art. Did it take you long to make it?"

"Three days."

Vivienne gave a low whistle. She hung it back on the wardrobe then studied it for a few moments longer. "You should be selling dresses like this," she told her. "They're as good as anything you see in the high-class shops and probably better made. You would make a lot more money than you earn from working in a shop."

"I enjoy working in the shop," Sarah said, a note of defence in her voice. Even when Vivienne was giving her a compliment, she suspected superior, critical thoughts behind her words. Since the row all those months ago, the medical student had given her no reason to feel like this, but Sarah reckoned that leopards didn't change their spots that easily.

Anna went over to feel the dress now and examined the beading at the neck. "She's right, Sarah. You could be working at dress-designing full time. You could have a simpler dress than this made in the same time it takes you to make curtains or fancy cushion-covers."

"If you made that dress in white," Vivienne said now, "it would be a fabulous wedding dress. Have you ever thought of making wedding dresses?"

Sarah's throat tightened. It was only a matter of months ago when she was stitching her own white satin and lace creation. But the girls didn't know that. "I'm happy doing this sort of thing for now."

* * *

As she gathered her taffeta dress up to step out of the black hackney car, Sarah felt a tinge of excitement run through her. After a pleasant but quiet Christmas with Lucy Harrison, it was nice to be mixing socially with people her own age again. She hadn't been to a dance since she left Ireland, and it was the first time she'd felt light and easy in all those months. It was the first time she'd felt good about anything outside of work, and she had never imagined herself wearing a dress as glamorous as this. There had never been the occasion. The girls back in Tullamore wore nice dresses and suits for special dances, but the Parochial Halls and the local ballrooms were not the sort of places for very glamorous evening wear.

Her confidence had been boosted by all the compliments she had got on her dress from the girls in the house and from Lucy and Lisha and her mother. And although she had never been particularly heavy, Sarah could see the stone or so she had lost since coming to Newcastle had made a definite difference to the way the dress looked.

There were two sparkling Christmas trees on either side of the hotel door and, as they stepped inside to the busy foyer, Bing Crosby's voice greeted them crooning "White Christmas". It was a big, luxurious hotel and Sarah could immediately see the difference in standard between it and the hotel she had worked in back in Tullamore. She caught her breath as she looked around at the beautiful decorations and the huge indoor tree with the silver and gold decorations.

"It's gorgeous, isn't it?" Anna said. "It's the last time we'll enjoy the Christmas stuff, so we might as well make the most of it."

Vivienne pointed to the double doors on the right. "We'll head over to the bar first for a drink," she said. "Jane and Elizabeth won't be here for another twenty minutes. If you two grab seats, I'll get us all a drink. Is a medium sherry all right?"

Anna grinned. "Anything for me!"

Vivienne looked at Sarah.

She nodded in agreement. "Sherry is fine." Whatever two medical students from refined families thought was okay, would be fine by her.

They walked into the busy bar full of men in tuxedos and women of all ages dressed in their finery. Immediately, the groups of men turned to look towards them. From the corner of her eye, Sarah saw one of a group of younger men nudge another and motion towards them. Instinctively she lowered her head and kept her gaze straight ahead.

"There's a table over there by the window," Anna said, propelling her by the arm. "Let's grab it."

As they made their way through the people, Sarah could also see some of the women looking at her and she suddenly felt self-conscious. She heard someone say something about her hair and she instantly regretted not having it put up to look the same as the others. They arrived at the table and four chairs the same time as the two young men who had been discussing them – one tall with dark hair and the other slightly shorter with fair hair.

"Sorry . . ." Anna said, raising her eyebrows and smiling, "but I think we got here first." She quickly claimed one of the chairs by sitting down in it.

Sarah lifted the hem of her long dress and sat in the chair beside her.

The dark-haired boy looked at Sarah and then laughed. "Oh, well," he said. "I suppose we'll just have to be gentlemen . . ."

"Or perhaps we could join you?" his friend said.

Sarah put her hand on the back of the chair next to her. "I'm sorry," she said, "but that chair's taken. Our friend will be here in a minute."

The fair-haired chap sat down in it. "I'll keep it warm for her," he said, smiling. He put his hand out. "Ben Livingstone and my friend is James Ryder."

Sarah felt slightly flustered. They were obviously not going to be put off easily. She had no option but to shake his hand. "I'm Sarah." She indicated to her house-mate, "And this is Anna."

Ben leaned forward to shake Anna's hand. "I know you," he said. "You were on the women's surgical ward last week, weren't you? I'm sure I saw you when I was doing the rounds."

Anna's face lit up, pleased that he had recognised her. "Yes, I'm a third-year medical student."

"Good for you. I think most people here tonight work in the hospital in some shape or form." He smiled. "Although it's hard to recognise some people in all their finery when we're used to seeing them in uniforms or theatre scrubs."

Sarah felt her throat tighten. This was a world she felt totally out of.

James Ryder came around the back of the chairs to crouch down beside Sarah. "What a lovely Irish accent you have. Do you mind me asking which county you're from?"

"Offaly. You probably won't know it – it's a very small county."

"I have heard of it," he told her, "but I've never been there. We often go over to Ireland for the racing – Kildare and Galway. My father's friends are big horsey people – they have a stud farm in Naas. Have you heard of Naas?"

"Yes, I've heard of it – but it's not somewhere I know well." She thought she was very unlikely to know the people either as most of the farms around her area were modest dairy farms.

Just then Vivienne arrived at the table with a young waiter who was carrying a silver tray with three large sherry glasses on it. "Dr Ryder and Dr Livingstone, I presume!" she said, laughing.

Ben Livingstone closed his eyes and shook his head. "I've heard that Dr Livingstone quote so many times it's got a beard on it."

"An oldie but a goldie!" Vivienne said, moving into the spare seat.

The waiter handed round the drinks and all three girls clinked glasses. Sarah took a bigger gulp than she intended to and had to hold her breath as the sweet but strong liquid went down.

"I didn't know these two lovely ladies were friends of yours," Ben said.

"We share a house together," Vivienne replied, taking a mouthful of her sherry. "And there's another two to come."

"All medical students?" James Ryder asked.

"No, no," Vivienne said quickly. "The other two are nurses and Sarah here is a . . ." She gestured with her glass towards in Sarah's direction, then moved her glass around as she thought.

Sarah looked at her, waiting for some kind of put-down.

"Sarah is a wonderful dress-designer," Vivienne said effusively. "She can make absolutely anything. She actually *made* that amazing creation she is wearing tonight."

"*Really?*" Both men said at exactly the same time.

"I did make it," Sarah said, laughing. She looked at her lodging partner now. "And thank you for the compliment about the dress, Vivienne."

A loud bang on a gong silenced everyone, and then an announcement was made regarding the time that dinner would be served, and advising people to check for their table number on a list inside the dining-room.

Ben checked his watch. "We have half an hour," he said. "Plenty of time for another drink. Same again, girls?"

"That would be lovely," Anna said, draining her drink.

Vivienne gave the two doctors a beaming smile. "Maybe a Martini this time?"

"I'm grand . . ." Sarah said, indicating her half-filled glass, but no one took any notice.

When the two men left for the bar, Vivienne turned to Anna. "How did you do it?"

Anna wrinkled her brow. "What?"

"Bag the two best-looking doctors in the hospital! I didn't know you knew them so well?"

"I don't," Anna said. "They just parked themselves down beside us. I've a feeling that it was Sarah who caught their eye."

"I'm sure I didn't –" Sarah started.

"Don't be so modest," Anna told her. "Surely you could tell by the way they looked at you?"

Sarah started to blush. "I didn't notice anyone looking at me." She felt false saying it, because of course she had noticed people looking at her, but it would sound vain to admit it.

"Well, I don't care how they ended up sitting with us," Vivienne said, throwing back the last of her sherry. "Let's just all try to make a good impression on them when they come back."

They sat chatting for a while, watching people and looking at all the lovely outfits as more guests arrived. Then, when a couple of chairs became vacant at a nearby table, Vivienne rushed over and pulled one of them up next to her own chair.

"That's a chair for both of them now," she said laughing. "We'll just have to find something interesting topics of conversation to keep them occupied, so they don't wander off to sit with some other girls."

"You two can do all the talking," Sarah said. "You have far more in common with them. I don't know the first thing about medical matters."

Vivienne raised one eyebrow. "My experience of doctors has taught me that the last thing they want to discuss on a night out are medical matters."

Anna laughed. "Unless it's to do with physiology and biology – especially the female form."

"They needn't bother studying my form," Sarah said. "Men are the last thing I'm interested in."

Vivienne's eyebrows shot up. "Are you joking? Surely you wouldn't turn down the chance of an amorous encounter with Dr Ryder or Dr Livingston? They're really good, eligible catches."

"I would turn it down quite easily."

Sarah felt the sherry had made her more relaxed, and even though the occasion was more formal than anything she had experienced before, she found she was actually enjoying herself. But even in the midst of all the glamour and excitement of the night, work was never far from her mind. As various females passed by their table, Sarah took in all the small details that made certain ball gowns stand out from the others. She made mental notes about the materials that sat well and the unusual diamante and lace finishes on necklines and cuffs, and the sorts of stoles and bags that made an outfit stand out.

She was discreetly studying a girl with a shiny black, twenties-style short bob who was wearing a green velvet Flapper-style dress when Vivienne leaned across the table and whispered. "Don't look now, but here they come again."

The doctors handed round the tray of drinks and then Ben sat in the chair beside Vivienne and James Ryder sat next to Sarah.

"So," James said, "how do you find Newcastle?"

"Grand. It's a nice city – I like it very much."

"Is it very different to where you come from in Ireland?"

"*Very*. I'm from a small country town about fifty miles from Dublin." Then, to deflect any further questions about herself, she asked. "Where are you from originally?"

"Just outside Manchester." He gave her a beaming smile. "Out in the country too, so we have something in common. In fact, my grandfather has a farm there."

Sarah took a drink from the full glass of sherry. "I grew up on a small farm. My brother and his wife have it now."

"And what about your parents?"

"They're both dead . . ." As she said it, she felt a catch in her chest and wished she had said nothing.

He looked surprised. "How awful for you! When did they die?"

There was nothing she could do now. "My mother died when I was thirteen and my father died nearly two years ago."

All eyes on the table suddenly turned towards her.

"Oh, Sarah!" Anna said. "I didn't realise . . ."

Vivienne leaned across the table and put her hand on top of hers. "I'm so sorry . . ."

"It doesn't matter now, I'm used to it," Sarah said, starting to blush with all the attention. She was furious with herself for having got into the conversation with the doctor that had led to her private life being discussed in front of everyone. She gently moved her hand from under Vivienne's and lifted her glass and took another sip. "I wonder when the others will arrive."

"They're always late! They've probably stopped to chat with people at work or maybe even out in the hotel foyer," Anna said, laughing.

A short while later Elizabeth and Jane came pushing their way through the crowds to get to their table. After all the introductory chat was over and everyone said how lovely everyone else looked in their evening wear, both girls immediately turned to Sarah.

"Where did you get the fabulous dress?" Elizabeth asked.

"I made it," Sarah said in a low voice, not wishing to be the centre of attention again.

"Did you bring it over from Ireland?"

Sarah shook her head. "I made it this week."

"But you were working on curtains the last time I saw you at the sewing machine," said Jane.

"I finished them on Wednesday, and then I started on the dress."

"You made it in *three* days?" Jane gasped.

Elizabeth studied her in amazement. "You're a dark horse. We'd no idea you were upstairs in your room making such a glamorous outfit."

"It was easy enough," Sarah said. She held up one end of her stole. "And this was only a matter of hemming and then putting the beads on the ends of it. I did it in a couple of hours." Whilst she found being the focus of any conversation difficult enough, it was preferable to talk about her work rather than herself.

"What else don't we know about you?" Vivienne asked.

"You sound a very intriguing lady indeed," James said. He glanced across at his doctor friend. "A little bit of mystery certainly keep things interesting, doesn't it?"

Sarah rolled her eyes and shook her head. "I can assure you there's nothing very interesting or mysterious about me."

The gong sounded and then the head waiter requested that all the ladies and gentlemen to please make their way into the dining room.

Ben stood up first. "Drink up, everyone," he said, and downed his glass in one. Sarah's four flatmates and James Ryder followed suit, so she lifted her glass and drank the remainder of her sherry. It was more alcohol than she was used to drinking in such short space of time, but she didn't want to stand out from the others. Her work and her background made her different enough.

Tonight she would do her best to fit in with the girls. Jane had been kind enough to buy her the ticket, and Vivienne had done everything possible to make up for their row. And, it was New Year's Night.

Vivienne leaned in close to Sarah as they moved towards the dining-room. "Unfortunately we're at an all-girls table. Our table places were fixed in advance, so we won't be able to sit beside our attentive friends."

Sarah looked up at her, wondering why Vivienne was explaining this to her. "I'm perfectly happy sitting with the girls."

Vivienne raised her eyebrows. "We'll watch where they sit and make sure we catch up with them when the meal is over."

Sarah wrinkled her brow and laughed. Vivienne must be very keen on the two doctors and was presuming she felt the same. Did her housemate imagine that she was the kind of girl who latched on to a fellow within an hour of meeting him? Did the other girls think the same? She decided she would give the doctors a wide berth for the rest of the evening.

The dining room was spectacular with each of the circular tables decorated in a white and purple theme. Heavy silver candlesticks towered over each one, and around the base of the candlesticks were vases filled with white flowers. Bottles of red and white wine rested in silver buckets on each table, and the waiters moved between them smartly dressed with cummerbunds and matching bow-ties.

Sarah didn't know whether to be relieved or disappointed when she recognised the menu as being fairly similar to what would have been served back in the hotel in Tullamore – melon or soup to start and a choice between turkey, steak or a fish dish. She supposed that it was better to be presented with familiar food on her first proper night out in Newcastle. After her first glass of white wine, she found she was relaxed about everything including Vivienne and the doctors.

The two girls who had been working in the hospital that night started telling them about a Peeping Tom who had been spotted looking in through the window of a ground ward. Two of the male nurses had chased him out of the area where the buildings were, but lost him in the darkness of the grounds. A few days previously, some of the female nurses mentioned that they felt there was someone lurking around outside, but this was the first proper sighting of him.

"It's bloody disgraceful," Vivienne stated, "that we can't go about our work without having to worry about being watched by some pervert."

"Matron sent a note around to say that the female staff should only go outside in twos," Jane said, "and that we should keep the ward curtains closed when it gets dark."

"Piffle!" Elizabeth said. "We often have to go from a ward in one building to a ward in another, and when we're short-staffed we don't have time to go and look for a partner to walk over with."

After the meal the tables were cleared and the band came onto the stage to sort out their instruments for the dance session. The girls went in groups to the ladies' to touch up their make-up and Sarah was delighted when Jane linked arms with her as they walked along.

"I'm so glad you came to live in the house with us," Jane said, as they applied fresh lipstick. "And I think that little run-in you had with Vivienne did us all a favour. She's been a different person since then, and is more inclined to think before she speaks."

"I'm glad it's sorted too," Sarah said. She still regarded the medical student's outburst as more than "a little run-in" but given that it was New Year's Eve, she said nothing more.

When they came back into the hall there was a group of four young men standing by their table chatting to the other three girls.

"Vivienne will be delighted," Jane laughed. "She told me that she plans to find herself a husband tonight."

"You're joking!"

"I'm not. She reckons that most of her friends back home are already married and she feels it's about time she met someone." She slowed down a little. "You know she was engaged before, don't you?"

"No," Sarah said, "I didn't."

"It was before she came to Newcastle – a friend of the family. They'd been going out since she was fifteen. They used to write to each other at boarding school – that kind of thing."

"What happened?"

"She got bored. She said she was too young, and couldn't bear the thought of only being allowed to kiss one man for the rest of her life." Jane giggled now. "So I think she's trying a few out before settling down."

"At least she was honest. It was better that she realised sooner than later. It must be awful to be married to someone you don't love." Sarah wondered now if she had really loved Con.

"Her fiancé didn't waste any time. He met someone else fairly quickly and was married within a year. I believe they have a baby."

232

She tightened her grip on Sarah's arm. "Look at her now, all over those fellows. There are times when I wonder if she regrets her broken engagement and is afraid of being left on the shelf."

"I don't think there's any fear of that," Sarah said. "She seems to be getting plenty of attention from the men tonight, and anyway, she's still only in her twenties."

By the time they got to their seats the band was striking up for the first waltz. Sarah had just sat down when James Ryder appeared behind her.

"Miss Love," he said, holding his hand out, "might we have the first dance together?"

As they moved onto the floor he bent to speak in her ear. "I should tell you that you've made a big hit here tonight." He laughed. "I had to move quickly or someone would have got to you first."

Sarah laughed but said nothing. As they circled the floor together, she was conscious of his hand on her waist, and she was suddenly reminded of herself and Con Tierney dancing together. The difference was that the young English doctor was holding her in a respectful manner, whereas Con – when he had a drink in him – had often gripped her too tightly and pulled her in frighteningly close.

It seemed such a long time ago. Con felt like a stranger from a faraway place she hardly remembered. As she moved amongst the other elegantly dressed dancers she couldn't even picture his face any more. Tonight, the people in this glittering ballroom were much more real to her, and she realised she was becoming more part of things. She felt comfortable on a night out with the girls from the house. She felt comfortable in her stunning dress. She felt as good as anyone else here tonight.

When the dance finished, Sarah had barely sat back down at the table when she was taken up for the next dance with someone from a table nearby. After that, she was asked up by Dr Livingstone.

The first part of the night flew in and Sarah was glad when the break came so she could relax at the table and rest her feet for a while. The girls were all in high spirits, drinking wine and giggling and laughing about who they had danced with.

Vivienne leaned back in her chair to check that no one apart from those at the table could hear, and then suddenly threw herself forward. "I'm in love!" she said in a loud whisper. "I've met the man of my dreams."

"Who?" the girls all asked together.

She took a gulp from her glass of wine. "Dr Livingstone – he's perfect! Absolutely perfect. Even my parents would love him."

"But you hardly know him!" Anna giggled.

"I know all I need to know," Vivienne said, pushing her dark hair back from her face. "And I have to make a good impression on him tonight or I might miss my chance." She turned to Sarah. "I need your help. Apparently James Ryder is besotted by you and your lovely blonde hair. They're best friends and it would be easier if the four of us were together."

"Sorry – not interested!" Sarah laughed and put her hands over her ears.

"But Dr Ryder is lovely!" Anna said.

Sarah shook her head. "I have no interest in any men. Men are off my list for the next few years."

"*Years*?" Elizabeth gasped. "Surely you don't mean that long?"

Sarah nodded vigorously. "I do mean it!"

Vivienne leaned across to move Sarah's hands down. "I have a plan," she said. "You only have to be nice to him for a little while. Just enough time to let me get chatting properly to Ben." She put her hands together as though in prayer. "*Please!*"

Sarah suddenly felt very hot. She lifted her wineglass and took a long drink from it. "If he comes over and asks me to dance I won't be rude, but I'm not going over to hang around their table or anything like that."

"Spoken like a woman who knows her own mind!" Jane held her glass up in a toast.

Vivienne held her glass out in agreement and then downed the remainder of her red wine in one go.

"I do know my own mind these days, but I had to learn the hard way . . ." Sarah felt a sudden compulsion to explain herself. "I was due to be married when I moved to Newcastle. I had the wedding booked, the dress made . . . everything." She looked around her and saw the other girls were staring at her in shock.

"My God, Sarah!" Anna's gasped. "Are you joking?"

"You know I'm not the sort of person to make jokes like that." Sarah could hear herself saying the words, but in a strange way it seemed as though someone else was speaking on her behalf. She looked down at her glass, realising she had said too much. "Anyway, it's all water under the bridge."

"You can't leave it like that," Anna said. "Tell us more."

"Do you regret it?" Vivienne asked.

Sarah shrugged, wishing they would change the subject. "I don't regret my decision not to get married. I know I did the right thing."

"So, you as good as jilted him?" Vivienne said.

"You walked out on him just a week or so before the wedding?" Jane sounded shocked. "You cancelled *everything*?"

Sarah cursed herself for letting her guard down – she had no option now but to explain. "Yes, I did. But I was betrayed in a very big way and he deserved it."

"Who deserved it?" an amused male voice interjected.

When they turned around Doctors Ryder and Livingstone were standing there with a waiter with a tray of cocktails for the girls.

"What's in them?" Anna asked.

"It's a surprise!" Ben Livingstone said. "Each cocktail is different, and you must drink the one the waiter places in front of you."

The girls all giggled and laughed as they were each given a drink, and Vivienne patted the empty chair beside her and told Ben to sit down. Although there were a couple of empty chairs, James Ryder stood to the side of Sarah's chair so he could talk to her. Eventually, Jane – who was seated next to her – moved her chair further along, to allow him to drag in a spare one.

Sarah sipped the cocktail through her straw. "This is lovely!" she said, sounding highly surprised. She had been wary of it, having already drunk so much, and was delighted that it seemed a harmless, sweet, fruity drink. She felt the wine was having some effect on her, so was happy to switch to a less potent drink.

The other girls took sips of their cocktails. Elizabeth spluttered when she was drinking hers, and everyone started laughing. Sarah laughed along with them, so much that she lost her breath and ended up red-faced and giggly.

The band came back on and the dancing re-commenced, and then, after what seemed like no time at all – the band-leader was telling everyone to go back to their tables for their glasses to toast in the New Year.

As she made her way through back to the table, Sarah caught herself stumbling a few times and had to really concentrate on what she was doing. All the other girls were grabbing tall glasses of sparkling wine which had been placed on each table for the midnight toast, so she did likewise. As she lifted her glass, the wine splashed out on to the tablecloth and she was relieved that it was white and not red and wouldn't stain it. The same happened when the other girls lifted their over-full glasses but nobody seemed concerned.

"Everyone take a big drink from your glass!" Vivienne instructed, lifting a half-full bottle from the ice bucket.

Without question, Sarah took a gulp of the sweet bubbly drink, and thought it tasted lovely. Then, Vivienne went around the table filling everyone's glass up to the top again. As she moved along, she caught her leg on the chain of an evening bag which was under a chair, and stumbled forward onto the table, spilling the wine everywhere.

"Oh, bugger!!" she said, using both hands to lever herself back into a standing position. After a few seconds steadying herself, she lifted the bottle up to the light and said, "Thankfully, I didn't lose it all!" She then proceeded to lift the bottle to her lips and in a few mouthfuls she had drained it.

Sarah watched the scene with a strangely detached amusement and at the back of her mind noted that the other girls didn't seem to find anything unusual about Vivienne falling across a table. She wondered that she had ever thought doctors were something special. They were the same as anyone else when they were out enjoying themselves. It was just that they did it in grander surroundings.

When everyone got into circles for the midnight countdown, Sarah was surprised to find herself holding hands with Ben Livingstone on one side and James Ryder on the other. She couldn't remember them coming back to join the girls. She shrugged and joined in with everyone else as they counted down the seconds to midnight, and then, as the start of the New Year was declared, they all cheered and crossed hands with the person next to them and started to sing "Auld Lang Syne".

The first verse started off with everyone knowing the words and then the song gradually descended into many people guessing the words, miming or humming along. At the end of the final verse all the people in the hall were cheering and hugging and kissing everyone else.

After he had kissed her lightly on the cheek, James Ryder held her at arm's length and then pulled her back and said loudly in her ear above the din, "I don't believe I've spent the New Year before in the company of such a beautiful and enchanting young lady. I hope this is going to be the start of something big?"

Sarah giggled and shook her head, not taking it seriously. On a night like this everyone was in high spirits and everything was exaggerated and, although she was enjoying herself, she had no intentions of allowing any man to get close to her.

James had just lifted her hand to kiss it when Jane rushed across the floor to sweep Sarah up in a big bear-hug.

"Happy New Year, Sarah!" she screeched above the loud music. "I'm so glad you came to live in our house, and we all think you are going to be a famous fashion designer in the next few years!"

"That's lovely of you!" Sarah said, hugging her back. She was delighted that she was now fully accepted in the house, and the compliment about her sewing talent was ringing loudly in her ears. Was it really possible, she wondered, that somebody like her could have a career in fashion designing?

The music changed to a tango, and just as James started to ask her to dance again, Vivienne appeared and put her arms around Sarah. "I need to tell you something in private," she said, carefully enunciating each word." She then guided Sarah back to the table, steadying herself on the other chairs as she went along.

When they sat down, the medical student lifted a glass of the sparkling wine and gave it to Sarah and then she started drinking one herself. As Sarah took a sip of the wine, she warned herself to slow down and be careful, as she had already drunk too much.

Vivienne reached over and took Sarah's hand. "I want to . . . I want to apologise properly to you . . ."

Sarah could tell that Vivienne was now clearly drunk. "For what?" she asked.

"For the bloody awful way I treated you. She waved her hand around. "When you first arrived. The horrendous way I was." She paused. "I can explain it . . ."

Sarah waited. There was no point in throwing Vivienne off her train of thought, and she wanted to hear what she had to say.

"It wasn't really about *you!*" Another pause. "It was really about my father . . ." Tears started spilling down her face. "He's a doctor, too. Did you know that?"

Sarah nodded. Vivienne often talked about going home to visit her parents, and she had a vague recollection of the other girls mentioning something about Vivienne's father when she first arrived.

"Well . . ." Vivienne slowly shook her head from side to side. "Years ago, he had an affair with one of the secretaries in his practice and when he broke it off the woman – Catriona Clarke – came to our house and told my mother all about it." She stopped and took a deep shuddering breath.

"Oh, Vivienne, I'm so sorry . . ."

"I was playing behind the sofa with my doll and my mother didn't realise." The tears were really falling now.

Sarah glanced around her, hoping no one would come and interrupt them. "When I realised they were talking about something very serious, I kept quiet. I heard her telling my mother all about the affair, and how she was now expecting Daddy's baby."

238

Sarah felt a stab of intense sorrow as she listened.

"I was only about ten years old, but I understood every single word. My poor mother was devastated. She had known nothing about it, and just sat listening in silence. When she did speak, I could tell from her voice that things would never be the same again. It was awful – it was like the end of the world had come to our house. My older brother and sister were at boarding school so they knew nothing about it."

Sarah reached over and touched her housemate's hand. "I am so, so sorry, Vivienne . . ." She wondered how on earth an apology for being nasty to her had led to Vivienne recalling this devastating childhood memory. "It's all a long time ago, and your family have obviously got over it. It's best to forget all about it."

Vivienne shook her head. "There were terrible rows in the house and I remember Daddy going away for about three weeks. I thought he was never coming back. I wrote letters to Brian and Penny telling them all about what had happened, but I was too scared to post them."

Sarah waited. Vivienne obviously needed to get it off her chest.

"Daddy came back. He and Mummy spent night after night either arguing about it or not talking at all. One night I was in bed and when I heard them rowing I started to cry. Daddy came upstairs and heard me and came into my bedroom. He asked me what was wrong and I told him what I had heard about Catriona Clarke."

Sarah held her breath for a few moments. "What happened?"

"He broke down and cried . . ." Vivienne's whole body started to tremble.

Sarah moved over to put her arms around her and comfort her. "It's a long time ago," she repeated, at a loss for any other words.

"But it's never gone away," she sobbed.

Sarah noticed James and Ben coming towards the table now and she caught Ben's eye and shook her head, motioning towards Vivienne. They seemed to get the gist of things and moved back towards the bar.

Sarah turned back to her housemate. "What happened afterwards?"

"Daddy told me that his friendship with Catriona Clarke was over and that she had left her job and moved away. She was never mentioned again."

"What about the baby?"

Vivienne shrugged. "Presumably she had it. I never felt I could mention it again . . . although I often wondered if I had a brother or sister somewhere." She dabbed the napkin to her eyes. "When you first arrived at the house, you brought it all back to me."

"Me? How could I have reminded you about that?"

"Because Catriona Clarke's voice sounded exactly like yours. And that's why I was so hostile. She was Irish too. After that I couldn't bear to hear anything about Ireland or Irish people. And all the awful things I said to you . . . I had heard my mother screaming them at my father when she found out. After that there was always a frosty atmosphere in our house if anything came up about Ireland in the news or that kind of thing." She swept her hand through her hair. "I was never told anything officially but I have a funny feeling she had the baby and then went back to live in Dublin."

Everything fell into place for Sarah. She felt relief for herself that there was a reason for the prejudice rather than total ignorance. And now, instead of feeling angry, she felt sorry for the privileged, intelligent, medical student. She put her arms tighter around Vivienne now.

"It's all right," she said, "I understand why you felt like that." She paused. "And I understand exactly how your mother felt . . ." She moved back a little, so Vivienne was at arms' length. "Earlier in the night when I was talking about how my wedding plans were called off, well, it was for similar reasons."

Vivienne looked at her with glassy eyes. "What do you mean?"

"I was betrayed by the man I was engaged to and my best friend."

"No . . ." Vivienne looked totally confused.

Sarah lowered her eyes. "She became pregnant too. I wouldn't

240

have sex with Con so since Patricia was obviously willing he took his chance with her."

"No!" Vivienne repeated.

"I was devastated, and when I had a chance to think things over, I went around everywhere and cancelled the church, the flowers, the hotel reception and all those things."

"And how long . . ." Vivienne tried to muster up all her concentration. "How long to the wedding?" She reached out for her wineglass again.

"Less than two weeks. But then everything changed. Patricia lost the baby, and Con and his mother had the cheek to come up to our house to ask me if I would go ahead with the wedding. He said we were free now that he didn't need to marry Patricia Quinn. That's when I knew I had to move away. I couldn't marry Con and I couldn't stay living in a small town where I could run into him."

"Terrible!" Vivienne said. "Absolutely terrible."

Sarah touched her hand. "But, you know, we have to get over things. And I know you will get over what happened to you."

Vivienne nodded and tried to smile. "Thank you, Sarah. I feel much better about everything." She lifted her glass. "Let's drink to our friendship." Then, realising her glass was empty, she reached across the table for a half-full bottle of red wine and filled her glass up. She then held the bottle out to Sarah.

Sarah's hand moved to cover the top of her sparkling-wine glass which still had some in it. "I've had more than enough," she said. "I'll be sick if I drink much more." When Vivienne put the bottle back on the table, Sarah held her glass up. "To friendship and to great success in the coming year!"

Vivienne's glass wavered as she held it up. "To friendship!" she repeated.

They clinked glasses and Sarah took another mouthful of her wine. She looked at Vivienne's face which was blotchy and streaked with black mascara. She picked up her evening bag and stood up. "Come on, I think we'll both feel and look better if we go to the ladies' room and tidy ourselves up a bit."

When they were in front of the full-length mirror Sarah helped Vivienne to re-do her make-up. A few times Vivienne staggered backwards and Sarah had to move quickly to steady her.

"I think you'd be best to have a lemonade or something when we get back into the hall," Sarah said. "I know I can't drink any more."

"I'm fine," Vivienne said, smiling brightly at her. "It's New Year, and if we can't let our hair down tonight, when can we?" She glanced at her reflection. "Do I look okay?"

"Yes, you look lovely again."

"Good." She smoothed her dress down and then straightened up. "Because I intend to go in for the kill now with Dr Livingstone. And you should do the same with Dr Ryder."

"But I'm not interested in men," Sarah told her.

Vivienne waved a knowing finger in front of her. "Don't let what happened to you back in Ireland put you off finding a good catch. You've got to get married some day, and fellows like that will be snapped up by some of those bloody nurses if we don't beat them to it. They're always gushing around the male doctors when they're on ward duty, offering them biscuits and cups of tea. It's very different when it's an all-female group of doctors. Oh, yes – they're always too busy then!" She wagged her finger again. "And don't be fooled by Jane and Elizabeth, they are just as bad as the others. They're all out to bag a doctor if they can."

Just then Elizabeth came into the ladies' and Vivienne went into a fit of giggles.

"What's the big joke?" Elizabeth asked.

"The male doctors," Vivienne spluttered, swaying on her feet. "I was just saying how all you nurses would just love to bag one for yourselves."

Elizabeth rolled her eyes and gave an exaggerated shrug. "Maybe it's the other way around – maybe the doctors would like to bag a nurse?"

"Well, you're all welcome to them," Sarah stated, "I haven't the slightest interest in any men."

They waited for Elizabeth and then all three went back into the ballroom together. Within minutes they all had offers of dances and Sarah was back on the floor again, this time with a male nurse she had not seen before. He was very chatty and told her that he had been watching her all night from a nearby table and had only plucked up the courage to ask her to dance when she seemed to have disappeared.

"I kept looking for the lovely blonde hair on the dance floor – it really makes you stand out. You look like Alice in Wonderland."

Sarah felt a stab of annoyance at having her hair compared to a little girl's. People felt they could say absolutely anything about her hair and expect her to not to mind. She ignored the comment and carried on dancing. He then further annoyed her by asking if she would like to go to the pictures with him the following weekend.

"I'm sorry," she said quickly, "but I'm much too busy with work and haven't got time for social outings."

Half an hour later she had the same conversation with James Ryder when they were dancing and he asked to take her out to dinner some night. Although she knew she would incur Vivienne's wrath, she turned him down as well. But she felt she owed him more of an explanation since he worked with her housemates and had been so nice to her over the evening.

"I'll be honest with you," she said as they sat at the table together. "I've just broken off an engagement a few months ago, and I'm not ready to start seeing anyone else yet. I've also committed myself to a lot of work in the evenings over the next month or two." She was amazed at how easily the difficult words had tripped off her tongue. Just a few days ago she could never have imagined explaining about her broken engagement to a complete stranger. Nor could she have imagined turning a date down so easily – especially a date with a doctor. She had come a long distance in her life in a short time – particularly with regards to confidence.

"Okay," he said. "I can't say I'm not disappointed but I do understand your reasons." He leaned over and touched her hand with a finger. "But when you are ready to have a night out, will you let me know?"

"I will," she said, smiling back at him. There was no point in snubbing him outright. By the time she was in the situation to consider going on a date, she was sure the handsome doctor would have forgotten all about her. Another round of cocktails was brought to the table and, since she hadn't drunk for the last hour or so, Sarah chanced another drink. A short while later when she checked the time on her watch, she could see two faces on it and realised it was time to go home.

"I'm going to get a taxi now," she told Jane, standing up. As she did so, her head started to spin again. If she drank any more she would be as bad as Vivienne. "If anyone else is ready to go home, then we can go together."

"Anna's gone off to the ladies'," Jane said, "and she said she was going home very soon." She craned her neck to check the dance floor. "It seems Elizabeth has caught the eye of one of the medical officers – they've been dancing together for the last half an hour. I'll wait for a while and come back with her and Vivienne."

"Where is Vivienne now?" Sarah asked.

Jane shrugged. "The last time I saw her she was draped over Ben Livingstone. She'll turn up soon."

Sarah lifted her stole and bag. "I'll go and see if Anna is coming with me and then I'll check if there are taxis outside." She went off in the direction of the ladies', taking care to walk in a straight line and not look the worse for wear. There was a queue for the toilets and as she waited outside for Anna, she saw the attractive woman with the short dark bob coming out. She was suddenly reminded of the fashion designer who had come into the shop the first week she worked there looking for sequins. Sarah thought she was the most elegant woman she had ever seen, and this woman was a similar type. She studied the slim, dark woman for a few minutes. She wouldn't be surprised if she was a surgeon or a psychiatrist or somebody important like that. Sarah thought that her hair made her look confident and professional – unlike her own hair which drew all the wrong sort of attention. The short style looked easy to manage, and looked as though it would only take half an hour or so for it to dry. It was something she was definitely going to consider.

Anna came out of the ladies' room and straight towards her. "Are you ready to go home now?" she asked. "I've had a lovely night but my feet are killing me in these shoes."

"Yes, I'm ready to go too," Sarah said, "I've had more than enough to drink, and if I stay I'm going to regret it in the morning."

"Me too!" Anna laughed.

"I'm just going to check if there's a taxi outside."

"I've left my wrap at the table," Anna said. "I'll meet you back here in a minute."

When she went out into the foyer a doorman told her there was a row of taxis just outside the door. She turned back towards the hall to check if Anna was ready when she saw James Ryder coming instead.

"Jane told me you were going and I couldn't let you leave without saying a proper goodbye." He came towards her with his arms held out.

As he gathered her up in a tight hug, Sarah could feel the warmth of his breath on her neck and could smell the woody spices in his cologne. As she softened in his arms she was suddenly reminded of Con – the smell of the hair cream he used and the slightly salty taste of the skin on his neck. That was the last time a man had held her in his arms.

James Ryder bent to kiss her gently on the lips. Then he moved back and studied her face for a few moments. "God, you are really beautiful," he said in a low voice, "and that hair makes you look like a little angel." Then he gathered her hair up in his hands and suddenly bent to kiss her much harder.

Sarah immediately froze. She felt herself sway in his tight embrace and then she felt a sense of panic. She pulled away from him, and then, realising he was surprised; she made a pretence of the situation. "I nearly lost my balance there," she said, laughing brightly. She looked behind him. "Ah, here comes Anna now!"

"I hope to see you again soon," he said, running a hand through his hair.

"It was lovely to meet you," she said, "but I've got to go. I've a lot of work to get on with in the morning."

He thought for a few moments, then he took a small notebook and a pen out of his inside pocket. "I'll give you my house number, and you can ring when you have a free night." He smiled. "Vivienne will keep me up to date with you."

Sarah kept a small smile pinned on her face which gave the impression of agreeing with him. He handed her the scribbled number and she put it in her bag. She had no intention of phoning him, but tonight wasn't the time to make an issue of it.

"Are we ready?" Anna asked.

"We are," Sarah told her.

She linked arms with her friend and walked out to the waiting taxis, leaving James Ryder staring after her.

CHAPTER 28

When Sarah first woke, she opened her eyes and then tried to turn her head towards the dark window. It felt as though a ton weight was attached to it. She lay for a few moments and then made a tentative move to sit up. The bedroom suddenly started to spin around. She sank back into her pillows, trying to work out what was happening. And then it hit her. She had drunk too much last night. Sherry, wine and later, other drinks she couldn't remember. A wave of shame washed over her, but she wasn't fit to deal with it.

She closed her eyes and went back to sleep.

The second time she woke, it was to the sound of the front door banging. She sat up more quickly, and the room started to move around her again. A feeling of alarm crept over her as fragments of the night before came flitting back to her memory. Fragments of the night she didn't want to relive. She looked over to the window. It was still dark outside. She turned her spinning head to the clock on her bedside table. The hands showed twenty past three. The door banging must have been the other girls returning. She closed her eyes again.

The clock showed eleven o'clock when the knocking on the bedroom door woke her up for the third time. When she sat up, she was grateful that the dramatic feelings of the night before had subsided enough to let her move more easily. But as she swung her legs out of the bed a wave of nausea hit her and the dizzy feeling closed in on her.

She was still sitting on the side of the bed when Jane opened the door. "Sarah," she started, "I'm really worried about Vivienne . . ." Then she stopped in her tracks. "My God!" she said, her hand flying to cover her mouth. "What have you done to your beautiful hair? You've cut it all off."

Her gaze moved to the long blonde strands which were scattered on the floor around the chair in front of the dressing-table.

"My hair?" Sarah looked back at her in a daze, and then she remembered. A bolt of alarm hit her. She remembered hacking at it with her scissors last night. She moved her hand to feel it now, and found a strange empty space where all the thick hair used to be. Her stomach started to churn. What on earth had she done? She took a deep breath. "I decided I wanted to have it short . . ."

"But you should have waited and gone to the hairdresser's. It's all up and down . . . all uneven . . ." Jane's voice trailed away.

Sarah felt a sense of panic now, which she struggled to keep hidden. She went over to the wardrobe mirror. And there, looking back at her, was a complete stranger. But, as she scrutinised herself with pin-hole eyes, it wasn't as bad as she had dreaded. When she turned her head to the side she could see that that the edges were up and down, but from the front it looked something like the bob the dark-haired girl at the dance had.

She turned to face Jane. "I've wanted to have it cut for ages, but I didn't have the courage . . ." She was surprised at her own words, but she knew they were true. Somewhere at the back of her mind she had been considering it for a while.

"What on earth made you do it last night?"

Sarah couldn't find an answer that would sound sensible or reasonable. She couldn't say that she had cut her hair off because it drew too much attention from men. Most girls would be grateful for an asset like that and would think she was mad. She shrugged. "I suppose all those drinks made me take the step I was afraid of . . ." She looked back at herself in the mirror. "I think I knew I would never get around to going into a hairdresser's to get it cut, so I took matters into my own hands."

"In a funny kind of way it suits you short," Jane told her. "But you would have been better to wait and have it done professionally."

"I know, but it's too late now. The shops aren't open until tomorrow. I'll have to wait until then" She looked at the nurse now. "Are you any good with scissors? Do you think you could straighten it up until I get to the hairdresser's in the morning?"

"Oh, Sarah!" Jane pulled an anguished face. "I'm not sure if I could do it any better."

"Would you have a go at it?" Sarah asked. "Please? Just to get rid of the raggy bits before anyone else sees it."

"Have you got a pair of decent scissors?"

"I cut it with my large scissors," Sarah said, going over to her work table. She opened a drawer. "But maybe if you used a finer pair, just to even it off."

"I'll do my best," Jane said. "But I'm no hairdresser."

A short while later they both looked at a tidier version of the hairstyle in the mirror.

"I like it," Sarah said, her voice full of conviction. "And thanks for doing it. It will be fine until I get to the hairdresser's."

"You're very brave . . ."

"I feel as though a weight has been lifted off me."

"It has," Jane said. "A blonde weight most girls would have killed for."

"It was difficult having it," Sarah told her. "It's always been a problem. It just draws too much attention. I'm glad it's short now." She moved away from the mirror, anxious to end the conversation. "What were you looking for when you came into my room?"

"Vivienne. She's not in her room – she mustn't have come home last night."

Sarah stared blankly at her. "Are you sure? Maybe she's downstairs . . ."

Jane shook her head vigorously, and Sarah wondered that she could do it so easily, as any sudden movement was still uncomfortable.

"She was in a terrible state last night," Jane said.

Sarah's brain was blank at first, and then she started to remember the long, involved conversation that she and Vivienne had. From what she could recall it had ended with them crying and hugging each other. God, she began to feel a sense of having behaved ridiculously. There was another memory lurking at the back of her mind. She had an uneasy feeling it was to do with one of the male doctors. "She didn't seem that bad to me . . ."

"Well, after you and Anna left she downed even more. I took one drink off her and moved a few glasses away from her but, even so, by the end of the night she wasn't able to stand up."

Sarah's face showed nothing of her feelings. That could have been me, she thought. Another drink or two and that could easily have been me . . .

"I know we all had a lot to drink, but she was far worse than the rest of us," Jane continued. "The last time I remember seeing her, she was collapsed in a chair in the cloakroom. I woke her up and told her to wait for us and we'd get a taxi home, then I went back into the hall to find Elizabeth. By the time we got back to the cloakroom, Vivienne had gone."

"She's obviously gone home with someone," Sarah said. "One of her other friends from the hospital."

"I don't know what to think," Jane said, "She was so drunk that anything could have happened to her."

It gave Sarah a small crumb of comfort to know that she wasn't the only one who had overdone it with alcohol, but something about the situation alarmed her. "What do you think we should do?"

Jane shrugged. "I don't know what we can do."

"I'll get dressed and come downstairs with you." She couldn't face the thought of a bath this morning. The manoeuvring in and out and the bending would be too much for her fragile state.

"I'll put the kettle on."

* * *

The tea and toast helped, and as she started on her second strong cup, Sarah was beginning to feel vaguely normal.

Then Elizabeth and Anna came into the kitchen, still in their dressing-gowns. They both stopped in their tracks.

"What have you done?" Anna gasped.

Sarah remembered her hair again. "I know, I know." Her cheeks reddened. "I know I should have waited until I went to a proper hairdresser's. But it's done now and I can't stick it back on. Anyway," she said in a manner braver than she felt, "I prefer it short."

"It's definitely different," Elizabeth said, pausing to find a better description.

"And even if it's short," Anna said, "it's still a lovely colour."

Small praise. She would have to brave this out for the next few days with every single person that knew her. An atonement for being stupid and for drinking too much. She had paid dearly for the lesson.

"Vivienne never came home," Jane said. "I'm beginning to get a bit worried about her."

"She'll be fine," Elizabeth said, going over to check the teapot. "She probably went back to one of the rooms in the hospital for another drink."

"She wasn't in any state to drink any more," Jane argued. "She was hardly in a state to walk."

They discussed the situation for a while and then Anna said she would go out to the phone box and ring around some of their friends.

A short while later she came back into the house, shaking her head. "No one has heard anything about her."

Elizabeth shrugged. "I think we should give it a few more hours before we start getting really worried. It was a New Year's party and she's just had too much to drink and gone off with some of her friends to sleep it off."

Sarah was upstairs lying on her bed when she heard the black Hackney cab pull up outside the house. She went over to the window and saw Vivienne getting out of the taxi. She was wearing a man's jumper with jeans that had the hems rolled up, and carrying a Marks and Spencer bag.

Sarah ran across the bedroom floor and into the hallway to call out to the others. "Vivienne's okay. She's just coming into the house now." Then she went back into her room and lifted a white angora, cloche-style hat she had knitted and pulled it over her hair.

Vivienne looked at all the concerned faces seated around the kitchen table. "What did you think had happened to me?" Her voice was high and incredulous.

"Well, anything could have . . ." Jane said.

Vivienne pulled a face as though they were all mad for worrying, then she grinned and shook her head. "I went back to the hospital for a drink with some of the doctors and decided it was easier to bunk down there in one of the rooms."

"Who gave you the clothes?" Elizabeth asked.

"One of the guys I work with."

Sarah looked at her, remembering all Vivienne had drunk. Remembering what they *all* had drunk. "How do you feel? I've got a terrible headache after all the wine."

Vivienne shrugged. "I've a bit of a hangover but no worse than any other New Year. Last year I was drunk much earlier and had no memory of getting home at all. I remember everything about last night." Then she laughed. "At least I think I do . . ." She threw a fleeting glance at Sarah. "Although anything I said is probably best forgotten. I tend to talk a lot of rubbish when I'm drunk."

Sarah lowered her gaze. Vivienne's message was quite clear. She wanted to forget all that she had said about her family and the Irishwoman the previous night. Sarah could understand it. She wouldn't like anyone to start talking about her aborted wedding plans this morning.

Jane's eyes narrowed. "As long as you're okay," she said. "Then what you do is entirely up to yourself."

"Yes," Vivienne said. "It is." She looked over at Sarah again. "Why on earth are you wearing a hat with your dressing-gown?"

Sarah's face reddened. She would just have to brave it out. She pulled the hat off.

"My God!" Vivienne said. "What have you done? You look like a completely different girl."

"Good," Sarah said. "That's exactly what I intended. A new

year and a new me. I'm fed up being called Alice in Wonderland or any of the stupid names people think they can call me because of my hair." She raised her eyebrows. "And before you say any more, I'll be going to a hairdresser's to have it properly shaped as soon as they're open."

"It's actually okay," Vivienne said. "When we get used to it, I think it will suit you very well shorter."

Sarah felt better. If it was anyone else she would have called it being damned by faint praise, but she knew Vivienne would speak her mind. Her hair would be a nine-day wonder. She had survived the cancelled wedding and telling everyone about it. She had survived the shaky start she had in the house with the girls. She had survived the row with Harriet and would cope whether the nurse dropped their friendship or not.

She would easily survive something as trivial as a haircut.

CHAPTER 29

1965

On the Friday after New Year's Day Sarah stood outside the door of Harrison's in the biting cold, trying to get the key in the frozen lock. When she eventually got inside, the shop was so cold her breath came out in clouds. She rushed around putting the heater on in the main shop and the small fan heater in the kitchen.

Lucy had dropped the shop key off to her the night before, saying she had to go to the doctor's first thing if Sarah wouldn't mind opening up for her. She had been taken aback when she saw Sarah's hair.

"I just fancied a change and was too impatient to wait until the hairdresser's opened," Sarah told her.

"I'm sure it will look very nice when it's evened off properly . . ."

"I hope you're okay?" Sarah had asked when she walked her out to the door.

"Yes," Lucy had said. "It's nothing of any importance."

Sarah had watched her walking back down the path and into her car, thinking back to what Harriet had said about her having a nervous breakdown.

By the time Lucy arrived at the shop at ten o'clock it had warmed up and there was a queue of customers waiting to be served. Sarah moved around the serving area quickly packing wool and needles into bags, measuring lengths of material and opening pattern books at the end of the counter for those who needed advice.

At eleven o'clock Lucy looked at her watch. "Why don't you go and have your hair done now, Sarah? We're not busy and it will be quiet at the hairdresser's at this time."

Sarah looked up at her. "That would be great. I'll work through my lunch hour to make up for it."

"I don't think we need to worry too much about an hour extra off. You give more than enough of your own time."

"You're very good," Sarah said. "And I meant to thank you for the tailor's dummy. I made a lovely dress for a New Year's Eve Ball and having it to fit the material on really made a difference."

"And I meant to ask you if you enjoyed the dance."

Sarah felt herself flush at the mention of the night. "Yes," she said. "The hotel was beautiful and we had a lovely meal."

"Did your friends all enjoy it?"

Sarah nodded. "I think everyone did." She thought for a moment, wondering if she should confide in her employer. "The only thing . . . everyone, me included, drank a lot. In fact I feel a bit stupid, because I felt the effects of it the next day."

"Well, it was New Year. I suppose everyone lets their hair down a bit."

"I got into a slightly awkward situation . . ." She saw Lucy's concerned face. "Nothing that bad. It was just that one of the doctors Vivienne knows took a bit of a shine to me. He asked me out for a meal; but I told him I wasn't ready to go on a date with anyone yet."

There was a small silence.

"I told the girls about my cancelled wedding," Sarah explained, "and I felt it was just as easy to tell the doctor about it as make up an excuse." She paused. "I'm going to do the same with David McGuire. After seeing how upset Harriet was when we went out to visit his family, I've got to do something to put him off me." She touched the back of her hair. "Although having this all cut off might help."

"You didn't really do it because of that?"

Sarah shook her head. "No, I was fed up with it. It got in the way, and it was heavy. And, I felt it made me look too young. I think I look more serious – more businesslike – with my hair shorter." She looked expectantly at Lucy.

"You suit it very well."

"Thanks, I'll get my coat and head off to the hairdresser's now."

The hairdresser had no idea how long her hair had previously been, so Sarah made a vague excuse about having asked a friend to trim it. The hairdresser laughed and said she'd seen worse jobs.

"I think you could take another couple of inches off," Sarah said, as she looked at herself in the mirror. Since she'd had a few days to get used to the new length, she thought she might as well go the whole way now and have it cut as short as the style she had admired.

"Okay," the hairdresser said. "If you don't like it, you can easily grow it out."

Back at the shop Lucy took a few moments to get used to it. "Yes," she said, smiling. "It looks even better now. It really frames your face. Your long hair was striking and beautiful, but you look equally nice now."

"Thanks," Sarah said, knowing most people would be kind enough to say that now, even if they thought it was awful. She would live with it. "Has Harriet called in yet?"

"No."

She felt a knot forming in her stomach. Harriet was obviously still annoyed with her.

"But David McGuire has been in. He said his grandmother asked him to give something to you and he'll call back later."

Sarah sighed. "He could just have left it."

Lucy smiled and said nothing.

After a reasonably busy morning, there was only a dribble of customers in the afternoon. Sarah kept busy dusting and washing shelves and sorting out the stockroom.

"It's always quiet at this time of the year," Lucy said. "People don't have much money after Christmas. It picks up again when the days get longer and then the customers start to think about decorating and getting new curtains."

Sarah suddenly remembered. "The cushions! We said at Christmas that I'd make those velvet ones for the window and a few extra for sale inside. I might as well go and get started. Before we know it, I'll be too busy with alterations to take time for the shop interior."

She had just finished hand-sewing the tassels on the first cushion when a knock came on the stockroom door and a moment later David McGuire came in. He held a bag up to show he was there on business. "Happy New Year – I haven't seen you since it started."

Sarah smiled. "Happy New Year to you."

"I like the new hairstyle," he said, leaning against the jamb of the door. "Very fashionable . . ."

Sarah could immediately tell by his muted reaction that Lucy had warned him about the hair, and she could tell by his eyes – like most other men – he had preferred it long. But he was nice enough not to say it.

"Thanks," she said. "Is that the christening gown and shawl?"

"Yes, I didn't dare forget it or she would have had a heart attack. She's been telling everyone about you, so don't be surprised if you get a rush of business from our neighbours." He handed her the bag.

"Well, I hope I don't disappoint her," Sarah said taking a square gold cardboard box out of the bag very carefully. She untied the satin ribbon and then took the lid off. She lifted out the cream silk and satin gown and held it up. "It's beautiful . . . a work of art." Her eyes moved to the hem to where the hot iron had melted the lace. She put it down and then took out the shawl. Again, the lace was damaged in a few areas. It would require careful unpicking and then replacing with new lace, and there were a couple of holes which would need repairing. The work would be slow and tedious but it would be worth it.

"I'm glad you came out to our house after Christmas," David said now. "I've got used to seeing you almost every day and it felt strange not seeing you for such a long time."

Sarah went to the door to check that Lucy couldn't hear. "Things were awkward afterwards with Harriet."

"I didn't expect you to bring her."

"I asked you if I could bring a friend."

He looked over to the row of small windows on the back wall. "I thought it would be one of the girls from the house."

"Harriet is as nice as any of them. You hardly spoke to her at the house."

He turned to look her in the eye. "I was the same as I always am with her – I only like her as a friend. I was afraid she would get the wrong impression. That she might read something into the fact she was at my family home."

Sarah took her chance. "Well, I suppose I can understand about not wanting to give the wrong impression." She looked down at the little gown in her lap. "I've recently had the same problem."

"What do you mean?"

"I was at a dance at New Year with the girls from the house . . ." She stopped to clear her throat. "And I was asked out on a date. He was a nice fellow – one of the doctors at the hospital where two of the girls work."

He waited.

"I told him I'm not interested in seeing anyone at the moment." She looked up at him, making sure he got the point. "I explained that apart from being too busy with work I'd just broken off an engagement before I came to Newcastle." It was all so easy to say now, like repeating the lines in a play. "I should have been married in September."

He looked startled. "I didn't know that . . ."

"Why would you?" She smiled. "I had no reason to tell you before."

The shop bell went and with the stockroom door half open, they could hear a customer asking about alterations.

Sarah folded the gown and put it back in the box. "Thanks for dropping this over. Tell your grandmother I'll start on it when I get a chance. I've a lot of orders in at the moment."

"She said there's no rush. I'll let you get on with your work."

For a moment, as he turned away, Sarah had to stop herself asking about the job in London. She wanted to tell him that he should forget her and go for it, that his career was much more important than any romance. But, he would know then that his grandmother had told her about it, and she might end up telling him that Harriet had heard it all too. She decided to say nothing.

* * *

On Saturday morning, as Lucy was serving a customer, Sarah answered the phone and a formal female voice asked for Miss Harrison. The woman apologised for disturbing her at work, but said it was an emergency.

When Sarah gave Lucy the phone, within seconds she knew by her face that there was something wrong. Then, when she saw Lucy rushing into the kitchen, she instinctively knew not to follow her. She finished serving the woman and as the door closed behind her, Lucy reappeared, with her handbag under her arm and holding her car keys. Sarah immediately knew she had been crying.

"I'm sorry, Sarah," she said, trying to sound normal, "but I'm going to have to leave you on your own. I have some business I need to attend to straight away." She went towards the door. "I won't be back before closing time today, so if you wouldn't mind locking up for me."

"That's fine," Sarah said. "And you can either pick the keys up at the house, or I'll come down early on Monday to open up for you."

Lucy turned back to look at her. "I don't know what I'd do without you, you know. You make even difficult things much easier for me."

Then, as she went off without any explanation as to what the emergency was, Sarah felt a small twinge of jealousy as she wondered whether Lucy would tell everything to Harriet.

* * *

Back at work the following Monday morning Lucy made no mention of her upsetting phone call and subsequent quick dash out of the shop.

Harriet appeared mid-morning and Sarah was relieved that she seemed almost back to her old chatty self. She sat in the kitchen with Lucy and Sarah drinking tea and telling them about the great party she had been to at New Year, then all the things that had been happening in the clinic since she'd come back to work.

When she was going, she and Lucy stood chatting at the door for ten minutes while Sarah measured material for a customer, and she heard Harriet saying, "It'll be fine," and then she caught something about "having the best professional care".

Once again she had the feeling of being left out in the cold.

CHAPTER 30

In the middle of February Lucy told Sarah that she was starting renovations in the three rooms above the shop. "If I don't do something, the rooms will go damp and be eventually unusable, and with everything so much busier, we could really do with more space for stock. I met up with my solicitor Peter Spencer recently and we got chatting. You know him of course, don't you, Sarah? He's your landlord."

Sarah nodded. "Yes, I've met him out at the house a few times, he's a nice man."

"Well, we were discussing some other subject and we got to talking about the shop and how much business has improved, and I told him my concerns about the upstairs part and he suggested I have a chat with this architect he knows. Anyway, to cut a long story short, he's suggested we move the kitchen and toilet upstairs, which will let us expand the shop area."

Sarah was curious now. "What will you change downstairs?"

"We'll have two work areas – we'll make the counter we have bigger with shelves behind for wool and craft things, and another counter area at the back for measuring material, a corner for a desk to do the accounts and a bigger changing area for the customers with a door on it." She narrowed her eyes, picturing it. "It will practically double the space in the shop."

Sarah was more than impressed the plans. "It sounds fantastic. We'll be able to put more stuff out on display."

"Ah," Lucy said, holding up a finger. "We're also having a new door and bigger deeper windows so we can have bigger displays of your wonderful work. I also thought we might expand our range of ready-made things – and maybe stock a gift range." She tilted her head to the side. "Things for the home like nice vases and ornaments."

Sarah's eyes widened. "My God . . . it sounds as though it's going to be huge! That's wonderful and –" She halted as a thought struck her. "But what will we do when all the work is going on?"

"We're going to have a week off," Lucy told her. "I've a lot of business and personal things I need to catch up on, and a week would make a big difference. I thought you could work your usual hours from home – take any shop alterations with you – and it means you will have your wages as normal."

"When does the building work start?"

"Next Monday, so we can start moving things towards the end of this week."

* * *

Sarah wasn't sure whether it was because a sign had gone up advising customers that they were closing Harrison's for the week, or because it was the month before Easter, but more customers than ever came asking for new curtains and soft furnishings, plus all the usual alterations.

Lucy made several car trips up to Victoria Street with boxes of material and trimmings. "Are you sure you don't mind having all this in your bedroom?" she said, looking at all the sewing machine and all the sewing paraphernalia, and the boxes and bags of carefully labelled material.

"Not at all," Sarah said. "It will be great to have everything to hand so I can get on with things any time of the day or night. It's just a case of keeping everything tidy."

"Does the machine disturb the other lodgers?"

"No one has ever said anything," Sarah told her. "They often play music so I don't think they would mind too much if it did."

Lucy paused at the door. "I think we should have a day off to relax. Would you like to take a trip out to one of the towns you haven't seen yet? We could go somewhere like Whitley Bay." She shrugged. "Of course it will be cold this time of the year, but we could wrap up well."

Sarah's brow deepened. "Could we see how we are toward the end of the week, in case I don't get everything finished?"

"No," Lucy said, wagging a finger. "We're going to take next Saturday off whether you're ahead with things or not. You haven't been anywhere since the Christmas holidays and you need a break." She smiled. "Even I take time out to play golf in the evenings and weekends. It's got to be bad if someone has a worse social life than me."

"Okay," Sarah said, laughing. "A day out would be lovely, although after Easter I'm actually going to be very busy myself."

"Doing what?"

"Evening classes. I've signed up for a course in fashion design at the university."

"Really? That's a fantastic idea." Lucy's face suddenly clouded. "But it's more work, Sarah – I hope you're not going to drive yourself too hard?"

"It doesn't feel like work. I'm really excited about it." She indicated the piles of boxes. "I'm going to get all the work I've accepted out of the way and after that I'll pace myself carefully. I won't be talked into doing rushed jobs for customers or promising things to be done overnight. I'll work out a proper schedule which will allow me so many hours studying for the course and the rest of the time doing alterations."

Lucy looked thoughtful "It's got much busier now and I feel bad leaving you on your own every Thursday. It's a day when you get no time for anything else but serving."

"It's a good complaint," Sarah said. "And isn't it great that the business is doing so well that you have to think of expanding the premises?"

"I probably wouldn't have thought of doing it now, but Peter Spencer said that if the building is well-maintained it will make it much easier to sell in the future. He pointed out that the premises next door to the bookshop have been empty for the last year, but no one has put in a bid for it because it's so dilapidated."

Sarah felt something cold clutch her. The thought of not working in Harrison's shop suddenly filled her with fear. "Surely you wouldn't think of selling up? Not when things are going so well."

"Not now," Lucy said quickly. "Although I won't deny it crossed my mind last year before you came. The responsibility had become like a millstone around my neck. It's different now. I've got a renewed interest and enjoyment in it, so you can rest assured that I'm in it for the long haul."

Sarah was relieved. "Good," she said. "So it looks as though we have a busy year ahead."

"If it gets busier when the new shop is ready," Lucy said, "then I might have to think about taking on another member of staff."

Sarah felt a sudden jolt. "I suppose there's no big rush," she said casually. "You will probably just want to take one step at a time."

After Lucy left Sarah went back up to her room and lay on the bed thinking about all the changes that were due to come about. To her they were big changes. She had been working in the shop for six months now and had got used to the way things were. She liked working with Lucy and she liked all their regular customers. She had a free hand with most things in the shop and could decide which way she wanted them done. She didn't really want anyone new coming into the shop who might want to do things differently. She liked the routine of her week in the shop and doing her sewing at home. And she had got used to the girls in the house and over the months had got to know quite a number of the neighbours in Victoria Street. Things were fine as they were. She realised she didn't really want any changes just now.

And then, she caught herself.

How could she mind the changes that were going to happen to Harrison's when it meant such an improvement in their working situation? How could she begrudge Lucy the chance to develop a small, old-fashioned shop into a bigger and better business? And how could she even think of holding herself back? The changes would bring a more professional tone to Harrison's, and the new gift section would widen their customer base.

She thought about the fashion-design course she was due to start straight after Easter. She wondered if it would be difficult, if it would be more advanced than anything she had ever done. She thought back to all the things she had made over the years – skirts, jackets, dresses, suits, pyjamas – and inevitably she found herself picturing the wedding dress and the bridesmaid dresses. She forced herself to push away the uncomfortable emotional memories and focus solely on the physical work that had gone into the intricate garments, and she was surprised that she could now feel a tiny spark of pride in the fact that she had made them.

Then, before any tentacles of self-pity could reach out and grab her, she moved from the bed and went across to the wardrobe to examine the dusky grey and navy ball gown she had made for New Year. By anybody's standards it was a good piece of work, from the choice of fabric to the hand-stitched details, and the compliments she had received bore this out.

As she closed the wardrobe door she had a flashback to the dance, to the conversation with the male doctors about her dress-making skills. She remembered all the things that Vivienne had said about her becoming a famous fashion designer. She had said nothing that night, but she had felt a wave of satisfaction – even pride about the work she did. She felt something like it now when she thought about the future.

A sense of hope – a sense of ambition.

She remembered the feeling from before, when she and Con Tierney used to talk about their plans for the future. She had given up all those plans and dreams after she left Ireland. Since then, she had only really been living day to day. Now, she knew, she could plan and dream of a better, bigger life. A life that she could create with her own hands. She wasn't looking to reach the grandiose heights that Vivienne had described – but any achievement in that direction would be worthwhile nonetheless.

She closed the wardrobe door, smiling to herself.

All the changes that lay ahead were going to be good for Lucy and good for her.

CHAPTER 31

Sarah finished working on Nora McGuire's christening gown the following Monday. It had been a slow, fiddly job, but in the end she felt very satisfied, knowing that it would take a very practised eye to see where she had mended it.

She decided to wait until she was back in the shop to give it to David. She wanted it to seem casual, just another job – but by Tuesday guilt had set in. She knew the old woman was anxious to have it back in its fully restored condition. She diligently worked until her usual lunchtime break at one o'clock and then she put her warm coat on and walked down to the bookshop. It was only when she approached the shop and saw the blinds down, that it dawned on her that it was closed. Annoyed at herself for making such a stupid mistake, she turned towards Harrison's. The windows were thick with dust and from what she could see, everything was covered with sheets.

She could tell from the muffled noises that the workmen were upstairs. She stood for a few minutes deciding whether or not to open the door and go in, when she heard the bookshop door opening. She turned around to see David McGuire coming out, doing the buttons up on his black overcoat.

"Come to keep an eye on them?" he said, smiling at her.

"I came to see *you* actually," she said, holding the bag out. "I've finished your grandmother's christening gown."

He took the bag from her. "That's great! She'll be delighted with it."

"Make sure you give it to her without anyone else seeing it," she reminded him.

He lifted his eyes heavenwards. "I'm not likely to forget. You would think she was conducting an illicit spy ring the way she's gone on about it."

Sarah laughed.

"Has she paid you?" he asked.

"The bill is in the bag. There's no rush."

"Thanks, that's good of you." He gestured towards the sewing shop. "Big changes. If you'd asked me last year did I ever think she would do the place up I would have said you were mad." He smiled and shook his head. "I'll say something – for a small, delicate-looking girl you know how to get things done. Before you came the shop was on its last legs."

Sarah looked at him in bemusement. "But it's not down to me. Lucy decided on her own about the renovations. I made no suggestions about it."

He raised his eyebrows. "Well, let's just say you gave her the incentive." There was a pause and then he said, "Have you had your lunch?"

"No," she told him. "I was going to have it when I get back to the house. I'm working from home this week."

"Away, man!" he said, nodding in the direction of the main shops. "You can surely take an hour off today?" He held the bag up. "I think I owe you a lunch after all the trouble you've gone to with this."

Sarah's immediate reaction was to refuse but before she got a chance he said, "It will probably be the last time. I'm heading off to London in the next few weeks. I'm going into partnership with my uncle. Originally he offered me the job of manager, but when he came up last week he suggested I go into ownership with him in the shop in Charing Cross Road."

She was taken aback. "Well, congratulations! Owning your own bookshop – that's a huge achievement." She smiled at him, all the tension leaving her. "I'll join you for lunch on the condition that it's my treat – to wish you well in your new business and new life in London."

"Okay," he shrugged. "I'm not going to argue with that." He looked at the bag Sarah had given him. "If you'll wait a minute I'll just drop it into the shop for safe-keeping."

Sarah waited for him at the door. She glanced around the shop and wondered how different the bright, welcoming place would be without its lively, enthusiastic manager.

As they walked along, Sarah thought he seemed different. He was easier, less animated, and less obvious in his delight at being with her. Lucy had warned her to expect him to say something before making his final decision about London. Sarah had half-rehearsed what she would say back, but now it seemed as though there was no need. He had made up his own mind.

They went to the café where they had gone the first day they met. David was his usual friendly self, and if he harboured any resentment at the rebuffs she'd given him over the past months he didn't show it.

"I'm looking forward to London," he told her. "It's an exciting place – I'm looking forward to the challenge." He narrowed his eyes. "You've settled well in Newcastle, haven't you?"

"Yes," she answered without hesitation. "I'm very happy here."

"There's more to you than meets the eye, Sarah," he said. "You came here without knowing a soul and you've made a new career and a new life. Look how you sorted out all that carry-on up at the house with the snooty doctor. You know how to look after yourself – you're a survivor."

"I had to be," she replied.

As they walked back to the shop, Sarah felt a pang of regret about David's departure. It was a pity he had changed their easy friendship by developing feelings for her, because he was someone she could count on to have her best interests at heart. She had shown her vulnerable side to him on several occasions and he had immediately dropped his chirpy banter to listen attentively and then advise her in a serious, intelligent way. She knew she hadn't been so caring about his feelings, and she wished it could have been different. As their steps kept time with each other, she knew she would miss his warm, easygoing ways

They slowed down as they came to the bookshop and then David turned towards her. "In case I don't get to talk to you on our own like this again, I just want to say I'm sorry if I put you in an awkward position with Harriet, and I'm sorry if giving you the poetry book made you embarrassed." He looked straight into her eyes. "My interfering, but well-meaning, grandmother told me that she put you in the picture about it. All I can say is that I made light of picking the book up for you because I thought if I explained what it meant to me personally that it would only embarrass you."

Sarah felt her face flush. "It was kind of you and I appreciate it, and I will take the time to read it properly."

He smiled. "I'm glad that's settled.

Since she knew he couldn't misconstrue her actions now, she moved towards him and gave him a hug. "I really wish you all the best, David."

His arms came around her waist and he pulled her close. "And I wish you all the best." For a brief moment he leaned his head against hers. "I'm not going to say anything more, because I've said enough already."

Then, just as she was walking away, David took a business card out of his pocket. "That's the shop address and the phone number. If you ever need anything, or if you fancy a trip down to London, just phone me."

Sarah took the card from him, and as their hands touched, she suddenly felt tears spring up in her eyes. "I'll miss you," she whispered, then she quickly walked away.

* * *

She was back at the house working on a curtain pelmet when she heard the gate clanging and then a knock on the door. She ran downstairs to see Lisha William standing on the step, her eyes red from crying.

"I hope you don't mind me coming over," she said, her whole body trembling, "but I didn't want to be on my own."

"Lisha, what's wrong?"

"My father died this morning. He was rushed into hospital last night."

Sarah's chest tightened. She had been right about the poor man.

Lisha wiped the back of her sleeve to her eyes, suddenly looking like a young girl again. "My mother and my brother, Mark, have had to go to see the solicitor or something like that . . . and she told me to come home to put coal on the fire and check everything was okay." Tears filled her eyes again. "I know it's stupid, but I feel afraid in the house on my own."

Sarah put her arms around the girl. "Come in," she said, guiding her along the hallway. "I'm glad you thought to come over."

Sarah made mugs of hot chocolate and listened while Lisha poured the story out about her stepfather's recent and swift decline. "He was in hospital between Christmas and New Year, but then he said he felt okay again. "They said he had heart failure. He'd had it quite a while and we thought if he took it easy he would get better."

Sarah nodded, trying to think of the right thing to say. "I understand how you feel," she ventured, "because I lost my mother when I was thirteen."

Lisha took a sip from the mug. "What happened?"

"She had some sort of blood disorder. I'm not sure exactly what it was, but it made her very tired and ill."

"That must have been terrible. I couldn't imagine what I'd do if anything happened my mum."

Sarah nodded and then took a drink of her hot chocolate. She rarely allowed herself to think how she felt about having lost her mother. It was so long ago and had somehow got overshadowed by her father's death. She tried to remember how she had coped – the things that had got her through both those difficult periods. The only thing she could come up with was keeping busy to distract herself from the devastation that had barged into her life. Reading was impossible for the first phase of the grieving. Words and sentences would be read over and over again, until they became strange unintelligible squiggles. Mundane household tasks had not been much better. Washing dishes or peeling vegetables still allowed her mind to wander, and she had often caught herself staring out of the kitchen window with her hands in a basin of stone-cold water.

"Have you done everything you need to do at home?" Sarah checked. "Because you know that you'll have lots of people calling around?"

Lisha nodded. "Yes, it's all ready."

"Well," Sarah said, "I think it's better if you keep yourself occupied, so would you like to come upstairs and help me? I've got some small beads that I'm sewing onto the corners of some cushions. It's an easy job . . . and you can sit by the window and watch for your mother coming back."

They went up to Sarah's room and sat with the radio on in the background, working away on the cushions. Sarah was surprised at how neatly and quickly the young girl worked. Gradually, she seemed to relax and she started to talk about school.

"Did you know that I've been picked for the county swimming team?"

"No," Sarah said, "That's brilliant news! I'd no idea you were such a good swimmer. I thought your mother said you played hockey?"

Lisha pushed a long black ringlet away from her face. "I play most sports, but recently I've won quite a few of the local swimming galas and now I've been put forward for the county championships."

"That is fantastic. I suppose there's a lot of training involved?"

"Yes, I'm going most evenings after school, and after Easter we'll start practising early in the mornings. The only thing is we have to pay for some of the training and the bus fares and things, and it can be quite expensive." She shrugged. "My dad wasn't able to work for the last year. I don't know how my mum will manage for money now he's dead."

By the time Fiona Williams pulled up in a black hackney cab, Lisha had finished all the cushions that Sarah needed and had also helped tacking an embroidered border onto a pelmet.

Sarah went out along with her to offer her condolences to her mother. As they crossed the road, she pushed two half-crowns into Lisha's pocket.

"No, no . . ." Lisha protested, trying to give her the money back.

"Take it," Sarah told her. "Working with those beads is very fiddly and you've saved me a lot of time." She smiled at her. "Your work was perfect – that's another new talent you have."

Lisha gave her a proper smile. "Thanks." She went on into the house.

Fiona Williams looked defeated and resigned. "I thought last year was bad," she said in a flat tone, "but this year has started off even worse."

"If there's anything I can do," Sarah offered. "Just call over any time."

"Thanks for being so good to Lisha," Fiona said. "I appreciate it. She's finding it tough at school and Tony being sick has really affected her." She looked at Sarah. "You know Tony wasn't her real father? It's obvious with her colour and everything that she couldn't have been his daughter, but they were close." She paused. "Lisha's father was an officer in the Navy. He was a nice man, and when we found out I was expecting Lisha he was full of plans about us getting married." She shrugged. "But he went off as usual on the ship one day and I never heard a word from him ever again."

Although she hid it well, Sarah was taken aback at Fiona Williams being so frank about having an illegitimate daughter. Back in Ireland things like that were shrouded in secrecy.

Fiona rubbed her eyes. "I was lucky then to meet Tony. They got on very well, better than many real fathers and daughters." She looked straight at Sarah, almost as though she was looking through her. "I'll tell you the kind of man he was – he never once made any issue about her colour or who her real father was. How many men could you say that about?"

"I only met him once," Sarah said, "but he seemed like a very nice man."

"He was. I'll never meet another one like him." She closed her eyes and shook her head. "All the men you meet day in and day out – and you're lucky if you come across a handful in the whole of your life that would make a decent husband. Well, I met mine, and now he's dead and gone. It'll be me and the kids from now on."

Sarah felt a shiver run through her. Had her father felt like that after her mother died? She couldn't remember any big difference in him. He must have suffered in silence.

* * *

Sarah worked long into the night to finish the most pressing orders. Several times she was tempted to run out to the phone box to phone Lucy and cancel the trip they'd planned to Whitely Bay, but she knew that it would only cause a row and draw more attention to the amount of work she did.

CHAPTER 32

On Thursday at five o'clock Sarah heard a car engine outside the house and wondered if it was Lucy. She had said she would call on her way home from Durham and give her an update on the work that was going on in the shop. When she heard the front door open she presumed it was one of the girls. Then, when there was usually a "Hi!" or "It's me!" there was only the sound of slow footsteps going along the hallway and then up the stairs.

Sarah tried to work out which one of the other lodgers it might be. They were all working various shifts today and by her reckoning none of them should be home at this time. She went out into the hallway and saw Vivienne standing with her hands rested on the banister halfway up the stairs. Her face looked chalk white and she still had her heavy camel duffle coat that she wore to work on and her pull-on hat and gloves. Her bag lay in the hallway downstairs.

"Are you okay?" Sarah asked.

"No . . . I've come home from work. I've had a very heavy period and I don't feel well . . ." She moved her hands and then slowly manoeuvred herself into a sitting-position on one of the stairs.

Sarah went quickly down the stairs beside her. "Can I get you something? Do you feel sick or faint or what?"

Vivienne now had her head in her hands. "I've got a bad pain in my stomach . . ."

"Have you taken anything?" Sarah checked. "I think I have some aspirin in a drawer somewhere."

She shook her head. "I've already been given something at work. They said it was fairly strong."

"It would be best if we got you up to bed. If I take your arm you'll find it easier."

The medical student took a deep breath and then she turned sideways and pulled herself up on the banister, and it was then that Sarah saw the dark red bloodstain on the back of her coat. She quickly decided that it was best not to alarm Vivienne – she would say nothing until she got her into the bedroom. As they slowly made their way up the stairs – Vivienne bent double with the pain in her stomach – she was working out where she would find a big towel to save the mattress.

When they got to the bedroom, Vivienne gave a little moan. "It's a bit of a tip. I haven't had a chance to tidy it yet."

"I wouldn't worry about that just now." Sarah guided her across a messy room to a wooden chair. She quickly moved the clothes from the back of it, and said "Sit there until I get the bed sorted for you." Then she went over and straightened the pillows and pulled the sheets and blankets up then went to the door. "I won't be a minute – I've got to get something." She ran along the hallway to the airing cupboard and grabbed two navy towels and went quickly back to Vivienne's bedroom.

"Have you got sanitary pads?" Sarah asked, as she spread the towels, one on top of the other.

Vivienne pointed over to a tallboy at the door. "I've some in the top drawer."

Sarah pulled the drawer open and lifted a packet of Dr White's out. "Have you any bigger ones?"

"Those should be okay . . ."

"I don't want to frighten you, but your coat's stained, so it must be pretty heavy."

Vivienne's face froze. She moved in the chair and pulled her coat out from under her. "Oh, God . . ." she said, struggling to get her arms out of the sleeves. "It's back really heavy again. It was like that this morning."

"Here, let me help you," Sarah said, coming around the back of the chair. She helped Vivienne take the coat off and saw that the back of her tweed skirt was soaked through as well. She bit her lip, not sure what to say. Vivienne was after all, a medical student who must know that there was a problem having a bleed as heavy as this. "I think if you could get changed you might see if it's finished or if you're still bleeding."

Vivienne gave a weary, frustrated sigh. "I got larger towels in work . . . they're downstairs in my bag."

"I'll get them for you," Sarah said, making for the door.

"No – honestly – thanks." Vivienne started to get up, then the pain made her sit back down again. "I should go to the bathroom . . . and get washed."

Sarah was getting frightened now. She'd often had bad period pains herself and the occasional heavy period, but this didn't seem normal. "I could bring a basin of hot water up."

"You're very kind," Vivienne said, "but I'd better go down." She stood up straight, then took several deep breaths. "I don't feel quite so bad now. I think I'll manage."

"We'll walk down together," Sarah told her.

When they got to the bottom of the stairs, Sarah lifted Vivienne's bag and went ahead to the bathroom, while Vivienne made her slow, painstaking way behind her.

Sarah then waited in the kitchen. She put the kettle on, thinking that a hot-water bottle and a hot drink might help the period pains.

For the next ten minutes she walked back and forward from the kitchen to the hallway, checking if Vivienne was okay. When she heard the bath water running she knocked on the door to see if there was anything else she could do.

"I need to have a proper bath," Vivienne called. "I think it might help me."

"Well, don't lock the door just in case you're not well," Sarah advised. She went back into the kitchen and filled the hot-water bottle, and then topped up the water in the kettle again from the tap to make tea. A few minutes later as she was scooping tea into the pot, the doorbell rang.

It was Lucy. Sarah brought her into the hallway.

"I've just called in at the shop," she told Sarah "and it's looking really, really well. They have removed the walls in the kitchen and plastered all the exposed areas. I can't believe the difference it's made. It looks huge."

"That's great news. Do you think they'll have it ready for Monday?"

"They say they'll have downstairs finished tomorrow and most of the work done upstairs by then. The plumbers are due in tomorrow to get the new toilet and kitchen fitted upstairs." Her eyes were shining. "It's going to look great. Now, there's something I want to ask you. Something that you might want to think about."

Sarah raised her eyebrows. "What is it?"

Lucy's hand moved to her neck, and Sarah recognised the gesture and knew she was anxious about something. "I've thought about it and I wondered if you would consider –" She stopped short as they both heard a noise in the bathroom.

"If you don't mind," Sarah said, starting off down the hallway. "I'll just go and check on Vivienne. She's not been too well."

Something made Lucy follow along after her and when she heard Sarah call out "She's fainted!" she rushed into the bathroom.

Sarah was kneeling on the floor with Vivienne's head cradled in her lap. She had obviously managed to have her bath and was wearing a quilted satin dressing-gown that one of the other girls had left behind the door.

"What's happened?" Lucy gasped.

"A very bad period – she's been bleeding heavily since this morning," Sarah said. "She's been sent home from work. She had pains in her stomach and she thought a bath might help her."

Lucy looked at the blood-stained clothes and the rusty-coloured water in the bath. "It looks more than a period to me, Sarah . . . I think the poor girl has had a haemorrhage."

"Do we need to call a doctor?" Sarah asked.

"I think it might be best if we get her straight to the hospital. I don't think we should waste any time."

Vivienne suddenly moaned, and a few seconds later she opened her eyes. "What's happened?" she asked. She looked at Sarah and then at Lucy as if she didn't recognise them.

Sarah's heart was pounding. "You're all right, Vivienne," she said, hoping she sounded calm.

Vivienne tried to sit up. "I feel dizzy . . . I think I'm going to be sick."

Both women moved quickly to help her over to the toilet where she vomited several times, then they helped her to sit on the side of the bath. She had beads of sweat on her chalk-white face and she was shivering.

"I think we need to get you into the hospital," Lucy said. She glanced anxiously at Sarah. "I'm sure it's not anything serious, but you need to get checked just in case."

"No, I can't . . ." Vivienne shook her head. "I'm not going to the hospital . . . I just want to go to bed . . . I'll be fine."

"Let's get you into the kitchen," Sarah said. "I've put the gas fire on and I've made some tea."

Vivienne struggled to stand up and with them both helping her she walked into the kitchen. "I'm feeling better," she said in a weak voice.

They sat her down in a chair by the fire and then Sarah brought her tea and a digestive biscuit on a small tray. "Hopefully that might stop you feeling so dizzy."

Vivienne lifted the cup but her hand was shaking so badly that Sarah had to take it from her and empty half of it down the sink. When she brought the cup back, she studied Vivienne as she sipped at the tea.

"How is your stomach?" she asked. "Do you still have the pain?"

"It's getting easier . . ."

Sarah went back to the sink to get the hot-water bottle. "Hold that to your stomach," she told her. "It will help to ease it."

"Do you usually have heavy periods?" Lucy asked.

Vivienne shrugged. "Occasionally . . . but I've never had it as bad as this." Her eyes suddenly opened wide. "Oh, no . . . I can feel it. The bleeding is starting again."

Lucy moved forward and caught the cup as Vivienne let it drop on the tray. "You'll be okay." There was a firm note in her voice. "But as soon as you feel you can move, we're going to get you into hospital. As a trainee doctor, you know it's the only safe option."

"No . . . no . . . I can't." Vivienne looked over at Sarah. "Would you please go to the phone box and make a call for me?" She gestured to her handbag and Lucy lifted it up for her. "It's one of my friends – a gynaecology doctor. He'll know what to do. Just tell him I'm still bleeding." She closed her eyes. "He'll bring stronger medication for me."

"No, Vivienne," Lucy said firmly. "This is too serious, we can't take a chance. We've got to get you in and get you properly examined. If you let it go any longer it could turn into something far more serious."

"No!" Vivienne started struggling to get up. "I'm not going in." Her eyes darted first to Sarah then over to Lucy. "It's *my* decision. It will ease in its own time."

"Lucy is right," Sarah told her. "You need to go into hospital. You've lost too much blood."

Vivienne got to her feet now, stood for a few seconds then walked slowly across the floor. She had just reached the door when she suddenly doubled in two, crying out in pain. The two women ran across to her as she sank down to her knees.

"That's it," Lucy said. "Run out to the phone-box, Sarah, and call an ambulance."

Vivienne started to cry. "But you don't understand . . ."

Lucy's face went rigid. "Why? What are you talking about?"

"Because . . ." her crying went into sobs, "because it's not just an ordinary situation . . . I had to have an abortion."

Sarah's hand came to cover her mouth. Surely she had heard wrong? Surely Vivienne hadn't just said she'd had *an abortion*? This was something she had only ever heard about in whispered conversations back in Ireland. Something she knew very little about. The one thing she did know – and had heard many times – was that it was a mortal sin. Surely Vivienne – a girl from a good middle-class family, a girl who was studying to be a doctor – hadn't done something as terrible as that?

"Okay, but we're going to have to do something to help you," Lucy said, her voice surprisingly normal. "Have you the phone number of the doctor who carried out the abortion?"

Five minutes later Sarah was in the cold, musty-smelling phonebox dialling a number which she had scribbled down on a scrap of paper. "Is that Dr Ferguson?" she asked, her voice strange to her own ears.

"Yes, this is Gordon Ferguson."

Sarah went on to explain the situation in the way that Lucy had directed her.

Apart from several short silences, the man seemed calm and considered. "I'll just have to sort a few things out here at the hospital," he told her in a brisk manner. "But you can tell Miss Taylor-Smith I should be out at the house in ten minutes with medication which will stop the bleeding." He paused. "Please tell her not to worry as this can often happen after such a procedure."

Sarah went rushing back to the house, her heart thumping in her chest. She couldn't believe this was all happening. That Vivienne had slept with someone and had become pregnant. As far as Sarah and the other girls knew, she didn't even have a regular boyfriend. How could she be so stupid – how could she have such low morals? She was supposed to be an intelligent girl – she was a medical student – the sort of person that people looked up to. The sort of girl who you'd think would be an example to others. "*Procedure*", the doctor had called it. Sarah was very ignorant of the subject, and wasn't even sure if abortion was legal in England or not – it certainly wasn't in Ireland. She wondered if maybe that's why Vivienne was so upset.

She arrived back at the house to find Vivienne asleep on the sofa and Lucy pacing up and down worriedly between the kitchen and hallway. She beckoned Sarah to stay out in the hallway.

"The doctor says he will be here in about ten minutes," Sarah whispered.

Lucy looked at her. "This is very, very serious. We have to be very careful about what we say and do."

"What do you mean?"

"Well, Vivienne could be in a lot of trouble. As you know, abortion is illegal and whoever has done this has taken a great risk."

Sarah now knew the situation was as bad as it would be back in Ireland. "When was it done?" she asked. So many questions were coming into her head now

"The day before yesterday. She said she just pretended she was going to work as normal but went to some clinic on the outskirts of Newcastle."

Sarah suddenly realised she had no idea of what Vivienne or any of the girls in the house were up to in their private lives. She wondered now if any of the others knew about Vivienne being pregnant. She herself had not noticed anything untoward. She hadn't heard the medical student getting sick in the mornings or noticed anything which might be associated with pregnancy.

She looked at Lucy. "What do you think?"

Lucy shrugged. "I don't know . . ." She tiptoed back to the sitting-room to peep in at Vivienne. "I'll be happier when somebody with medical qualifications has a look at her. I had to help her to the bathroom when you were out and she is still bleeding heavily."

"Oh, God . . . I just can't believe it. Imagine a girl like Vivienne getting herself into this kind of situation. You would think she would know better – know more than most girls about what to do." She shook her head. "I didn't think she was the kind of girl to have sex before she was married. To have sex with a man who she wasn't even engaged to . . . or someone she was going out with for a long time. I have no idea who the father of the baby could be."

"Sarah," Lucy said, "you can't go thinking about it as a real live baby. She was only seven or eight weeks pregnant." She looked her straight in the eye. "And you can't go judging Vivienne – it's her business and she has her own reasons for doing what she's done. She must have been in a desperate situation."

Sarah felt after all this business that she didn't know Vivienne at all. And, as she stared at her employer, she began to think she didn't know Lucy very well either.

She had expected Lucy to be outraged and shocked at the predicament Vivienne had got herself into. What could be worse than a doctor having an illegal abortion?

A short while later a car drew up outside the house and Sarah went to the door to let the doctor in. She hadn't really thought about the sort of doctor she expected, but the ordinary thirty-odd-looking man on the doorstep – average height, red-haired and bespectacled – was not him.

"Miss Taylor-Smith's address?" he checked.

Sarah showed him down to the kitchen where Vivienne was now sitting up on the sofa, white-faced and anxious.

Sarah and Lucy then went into the hallway, closing the door behind them.

"What should we do?" Sarah asked.

They stood in silence for a few minutes then Sarah said, "Do you want to come up to my bedroom to see the orders I've completed?"

"This is great," Lucy said, when she saw the carefully pressed curtains and other items in separate tidy piles. "I was actually thinking earlier that I could deliver some of them to the customers and get them out of your way."

Sarah lifted a cream linen bundle. "I've also finished this embroidered tablecloth and napkins that a customer asked me to do for a silver anniversary present . . ." She felt as though someone else was speaking and not her. She felt as though she was standing outside herself watching someone else holding up the sewing and talking as if all the terrible things downstairs weren't happening.

Lucy touched her hand. "Are you okay?"

Sarah looked at her. "I don't understand what's happening. I can't make sense of it. If her parents wouldn't allow her to keep the baby, maybe an aunt or someone could bring it up or she could have had it adopted. I know girls who have illegitimate babies in Ireland are thought badly of but I thought it was different in England . . ." Her mind flew back to the conversation she had had with Fiona Williams and she knew for certain that other people handled things differently.

"But her life would change," Lucy said. "All the things she planned like her medical career would never happen. As you explained, she doesn't seem to have a man to help her . . ." Lucy bit her lip. "You've lived a very different life from Vivienne, Sarah, and it might seem hard to understand but she obviously felt she had no other option."

Tears suddenly came into Sarah's eyes. "I'm just trying to understand it all . . ." She went over to her bedside table to get a tissue. "Every time I think things are settling down in my life, something else – something bad seems to happen." She rubbed her eyes then blew her nose. "I suppose it's making me think back to everything that happened with Con and Patricia and the baby they were expecting . . ."

"Of course."

"And you know I had problems with Vivienne when I first moved here, and then . . ." She closed her eyes. "And I still feel bad about what happened with Harriet." She swallowed. "I suppose I feel sad that David's going away. He was one of the people I first got to know here. I'd got used to seeing him . . ." She gave a teary smile. "It's so stupid, because half the time I didn't want to see him – but I liked him a lot as a friend."

"All the things you've just said make perfect sense," Lucy told her. "And if it helps, I feel very uncomfortable with what's going on downstairs. I don't even know Vivienne but I now feel involved in some way." She took Sarah's hand. "It will all sort out. Someone once told me that to sort out what's important in your life, you have to ask yourself, 'Will this matter in ten days, ten months or ten years time?'"

"What does that mean?"

"I think it's to make you see how big the situation is and what effect any decision is likely to have on you in the future." She smiled. "In ten days you will still be thinking of Vivienne's predicament, but in ten months it will seem like a long time ago. In ten years time, you're likely to have forgotten all about it." She raised her eyebrows and gave a little sigh. "I imagine it will be very different for Vivienne. The decision she made will be with her for a long time."

Sarah thought she understood what Lucy was saying and found herself nodding. They talked about more mundane things and Sarah said she was going to Lisha's father's funeral the following morning.

Sometime later they heard the kitchen door opening and they both moved.

"I've given her medication which will stop the bleeding," the doctor said. "And an injection to help any pain. She also has painkillers for tomorrow and something to help her sleep. I'll let them know that she's sick at the hospital and won't be in for the rest of the week."

"Is there likely to be any other complications?" Lucy asked.

He pursed his lips together. "I've examined her and I think it should all be okay now. If there are any other problems you can ring me immediately. Just make sure you don't talk to anyone else except me."

Sarah looked away. She didn't know whether this was the doctor who had performed the abortion and she didn't want to think about it.

When they went into the kitchen Vivienne was sitting up. She was still pale but she looked a little brighter.

"I'm so sorry for involving you in all this and I'm very grateful for all your help."

"As long as you are okay," Lucy told her. "I'm just glad we were both here."

"Yes, I'm glad you are okay." Sarah could see Vivienne needed reassurance.

"If you wouldn't mind walking me to the bathroom, please," she said, "and I'll freshen up again."

When she was washed and changed into clean pyjamas they walked her back upstairs and got her into bed. She seemed suddenly sleepy, but just as her eyes were starting to close, Vivienne looked at Sarah.

"Please don't tell any of the other girls," she said in a half-whisper. "They don't know anything about this and I don't want them to. . . . I'm ashamed of myself and I'm so sorry I've had to involve you with the doctor and everything."

"It's okay," Lucy said. "We won't breathe a word. The less people who know the better."

When Lucy left, Sarah went back to her work, stopping every so often to check on the sleeping Vivienne. The other girls arrived at different times throughout the evening and Sarah told each one that the medical student was in bed with bad period pains and didn't want to be disturbed.

Around nine o'clock Sarah took some tea and toast for them both up to Vivienne's bedroom.

"I'm feeling much more human now," Vivienne said, munching on the toast. "I should have listened to the doctor's advice yesterday and not gone into work. I was silly trying to pretend nothing had happened . . . trying to get back to normal too soon."

"You've been through a lot."

"It's all my own fault," Vivienne said. "I can't believe I was so stupid." Her eyes filled. "It was after the party at New Year . . . I was very drunk"

Sarah had guessed as much. "Don't feel you have to explain to me."

"I want to, so you understand. I went back to the doctor's quarters with Ben Livingstone . . ."

"Was it him?"

Vivienne shook her head. "No." She closed her eyes. "He told me he had a girlfriend back home and I felt so bloody stupid for having tagged along with him instead of coming back home. When

I think back to the drunken state I was in, I feel mortified. I went out to one of the mess-rooms to phone a taxi, but I was so drunk I couldn't find the right number and one of the doctors who I vaguely knew came over to help me. He asked me if I wanted to go back to his room for a drink and stupidly I did." She covered her face with her hands. "I think I felt so embarrassed for being rejected by Ben Livingstone that I just wanted to prove that it wasn't because I was unattractive. Oh, I don't know . . . but I ended up staying the night." She moved her hands away to look at Sarah. "It was as simple and as stupid as that – one mistake that could have changed my life forever."

Sarah wondered how Vivienne could have ended up in bed with a total stranger. She thought back to all the times she had pushed Con away from her. She had known him for years and had still been afraid to let him too close to her. The furthest she had allowed him was his hands on her breasts. If he had moved his hands anywhere further down than her waist she had immediately pulled away.

Vivienne had obviously allowed someone she hardly knew to do much more than touch her. They had been as intimate as a man and woman can possibly be.

"I realised a few weeks ago that I was pregnant," Vivienne continued, "and I had no option but to go to the fellow and tell him."

"What did he say?"

"He was shocked – horrified. He seemed a decent enough chap and he said he'd do his best to sort things out."

Sarah caught her breath at the casual way Vivienne referred to the man who made her pregnant: '*He seemed a decent enough chap.*' She was describing a total stranger. How could an intelligent, educated girl behave in such a cheap way?

"It turned out that the chap is close friends with James Ryder." She paused. "You know, the doctor who was so smitten with you at the ball.

Sarah didn't react, waiting for Vivienne to carry on.

"Anyway, James happened to know a gynaecologist who was

sympathetic to silly women in my situation, and we got it all sorted as soon as it could be arranged. All highly confidential as there could be terrible trouble if it got out."

Sarah nodded, thinking that she had made the right decision not going out with James Ryder. After hearing his involvement in this incident, there was no way she would have anything to do with him now.

Vivienne finished her tea then lay back on her pillows. "It's all over now and I just want to forget it. The injection he gave me seems to have worked. The bleeding has eased off and the pains have gone."

"I'm glad," Sarah told her. "And a good night's rest will make all the difference."

When Sarah went back to her own room she suddenly felt exhausted. She got undressed and got into bed. She drifted off to sleep and fell into dreams where she was standing at the side of Con Tierney's house while Patricia Quinn told James Ryder about the baby she had been expecting.

CHAPTER 33

Lucy came to pick up Sarah at ten o'clock on Saturday morning for their day out. It was a dry, clear day and Sarah found herself looking forward to it. She dressed casually in black slacks with a warm beige jumper and a silk black-and-cream checked Burberry scarf she had bought from Fenwick's.

"You look very stylish, Miss Love!" Lucy told her. "And I've definitely come around to your shorter hair. In fact, I really prefer it."

Sarah felt a small glow from the compliments, because she knew anything her employer said was genuine. If Lucy had nothing good to say, she said nothing. Vivienne – who had been up early to catch Lucy and quietly thank her again – had said similar things about Sarah's outfit. She hadn't taken the compliments too seriously, sensing that the medical student would say anything nice to keep on the right side of her after the drama earlier in the week.

Vivienne seemed to have made a good recovery, and was more or less back to her old self. But Sarah saw a vulnerable look in her eyes that had never been there before. The subject of the abortion had not been raised between them since that night, and they both circled around it carefully, with Sarah asking if her heavy period had eased and Vivienne referring to it as "the night I had the haemorrhage".

Sarah found herself praying a lot in the last few days. She had knelt down in the Church of England at Tony Williams' funeral the morning after the incident, and asked for the return of Vivienne's good health, and for guidance in the way she should advise her housemate about her future behaviour.

She didn't know how she should act with Vivienne now the health scare was over, because deep down she felt the whole thing had been morally wrong.

As she and Lucy drove out of Newcastle, Sarah confided that she found it hard to accept that a little life had been lost so casually, and that she felt a need for some sort of reassurance that Vivienne had learned something from the terrible ordeal.

"Believe me," Lucy said, "she will undoubtedly have learned something from it."

"But she seemed to have no remorse . . . no awareness of what a serious thing she has done," Sarah said.

Lucy was silent for a few moments as she negotiated a junction. "She has to find her own way of dealing with it," she eventually said. "And you must find your own way of dealing with it too, Sarah, because I think you're feeling some sort of guilt over the situation, as if you were somehow involved by having helped her." Her brow wrinkled in thought. "Maybe if you spoke to someone who understood?"

"Who do you mean?" Sarah wondered if she meant Harriet. Whilst she liked the District Nurse, and knew she had obviously been of great help to Lucy, she felt that Harriet did not have the necessary gravitas to help her with this situation.

"I was thinking of someone who would know exactly about the type of feelings you have – maybe one of the priests from your church. As you know, I'm not very religious myself and rarely attend church, but I think it might help someone who is as committed to their faith as you are."

Sarah felt a weight lift from her shoulders. "That is a really good suggestion." She smiled brightly at Lucy. "Sometimes I forget that it was a priest who helped me start a new life when I was lost."

They had been driving some time when it dawned on Sarah that there was still no sign of the coastal roads she had expected to see by now. "How far is it to Whitley Bay?" she asked.

"I hope you don't mind," Lucy said, "but I decided to change our plans. I'm taking you somewhere today that I've often thought I should have taken you before."

Sarah looked at her, intrigued. "Where is it?"

"I'll explain everything when we get there." Lucy switched the car radio on and they sat in companionable silence listening to the music and news reports.

Twenty minutes later when she saw the sign for Durham, Sarah felt that today was going to be very different from the seaside walk she had envisaged. She had no idea what to expect or who they were going to meet.

When they came to large gates that led into a long winding driveway, she felt a little knot in her stomach. They went slowly up the gravel drive, past a sign that said *Meadow Hall* and on to the car park at the front of a large, rambling grey-stone building which had a bright red and gold Virginia creeper covering the middle part of it. Sarah immediately thought that whoever owned the property obviously had a lot of money, and this was confirmed when she saw stables to the side of the house and spotted a young man around the same age as herself leading a pony around the grounds.

"You're going to meet some people who are very special to me here," Lucy said. "And you'll understand why I come here every week."

Sarah felt almost fearful as she got out of the car. After all the months of feeling left out of Lucy and Harriet's secret, she now had a feeling that she had pushed her way in and was intruding into an area of Lucy's life that she had no business being in. "You don't have to . . ." She was stumbling over her words. "You're entitled to your own privacy . . ."

"I brought you here because I wanted to." Lucy's face had

relaxed and she was smiling warmly at her. "And because I think you will enjoy your visit. My biggest problem coming here is that I don't want to leave."

They walked up the front steps and into the hallway.

"Lucy!" A blonde, middle-aged woman wearing a smart red-and-black suit and pearls and high heels came towards her. "It's lovely to see you on a Saturday. I was delighted when you rang to say you were coming over."

Sarah guessed the attractive woman was the owner, and wondered if the lad she had seen was her son. She had deduced by now that the people were wealthy relatives or friends of Lucy.

"We're having work done at the shop," Lucy told her, "so I thought I'd take advantage of the day off." She turned to Sarah. "This is a young friend of mine, Sarah Love. Sarah, this is Millicent Turner."

"Welcome to Meadow Hall," Millicent said, shaking Sarah's hand. We're always delighted to have new visitors. Now, would you like tea first or do you want to stick to your usual routine and then join us for lunch?"

"The usual routine," Lucy said, taking off her coat. She looked at Sarah. "We can leave our coats – there's a cloakroom just across the hall."

Sarah took her coat off and after they had hung them up, she followed the two women down a thickly carpeted hallway. She could hear music coming from several of the rooms they passed and she was just wondering if they might actually be in a hotel, when they came to a halt outside one of the doors.

"This will be a great surprise for them," Millicent said, her eyes twinkling. "And for one person in particular."

Lucy turned to Sarah and squeezed her arm. "Just relax and go with the way things are here. There's nothing at all to worry about."

Sarah went through the open door behind them, and immediately she could feel the pleasant hum of activity in the bright airy room. She first noticed two girls around the same age as herself holding court in the middle of the room, then her gaze was drawn to a man in his thirties who was holding up a puppet in his hands.

She stood on the edge of the floor and watched as Lucy went across the room. There was a whoop of surprise as Lucy bent down over a chair and then she stood watching in amazement as Lucy came towards her pushing a low, long wheelchair.

"Charlotte," she said, "I'd like you to meet my friend, Sarah."

Sarah looked down at the wheelchair and saw a little girl with long dark ringlets and big brown eyes smiling up at her.

"Hell – o, Sarah."

"Sarah," Lucy said, tears glistening in the corner of her eyes, "I'd like you to meet my daughter, Charlotte."

* * *

"Charlotte has Spina Bifida complicated by epilepsy and a heart defect," Lucy explained in a quiet voice as they walked along the corridor to the dining-room for lunch, Sarah pushing the wheelchair.

"She's lovely," Sarah said. "So bubbly and bright. I can see why you find it hard leaving her every week." She manoeuvred the wheelchair round a corner then through open double doors.

"Mummy," Charlotte said, "can we sit at the table beside Angela?"

"Yes, darling," Lucy said, wheeling the chair across the wooden floor to a table by one of the big bay windows.

"She's actually ten years old," Lucy said, when they had parked the wheelchair next to her friend's chair, "but she operates at about the level of a five-year-old. I'd love to have her home full-time but it's impossible. I've got used to her difficulties from the Spina Bifida but the epilepsy is severe and unpredictable and needs specialist care." She looked at Sarah. "Do you remember the phone call I got a few weeks ago? The time when I had to rush off?"

"Yes," Sarah said.

"She had a bad seizure then, and the staff couldn't get her out of it so she was taken to the general hospital. She had some sort of chest infection and her temperature had risen dramatically."

Sarah felt a wave of sympathy. "That sounds very serious."

"But," Lucy said, smiling brightly, "most of the time she's the cheery, chatty little girl you see today. She has friends who have been with her since she was very little, and they have a time-table full of activities every day with things like story time, art and crafts, swimming and individual physiotherapy." She smiled. "They even have dance classes for the children in wheelchairs, and the older children do baking and domestic skills."

"Did I notice ponies?" Sarah said.

"Yes. They cater for the individual child and encourage them to reach their full potential." Lucy shrugged. "How could I give her all that?"

After lunch Sarah went with Lucy to watch Charlotte in the swimming pool. Again, her heart went out to both the mother and daughter as she observed the carers from Meadow Hall lift the child from the wheelchair into the pool. Everything was carefully timed and manoeuvred and the hard work involved was obvious.

"I often come here on a Saturday afternoon to watch her swim," Lucy told Sarah while they sat at the side of the pool, waving and shouting words of encouragement to Charlotte, "and since my father has been in the home I sometimes come on a Sunday. Believe it or not, it's the place I feel most relaxed and at peace in."

Sarah looked at her in surprise. "I thought you played golf all weekend."

Lucy smiled. "I do play, but not as much as I make out." She had to raise her voice a little to be heard above the screams of laughter. "It was easier to suggest I was on the golf course than explain about coming here."

Afterwards, Sarah went for a walk in the grounds while Lucy went with the care staff to help dry and dress Charlotte. As she walked around the beautiful gardens and the play area for the children, she could understand how Lucy liked this place so much. It was a bright and beautiful place, full of happy, laughing children and staff who seemed to be enjoying themselves too. Lucy had told her that she was on the parents' committee for fund-raising and had become friends with a number of the families.

"We have picnics and a summer and Christmas Sale of Work," Lucy said. "The parents bring things for raffles and tombola and that sort of thing."

"But you could have asked me to make things for it," Sarah told her. "I would have been delighted."

"I did think of it, but I felt it might sound strange that I was involved with a children's hospital." She gave a small sigh. "I just wasn't ready to explain things . . ."

Sarah wondered what had made Lucy open up to her today, and she found out as they drove back to Newcastle in the afternoon.

"I'd thought of telling you about Charlotte over Christmas, but I just didn't have the emotional strength to go into all the details." She glanced at Sarah. "I know you must wonder about a lot of things . . ."

"You're entitled to your privacy," Sarah said. "You really don't owe me any explanations. I know how I felt having to explain things about Con and the wedding."

"I wanted to tell you," Lucy went on. "I know how decent and trustworthy you are, and I feel you're almost like a younger sister to me."

Sarah's eyes welled up. "That's a lovely thing to say."

They passed an old Tudor-style hotel that was open for late afternoon teas.

"Let's have a stop," Lucy said, reversing the car on the empty road. "It will be easier to chat when I'm not driving."

They got a quiet table at the back of the old-fashioned dining-room beside a brightly burning fire. Over tea and scones and cakes, Lucy told her story from the beginning.

"I think I explained to your before that I was educated in London, and it was hard for me to maintain friendships when I was travelling back and forth so much. When I finished school and came to work in a large shipping office in Newcastle, I made friends with a lot of the other girls and we did all the usual things like going out to dances and to the cinema." She smiled. "And of course we met young men – the natural order of things, I suppose. I met a particularly nice fellow – Simon Hall, a history lecturer at the university. We went out for over two years and we talked about getting engaged and married – all the usual things. My parents liked him well enough . . ."

Her head suddenly drooped and Sarah saw shades of the old Lucy again – the anxious, angst-ridden woman who had met her in the station.

"To be honest," Lucy continued, "my mother and father were going through a bad patch in their marriage – constantly arguing and niggling at each other, and my father was inclined to stay out when things were bad. He would go straight to a bar from work – and my mother would be ranting and raving to me about the meal she had cooked that was now wasted. She would usually end up going to bed in the spare room before he came in. If it got really bad, she would take herself off to London on the train to stay with my grandparents or one of her sisters. My father maintained that my mother was the awkward one and had gone highly-strung with the change of life." She shook her head. "I always felt like piggy in the middle with them. I felt as long as I was there they would make more effort to be civil to each other, so there were nights when I would cancel going out with Simon at the last minute."

Sarah absent-mindedly spread butter on a scone. "Was he understanding about things?" she asked. She found Lucy's revelations so much at odds with the quiet, serious-minded person she thought she had come to know. But then she remembered the reaction she had got from her fellow lodgers when she told them about her cancelled wedding. They had seen her only as a person who was interested in nothing but work and were almost amused that she had been closer to marriage than any of them.

Lucy sighed. "Yes, he was very good, but then my mother took ill – bowel cancer – and she decided that the hospital in London was the best for her treatment. She moved back down there – partly to be near her own family and partly to spite my father. When she got really ill I gave up my job and went to stay with her."

"How long were you down in London?"

"Over a year," Lucy said. "And looking back I can see how badly I neglected Simon. I got caught up in things in London – hospital visits, catching up with old friends, invites out with relatives." She gave a wry smile. "I met up with an old boyfriend from school and we started going to the theatre and museums and all those sorts of things. It was fairly innocent, but I was enjoying things I should have been doing with a boyfriend. I went back to Newcastle for the odd weekend and I suppose I just thought Simon would always be there waiting for me." She shrugged. "My mother seemed to recover and stayed down in London, but when I moved back to Newcastle I discovered he had met someone else, a new, younger female colleague who got him out of the university to go on weekend field-trips all over the country. Apparently they both shared a passion for visiting old castles – something I was always too busy to do with him." She gave a weak smile. "Oh, I can't blame him, and he was upset when he told me."

"Did you regret it when it finished?"

"It didn't really hit me at the time. In fact, I think if I'd put up a fight for him – said I'd realised how badly I'd treated him, and how I would make more of an effort – I'm sure I could have wooed him back because I know he did love me. But I didn't even try. I suppose I thought I'd meet someone like him or even better." She lifted her teacup and took a sip. "Unfortunately it was just after that I met Charlotte's father."

The bitter tone in Lucy's voice made Sarah glance up at her. Apart from the obvious tension in her face, she had unconsciously gripped the linen napkin and scrunched it into a ball in the palm of her hand.

"I've told you everything else," Lucy said, "but I have to tell this part quickly because I still find it very, very difficult. I met him in the office when I came back to Newcastle. He was one of the main customers, a well-dressed, fine-looking man from Manchester. When he came up to Newcastle he always stayed in one of the city-centre hotels, and he asked me to join him for dinner or the theatre on a few occasions. In the beginning I refused, because everyone knew he was married, although as time went on it was mentioned that he had separated from his wife." She halted, her voice faltering. She looked down at the crumpled napkin in her hand, and then she shook it out and put it back on the table. "But, because I was struggling at home with my father and didn't have any single friends I could go out with, one night I agreed to go to a concert with him. I reasoned that as long as I kept it on a platonic basis it wouldn't do any real harm." She shook her head. "A big, serious mistake . . . I didn't realise that this handsome, well-dressed biddable man had another side to him."

The waitress came over to check if they wanted more tea or hot water.

Sarah looked over at Lucy. "I think we're okay, aren't we?"

"Yes, yes," Lucy said nodding her head vigorously. She waited a few seconds until the waitress had moved on to another table. "Anyway . . . after about three or four trips to the theatre or cinema, I had a meal in his hotel and I stupidly went back to his room." She closed her eyes. "This still sounds unbelievable but . . . we were hardly inside the bedroom door when he pinned me to the bed and . . ." She had to stop to collect herself. "Looking back, there are no other words to describe what happened, other than he *raped* me . . ."

"Oh, my God!" Sarah gasped. "Did you report him?"

"That," Lucy said, "is where all reason totally left me." She lifted the napkin again and started to twist it between both hands. "He convinced me that it was my fault for having strung him along for months, he convinced me that he was only being rough because he had been so frustrated." Her face was totally anguished now. "And because I was so naïve, stupid, desperate for affection – I continued to see him."

"Oh, Lucy . . ." Sarah couldn't find the words.

"I can't explain what I saw in him apart from his looks and his charming manner, and I cannot excuse the pathetic way I behaved." She shook her head. "The abusive way he treated me I now know wasn't lovemaking – it was weird and controlling and at times physically unpleasant." She lifted the napkin to her face. "There were times when he made me do the most appalling things . . ." Tears slid down her face.

Sarah reached forward to put a hand on top of hers. "It's a long time ago – it doesn't matter now."

Lucy nodded and dabbed her face with the napkin. "Then, one weekend we had a huge row and he told me it was all finished, that he had reconciled with his wife and she was expecting a baby in the next few months. It shows you how bad things were, that my only feeling was one of relief. He got transferred down south somewhere and just as I felt I was getting back on my feet, I discovered I was pregnant with Charlotte."

"Did you tell him?" Sarah asked.

"No," Lucy said. "I couldn't bear to." She hesitated. "You won't like this, Sarah, but initially, I wasn't going to keep the baby. I'm afraid I considered the exact same solution as Vivienne – an abortion."

Sarah tried to keep her face impassive – tried not to show how shocked she felt. "It must have been difficult for you . . ."

Lucy nodded and gave a bitter laugh. "You have no idea. Anyway, it was ten years ago and I wasn't as worldly-wise as your friend and I didn't go through with it. I didn't have anyone to advise me where I could go to have an abortion – and if it happened again today, I still wouldn't have a clue. My father was horrendous to me when he found out – he still is – he's never forgiven me. You see, I had only just explained to my mother that I was pregnant and unfortunately within a few months she deteriorated and died. The doctors said it was the cancer which had spread through her, but my father chose to believe that the shock of my pregnancy killed her, And even though he's losing his mental faculties now, it's one of the things he still remembers." She closed her eyes for a few moments, then composed herself again. "Anyway . . . before my condition became obvious, I left the office and moved back to London. My grandparents had both died, but I had an aunt who was sympathetic, so I stayed with her until Charlotte was born."

Sarah listened as Lucy went on to explain how the baby had

been rushed to a special hospital unit to be assessed, and how she had then suffered from severe post-natal depression for almost a year when she discovered that the child had Spina Bifida and epilepsy and all the other complications. Trying to cope with a sick baby had made things more difficult and eventually she was advised that long-term specialist care was the only solution. She was still deciding what to do when her aunt in Newcastle died, leaving Harrison's shop to the family. The unit outside Durham – Meadow Hall – was regarded as one of the best in the country for children like Charlotte.

"So," Lucy said, sounding exhausted, "my life has revolved around my visits to Charlotte ever since."

"It must get on top of you at times," Sarah said.

"Yes, especially since my father has started to decline. A few years ago I'm afraid I just caved in with a complete nervous breakdown. I was in hospital for two months." She looked at Sarah. "I was off work for about six months altogether. I just couldn't face people, couldn't face going out of the house. Of course, that's when the shop went downhill. Miss Shaftoe, Mary, couldn't manage on her own. She did her best, but she wasn't too good with the customers and a lot of them drifted away."

"But things did improve," Sarah said. "And you did get back to work."

"Yes, indeed – that's when Harriet came out to see me in her District Nurse capacity. She was the first person who took a real interest in me. She got me up and dressed and brought me newspapers and magazines. She got me to buy a television and to start listening to the radio and music. Bit by bit I found my old self again." She went to say something then stopped and her face clouded over again. "To be honest, I'm still not a hundred per cent . . . I'm still on medication and I still take tablets most nights to help me to sleep. I'm sure you've noticed odd little things, Sarah?"

"I've noticed a big change in you since I first arrived – a big improvement."

"Good!" Lucy said. "I'm glad because I feel the best I have in ages. When things are running smoothly with the shop and Charlotte is well, I feel great – but it only takes a difficult visit with my father and I seem to go backwards again."

"From the way you've described him, I think anyone would feel the same," Sarah said gently. "I think you're to be admired for still caring for him after the way he's been with you."

Lucy looked at Sarah now. "Do you think I'm an awful person – after hearing all this? I know you struggled with the situation with Vivienne, and I just couldn't be a hypocrite and keep silent about my own experiences. I feel better that I've told you, that there are no secrets between us. We spend almost every day together and it was difficult keeping all these huge things hidden. I dreaded Thursdays, knowing you were obviously wondering who I was visiting in Durham." She paused for breath. "After all this, you probably think at the least that I'm very stupid and naïve? Or maybe you think I'm wicked for contemplating getting rid of Charlotte? Some people might even think it's my fault that she's so badly handicapped. My father says it was a punishment from God for my behaviour."

Sarah felt her chest tighten. That was exactly the sort of thing that people back in Ireland might say. "Lucy," she said, moving out of her chair, "I think *none* of those things about you." She put her arms around Lucy now, oblivious to the people at the other tables. "You're one of the nicest, kindest people I've met in my whole life, and a wonderful, loving mother."

"Thank you," Lucy whispered, "Thank you, thank you . . . thank you."

CHAPTER 34

Harrison's re-opened the following week, although decorating work was still continuing on upstairs. Sarah and Lucy came into the shop an hour early to wash down shelves and counters and try to get the place back into some sort of order.

"I can't believe the size of it," Lucy said as they walked around the downstairs area.

"It's very deceptive," Sarah said. "When you come in first it looks the same, but then you see the openings on either side of the counter wall, and you realise that there is another area almost the same size behind." She went towards the back area. "I'm so delighted with the new changing room. It's much more private and the way the door swings out means you can measure customers without everyone else seeing it."

Lucy's eyes scanned the open area that used to be the kitchen. "The new counter down here for measuring and showing customers large pieces of material is much bigger than the one we have at the till. It just means we can move about more freely without being on top of each other. We'll know just how big it is when we get the stock back into place. We've got lots of shelves and the pigeon-hole boxes are perfect for displaying the wool and craft items."

Sarah grinned at her. "I'm really excited about it! I can't wait to see how things look when they're all in their new places." She took her coat off. "Let's get started straight away."

Lucy put her hand on her hips and raised her eyebrows. "Now, Miss Love," she said in mock-seriousness, "I believe it should be the employer who gives the orders and not the worker!"

Sarah laughed. "I'm sure there's no better woman to put me back in my place if I step out of it." She held up her coat and bag. "Now, where are we hanging up our belongings, since the coat-stand seems to have disappeared along with the kitchen?"

"There's a little cloakroom upstairs," Lucy said, moving towards the back of the shop. "Let's go up."

Their steps echoed loudly as they went up the wooden stairs, bare since the workmen had removed the red-and-black striped runner. There was a smell of fresh wood in the air and a thick layer of pale yellow sawdust on the stairs and the handrails.

"Let's check how the kitchen is looking," Lucy said. "That's the most important place for us." She opened the stripped pine door and went in. "My goodness!" She stood in silence looking around her.

Sarah followed her in, then they both walked around looking at the pink, freshly plastered walls, opening the pine wooden cupboards and checking out where the electric points were.

"This is much better than I envisaged," Lucy said. "And it's almost finished."

Another door in the corridor opened into a small cloakroom, which then led on to a bathroom with a full porcelain floral suite of sink, lavatory system and a curved bath on gold legs.

Sarah looked around her. "This is beautiful! Was there a bathroom here before?" Her voice was high with surprise.

"No, but Peter Spencer advised me to have one put in now. He said if I ever wanted to let the rooms out up here, then it would be more difficult to put a bath in later."

They had a look at the good-sized stockroom and then went to investigate the rooms on the other side of the corridor.

In the first bedroom there were two windows on the back wall which looked out over the tops of the immediate buildings and then further back towards Grey Street and the tall monument. A new shiny black cast-iron fireplace had been installed with a tiled insert featuring delicate stemmed cream, pink and purple flowers, and there were new cupboards fitted in either side of it, just waiting to be painted.

Sarah immediately thought if she had a free hand in the decorating, she would pick out the cream in the flowers to paint the cupboards, doors and skirting boards. Apart from a few new electric sockets, the rest of the room was bare.

"This will probably be a double bedroom," Lucy said. "There's another – more like a box room in size."

"This isn't that small," Sarah said, laughing, as she surveyed the "box room". "This is bigger than the bedroom I had back in Ireland!"

"It's not a bad size." Lucy looked thoughtful. "I'm sure it could be used for lots of things."

They moved to the last room at the end of the corridor, the sitting-room which was at the front of the building. It was more than double the size of the biggest bedroom and had a steel-grey, ornate cast-iron fireplace and a lovely bay window.

"Gosh, the window is huge," Sarah said, walking over to look down onto Pilgrims Lane. She examined the wooden shutters which had been stripped back to the bare wood for painting, then she patted the wooden window seat which followed the curve of the window. "I particularly like this. It's a real feature and handy for storage."

"I thought if we got pads and cushions made to match the curtains it would look nice," Lucy said. "I'm going to buy new furniture for all the rooms. The stuff that was already here was damp and beyond repair. I told them to get rid of the lot."

"That sounds very expensive," Sarah said.

"It will be worth it. As Peter Spencer said, if I let the place fall into disrepair, I'll only lose money on it in the long run." She suddenly smiled. "I'm quite excited about doing it all up. And that shows how much better I feel. Six months ago I would have felt totally overwhelmed with the slightest change in things."

Sarah's mind flitted back to the day when Lucy had come back to find the shop window all changed, and how she had almost flipped. The look on Lucy's face made her think she remembered it too.

"If you like, I'll help you with the soft furnishings," Sarah offered. "I would love to see how you can transform an empty space into a cosy, welcoming room." She thought for a moment. "I saw a magazine recently that had design and furniture suggestions for sitting-rooms and bedrooms. It looked really interesting, but I didn't have any need for it at the time. I might pick it up at lunch-time."

"Was it *Interior Design*?" Lucy checked. "Or *Ideal Home* magazine?"

"I'm not sure what it was called . . ." Sarah paused, thinking. "I've never heard the expression *Interior Design* before, but I suppose it really does describe what you're doing."

Lucy walked slowly around the room, a thoughtful look on her face. She came to stand by the fireplace. "How are you getting on at the house with the girls?"

"Grand," Sarah said, wondering what had prompted the question. "Vivienne has been quiet since the . . . since she was ill, but she's been quiet with everyone."

"How would you feel about moving in here?"

Sarah looked at her, stunned. "Me? To live here above the shop?"

"You don't need to decide straight away. The painting and decorating won't be finished for another week or two, and even then there's no rush."

"I think it's beautiful . . . but I wasn't expecting it. I really don't know what to say . . ."

"Think about it. Take your time."

Sarah walked around the room, and then came to sit on the window seat and look out onto Pilgrims Lane. She could see several upstairs parts of houses that she knew were occupied by shopkeepers and staff. There was only one family living in the lane as it wasn't really suitable for children, as there were cars and delivery vans constantly bumping up and down the cobbles during the day. Her gaze fell on the bookshop below and she immediately thought of David McGuire. It would be strange being in the shop knowing that he wasn't across the lane any more.

"I thought you might find it easier to do your sewing and alterations here without having to lug things back to Victoria Street. You could have the small room up here and if you needed any materials, patterns thread etc you would only have to walk downstairs."

"It would certainly be very convenient," Sarah said. "I can just imagine how lovely it will look when the decorating is finished and the furniture is in place."

"You have a good eye for colour and design so if you'd like to help me to pick wallpaper and paint and the furniture, I'd be grateful." She halted. "If you decide you do want to move into the flat then it will be exactly as you would like it, and if you don't want to move in, then it will be all ready for someone else."

"Wouldn't you mind someone coming in through the shop to come up here every day?"

Lucy's hand came up to push a stray dark curl behind her ear. "I would have to pick the tenant very carefully." She suddenly looked flustered, as though the idea didn't appeal to her, and she moved towards the door. "I shouldn't really have asked you. I think you're very settled in Victoria Street with the other girls, and it might be too lonely for you down here."

"But it would be a great opportunity." Sarah was turning things over in her mind. The opportunity was too good to miss, but something was holding her back.

"If you decide you want it, I would only charge a nominal rent. Take a week or two to think about it. Put it out of your mind for the time being."

The workmen appeared just before opening time and Lucy asked them to carry the rolls of material from the back area where they had been stacked and covered to the new stacking shelves that would allow easy viewing and access to them.

By the time the first customers arrived, the floor had been swept and the counters and shelves and the silver till had been washed down, and the account books and the pattern books were all back in their place. Sarah had quickly filled the pigeon-hole boxes with a mixture of coloured wool but, even as she was doing it, she knew as soon as she got time she would go back and re-arrange it so that the wool was in the exact order of shades.

Throughout the morning, every time the door closed after a customer, they moved quickly to empty boxes of threads and knitting needles and put them into their new homes. The workmen kept the noise upstairs to a minimum but inevitably there was the sound of voices and heavy footsteps competing against the background music from their transistor radio. Every so often one of the workmen came tramping down the stairs to collect something from the van parked outside, and when the door opened clouds of sawdust escaped.

"I think we should close the shop for an hour at lunch today," Lucy said. "We need a break from the noise upstairs and it was uncomfortable fighting our way through the mess to make tea earlier."

"Where do you fancy going?" Sarah asked.

"We could go to Fenwick's tearoom – they always have a good choice and it will give us a decent walk out in the fresh air to clear all that dust out of our lungs."

After lunch, they had a wander around Fenwick's ladies' department looking at the new spring fashions which had just arrived.

"Look at that!" Sarah gasped, holding out the price-tag on a simple straight dress. "I could make that in a couple of hours for a fraction of the price and still make a profit."

"Well, you should!" Lucy whispered back. "There are lots of people who would buy dresses like that if they could afford it, and the new shorter lengths mean you're using less material."

"But I have a lot of orders for curtains and things like that, and with the shop busy it's getting harder to get the time during the day like I used to." She suddenly stopped. "I didn't mean that to sound as though I was complaining – I enjoy sewing whatever it is I'm doing."

"I know that, and it's good that you're so adaptable because it keeps us in business," Lucy said. "Let's see how things go over the next few weeks," She checked her watch. "I have to go to the post-office. I'll meet you back at the shop."

Sarah walked along to the newsagent's and bought three house magazines which all had features on the latest designs in decorating and in soft furnishings. She went over the advantages and disadvantages of moving to the flat in Pilgrims Land in her mind, but still couldn't come to any decision. In many ways she knew it was only the fear of changing things yet again.

The shop was more or less organised by the time they closed up. The existing stock was now sorted onto the new display shelves, and the bigger, improved changing room had the chair and the clothes hooks all back in place. The windows had been washed and cleaned ready for the new gift-ware items that were due to arrive the following week.

"There are still things to do," Lucy said, as she locked up, "but the workmen have said they'll finish off the downstairs paintwork on Wednesday afternoon and they said the kitchen will be finished tomorrow. They expect to have the rooms papered and painted by Friday."

"And you and I will go and look at furniture on Saturday afternoon?"

"Yes, I suppose the quicker we start the sooner it will be finished."

* * *

On Friday evening there was a letter from Sheila Brady waiting for Sarah on the coat-stand table by the door. Sarah took it into the kitchen with her and stood reading it while the kettle boiled.

The first paragraph was all about Tom Lafferty, the fellow she had met over Christmas and how great they were still getting on. The whole family had met him and in fact her mother had discovered that she knew his granny and some of his uncles who had emigrated to America. Sarah smiled as she read it. There was no doubt that this was a serious romance.

The rest of the letter was full of a court report about a fight between two local doctors which had given much amusement to the local townspeople. Sheila had copied long sections from the local newspaper which had quoted the judge's witty comments on the fight and had highlighted the pettiness between two so-called pillars of society.

She mentioned she had seen Martina and James in town, and how Martina had been odd with her when Sheila had pointed to her expanded stomach and remarked how "blooming" she looked. Sarah gave a wry smile thinking that that's exactly how her sister-in-law would have reacted. Martina managed to find a slight in everything.

The letter then went on to say that Con Tierney was still up in Dublin working for the big decorating firm and that Sheila's mother had heard that he had got his younger sister, Carmel, a job working in the company's shop out in Donnybrook.

She said she also heard that Patricia Quinn was still going out with the farmer from Mullingar, but she had never seen hide nor hair of her since last September, and she didn't know how she would react if they ever met up. "*I can't ever forgive her for what she did to you,*" Sheila wrote. "*You lost your husband and then when you moved to England, I lost my best friend. Patricia Quinn has a lot to answer for. If it wasn't for meeting Tom, I don't know what I would have done.*"

Sheila's letter ended the same way her other ones did, asking Sarah when she was thinking of coming home and saying how everyone was asking for her. It dawned on Sarah that she would find herself short on company if she were to take a trip home, as it sounded as though Sheila was seeing Tom Lafferty almost every night. If they weren't at the pictures or a dance together, Tom was up at her house or she was out at his family's. She no longer had Patricia Quinn to go out with and soon Martina and James would be too wrapped up their new baby to go anywhere.

Sarah pondered over the situation for a few minutes, then told herself that it didn't matter because she had no plans to return to Ireland in the foreseeable future. What was there in Tullamore for her now? As the weeks went by, her hometown had become more of a dim and distant place in her memory. She would have a couple of weeks off in the summer and she would take days out here and there getting to know the surrounding places. Jane had asked her recently if she fancied a day out to Edinburgh over Easter as there was a direct train from Newcastle and it could be done in a day.

Vivienne and Anna came in shortly after her and Anna offered to run over to the shop to get them fish and chips. Sarah was always happy not to have to cook, and since it was Friday evening she would only have been frying fish in any case.

In all the months she had been living in the house as the only Catholic, she still kept up her religious observance of Mass every Sunday in the cathedral and not eating meat on Fridays. Occasionally she wondered if she was doing it out of sheer habit or whether it meant that she had a strong religious conviction. Most of the time she came to the conclusion that it was ingrained routine, something that everyone back home did without question. Here, she thought, there was no one checking up on her, but something still got her out of bed on even the darkest, dreariest Sunday mornings.

She went over to the cupboard now to help Vivienne get the plates and cutlery out for Anna's return. Since it was the first time they'd been on their own for a while, she took the chance to check how Vivienne was.

"I hope you don't mind me asking, but has everything settled back down to normal?" She chose her words carefully. "Are you feeling back to your old self?"

Vivienne's face coloured. "I'm fine, thank you . . . I've really learned from that episode and will make sure nothing like that ever happens again."

Sarah immediately regretted saying anything as Vivienne seemed uncomfortable with the reminder of the incident. "Don't be too hard on yourself," she said. "We all make mistakes." She went to the cupboard to get the salt and vinegar.

"I'll certainly watch what I drink in future and make absolutely sure that I never get into that state again. If I'd turned up at home pregnant, my parents would have disowned me forever." She smiled. "I don't know what I would have done without James's help – his friend quickly solved the problem."

Sarah felt herself tense up at the description of James Ryder's friend having *"solved the problem"*, as if it had been something trivial. Then, she caught herself. She knew she shouldn't judge. She forced a smile. "As you say, it won't happen again."

Vivienne rolled her eyes. "In future I'll make sure the man has French letters and, when I meet someone I'm seeing regularly, I'm going to go on the pill."

Sarah's face stiffened at the medical student flaunting her sexual attitudes so blatantly, as if anyone else's religious or moral view were of no consequence.

Vivienne gave a casual shrug. "You're a modern young woman – you know what it's like to be close to a man. You've been engaged . . ."

Vivienne suddenly faltered and Sarah knew she had realised that in order to defend her own position, she had touched on Sarah's rawest nerve.

Sarah turned away, fighting back the urge to retaliate – to say something equally hurtful in return. But she knew there was no point. For all she had a nicer, more decent side to her, there was some little glitch in Vivienne that would always make her unpredictable and self-serving.

Sarah swallowed back her feelings, telling herself that she must stop feeling personally responsible for pointing out Vivienne's faults. She had tackled the medical student when she first arrived about her prejudices, initially thinking that was her only weakness.

But, as the time had gone on, Sarah realised Vivienne was awkward with everyone. All the other girls openly acknowledged their exasperation with her outspoken ways – and behind her back often mocked her for it and imitated her high-handed ways with colleagues at work.

Sarah reckoned Vivienne would come a cropper soon. She had managed to avoid anything really serious happening up until now – but the day would come when she would meet her match.

Over the fish and chips there was a discussion about a new film that was on in the cinema and whether anyone fancied going to it. Sarah said she might go if the film didn't finish too late, as she still had a few things she wanted to finish off for the shop display.

"Don't tell me you're still sewing eyes on knitted dolls?" Vivienne laughed and looked around the rest of the group for support in what she called friendly teasing.

"They're actually sewing kits," Sarah said, not rising to the bait. "And people are more prepared to buy things when they can see what they look like finished." She finished the last bite of her fish and put her knife and fork down on the plate. "If no one else has planned to use the bathroom, I'm going to go and have a bath now."

Later on she heard Elizabeth coming in the front door and a few minutes later the nurse came bounding up the stairs to knock on the bedroom door.

"Sarah," she said, sticking her head around the door, "there was a mistake on the ward rota and they've more staff than they need, so I've got tonight off!" She grinned in delight. "*And* I just heard there's a dance on in the Station Hotel tonight that a lot of the hospital staff are going to. It's only five minutes' walk down the road and finishes at half ten. Do you fancy coming? Vivienne and Anna are dead keen to go."

"If you don't mind," Sarah said, "I'll give it a miss. I've some things I need to get on with." The cinema on a Friday night was one thing but a dance was another when she had to be up for work in the morning. There was also a serial radio play that she wanted to catch the final episode of.

The girls called to say they were going out just before eight o'clock and shortly afterwards the doorbell rang. For a moment Sarah thought one of them might have forgotten something and then it dawned on her they would have used their key. She ran downstairs to find Lisha Williams standing on the doorstep with her arms folded.

"Hi, Sarah," she said. "I've nothing to do at home and I wondered if you had any sewing or anything that you wanted me to help you with?"

"Come in," Sarah said. "I was just going to make some tea if you fancy it, or I think there might be some lemonade in the pantry."

"Oh, lemonade, please," the girl said, following her down the hallway.

Sarah sorted the drinks and went over what things Lisha could help her with. This had been the third or fourth time since the funeral that Lisha had come over to the house and she felt things must be bad at home if she needed to get away so often.

When they were back up in her bedroom, Sarah went over to a box which held the kits for the soft toys. "It would be real help if you could finish this off," she said, holding out a naked pink rag-doll. Then she lifted the bag that held the rest of the materials for the doll. "The instructions are in here along with the wool for her hair and the pattern for her clothes."

"That's brilliant!" Lisha said, grinning. She went over to the armchair by the window and Sarah brought her a small stool to put her things on. She switched the radio on and found a pop station she knew the girl would like, and then settled down at the sewing machine to finish yet another pair of curtains that someone wanted for Easter.

They worked solidly for a while, Sarah glancing over every so often to check how Lisha was doing. After a while Billy J Kramer came on the radio singing "Do You Want to Know a Secret?" and Lisha joined in with it.

"You have a lovely voice," Sarah said.

"I love that song. I love music of any sort really."

"You're a very talented girl. How is your swimming training coming on?"

"Great, we have a new coach and he really pushes us. I did my best time yesterday."

"How is your mother?" Sarah asked.

"She's okay . . ." There was a hesitancy in Lisha's voice.

"She's a very strong woman," Sarah told her. "You and Mark are lucky to have her."

They worked a while longer, then Lisha lifted up the doll, complete now with a full head of brown hair and a dress and black shoes. "What do you think?"

"That looks perfect!" Sarah's voice was high with surprise. "You're really getting the hang of sewing, Lisha."

"Will I do another one or have you something else?"

"There should be another rag-doll pattern in the box," Sarah said. "One with blonde hair. It would be nice to have them side by side in the window."

"You have a lovely job," Lisha said. "It must be great doing things like that all day."

"It is a lovely job," Sarah said, "but there's more to it than just sewing. You have to order the material and work out what's likely to sell, and then you're on your feet all day. It suits me great but it mightn't suit everyone."

They worked away together and some time later Sarah looked at her watch. "It's quarter to ten, Lisha, I think you should call a halt. Your mother might want to get to bed."

"She won't mind," Lisha said. "Are you finishing now?"

"I'll probably work on for another half an hour," Sarah said. "There's a play on the radio I was going to listen to, and I'll do my hand-hemming while it's on."

"I could finish this second doll if I stayed on with you," Lisha said. "I've just finished sewing the stuffing in and I've only the eyes and the dress to do." When she saw Sarah pursing her lips together she said quickly, "I'll run across now and check that my mother is okay. I'll leave the door on the latch."

She was back in minutes carrying a plate with two thick pieces of ginger cake on it. "My mum made that earlier on and she said we could have it for supper." She held up a key. "She and Mark are going to bed and she said I could let myself in when we're finished."

"That was really nice of her."

"She's been doing a lot of knitting and baking since the funeral – she says it keeps her busy."

"What sort of things does she knit?" Sarah asked.

"She's doing baby clothes for someone from work. She's really good. She can do lace and all that sort of thing."

"I must have a look at what she does," Sarah said. "Lucy was saying that we might take in some craft work to sell in the shop, as I haven't got so much time to spend on things like baby shawls." Sarah knew that Fiona Williams was still very down-hearted about losing her husband, and she thought that something like knitting might keep her busy and help the shop at the same time.

She ran the machine on the last seam of the curtain she was working on, then held the material up to the little blade on the side of the machine and cut the threads. She gave a sigh of satisfaction, then switched the machine off.

She went downstairs and quickly boiled some milk to make cocoa. When she came back upstairs and they sat drinking and eating the cake while listening to the drama on the radio. When they finished the supper they began to stitch as they listened.

It was gone eleven o'clock when Sarah heard the gate banging and then the front door open. The loud male voices and Vivienne's unmistakable shrieks of laughter told her that the girls had brought company home. They occasionally had female friends to stay overnight from the hospital, and they were often picked up in cars and taxis by fellows they were dating, but she had never known any of them to bring lads back after a night out.

Sarah stood up. "I think you should be heading home now, Lisha," she said. "I'll walk you across the road."

"Can I help you again tomorrow? I'd really love to do the teddy-bear pattern."

Sarah smiled at her. "I'm not going to say 'no' because you've done great work on the dolls tonight and –" she raised her eyebrows "– you've done them much quicker than I do." She winked. "We'll work out what I'm paying you tomorrow."

Lisha shook her head. "I didn't do it to get paid," she said. "I enjoy it and I like being over here with you." The Beatles singing "From Me to You" suddenly blasted out from the radiogram downstairs. An excited glint came into her eyes. "I think your friends are having a party downstairs."

"I think they're just playing a few records," Sarah said. "I know two of the girls are up early for work in the morning so it won't be a late night."

They were just at the bottom of the stairs when Vivienne, who was standing at the kitchen door, came rushing towards her saying. "Ah, she's not asleep! Here she is, James!"

Sarah's heart sank. Surely she hadn't brought James Ryder back?

Vivienne grabbed Sarah by the hand and started tugging her towards the kitchen and Sarah suddenly realised that she had been drinking again.

She jerked her arm back hard, pulling out of Vivienne's grasp. "I'm just seeing Lisha back across the road."

Several other people came out to the hall now, most of whom Sarah did not recognise. She turned back towards the door and just as she was ushering the girl out she heard James Ryder's voice saying, "Goldilocks! What have you done to your hair?"

It dawned on Sarah that of course he hadn't seen her since she'd had it all cut off and she felt a wave of satisfaction. Hopefully, her changed appearance might encourage him to divert his attention elsewhere – perhaps even in Vivienne's direction. From what she had learned about him and her recently, they were obviously well suited.

When she came back into the house James Ryder was still waiting in the hallway and she knew there was no escape.

"Miss Sarah Love!" His eyes lit up. "You look lovelier than ever. The new hairstyle is most becoming on you." He took her hand.

"We have some wine," he told her. "Come and have a glass and tell me all about your bid to take over the fashion industry."

Vivienne waved her glass in front of Sarah's face. "My last drink," she said, raising her eyebrows meaningfully.

They went into the kitchen and after James poured her a glass of white wine, Elizabeth introduced a nurse she worked with and James introduced two men who were medical students.

After they had shaken hands, one of the men looked at Sarah. "Who," he asked, "was the dusky young creature you were with earlier on?"

Sarah's brow furrowed. "Do you mean Lisha?"

"A real beauty," he said. "Is she coming back?"

Sarah stared at him in shock. "She's actually a schoolgirl – she's only seventeen years old."

He raised his eyebrows. "There are young seventeen-year-olds – and there are old seventeen-year-olds . . ."

"Well," Sarah said, "Lisha is definitely one of the young ones."

James then guided her towards a couple who were entwined in a passionate embrace behind the door. He put a curled fist to his mouth and gave a loud theatrical cough which prompted them to spring apart.

Sarah smiled when she saw it was Anna and then her face froze when she recognised the red-haired man who was with her.

James put his arm around Sarah's shoulder. "This is Gordon Ferguson," he said gesturing with his wineglass. "And this, Gordon, is the lovely Irish colleen I told you all about."

Gordon Ferguson pushed his dark glasses higher on his nose. "Delighted to meet you, Sarah," he said, shaking her hand. His eyes betrayed not a flicker of recognition.

The gynaecologist turned towards Anna. "And are there many more of you lovely young ladies in the house?"

"You've met everyone now apart from Jane," Anna said, sliding her arm through his.

Sarah noticed the smitten look on her housemate's face and wondered if she knew the kind of man she had just been kissing.

And if she did know about what had happened to Vivienne, would Anna care? Would Jane or Elizabeth care? A cold shiver ran through her. As she watched Vivienne leaning on the table looking as if she hadn't a care in the world, Sarah felt, after months of living with them, that she hardly knew the other girls at all.

* * *

"Are you sure?" Lucy asked Sarah the following morning when they were hanging up their coats in the newly painted cloakroom. "You really don't have to make up your mind straight away."

"I'm definitely sure," Sarah said. "I just have to give a month's notice and then I'm free to move out."

Lucy studied her for a few moments. "Has something happened? I thought you were too settled in the house to move."

Sarah wondered if she should try to explain, but she decided against it. She couldn't bear it if Lucy told her she was being silly and old-fashioned about Vivienne's morals or that she was being too judgemental about what Gordon Ferguson had done. She also didn't want to explain that she had turned down an eligible doctor for the second time.

"No, nothing in particular has happened." Her voice gave nothing away. "I just feel it makes more sense for me to move in here. It's much bigger and better than anything I could ever have hoped for and I won't have to carry things back and forward to the shop." She gave a weak smile. "And I won't have to queue for the bathroom in the morning."

Lucy's face lit up. "Oh, Sarah, I'm delighted!" she said, clapping her hands together. "The minute I saw you walking around the rooms I knew it was perfect for you."

"It is perfect," Sarah said, looking around her. "And I know how lucky I am to have it."

Lucy's face suddenly became serious. "There is only one concern – I'm worried that you might get too used to your own company down here. I want you to promise me that you'll get out and about and mix with people – make a regular night when you go to the

318

cinema or dancing with your friends." She waved her hand around. "It would be too easy to just lock the shop door here and hide away working all night."

"I won't," Sarah told her. "I'll still go to the cinema with Jane and some of the other girls." She had decided when she was lying awake last night that the quieter, more strait-laced Jane definitely wouldn't have condoned Vivienne's wayward behaviour, and she was fairly sure that Elizabeth didn't know either. She couldn't speak for Anna, but if her romance with Gordon Ferguson continued, she was bound to find out what he was like soon enough.

"Don't forget I'll be starting my fashion-design course in a few weeks' time so I'll be out of the flat two nights of the week for that." Sarah smiled. "In fact it will suit me just grand, because I'll be much nearer the college living here than in Victoria Street." She halted. "We'll have to sort out rent and bills and that kind of thing."

"You can cover the electricity and gas bills, but there will be no rent," Lucy told her. "I've been thinking of giving you a rise for all the extra work you do, and this is a perfect solution."

Sarah shook her head vehemently. "I couldn't . . . it's far too much."

"I'm not arguing about it, Sarah," Lucy said lightly. "You can consider yourself as being in a kind of caretaking capacity – you'll be looking after the building for me and keeping it well maintained." She shrugged. "With all the extra work you do for the shop, I know I'm coming out of the deal better, so let's leave it at that. Besides, you can save the rent money for your future business plans."

"But, I don't have any plans . . ."

"Well," Lucy said, "I'm very happy to keep the shop going for the foreseeable future, and as you know it's doing well at the moment, but the time may come when I might want to sell up. When my father's gone I will have his house as well as my own and I won't have to rely on the business. As long as I have the time and the money to visit Charlotte and make sure she has everything she needs, that's enough for me. You're a young extremely talented woman at the start of your career and you should start planning now for the future."

"But I'm very happy with what I'm doing," Sarah said. "And we've expanded the sewing service so that I'm doing household things as well as alterations."

"Why are you doing the fashion-design course, Sarah?"

"It's something I've always wanted to do, and I suppose it's the most challenging, the most exciting area in the business."

"Exactly – so presumably you will want to one day create your own designs and sell them?"

Sarah bit her lip. "Yes . . . I suppose I do."

"Start saving now," Lucy advised her. "You never know what the future will bring."

"You're right, but I still feel I should pay you some rent."

"The subject is closed," Lucy told her, "and don't forget we're going furniture-hunting when we close at one o'clock today." She smiled. "If it makes you feel better, you can think of trading your interior design ideas in lieu of rent."

CHAPTER 35

The winter weather moved into spring and in March Sarah packed her belongings and said her goodbyes to the girls in Victoria Street. They were all surprised and even upset she was going, but she promised to call up regularly and told them they could drop up to her flat any time. Jane made her promise that they would go to the cinema every Friday night that she wasn't working, and if there wasn't a good film on they would find something else to do like the theatre or for a meal. Sarah promised her that she would keep to their nights out as Jane often worked two out of four Fridays, and she knew the arrangement would keep Lucy happy too.

What Sarah hadn't reckoned on was the effect it would have on Lisha. When she told her she was moving out of Victoria Street the girl broke down crying and said that she had already lost her father and now she was losing Sarah.

"But I'm only moving half a mile away," Sarah told her, "and you can call into me any evenings. In fact," she said, "now I'm living in my own place, you can even come and stay the night." Sarah didn't know where the suggestion had come from as she hadn't considered it before, but she supposed it wouldn't do any harm.

321

"Really?" Lisha said. "That would be great. Some of the girls at school stay at each other's houses, but I've never done it."

"The couch on the three-piece suite goes down into a double bed, and I have spare blankets and pillows. You just have to check that it's okay with your mother." Sarah hadn't imagined that she'd use the pull-down bed so soon, and she was grateful now that Lucy had suggested buying it. She had pointed out that Sarah might want any of the girls to stay overnight and in the summer she might want to put up friends or family from Ireland.

"Oh, I'm so excited now," Lisha said. "So when can I come and see your new flat?"

Sarah thought quickly. "Saturday afternoon when the shop shuts at one o'clock. We could have a walk around the shops and maybe go for a Coke or something."

* * *

The following Saturday Lisha arrived at the shop just as Lucy was putting the *Closed* sign on the door. "You're very prompt," she said, opening the door to let her in.

"I've nothing else to do." Lisha glanced towards the back of the shop where Sarah was sorting out boxes of embroidery threads. "I was up for swimming training at eight o'clock this morning and I've just been hanging about the house since I got back." She gave Lucy a sidelong glance. "I wasn't sitting about doing nothing – I helped my mum with the hoovering and things like that . . ."

"I've heard you're a busy girl. Sarah has shown me the lovely work you've done for her, haven't you, Sarah?"

"Indeed I have," Sarah said, coming over to them. "She should do very well in her sewing exams at school."

"I'm not too sure about that," Lisha said, rolling her eyes. "We have the grumpiest teacher in the school for sewing and she marks you down for the least little thing."

Sarah brought her upstairs and was delighted at the girl's reaction to all the new decorating and the modern furniture.

"Wow!" Lisha said, running a hand across the back of the new-style grey linen sofa with the wooden frame and arms. "I wish our house was like this." She picked up a darker grey cushion with a pink heart appliquéd on it which picked up the tones in the grey and pink floral wallpaper. "That is gorgeous! I'd love something like that in my bedroom. All the girls in school would love it."

"I'll show you how to make one," Sarah told her. "It's really easy."

Lisha looked around the room again, then she suddenly said, "Haven't you got a telly in here?"

"Not yet," Sarah said, "but I might get one later."

They moved into the bedroom and Lisha was equally enthusiastic about the lilac and white abstract wallpaper and the teak bedroom suite. She posed in front of the double wardrobe which had an oval mirror in the centre and white marbled melamine inserts on the doors and sides. There was a matching dressing table, bedside cabinet and headboard for the double bed.

"Is it okay if I look inside the wardrobe?" Lisha checked, and when Sarah nodded she opened the door wide to reveal the rail of coats and suits and skirts and dresses.

"Did you make all those?"

"Not all," Sarah said. "I've bought a few of the dresses and blouses."

"They're lovely," Lisha said. She lifted out a short sleeveless dress with all different coloured panels. "Wow . . . I've never seen you wearing that. That's the new short style that I saw a singer wearing on telly. Did you make it?"

"Yes, I saw something like it in a magazine and I thought I'd have a go at it." Sarah was enjoying chatting to someone young and so enthusiastic. "It was really easy. It's not a totally new idea – it's based on the sack dresses that have been out for a while, but when you look at the fashion pages in the newspapers and magazines you can see the lengths are getting shorter every year." She laughed. "I'm not brave enough to wear it yet. I've only gone as far as the knee with skirts."

"Could I try it on?" Lisha asked.

"Go on," Sarah said, curious to see how it would look on the tall slim girl. She went out into the hallway to let Lisha change in private. A few moments later she came out bare-footed, wearing the dress.

"You look like a model in it!" Sarah wasn't just flattering her – she had seen dark-skinned girls in the fashion magazines and she looked very similar to them. "It's really lovely on you." Lisha twirled around, delighted with the compliments. "The only thing is, I think your mother might think it's a bit short."

Lisha's face was suddenly solemn. "At the moment she wouldn't notice anything."

"I suppose she's still thinking about your father. It will take her time to get over it . . . it's only to be expected."

Lisha nodded but didn't meet Sarah's eyes. "I'll just get changed."

Sarah could sense things were worse at home than the girl was saying and she wished she could help.

"I was just thinking, Lisha," she said when they were walking around the shops, "I could show you how to make a dress like the one you tried on. I have the pattern and I'm sure I have a remnant of material big enough to do it. Chat to your mum and see if you can stay next Friday or Saturday night and we could get started on it."

"Oh, brilliant!" Lisha said. She suddenly pointed across the street. "There's a great café with a juke-box just behind there that my mum sometimes take me into."

Sarah immediately knew it was the café that she had been in with David McGuire. "Okay," she said. "We'll go and have some chips and a Coke."

When they walked into the café, Sarah felt a strange little empty feeling inside. It was almost like the feeling she first had when she had arrived in Newcastle and knew no one. They went to a booth which was just across from the one she and David had sat in the day she told him all about Vivienne being horrible about Irish people.

As Lisha scanned the menu, Sarah remembered how he had

made no issue about leaving his friends and had walked her all the way back up to the house. Compared to the crowd from the hospital that had been in the house the night before, he seemed so straightforward and so decent, and she knew he would have understood her feelings about Vivienne's abortion. And being a Catholic, he would have understood it even more than Lucy would.

It was a pity, Sarah thought, that the one person she felt she could talk to about absolutely anything – the one person she could have the best laugh with – had to be someone who fancied her. If he had just been happy to be friends with her – given her a bit of time . . . but he hadn't. And then, of course, there had been all the complications with Harriet.

Thank goodness she seemed to have got over it. When they were having a cup of tea in the mornings that the District Nurse dropped in, David McGuire was never referred to. It was almost as if he had never worked in the bookshop just a few yards away from them. And strangely, the shop now seemed like a different place. Sarah thought the new manager, Robert Wright, was a nice enough man, but an older and much more serious sort than his young devil-may-care predecessor.

Sarah's thoughts were interrupted when she suddenly noticed a middle-aged couple who were staring across at her and Lisha and obviously talking about them. From the snatches of conversation she overheard, she knew they were discussing her Irish accent and the colour of the young girl's skin. Sarah lifted her head up as high as she could and then gave them a long, cool look which made them turn away.

"Is it okay if I put a record on the juke-box?" Lisha asked, oblivious to the attention they had been receiving. "I have my own pocket money."

"Hang on a second," Sarah said, delving into her handbag. She slid a shilling across the table. "You'll get a few for that."

"Are you sure? Oh, thanks." She moved out of the booth. "I'll play one for you. Who would you like?"

"I don't mind . . ." Sarah was trying to sound relaxed and

casual, because she didn't want Lisha to know how annoyed she was at the ignorant people.

"Oh, no, you've got to pick one."

She thought for a moment. "See if they've got Gerry and the Pacemakers, 'You'll Never Walk Alone' or the other big hit they had."

"D'you mean 'How Do You Do It'?"

"Yes, that's the one."

As she watched Lisha intently studying the lists of records, it suddenly struck Sarah what people in Ireland would think if they saw them together. Most of them, she thought, would gawk at them like the couple across the way – especially people like Martina and maybe even James and possibly her friend, Sheila. She supposed it was because they had no experience of foreigners, but then, she reasoned, neither did she. And yet, as far back as she could remember, she had always thought that people coming from different countries and having different coloured skin was an interesting, exciting thing. In school she had loved looking at all the different countries on the huge map they had on the wall. It reminded her that Ireland was only a tiny country in a very big world. And now she had got to know someone like Lisha fairly well, she knew there was even less of a difference than she had thought. People were either nice or not nice – that was all that mattered.

Later, as they sat eating chips and hotdogs, Sarah noticed two young lads who had just sat down in a booth at the opposite side nudging each other and grinning across at her and Lisha. Although their attentions were obviously of admiration, they were still irritating so she turned at an angle in the seat so she couldn't see them.

When they parted outside Harrison's shop, Lisha said, "I don't know why I was worrying about you moving out of Victoria Street; it's actually better coming down into town to see you, and now I'm even going to be able to stay the night."

"I'm looking forward to it too," Sarah said, "But will you just ask your mum to pop in to see me the next time she's down at the shops? I'd feel better if I've had a word with her before you come to stay over."

"She won't mind at all," Lisha said, beaming at her. "She really likes you."

* * *

When they closed on the Thursday for Easter, Lucy told Sarah that she was going to advertise for another member of staff.

"The shop is busier than ever," Lucy reasoned, "and a lot of the time I think we need another person serving while you're dealing with the customers. I also think we're losing a lot of customers by closing half-day Wednesdays and definitely on Saturdays. I'm going to do it professionally. I'll put an advertisement in the *Evening Chronicle* for a fully qualified seamstress with experience working in a shop. I'll draw up a short-list of the best applicants and we'll interview them on a Wednesday afternoon."

Sarah raised her eyebrows. "Aren't you going to interview them on your own?"

"No, you and me. You actually spend more time working in the shop than me, so we've got to make sure we're both happy with the choice."

Sarah looked alarmed. "But I wouldn't know what to do or say in an interview."

"Then we'll practise beforehand," Lucy said, "and it will give you experience for the future."

* * *

The Easter weekend went by quickly as Sarah and Jane took an early train on the Saturday up to Edinburgh, and spent the day walking around the shops and the lovely gardens on Princes Street, and then they walked along the Royal Mile and afterwards went on a tour of the castle.

On Easter Sunday she went to Mass in the cathedral in the morning and she wondered if she might see David McGuire and his mother. In a way she wouldn't have minded meeting him and hearing all about his new job in London but there was no sign of them there. He had either not come home for Easter or he had gone to a different Mass. After church, she went with Lucy to Durham to visit Charlotte and then they came back into Newcastle and had dinner in the Station Hotel.

"I feel I've got to know the area quite well in the last few months," Sarah said, as they sat chatting over a glass of white wine.

"Yes, you kept your promise about not working all the time and I'm really glad you've kept up with the girls in the house, and that you went off to Edinburgh with Jane." Lucy smiled now. "You've seen a good bit of the North-East now – so far we've been to Whitley Bay, Blyth, Lindisfarne, Darlington and Redcar – and we must go to Harrogate and York in the summer – you'll love those."

"I'll look forward to it," Sarah said. "Out of all the places I've been so far, I feel I've got to know Durham fairly well."

Lucy's face brightened. "Charlotte loves you visiting," she said. "She's really taken to you."

"I'm very fond of her as well."

"I have explained to her that you won't be coming so often because you'll be studying for your course."

"Oh, I'll still make the time," Sarah said. "She's like a little niece to me." She paused. "I have a real niece or nephew due in the next few weeks, but I don't think I'll be allowed to get to know them as well as I know Charlotte."

"Have you given your brother my home phone number as well as the shop one?" Lucy checked. "Because if the baby is born in the evening or Sunday, he can give me the message and I'll drive straight down to you."

"Yes," Sarah said, "they have both numbers."

"It will be lovely for you to have a nephew or a niece, and it will probably make things easier between you and your sister-in-law. Babies make such a difference. I think it would be nice if you went over to see them in the summer." She paused. "It will be almost a year since you came. When Kitty Reynolds wrote to me a few weeks ago she was asking if you had any plans to go back for a visit."

"No, I won't be going there any time soon. I'll only go back when there's a genuine welcome there for me," She paused. "And when the wedding business with me and Con Tierney is long forgotten."

* * *

Sarah started her Advanced Fashion Design course during the third week in April. She would attend college on Tuesday and Thursday nights in a class of only eight students. On her first night, as she listened to the lecturer explaining all the areas they would be covering in the course, Sarah felt her heart soaring. She knew practically everything that was mentioned, but she was excited to hear that in the first half-term the students would be given projects to do which would involve tailored sleeves, tailored pockets, and bound buttonholes, plus various styles of bodice, sleeves and collars. These were all areas she had taught herself and that she knew she could improve on. The second half-term would then move on to making and adapting their own patterns which was another area that Sarah was keen to learn more about.

The teacher came across as both inspiring and helpful, and the other students – five women and, surprisingly, two young men – were as intent as Sarah on improving their fashion designing skills. Since they had a lot in common, the group bonded together naturally and from the outset Sarah looked forward to going to classes.

Meanwhile, Lucy was busy in Harrison's organising interviews for new staff. Out of eighteen applicants, four women were to be interviewed on the last Wednesday in April, and the others had been thanked for their interest by letter and then been told that they had been unsuccessful.

On the Monday afternoon before the interviews, as she was checking the button drawers, Sarah noticed two women standing outside the door of Harrison's, engaged in a heated discussion. One was a heavy, unkempt middle-aged woman with strands of grey-streaked hair escaping from under a headscarf, and the younger, thinner girl was equally untidy with badly dyed blonde hair. They were both smoking cigarettes.

After she got a look at them from a few different angles, Sarah reckoned they were mother and daughter, and the girl looked to be in her late teens. They moved out of the doorway and walked a few yards along the lane, still talking in an animated fashion. Sarah went back to her buttons, forgetting about them, but a few minutes later she saw them both staring in the window, then the older woman started jabbing her finger on the glass. They went to walk away and then the mother started poking the daughter in the chest as though making a point.

Sarah went towards the back of the shop where Lucy was sitting at a table, entering figures in a ledger book. "I think we might have a bit of a problem," she said, thumbing in the direction of the door. "They've been there for the last few minutes. They keep going back and forward looking at something in the shop window. There's definitely something going on."

Lucy stood up. "I'd better go and have a word – see if there's something wrong."

Sarah watched as Lucy went out to the door. She heard raised voices and then a short while later the shopkeeper came back inside, and stood holding the door open for the two women.

"I'd much rather we discussed this in the shop," Lucy said in a quiet voice. "I'm not prepared to talk about it out in the street. I have customers to think about, so I'd be grateful if we can talk inside here in a friendly, civilised way."

Sarah felt her heart quicken. She moved towards the back of the shop to unpack a box of yarn and give Lucy privacy to talk to them.

"Well, you weren't exactly civil to our Isobel when you didn't even give her an interview!" the older, dumpy woman said. She took a folded envelope from her pocket and waved about. "You didn't have the decency to say why you didn't want her!"

The blonde girl's eyes darted between Lucy and the woman. "Mam," she said, reaching a hand to catch her mother's sleeve, "it's not worth it. If she doesn't think I'm good enough for the job, I don't want it."

"Give me one minute please," Lucy said, going to the desk at the back of the shop where she did her accounts and suchlike. As she passed Sarah she rolled her eyes to the ceiling. She opened a drawer in the desk and took a folder out. "Can I just check your name please?"

"It's Isobel Brown," the woman said. "Don't you recognise us? We've bought wool out of here before."

"I'm sorry," Lucy said, trying to sound calm, "but we get lots of different customers here and it's hard to keep track."

Lucy looked through the folder and lifted out a few sheaves of paper. She glanced through them and then came back to the counter. "I have your application letter here and I can see from the notes I made that you don't have any experience working in a shop. That's the reason I couldn't consider you."

"But she's a canny sewer, our Isobel!" the woman said, her voice high with indignation. "She can make flippin' anythin'. We looked at all the stuff in the window – all those cushions and embroidered things – and she can easily do as good as that if not better. She's made skirts and dresses an' all sorts of thing." She jabbed a finger in Lucy's direction. "You didn't even give her a fucking chance!"

"There's no need for abusive language," the shopkeeper told her.

Sarah put the yarn down now and approached them. "Is everything okay here, Lucy?"

Mrs Brown turned around to look Sarah up and down.

"Everything is fine thanks, Sarah." Lucy said. She looked at the woman. "I'm very sorry but the advertisement specified that I needed someone with experience in both sewing *and* shop work. It's as simple as that. There were several other people who applied who hadn't worked in shops before, and I'm not interviewing them either." She looked straight at Isobel. "I'm sorry, dear, but I've treated everyone as fairly as I could. The people who are being considered for the job can all sew and knit and have worked in shops."

"It's not good enough," the woman said, folding her arms high up on her chest. "How is she supposed to learn about working in a shop if she can't get a job in one?"

"For Christ's sake, Mam! They don't want us an' I'm not hanging about here to make a fool of meself any longer."

"I don't think we need to use language like that," Lucy repeated, her face tight and anxious looking. "I'm afraid I haven't the time to train someone in the ways of working the till and doing stock-keeping and all that sort of thing. I need someone who knows how to do it already. I suggest that Isobel apply for a job in one of the department stores or grocery shops or something like that until she's gained the necessary skills in shop-keeping." She paused. "There are quite a few sewing shops in the city and in places like Gosforth or Jarrow."

Isobel looked scornfully at her. "Ah, you can stuff your flamin' job! I wouldn't take it now if you paid me. Come on, Mam, I told you we shouldn't have bothered." She turned on her heel and headed for the door.

Mrs Brown looked at Lucy, her eyes blazing. "You won't get anyone better than her." She waved her hand around the shop. "She's far too good for this place. You can paint it up and put new shelves and things in, but it's still only an oul' dump. Always was and always will be."

Sarah looked at Lucy's stricken face and something snapped. She moved towards the woman. "That's quite enough – you can't just walk in here and start shouting and swearing and abusing people. You can get out of the shop right now!" She rushed to the door and opened it wide. "Out – and if you dare to come back we'll call the police. Your behaviour is out of order and illegal."

The woman walked towards the door with her head in the air and as much dignity as she could muster. "You needn't worry! I don't want to waste another minute in here." She halted on the threshold and stared at Sarah. "If we'd known there was your sort working in the shop, she wouldn't have applied for it in the first place!"

It was much later in the day when Sarah finally got Lucy to see the lighter side of the incident. "Look," she said, "the woman obviously has a slate missing and she's dragged that poor girl in here. Who in their right mind would do such a thing?"

"I still feel bad about it," Lucy said.

"The cheek of her!" Sarah's eyes were wide with indignation. "And the work that's been done to make the shop lovely and more modern and all she can do is call it a dump! And she even had the cheek to criticise my work. All that time she was outside smoking and pointing at the window, she was probably saying that all the things I'd made were rubbish." She paused. "And I'm sure when she said 'your sort' she was referring to me being Irish."

"Oh, let's forget about them," Lucy said. "And just be grateful we didn't have any customers in at the time or she would have driven them all away."

On Wednesday afternoon all four women were interviewed and a bright, red-haired woman in her thirties, Margaret Davies, was told at the end of the day that she had the job.

"This means that we can stay open all day Saturday and Wednesday from now on," Lucy said, "and we can sort individual days off to suit us throughout the week."

* * *

Over the following weeks, to Sarah's relief, she found Margaret an easy person to work with. She listened carefully to anything she was told and she asked questions about anything she wasn't sure about, and on Lucy's days off, she gave Sarah her place as being in charge of things. Sarah had been concerned that an older person might not take suggestions from her, but there was no conflict between them.

Sarah's old landlord, Peter Spencer, called in one Saturday afternoon to take a look at the refurbished shop and Sarah told Lucy to show him around upstairs. She was surprised when she heard them coming down the stairs together laughing, and was even more surprised when Lucy told her later that he had invited her to come to a wedding with him at the end of June.

"A younger colleague of Peter's is getting married and he's been asked along with a partner. He wasn't going to go, and then he remembered that the bride is a member of the same ladies' golf team as me, so he thought it would help if the friend he brought knew some of the other guests."

"He's a lovely man," Sarah said. "And I'm sure you'll have a great time."

"I've said I'll have to think about it. I haven't accepted yet . . ." Two pink circles appeared on Lucy's cheeks.

"What's to stop you? You've known him for ages." Sarah paused. "He's a widower, so it's not as if you don't know his situation or anything."

"Oh, it's not that," Lucy said. "In fact, he's one of the few men that I feel comfortable with because he knows the situation about Charlotte. I had to give all that information to my old solicitor when I was making out a will and the files were automatically transferred to Peter Spencer when he took over. He's been the height of discretion and he's very understanding. He actually knows more about me than anyone else. He knew when I was ill and he's given me advice about my father and nursing homes and all that sort of thing." She lifted her eyes to heaven. "God knows why he's asked someone who's been through all the things I have."

"He obviously likes you and sees beyond all those things," Sarah said. "I've always thought he was a really nice, fair man," Sarah said. "Any time we had any trouble with the house in Victoria Street he either sent the plumber or electrician around and if he couldn't get anyone, he tried to sort things out himself."

Lucy looked down at her hands. "It's not really Peter I'm worried about, it's the fact that I've not been out with a man since before Charlotte was born. I'm not sure if I would be very good company – I'm not sure if I would know what to talk about for a whole day and evening."

"You'll be grand," Sarah said. "Just think – a lovely summer wedding! You'll have to get a new outfit for it."

Lucy took a deep breath. "If I do decide to go, I might get you to make me something for it. I imagine with the sort of people who will be going that it will be quite an up-scale affair."

"I'd love to make something special for you," Sarah said in an excited tone. "I've got loads of new ideas from the course. We've been studying the work of Coco Chanel and André Courrèges and some of the new designers like Mary Quant. And I can't believe how much I've learned already. I know how to do perfect tailored finishes on sleeves and pockets and all those sorts of things now. If you have any really intricate patterns, I can always ask for help from the teacher or even some of the other students. Some of them are really talented."

"I've no doubt that you'll make something fantastic, but I'll have to think about it . . . I'm not sure what would suit me."

Sarah suddenly felt brave. "Lucy, you have the most beautiful thick curly hair, but I think it might look even nicer if you tried a colour rinse in it to blend that little bit of grey at the front. If you don't mind me saying, I think it would make you look younger."

Lucy's hand came fluttering up to her neck. "Oh, I'm not so sure about dying my hair. I made a big mistake with it when I was younger. I tried to go lighter . . . sort of blonde. It was in terrible condition and my father said it looked ridiculous. I've been afraid to try anything since."

"I think going from dark to blond strips the colour out of your hair and leaves it very dry, but putting a dark colour over grey doesn't do any harm. One of the girls at the house – Anna – has quite a few grey streaks in her hair and she's only twenty-four. She puts a tint through her hair every few weeks and it looks really natural. If you like, I could do it for you."

Lucy looked at Sarah and then she smiled. "What have I got to lose? Even if I don't go to the wedding, putting a bit of colour in my hair isn't going to kill me."

The following Saturday, when the shop was packed with customers and all three women were run off their feet, Lucy came rushing over to Sarah to tell her that her brother was on the phone from Ireland.

"It's a baby girl," James told her. "We're calling her Teresa Bridget after Martina's two grannies."

"That's lovely," Sarah said. "And how is Martina?"

"She had a tough enough time," James said. His telephone voice was always formal as though he was speaking to a stranger. "But thank God she's doing all right, and the baby is coming on fine. Martina's mother has come to stay for a month to give her a hand. She's in your old room, so we moved anything you left into the shed for the time being."

"I'm delighted everything is fine," Sarah said. "Give my regards to Martina. She's probably exhausted now after it all. Was the baby born this morning or last night?"

"Ah, she was actually born on Monday morning," James said. "But by the time she got out of the hospital and everything, I never got a chance to phone before. To tell you the truth, I was so busy I never even thought."

When she came off the phone, Lucy could tell there was something wrong. As soon as there was a lull in the shop, she asked Margaret to keep an eye on things and she told Sarah they were going upstairs for a cup of tea.

"What's wrong?" Lucy asked when they sat down at the table.

"The baby was born last Monday and he never even bothered to let me know." Sarah pursed her lips tightly together.

"Maybe they tried and couldn't get through. The lines can be bad at times."

"He didn't try to phone. He told me he forgot all about me. And there was I, thinking just the other night that they might ask me to take a week off to come over to see the baby and maybe give Martina a hand." She lifted her hands. "I know I'd said before that I didn't want to meet people, but I was thinking that I could just stay in the house, that I needn't have gone near the town . . ."

"You could go anyway," Lucy told her. "Go as a surprise. Margaret and I can manage on our own for a week."

"Martina's mother has moved into my room to help them." Her eyes filled up. "James made it quite clear that they don't need me. He as good as told me that they had forgotten all about me."

"I'm sure they haven't," Lucy said, trying to console her.

Sarah stood up. "It really doesn't matter," she said briskly. "I have the present all ready and I'll get it in the post today."

CHAPTER 36

In the middle of June Sarah received a letter from Sheila Brady telling her that Tom Lafferty had surprised her with an engagement ring on her birthday. She went on to say that they had set a date for August of the following year and she wanted Sarah to be her bridesmaid.

"*I know you said you won't be able to make it over this summer,*" Sheila wrote, "*but surely your boss will give you the time off for your best friend's wedding? If you don't get over soon, James's little girl will be all grown up and running about.*"

Sarah showed Lucy the letter when Margaret was on her lunch break and they were on their own.

"I think you should reassure your friend that you'll definitely go home for her wedding," Lucy said. Then she raised her eyebrows and smiled. "Even if it's just to let people know that your employer isn't the terrible ogress they all obviously think I am."

Sarah looked at her from under her lashes. "I didn't actually say that. I just said we were mad busy in the shop and, with my course and everything, I didn't feel I could spare the time."

"I understand!" Lucy laughed. "I meant to tell you that I got a letter from Ireland recently, from my cousin and our mutual friend in Tullamore."

"Miss Reynolds?" Sarah asked.

"Yes, she's coming over in July with Father Kelly. Apparently, they're going to visit an elderly nun who's ill in a convent in York and they said they would come up to Newcastle for a few days to see us both and for Miss Reynolds to visit my father. They're going to stay in a convent in Newcastle, so they'll probably only see us for an afternoon."

Sarah looked at Lucy for a moment. "How do you feel about it?"

"It will be nice to see them," Lucy said, "but I feel rather awkward having to explain to people about my father's condition." Her face darkened as it always did when she talked about him. "He's got much worse recently, and there are times when he hardly recognises me." She closed her eyes. "And his language can be quite appalling."

"They'll understand." Sarah thought of the well-meaning, upstanding, old-fashioned teacher and the friendly priest and hoped she was right.

When they were locking up that evening, Lucy asked Sarah when she was likely to see Lisha again.

"Tomorrow night," Sarah said. "She was so pleased with the dress she made that she's bought material to make a similar one for her mum. They're both coming down to the flat so we can measure the pattern for Fiona."

"I was just thinking that we could do with a Saturday girl and Lisha came into my mind. She wouldn't have to do anything very complicated, just serve the customers who need basic things like needles and wool and that sort of thing, and bring the people who want alterations done down to the changing room. She could also make tea for us and tidy around the kitchen. What do you think?"

"I think it's a great idea. It will give her a bit of pocket money and get her out of the house."

"Well, when you next see her, ask her to call in to the shop on her way home from school and we can show her where things are and how to use the till. If she could start this Saturday it would be great as it would give her a couple of weeks to get used to things before I have the day off for the wedding."

"Is it that close?" Sarah asked. "Have you got your hat yet?"

"I bought a little feathery thing, but I'm not sure if it's right."

"You must bring it in to let me see it. Have you decided how you're wearing your hair?"

"I think I'm going to have it put up in a French roll."

Sarah tilted her head to the side, trying to picture it. "I've never seen you with your hair up. I bet you'll look lovely, and it will really suit your outfit, but you're going to have to be careful about what to wear on your head. A little fascinator works better than a hat if you have your hair up."

"Well, you were right about having my hair coloured, it's made such a difference. The hairdresser said the grey made me look washed out."

"Well, you certainly didn't look washed out the other evening when you tried on your outfit – you were absolutely glowing." Sarah paused, choosing her words. "I think you look so well these days, Lucy, and Harriet commented on it on Monday. She said how well rested you looked after the weekend. Do you feel any different?"

"Yes," Lucy said, "I do, actually. The doctor has also reduced my medication and I feel less tired and sluggish. I think it was the side-effects." She smiled. "I feel a huge weight was lifted off me when I told you about Charlotte and, since we did all the renovations in the shop, I feel so much more positive about the business. Our takings are up practically every week and we're still getting new customers."

"Having Margaret has made a big difference," Sarah said. "We're getting through alterations much more quickly now. I'm able to spend a good bit of the working day on them and we're getting bigger sewing jobs. I checked the books and we did curtains for an office this month, bed curtains for the new ward in the hospital and curtains and cushions for a small hotel."

"That's wonderful, but I hope it's not tiring you out too much. I know you're still working away here in the evenings and you have the work from the course as well."

"It's all going fine," Sarah reassured her. "And I love the course. It's so interesting; we're learned so much about the history of fashion, and the influence of different designers. This week we're studying accessories, so if you bring your suit in later in the week then we can go down to Fenwick's one lunchtime and find something to wear on your head."

* * *

Lucy came down to the flat on the Sunday afternoon – the day after the wedding – to check how things had gone in her absence. Sarah made them both a cup of Camp coffee with boiled milk, then she told Lucy how good Lisha had been and how well Margaret and the young girl were getting on.

"Ah, that's good," Lucy said. "And no problems from the customers about Lisha's colour?" They had noticed some shocked faces the first Saturday that the girl was behind the counter, and one or two of the regulars had asked why Lucy had picked a foreign girl to work in the shop. They had been politely told that Lisha wasn't foreign having been born and bred in Newcastle, and that she had been picked because she was great at sewing and was a hard worker.

"No," Sarah said. "They're getting used to her, and she's such a cheery, helpful girl that after a while I'm sure they won't notice anything different about her." She looked at Lucy and smiled. "Now, tell me all about the wedding. Were you happy with your dress and jacket?"

"I was thrilled with it! And I received countless compliments on it. Several women thought it was an actual Chanel design and couldn't believe it when I said you had made it." She lifted her brows and smiled. "I think I've got you a few commissions. I hope it won't put you under pressure with the work you have to do for the course."

"I'm well ahead with all my projects," Sarah told her, "and besides, you know I thrive on pressure."

340

"Oh, the outfit was perfect for the church with the jacket on, and then later when we were dancing I felt very comfortable just wearing the dress."

"Oh . . . dancing!" Sarah said, raising her eyebrows and laughing.

Lucy laughed too and made a little waving gesture with her hand. "Oh, don't tease me now." She composed herself. "I had a lovely time and Peter was an absolute gentleman. Although he knew lots of the guests, he stayed beside me all through the day. He's a really nice man, Sarah . . . I can't believe how well we get on and how relaxed I feel with him. His poor wife was sick for over three years before she died and he helped nurse her. He actually took the last three months off work to care for her full time." Lucy shook her head. "That is not easy for a man to do. And we were chatting so easily I was able to explain about my father and he just said how sad it was that the brain can be so affected, and that he could understand how hard it is for the family." She shrugged. "I'm just amazed that in the last year I've met someone like you who I can confide in totally, and now I've met a man who I feel very relaxed with as well."

"You like him a lot," Sarah said. "Don't you?"

"Yes," Lucy replied, "I think I do. He's asked me to go to the theatre on Wednesday night and I told him I would. At my age, what have I got to lose?"

* * *

The following Saturday when Lucy and Sarah came back from their lunch break, Lisha looked very awkward and flustered. As the afternoon went on she seemed to get quieter and only spoke when the others asked her a question. Lucy checked with Margaret if there had been any problems when they were out and she said no, things had just been normal.

Eventually, Sarah brought her upstairs to the kitchen on the pretext of making tea. "Lisha," she said. "I feel there's something upsetting you – what's wrong?"

Lisha looked down at the floor. "It's nothing," she said. "I shouldn't let it bother me."

"You'll have to tell me," Sarah said, "or I will start to imagine all sorts of things."

Lisha rubbed her hands to her eyes as though just waking up. "It was when I went to the shop for milk – when you and Miss Harrison were out. I was just walking back when his woman came up to me and asked if I was working in Harrison's . . ."

"And?" Sarah prompted.

"When I told her I was she started shouting and swearing at me. She said Miss Harrison should be reported for only taking on foreign workers when there are plenty of local people who need jobs. I tried to tell her I was English, but she called me a '*darkie*' and a '*nigger*'!"

Sarah's heart quickened. "Oh, no . . ."

Lisha's eyes filled up. "I'm used to it at school and I've learned to ignore it, but adults usually just stare at me – they don't usually say things like that."

Sarah moved out of the chair and went to put her arms around the girl. "If you see the woman again, tell me and I'll sort her out."

"She doesn't come into Harrison's, she told me. She said she wouldn't buy anything out of it if it was the last shop in Newcastle."

It suddenly clicked with Sarah. "What did she look like?"

The description could only have been Isobel Brown's mother.

"I have an idea who it could be," Sarah said. She squeezed Lisha's arm. "Try not to take it personally. We've had trouble from her before because her daughter wasn't given a job in the shop. I'll make it my business to keep an eye out for her."

* * *

Sarah studied for hours on the Saturday night for an exam the following week. She went to bed around half past ten with the names of different designers rattling around in her head. She woke to the sound of voices outside and when she checked the clock it was going on for midnight. Noise outside was nothing new at the weekends as people often used Pilgrims Lane as a shortcut walking back from the pubs. When she heard the drunken attempts of a group singing "Rule, Britannia", she pulled the bed covers over her head and tried to get back to sleep.

The singing went on for a while – "Rule, Britannia" repeated over and over again in a mixture of tuneless male and female tones. It was some time later when there was a loud cracking noise which made Sarah sit bolt upright in the bed. She took a few seconds to gather herself together, to come to the realisation that she had heard the sound of breaking glass. She threw the covers back and ran across the floor to the window. There was nothing to be seen. She switched the light on, put her dressing gown on over her pyjamas then slipped her feet into slippers and went out into the hallway. She stood still and listened – but the only sound was the ticking from her bedroom clock.

With her heart thudding she went down the stairs and into the shop, telling herself that there were neighbours close by in the surrounding buildings. The light from the streetlamp showed her all she needed to know. There was a huge, open crack in the window and when she went over to check there was a large brick lying in the middle of her new tableware display.

She went straight to the phone and rang Lucy's number.

"I'll call the police," Lucy said, "and then I'll be with you in ten minutes."

Before the police arrived, half a dozen of the neighbours had come to investigate the noise.

"Ah, it will be some of those drunken hooligans that have nothing better to do than cause trouble on a Saturday night," the baker from the shop further up the lane said. "But you'd wonder at them attacking a sewing shop. What the hell would they get out of doing that?"

When the police car arrived, the two officers checked if any of the neighbours had actually seen or heard anything of the perpetrators, and when they drew a blank, the group all dribbled away. Sarah was in the middle of giving any details she could remember when Lucy arrived. They all went upstairs into the kitchen and Sarah made tea and toast for the four of them while the officers took notes.

"I'm afraid we've nothing much to go on," the older of the two men said, shrugging. "We can only hope that some other witnesses might call in at the shop over the next few days and give us more information." He stood up and put his hat on. "Call us if you hear anything else."

When they left Lucy and Sarah went to the stockroom and got big pieces of cardboard and some duct tape to cover the hole in the window until the glazier could come on Monday.

Lucy then told Sarah to pack an overnight case.

"You're not staying here on your own until we've got the window sorted. You can stay with me until Monday."

Sarah shivered, suddenly feeling tired and drained. "I'm not going to argue with you," she said, "but I'll come back here to study during the day, as I have all my books and materials here." She gave a deep sigh. "I have a horrible feeling I know who did this – or who organised someone else to do it."

Lucy nodded. "The lovely Mrs Brown." She walked over to the boarded-up window. "The problem is, we have no evidence. We can call the police and tell them that we're sure we know who did it, but unless we have a witness who saw her, there's not a single thing they can do.

* * *

It was a few weeks later, when the incident with the window had faded, that Sarah came face to face with Isobel Brown outside the bank. She had been standing checking her bank slip when the thin, blonde girl came walking towards her. Before she had time to think about it, Sarah stepped right in front of her, barring her way.

"I want a word with you," Sarah said, guiding her over to the wall of the bank where they wouldn't be in anyone else's path.

"I haven't done anything!"" The girl's face was stiff and defensive.

"Do you know that your mother was very abusive to one of our staff out in the street? She called her the most terrible names. The sort of names that people are not allowed to use."

"It was nothing to do with me," Isobel said, her eyes darting around, checking no one could hear them. "I'm not to blame for the way my mother behaves. I told her not to go near the shop but she dragged me there. I didn't even want the job in the first place."

"I know it's not your fault," Sarah said, "but your mother is going to get into very serious trouble if she keeps this behaviour up. Do you want the police calling out to your house?"

"What d'you mean?" Isobel looked incredulous. "The police won't come out for people havin' a row."

"We also had another incident – a more dangerous one," Sarah informed her. The girl went to move, and Sarah again moved in front of her to bar her way. "We had the police at the shop and they're carrying out investigations about a brick which was thrown through the shop window the night after your mother abused Lisha."

Isobel's face suddenly paled. "It wasn't her – it couldn't have been her."

"How do you know?"

Isobel turned her face towards the wall. "Because . . . because she told me da that she'd had a word with the black girl and he went mad. She didn't say owt about calling the girl names, but she said she'd had a word about her stealing English people's jobs." She looked at Sarah directly now. "Me da gave her a belt for causin' trouble again and she said she wouldn't go anywhere near the shop. She's terrified of him when he gets his temper up, so I know she wouldn't have dared go back near your shop."

Sarah looked at her, unconvinced. "I still think the police need to know about the things she said to Lisha."

"Look," the girl said, "I promise you that you won't get any more trouble off her. I'm gonna go straight home now and tell her that the police know and she'll be terrified. We had them at the door before Christmas because she had a run-in with a neighbour over his dog and then the dog ate some rat poison by mistake and the man blamed her . . ." Her voice tailed off as though she suddenly realised she had said too much. "Anyway, me dad gave her a good hidin' for the police coming to the house, so I know she wouldn't so anything that would get her into trouble again." She shook her head. "She definitely wouldn't lob a brick through a window."

Sarah's mind worked quickly. "Well," she said, moving back a bit now, "the police have taken the brick away to be examined for finger-prints." She lowered her voice. "If I were you I'd have a private word with your mother and tell her that she'd better keep well away from the shop because the police will be keeping an eye out for her."

"I will," Isobel said.

"I'm not saying that you should go and cause trouble between her and your father, because he sounds like a violent man."

"He is," she said. "He'd kill her if he thought she'd put a brick through a window." She paused. "Not that I'm sayin' she did, like . . ."

"Well," Sarah said, "let's just leave it at that, and hope there's no more trouble."

Isobel started to move away and then she stopped. "Tell the young girl – the coloured one – that I'm sorry for what me mam said. It wasn't right."

When Sarah got back to the shop she took Lucy aside and explained the situation to her.

"Well done," Lucy said. "You certainly sound as though you handled that very well. I'd say that's the last we'll hear of Mrs Brown." She paused. "Do you think we should tell Lisha that you spoke to the woman's daughter or is it best to leave well alone?"

"We'll tell her," Sarah decided. "She needs to know that we didn't sweep what happened under the carpet. She needs to know that people have to stand up against ignorant people like Mrs Brown."

CHAPTER 37

The summer passed quickly. Secretly, Sarah had dreaded seeing Father Kelly and Miss Reynolds in July, but the afternoon of their visit went off much better than she had hoped. Lucy's father had deteriorated further, hardly recognising anyone, so Lucy told the teacher there was no point in visiting him and that it would be best to remember him as he was. Instead, she and Sarah took them for a run out to Whitley Bay. They went for a meal in a nice restaurant, and the visitors protested when Lucy and Sarah insisted that they share the bill. Afterwards they had a stroll along the seafront since the weather was lovely.

Both the priest and the teacher thought that Sarah looked almost like a different girl with her short modern haircut, and Miss Reynolds said she had matured and grown more sophisticated since living in England.

"They'll all get a big surprise when you come back for a visit," the elderly teacher said. "Sure, they'll hardly recognise you with your hair and your lovely new clothes. Have you made any holiday plans yet?"

Sarah told her that she hadn't as she was busy working and studying but that she would be over when a convenient time came up. Ireland in fact wasn't on her agenda, as she had been given a list by the college of fashion shows that were on throughout the year in London, and she planned to go there instead.

When she was walking on her own with Miss Reynolds, the teacher said, "You know, Sarah, you don't have to worry about coming back to Tullamore because of Con Tierney. He's up in Dublin all the time – in fact, I've only seen him once since you left. He and his sister Orla are both doing very well there, working for a decorating firm. Orla goes out to people's houses and advises them on the colours and wallpaper and furniture that would suit their house. I was talking to his mother and she tells me they have big plans to open up their own company in the not too distant future. Seemingly, they've already saved quite a bit and their grandfather died and left a house and they got a good share out of it."

Sarah didn't say that Sheila Brady had already told her all this, apart from the inheritance bit which must have been kept quiet. Neither did she say she wasn't a bit surprised that Con was doing well – he had always had big plans.

"Mrs Tierney asked me to send you her best wishes and to say she often thinks about you."

Sarah felt herself squirm at the memory of the last occasion that they spoke up in the cottage. It all seemed so far away and foreign.

"She says that Con has never got over you and never will." Miss Reynolds turned to look at her. "Do you think that time could make a difference to you, Sarah?"

"In what way?"

"If Con was to do well with his business and maybe you were to think of moving back to Dublin. You would easily find work there, and you'd be away from any tittle-tattle but still living at home in Ireland. Sometimes these things work out much better the second time around when hard lessons have been learned. He's not the first to make a mistake and you could fare a lot worse."

"No," Sarah said. "Time would make no difference at all."

* * *

Sarah's first term finished in July and she was delighted when she received her results and found she had received A's for most of her projects. She knew that put her up at the top of the class and it gave her a great sense of achievement.

In August David McGuire paid a surprise visit into Harrison's when he was having a week's holiday back home.

"I heard there were big changes here," he said, winking at Sarah, "so I thought I'd come down and see how you were all getting on." He waved his hand around. "You wouldn't recognise it with all the fancy décor and the vases and things in the window. Is it doing well?"

"It's going very well," Lucy told him. "We've now got three full-time staff including Margaret and we have a Saturday girl, Lisha, who worked over the summer to let us have holidays."

David thumbed in Sarah's direction. "I'd be surprised if this one has taken any holidays."

"Excuse me!" Sarah said, with mock-seriousness. "I often have day trips out."

Lucy looked at Sarah too, and raised her eyebrows. "She hasn't taken any proper holidays yet, but she will be having them later whether she wants them or not."

After chatting for a while about the shop and the new manager over in the bookshop, Lucy told Sarah take David upstairs to see her apartment and to make him a cup of coffee.

"I can't believe it," he said as he looked around upstairs. "This building was an absolute wreck. Fair play to her, she's turned it into a beautiful flat, and whoever has picked the furniture and curtains and things has a very good eye."

"Thank you!" Sarah laughed. "It was me."

When they came to Sarah's bedroom she opened the door but, presumably thinking that it was too personal, he just glanced inside and carried on down the hallway.

After he had admired the sitting-room, they went back to the kitchen. Sarah put coffee and a tin of chocolate biscuits on the table, and as they sat talking – often cutting across each other –

Sarah realised that she had missed their chats. Before things had got awkward between them, she liked his easy-going ways, his joking banter – the things he made fun of that took her back to her carefree teenage years in Ireland. And yet, as they sat across the Formica table from each other, she felt there was a change in him, something she couldn't put her finger on.

Certainly, his clothes were more modern and his thick dark hair was fashionably longer. Sarah had teased him about it, and called him a "Mod" – but there was something other than clothes that had changed about him.

David laughed when she commented on his Italian-look narrow trousers, narrow lapels and thin tie and said he looked like someone from the Beatles or Rolling Stones.

"You probably know a lot more about men's fashions than me. I actually haven't got a clue, I just pick what looks kind of modern but not too outlandish." He looked vaguely embarrassed.

"I'm only kidding. Your clothes are lovely, David. They're very stylish and you look really well."

"Well, thank you," he said, laughing. "There are record shops and clothes shops springing up all over London, and everybody goes for a walk down Carnaby Street or The King's Road at the weekends. There's such a great buzz around the place, you end up buying things without realising."

"Oh, it sounds really exciting," Sarah said, her eyes shining. "I'd love to see all the new boutiques they have down there especially Biba and the Mary Quant shop, Bazaar. We've been studying all those new designers on my fashion course."

He looked impressed. "You certainly sound as if you're well up on things." He took a sip of his coffee. "I see you've branched into clothes, I noticed some dresses downstairs."

"It's really just a few styles," Sarah said. "We haven't really room for clothes-racks. I made a few of those simple dresses for myself and Lucy, and she suggested that I make up a few samples to see if there's any interest. I just put them out in the shop the other day and I think we've sold half of them already."

"Well," David said, "maybe that's the way to go. It's a case of making something cheaply and getting a good profit from it. I wish selling books was so simple." He glanced towards the door and then lowered his voice. "Hey, what's happened to Miss Harrison with her new hairstyle and modern clothes? I can't believe the change in her – she looks about twenty years younger."

Sarah rolled her eyes at him. "You are *terrible* . . . Actually, I talked her into colouring her hair and we've gone shopping together around the boutiques here and in Durham and bought some of the new styles. She's really lovely, David. I know she's a bit older than me, but Lucy is the best friend I ever had."

"I know," he said, "I'm just kidding about her. She is a very nice lady." He paused. "Look, I've got a nice apartment down in Chelsea. Why don't you come down for a few days and I'll take you around? I know where all the main shops are and we could go to concert or a show or something like that."

Sarah's eyes narrowed. "I'll have to think about it."

He held his hands up. "You don't need to worry about me getting any ideas about us being more than friends. I got the message loud and clear. Besides, I'm seeing a girl in London at the moment." He leaned across and took a Kit-Kat from the tin.

Sarah was amazed to feel a sudden stab of disappointment – of jealousy almost. As soon as she felt it, she immediately realised how ridiculous it was. She had only ever seen him as a friend and couldn't begin to imagine how they would be as a couple, and, apart from the fact that he now lived in London, there would always be the problem of Harriet.

She stole a glance at him as he unwrapped the biscuit and it dawned on her that the change was not in his hair or clothes – it was in his eyes. He no longer looked at her with the lingering interest that had been there since the first day they met. He had got over her. He saw her just like any girl – she was no longer important to him.

As he was leaving, David reminded Sarah of his invitation to London.

"I promise I'll think about it," she said,

"Bring one of your friends. I have a spare twin room." He smiled. "You can even bring Miss Harrison."

Neither of them mentioned Harriet as the memory of last Christmas was still lurking in the background, although he had asked after the District Nurse earlier.

"I might bring one of the other girls. Lucy will probably be busy as she has a new man friend," Sarah told him. "He's a widower and he's very nice."

He tutted loudly. "Dear, dear, dear – all the years I was here and nothing exciting ever happened. I go away for a few months and everything has changed."

As she closed the shop door after him, Sarah felt as though the sunny day had suddenly become overcast and grey.

It was incomprehensible – since she was the one that had sent him away – but she felt she had lost something warm and familiar. Something of herself.

* * *

Lucy's father died suddenly in August. Sarah took over the running of the shop to let her employer take a couple of weeks to sort out the funeral and all the legal paperwork.

When Lucy had got the phone call on a Sunday night, saying he had died, Sarah wasn't sure how her employer would feel about things. Lucy's life had totally changed since she had started seeing Peter Spencer, and although they had taken it very slow and steady due to him recently being widowed, there was no doubt that their relationship was serious. Sarah was afraid that all the improvement in her friend's health might be undone by losing her father, without having had a chance to reconcile things properly with him.

Sarah called out to the house on the Tuesday and was relieved to see Lucy there with Peter, looking both bright and calm. Lucy brought her into the sitting-room while Peter went to pour them both a sherry.

"There's nothing I can do to change what happened," Lucy said, "so I've just got to accept it. To be honest, Sarah, I grieved for my father a long time ago. He was always a difficult man and there was nothing I could do to change that, but when his mental faculties started to deteriorate he was like a total stranger. I looked after him when my mother died, while he was still capable of living at home. I visited and cared for him when he was in hospital and the nursing home. I kept visiting him when he was abusive and even violent towards me. Each day I went into the nursing home I never knew what sort of reception I was going to get." She shrugged. "How can I be upset that all that pressure is gone?"

"I'm so glad you feel like that," Sarah said, going over to embrace her. "I know you put up with more than most daughters would have done, and you have nothing to reproach yourself for."

As Sarah went to move away, Lucy kissed her on the cheek. "Thank you, my dear friend – you're so good at saying the right things." She cleared her throat. "I know the worst of his condition was caused by his brain deteriorating with age, and I forgive his behaviour because of that. Now, I have to look to the future –" She halted as the drawing-room door opened.

"And hopefully," Peter said, coming into the room carrying two sherry glasses, "you'll be able to find more time to spend with Charlotte and with me." He gave them both a glass and then stooped to fleetingly kiss Lucy on the top of her curly head.

As she watched the touching scene, Sarah felt a great rush of emotion. She suddenly knew the tide had turned for Lucy. Peter Spencer would look after her and make up for all the terrible things that had gone before.

CHAPTER 38

In September, Sarah decided that she would go to London and she asked Jane if she would like to come with her. The nurse said she would love to go, as she had holidays still to take. She also said that she'd only been to London once when she was a teenager at school, and that she had a friend from college who was working at a hospital in the city who she would like to catch up with. She was delighted when Sarah explained that they would have a place to stay with her friend, and that she could get them reduced-priced tickets for a fashion show.

Lucy was pleased when she heard that Sarah had finally made plans to take a holiday. She had taken the fortnight in August to sort out her father's business and Margaret had taken a week in July and was on her second week now.

"I'm going the Saturday after next if that's okay," Sarah told her, as they were going over an order for material. "And I should have another dozen of those Crimplene short skirts with the belts ready before I go, and the multicoloured cotton dresses." She paused to think. "You might be best to order some more of the blue and pink Crimplene and the striped cotton too."

"You know we sold more of your clothes last week than wool or materials?"

Sarah looked up. "Did we?"

"We did," Lucy said. "Peter says we should think of opening a clothes shop, but I told him he was mad, that we're busy enough without taking on another business."

"You're right," Sarah said. "Could you imagine the work involved in that? Definitely not! Things are perfect just as they are. The staff are all paid well and you're making a nice profit, which is only as it should be."

Lucy gently tapped her pen on the desk. "Businessmen have a different way of looking at things. I reckon that if you start to get greedy – have your finger in too many pies – then that's when things start to go wrong. There's no point in fixing something that isn't broken."

They finished the order, then, just as Lucy was going to phone it through, she stopped and looked at Sarah. "Who are you going to London with? You said you were taking a friend."

"Jane," Sarah said. "You know her – it's the small dark-haired girl from the house in Victoria Street. You know we're staying at David's house? I wrote to him to check it was still okay and he said it was fine and that he was looking forward to being our tour guide."

"Yes, he'll be a great host to show you around London. I like David a lot, and I'm pleased that you're still friends with him." She tucked a stray curl behind her ear. "You know that Harriet has been seeing a new fellow for the last month or so?"

"I wasn't sure," Sarah said. "She said she'd been at the cinema with somebody called Kevin recently, but she didn't elaborate."

They didn't speak for a few moments.

"I think she's got over David, you know," Lucy finally said. "So you can tell her you're going to London. You gave her every opportunity to see if she had a chance with him – you wouldn't need to feel awkward about anything."

"I was going to tell her this week." Sarah looked out towards the window. "I don't think there will be any awkwardness when I explain that Jane is coming with me and that David also has a girlfriend down in London."

"Oh! You didn't mention that before."

"Didn't I?" Sarah said. "I must have forgotten."

* * *

When the train pulled in at King's Cross on the Saturday afternoon, David was there to meet the girls.

"You didn't tell me he was so good-looking and such a trendy dresser," Jane giggled as they walked along the station concourse.

Sarah just laughed and reminded Jane that he already had a girlfriend. The girls' attention was taken up by the fashions many of the people were wearing – their eyes were particularly drawn to the much shorter skirts the women were wearing compared to the ones seen in Newcastle.

Sarah was delighted when she saw lots of girls wearing the style of dresses that she was selling in Harrison's although she had to admit that the abstract patterns she saw were more adventurous than the ones she had used. The girls nudged each other every time they saw a particularly outrageous outfit like a shift dress with triangular holes around the waistline, or strange spaceman-type outfits. Sarah was particularly taken by the accessories like polka-dot scarves – which she knew she could make in five minute – and the baker-boy style hats. Everything she saw gave her ideas for stuff they could sell in the shop.

They went down to the underground and David guided them through a series of different Tubes and stations until they arrived at the nearest station to his house, and then he flagged down a taxi to take them on the final leg.

Sarah was quite overwhelmed by the noise and speed of the Tube and the bustling crowds and thought she would never manage to get around London on her own. It was lucky for her that Lucy Harrison's shop was in Newcastle, because she felt she would never have survived in anywhere bigger.

The two-bedroom, basement apartment was surprisingly bright and spacious, and decorated with an artistic eye. Sarah and Jane walked around the ornate sitting-room and dining-room in amazed silence, and were equally impressed when they went up several steps to the open-plan, white fitted kitchen.

"Nothing to do with me," David said, waving away compliments about the art deco furniture, the pale walls and the flamboyant gilt mirrors and dining chairs. "Nick, my uncle, sorted it all out for me. It's rented from a friend of his. He owns several houses in this road, and he brought in an interior-design company to do them all in one fell swoop."

He was equally modest about the beautiful spacious bathroom, with its own separate shower, and the two neat bedrooms. The beds in both rooms – David's own double room and the twin guestroom – had green and gold counterpanes and bolsters, and teak cabinets on either side which held gold-stemmed lamps.

"I have to say I'm pleased with it," David said. "I definitely landed on my feet. I've even got a lady who comes in on a Friday to make sure it's decent for the weekend if I've got friends around."

Sarah wondered if he brought his girlfriend here, and assumed he would. People in English cities seemed to do whatever they liked. She thought back to the cottage she and Con had been planning to live in, and the times she had to almost fight him off. Back in Ireland couples would have been the talk of the place if it was discovered they were in a house on their own, and it would be presumed they were "getting up to no good". In England everything seemed different. People were more open about sex and relationships, and Lucy had recently told her that Peter now stayed the odd weekend. Strangely enough, she hadn't been a bit shocked. They were both mature people and Peter had been married before and Sarah had a child, and it wasn't as if they were Catholics. It was too soon for them to get married but that didn't mean they didn't want to be close to each other. Sarah supposed that times were changing generally and, at the end of the day, people were entitled to do what they wanted.

The girls had brought wine and chocolates and a couple of Stottie Cakes – a speciality bread from Newcastle – which Sarah knew David loved.

He laughed as he opened the bag to see the flat, round loaves with the familiar indent in the middle. "Aw, thanks! We'll have them later with ham and tomatoes, or maybe in the morning with bacon and eggs." Then he opened a bottle of wine he had in the fridge and they sat chatting about the journey down and the people they had met.

Sarah listened to the way he modestly explained everything or made light of it, and when Jane went to use the bathroom she held her glass out to him.

"Congratulations, David," she said. "You certainly made a good move coming here."

"I can't complain," he said, smiling at her. "In six months it's gone far better than I could have imagined." He took a drink from his glass. "The only negative thing is not being able to see the people you're used to so often."

"Knowing you, I bet you've made lots of new friends."

"Ah, yeah. There's plenty of nice people in London – the same as anywhere else."

They went out to an Italian restaurant for their first night and David waved away their offers of paying the bill. "We have nearly a week ahead of us," he told them, "so you can catch the bill another night."

Sarah had never eaten Italian food before and was pleasantly surprised by the spaghetti and meat and tomato sauce and both girls said how much they enjoyed the sweet red Italian wine. She wondered whether David's girlfriend was going to join them at some point, but there was no mention of her. They went back to the flat and watched television and then later David brought out a pile of LPs and single records to let the girls choose which music they wanted to put on the record player. They started off with Jane's choice of Roy Orbison's "Pretty Woman", then Sarah chose The Supremes' "Baby Love", then David picked a Moody Blues hit. They took turns throughout the night while the girls sipped on wine and were entertained by David pretending to be a DJ, commenting on each record he put on the turntable.

"What a really nice guy," Jane said, when they were lying in bed. "I wonder if we're going to meet his girlfriend?"

"I'm sure we will at some point," Sarah said. She paused. "David and I are going to go to ten o'clock Mass in the morning, if you don't mind staying on your own?"

"Not at all," Jane said, "I'm very happy to have a long lie."

"We'll have breakfast when we come back, and then David said he's taking us around the sights in the afternoon."

Jane leaned out of bed and switched her lamp off. "Sounds good to me."

* * *

Sarah enjoyed the ten-minute walk with David to and from his local church. He asked her all about her fashion-design course and listened intently as she told him about all the projects she had done and about her end-of-term results.

"I'd be surprised if you didn't come top of the class," he teased. "A little swot like you!"

She laughed and gave him a friendly push.

"No, seriously," he said, "I'm very proud of you. You're an extremely talented woman and you've worked harder than anyone I know and you deserve all the success you get.

"That's very kind of you," Sarah said, feeling a warm glow at all his praise.

She then listened as David brought her up to date with the world of books, explaining about the different authors and publishers that he met and all the book fairs and events he attended.

On Sunday afternoon they saw Buckingham Palace and the Tower of London and later on they took the Tube to Carnaby Street, where they went into a pub and had a roast beef lunch with Yorkshire puddings. Afterwards they walked around the shops and Sarah was surprised that the Carnaby Street shopping area was actually only a few buildings long, when she imagined it to be about a mile.

The shops themselves didn't disappoint and she found herself almost giddy with excitement as she examined the T-shirt dresses, floppy hats and coloured tights. All wonderful things she could easily make and sell in Harrison's.

At one point, David came across her as she stood outside a shop taking notes on all the things they had on display in the window.

David laughed at her. "Trust you! You can't even come away on holiday without turning it into a work thing." He put his hand on her shoulder. "We can come back on Friday and take photographs of the shop windows if that would save you all the writing."

"That," Sarah said seriously, "is a brilliant idea. I could take them home and show Lucy."

* * *

On Monday David had to go into work, so the girls had a lazy day around the apartment, taking a couple of hours in the afternoon to look at the shops in Chelsea and buy newspapers and magazines.

It was Tuesday before Sarah was introduced to Camilla Jones, David's girlfriend. He had the day off work, so they went back into London to see Covent Garden and meet up with Camilla for lunch in one of the little restaurants in the area.

Sarah didn't know what to expect, but she was pleasantly surprised with the curvy, bubbly dark-haired girl who gave her and Jane a run-down on all the things they should try to see on their visit. She told them she worked as a photographer on one of the newspapers in Fleet Street.

"I've been told she's one of the best, with a great future ahead of her," David said, putting his arm around her.

"I've still a lot to learn," Camilla said, "but I'm enjoying it."

"Apart from the dogs . . ." David winked at them.

"Oh, don't remind me!" Camilla said, going into a fit of giggles.

David went on to explain that Camilla had been sent to cover a pedigree dog show in the Olympia Exhibition Centre.

"It's a huge place where they hold things like the Ideal Homes Exhibition," Camilla said. "They've always got something interesting on in it."

"That's actually where our fashion show is on Friday afternoon," Sarah suddenly realised.

"It's easy to get to," David said. "It's out in Kensington. I'm off, so I'll go out there with you and meet up with you afterwards."

"I might actually come too," Camilla said. "I'll see if I can juggle my appointments around."

Sarah thought. "You might have to ring about tickets – when I bought them they said they didn't have many left."

David put out his hand. "Don't give her the chance to brag," he said, laughing. "She loves to tell you how she only has to wave her Press Pass at the door and they let her in anywhere for nothing."

Camilla gave David a friendly punch and then she started tickling him, which made Sarah feel awkward and look away.

"Get back to the dogs before we get put out of this restaurant," David said, standing up to straighten his tie and jumper.

Camilla started into her story again and spent about ten minutes relating a catalogue of catastrophes with the dogs.

"Anyway, I eventually got the winners of the obedience category and their owners all into position for the photograph, when one of the dogs got stung by a wasp and it suddenly went mad howling and snapping at the other dogs. The owners all got involved and in the end two of the men ended up rolling around the ring in the sawdust fighting with each other!"

"Oh, no!" Jane said, covering her hands with her mouth.

"And then I went to help grab one of the escaping dogs," Camilla said, wiping away a tear of laughter, "when the little bugger turned on me and bit me in the leg."

"Was it sore?" Sarah asked.

"Bad enough – I needed a tetanus injection. But to cap it all, when I got back to the office, all the reporter wanted to know was whether I'd got the photo or not."

As they strolled around the Embankment, both Camilla and David kept the girls entertained with information about the area or more funny stories or jokes.

"They're well-suited, aren't they?" Jane said, as they walked behind the couple into a Wimpy Bar.

"Yes," Sarah said, "they really are." She wondered now if David felt embarrassed at having pursued her so openly back in Newcastle. He probably felt a sense of relief, she thought, that things had turned out the way they had. He probably felt glad that he'd been turned down, as it meant he had met someone more exciting and more suited to him, like Camilla.

* * *

David worked Wednesday and Thursday so he could have Friday off. The girls stayed around Chelsea again on the Wednesday and then, having got braver about the Tubes, decided to go into London on Thursday on their own to meet up with Jane's old friend and do some more shopping.

They spent time at each of the stations negotiating the complicated Tube maps and then deliberating which line and then platform they should head for. Sarah felt a great sense of achievement when they came out of the station in Oxford Circus to find the girl waiting for them at the exact point they had planned.

Jane's friend, Millie, took the girls first to Biba. Sarah's heart quickened when she saw the familiar black and gold logo outside the shop that she had seen in magazines and in her course notes. When she went inside, she was surprised how dark it was and it took a few seconds for it to dawn on her that the store had blacked-out windows which gave more atmosphere to the art-nouveau interior. Sarah's eyes were immediately drawn to the décor and the decadent furniture scattered with random items like feather boas and hats in all shapes and sizes. Every so often, she took her little notebook out and scribbled down any details she feared she might forget, so she could tell Lucy and use them in the shop.

The girls wandered around looking at all the amazing designs in unusual shades of blackish mulberry, blueberry, rusts and plums – and found themselves picking things up and taking them to the changing room to try them on. Sarah went over to study the Biba make-up and ended up buying eye-shadow palettes and lipsticks for herself, Lucy and the other girls back at the house.

They moved on to Mary Quant's Bazaar, which they noticed was pricier, but Sarah fell in love with lots of the designs and within half an hour she had bought stretchy long black boots, a white PVC coat with a navy and white flowery lining, and a pretty Empire high-waisted dress in small-flower-printed lawn, which came about two inches above her knee. Jane was braver and bought a black belted skirt which was a good four inches above her knee and a purple skinny-rib jumper.

They were just ready to leave when Sarah spotted a black sleeveless straight dress which had white daisies with black buttons going all the way down the front. "That is just amazing!" she said, running over to the clothes-rail. "I won't be a minute," she told the other two girls. "I've just got to try it on – I know it will look perfect with my boots and coat." Five minutes later she came out with another black bag with the famous white daisy logo on.

In a shop further along the girls all bought earrings: Sarah's had a black plastic cube dangling from a smaller black cube and Jane bought a pair with mauve droplets ending up in a big circle. Millie bought large black plastic hoops with a smaller white circle in the centre.

When Sarah told Jane she had bought Biba make-up for Anna, Elizabeth and Vivienne, she said, "They'll kill me if I don't bring something back for them too!" She rushed back to the basket of jewellery and chose two long, colourful necklaces for each of the girls.

* * *

On Friday after a long lie-in, David made them a fried breakfast of bacon and sausages and eggs and then the girls went to get ready.

"Well, would you look at the style!" he said when they came back into the sitting-room – Sarah in her Mary Quant dress and Jane in her short skirt and purple skinny-rib top.

"I don't know what the Newcastle people are going to make of you two when you walk down Grey Street wearing those short skirts!" He shook his head. "Poor Miss Harrison will take a heart attack and drop dead when she sees you!"

Sarah gasped and then started to laugh. "What have I told you about bad-mouthing Lucy?" She went over with her hand raised as though she was going to slap him.

His hand shot out to playfully grab her wrist, and when she looked up at him, his eyes caught hers and somehow the laughter disappeared and suddenly both their faces were serious.

David eased his grip on her wrist and then he stepped back. "I give in," he said, holding both hands up now, but his face looked flushed. He glanced over at Jane and winked. "I'll never say anything about Miss Harrison again. The next time I'm up in Newcastle she'll be wearing one of the dresses herself."

"You are terrible!" Sarah said. She went to laugh but her face felt strangely rigid. She shook her head and went over to stand by the window, to catch her breath.

A short while later they left and were soon on the merry-go-round of the Tube stations again. When they arrived at Kensington they had a look around the shops and then David walked them up to The Olympia Exhibition Centre for the fashion show which started at two o'clock. As it had turned out, Camilla was working and couldn't come. The place was busy with people milling around everywhere.

David checked the information notice at the door. "It looks like there are a few exhibitions on today."

The girls gathered beside him to see what else was on, but Sarah made sure she didn't catch his eye or get too close after their strange little encounter earlier on.

Sarah pointed to one of the posters. "Oh, there's a furniture and interior design show on all day in one of the other halls."

"That's sounds interesting," Jane said. "We might have a look at that when the fashion show's finished." She looked at David. "Do you fancy coming to that? We could meet you in the foyer here."

"Are you joking?" he laughed. "I told you the decoration in the house is nothing to do with me. I'll meet you in The Old Shakespeare pub when you're ready."

"Won't you be bored just hanging around?" Jane asked.

"I'm going to walk down and buy a couple of papers and when I've finished them, I have this." He went into his inside pocket and brought out a Penguin paperback. "And I might go mad and have a couple of pints too. I can't think of a nicer way to spend a Friday afternoon off." He gave them a broad grin and pointed to a large building. "It's just behind there. I'll be in the lounge waiting for you, ladies, and if you're nice to me I might even buy you a drink."

"Oh, my God," Jane said as they walked into the hall where the show was being held, "Camilla is one lucky girl. Why are all the best ones always taken?"

*　*　*

Sarah thought the show was a spectacle and her eyes were glued to the runway as she took in every model that came down it wearing the Spring and Summer Collection for 1966. At times her breath was taken away by the perfection of some of the classic outfits and the sheer artistry involved in the new innovative styles. She found herself shaking her head in bemusement at some of the combinations the models wore like white ankle boots with spotty tights and tartan shorts and at other times she and Jane clutched each other in silent laughter at the more bizarre outfits. She came out of the hall at the end with a folder full of leaflets about the designers and which shops would be selling the new collections.

They went across the hallway to the homes exhibition and, when they told the cheery Cockney lad on the door that they had just come out of another show, he waved them in for free. "The prices are bad enough for one show," he said, "without paying for two."

They had a walk around the show looking at all the stands and the new kitchen and bathroom designs. Sarah was interested in the soft furnishing displays and once again her notebook came out to take down details of curtain tie-backs and edgings and anything else that caught her eye. An hour passed and then Jane, who wasn't as interested in the displays as her friend, looked at her watch.

"I think we should get back, I feel bad leaving poor David on his own."

They walked out into the busy foyer and then Jane said she was just going to run to the toilet. Sarah was standing reading a poster when she suddenly felt a hand on her shoulder.

"Sarah," a female Irish voice said, "it is you, isn't it?"

Sarah turned round to find herself face to face with a familiar face from Tullamore. Her heart started to race when she realised it was Orla Tierney – Con's sister.

CHAPTER 39

Sarah eyes widened with shock. "Orla!" She could not think what to do or say.

"It is you!" Orla said. "I saw you earlier on walking around the show, but I just couldn't be sure it was you." She stepped back and looked Sarah up and down. "It was mainly the hair," she said, "but the clothes are so different. They're lovely and so is your short hair. You look like a totally different girl."

Sarah swallowed and felt as though she had something stuck in her throat. It was too late to walk away now. "So," she said, trying to smile. "What are you doing here in London?"

"The home exhibition," Orla said nodding. "I'm working for an interior design and decorating firm in Dublin. We come over to London when any of the exhibitions are on." She smiled. "Trying to keep ahead of the competition."

Sarah listened to her explaining all about her job as if she did not already know.

Then, she felt a hand on her arm. Her nerves were still jangling from meeting Orla so she whirled around.

"I can see you're chatting," Jane said, smiling at Orla, "I'll meet you over in The Old Shakespeare."

"It's okay," Sarah said quickly. "I'm coming now . . ." She looked at Orla. "I'm with my friend and we've someone else waiting for us." When she turned back, Jane was making for the big glass doors. Sarah moved to follow her, but Orla kept talking.

"I didn't know you were in London, I thought you were in Newcastle. Miss Reynolds was down in the house and she told my mother how well you were doing."

"We're down in London for a visit . . ." Sarah was completely thrown now, not knowing what to say or how to say it, and trying not to give too much information away. The very last thing in the world she expected was to run into someone like Orla Tierney in the middle of hundreds of strangers in London.

"You look fantastic," Orla said. Her hand came out to feel the material of Sarah's white PVC coat. "You look like a model."

"Thanks, you look well yourself!" Sarah took a couple of steps backward.

"Oh don't!" Orla laughed. She held out the skirt of her plain navy mid-length skirt which matched her jacket. It was the sort of thing that Sarah was wearing a few years ago. "I think I'm well behind the times when I look at all the fashions here. I think I need to come over some weekend when I'm not working and go round all the shops. When you're at these trade things you don't get any time." She suddenly stopped.

"So, what are you doing here? Are you at the trade show?"

"No," Sarah said, "We were in at a fashion show in one of the other areas."

"Fashion?" Orla looked interested.

"The sewing shop I work in, we've branched out into womenwear – dresses and skirts, that kind of thing."

"Very good." Orla gave a grin – a forced grin.

Sarah could see the girl was trying to act as though the events of the last year hadn't happened. Trying to pretend that her brother back in Ireland hadn't done the dirty on her with Patricia Quinn.

"How are you in yourself, Sarah? Are things going well for you?" A little pause. "Have you met anyone else yet?"

Sarah looked straight at the girl who should have been her sister-in-law. "I'm grand, Orla – I've never been happier. I love my new life and my new job."

Orla nodded. "Good, I'm delighted for you. And did you meet anyone else yet?"

"I've met lots of people," Sarah said, determined not to give her any gossip to take back home to Con. "I have lots of friends." She hitched her bag up on her shoulder. "It was nice to see you . . ."

Orla had one last shot at getting information. "Have you been back in Tullamore recently?"

Sarah shook her head. "No, I'm too busy. I've got to go," she said. "I hope the rest of your trip goes well."

When she found the pub she stood outside for a few minutes composing herself, then when she went inside and saw a sign for the Ladies', she went straight there. She stood in front of the mirror at the sink and stared at her red, flushed face. Then she turned the cold tap on and started to splash water all over her face until she felt it beginning to cool down. She dug into her handbag and got her new Mary Quant stick foundation out and with a shaking hand she applied it all over her face. She then powdered it and put fresh pink lipstick on which she thought helped to detract from her high colour. She stood for a few minutes taking deep breaths until she finally felt composed enough to go in and join her friends.

The old Tudor-style pub was half-full, with walls papered in deep wine and green colours which made everything seem cosy and warm. David and Jane were sitting at a table to the side of the bar in deep-buttoned green-leather chairs. She told them that Orla was an old school friend, and then listened to David and Jane saying what they thought the odds were of meeting someone from a small town in Ireland in the middle of London. When she explained that the girl worked in the home-decorating business David laughed and said that maybe the odds weren't so high after all.

David stood up. "What do you fancy to drink?"

Sarah stared over at the bar for inspiration and when none came she looked at Jane's sparkling drink. "I'll have what Jane's having, please."

David came back with two Babychams and a pint of bitter for himself.

When they were almost at the end of their drinks Sarah slipped out of her seat and went to the bar to buy another round. David made a fuss when she gave him the bitter, saying women shouldn't go to the bar, but she was pleased with herself as it gave her a feeling of independence.

Jane bought another round and then went over to the juke-box. She put several coins in it and then stood going through the list page by page. The first one she chose was "The House of the Rising Sun" by The Animals.

Sarah found herself more relaxed now with the comfortable atmosphere in the pub, the music and the Babychams. She felt it was one of the nicest pubs she'd ever been in. In fact, all the places – the shops, the restaurants and cafés – were nicer than anything she had ever been used to. She looked over at David who was looking across the pub at Jane picking her records and realised that they wouldn't be here if it wasn't for his big-hearted generosity. She wondered now if she had made that plain to him.

"David," she said, leaning forward to rest her clasped hands on the table, "I want to thank you very much for having me and Jane to stay this week. You've been a brilliant host and we've had a fantastic time. I'm very grateful. It's the first time I've felt truly relaxed since I came to England a year ago."

He turned towards her now and smiled, and she noticed that his gaze was somewhere over her shoulder rather than looking directly at her. "You're very welcome, Sarah. It's lovely to have people I know from Newcastle visiting, because in certain ways I miss it. I enjoy seeing them and taking them round the sights."

She hesitated. "I know you have other friends," she said, "but I'm thanking you because I realise I've not always been the best of friends to you . . ."

He shook his head. "You don't need to say any more," he said, still looking past her. "Everything is fine. We're fine."

But she couldn't let it rest. She felt compelled to explain herself further. To make things right between them. "I've never meant to hurt you or be rude to you." The words were tumbling out. "And I know at times I have been rude. It's just that things were so difficult when I first came over." She swallowed hard. "All the business about my cancelled wedding and then the situation with Harriet . . ."

He nodded. "You don't need to explain." His voice sounded strained and weary.

"But I do." Then, she felt tears welling up. "I feel awful that you left your family and friends to come down here when maybe . . . maybe if I had been different . . ."

He sat up and looked properly at her now. "Sarah . . . what's wrong? What are you trying to say?"

She realised then she didn't know what she wanted to say. She looked at him now and as their eyes held again, she felt something she had never felt before. An intense hot feeling moved from her chest to her stomach and then moved rapidly downwards to an area of her body she had hardly been aware of before.

Embarrassed in case he sensed what she was feeling, she looked away – looked over at Jane and the juke-box.

David lifted his drink and took a mouthful of it, then put it back down on the table.

A few moments later she stole another glance at him and this time she had the strangest, almost overwhelming urge to reach over and touch his face.

When he looked at her again she stood up and without saying anything went over to join her friend. Jane had still two choices left before her two-shillings ran out.

"I'm looking for the Righteous Brothers' 'You've Lost that Lovin' Feeling'," she said.

They flicked through a few of the pages until Sarah spotted it.

"Well done, you can pick the last one."

Sarah took her time going through the lists, trying not to think of the weird feelings she seemed to be developing for David McGuire. All the months he had been after her, all the times she had rejected him. As the melodious tones of the song started to play, Sarah thought how ironic it was that she had suddenly *found* something like a loving feeling – when it was all too late.

"Sarah," Jane whispered. "Are you all right?"

Sarah looked at her.

"It's just you seem a bit off – or quiet – with David." She glanced over at the table. "And he doesn't look as cheery as he usually does. Have you had a row with him or something?"

"Not at all," Sarah said. "We're getting on great. I was just thanking him for being so good to us." She leaned in closer to her friend. "Don't forget he's been in here drinking all afternoon. I'm not saying he's drunk or anything, but it's bound to have an effect."

Jane raised her eyebrows. "True. I never thought of that."

Sarah quickly picked "Mr Tamburine Man" as she thought it might cheer things up, and then they went back to the table.

"Right," David said, clapping his hands and looking from one to the other. "What's the plan? We need to go and eat somewhere."

The girls looked at each other.

"You decide," Jane said.

"Ah no," David replied, "it's your last night and it's got to be what you two want."

"Is Camilla joining us for the meal?" Sarah asked.

"I have to ring her and let her know where we're going. She was working until five and then going home to get changed." He nodded out to the door. "There's a phone box outside."

"What about that lovely Italian restaurant you took us to the first night?" Jane asked. "It's near your flat and we can just walk home."

"Great – that's fine by me. Sarah?"

"Yes," she agreed, "it was lovely. One of the best places we've been." She lifted her half-full glass of Babycham and took a sip. "I don't know if I should finish this – I've had enough already!"

David grinned at her now – looking like his old self. "Go on," he said, "live life dangerously for once."

Sarah lifted the glass to her lips and took another mouthful and then she caught Jane's eye and they both started to giggle. Then, she was vaguely aware of someone at the bar watching them. When she glanced over she saw it was a tall, dark-haired young man in a smart business suit. She looked quickly away in case he thought she was eyeing him up, and then a few seconds later, something made her look over again and she saw he was coming towards their table.

Recognition suddenly hit her and her whole body froze. *My God,* she thought, this *can't be happening . . .*

But it was happening. She looked up properly and there was Con Tierney standing right in front of her.

"Hello, Sarah," he said, "Orla told me you might be in here." He glanced at David and Jane. "Is there any chance we might have a few words?"

Her heart was thumping hard against her ribcage. "No, Con. I don't think that would be a good idea."

"Please," he said. "There are some things I need to say. I'm not going to get this chance again."

David suddenly stood up. "Look, I don't know who you are – but you heard her, she doesn't want to talk to you."

Con straightened up and it was obvious that he was good three or four inches taller than David. "I don't mean to cause any problem here or anything but –"

"You heard her," David repeated, his tone more definite.

Sarah moved now, sensing that things might take a wrong turn. She couldn't do that to David. "Right," she said to Con, pointing to a table over at the window. "You have exactly five minutes."

Con started moving towards the table and David slowly sat back down.

"I'm sorry," Sarah said to David. "I'll explain later."

"Is it him?" David asked. "Is it the guy you were going to marry?"

"Yes," she said. "I met his sister in the exhibition hall – but she didn't tell me he was with her."

"I'll be watching," David told her. "I'll watch every move he makes."

"It'll be okay," she said. "He's not going to do anything."

Sarah listened while Con told her how much he'd missed her, how his life was ruined after she left and how he had only just started to pick himself back up.

"I miss you every single day," he told her. "And I blame myself every single day for what happened."

"It's all in the past, Con," she told him. "I've forgotten what happened. I'm grand." She talked faster to get it over with. "I told Orla earlier that I was settled and happy in England, and it's the truth." She looked him straight in the eye. "I think you might have done me a favour."

"How?" he said, a note of desperation in his voice.

"I don't think we were really suited." Her voice was quiet and calm. "I don't think we would have been that happy together."

"You only think that because of what happened. You're forgetting how well we got on before I feckin' well ruined it . . ." He rubbed a hand over his face. "I can't believe I was such a fool, throwing everything away for a few minutes of – what?"

Sarah raised her eyebrows. "You should have thought of that at the time. And you should have thought of the little life it might create . . . the little life Patricia lost."

"Aw, Sarah," he said, shaking his head. "She meant nothing to me."

"More shame on you," Sarah said. "If you caused all that devastation for nothing."

He dropped his head in his hands. "I've learned my lesson. I've not had a happy day since it all happened." He was silent for a few moments then he looked up at her. "You've changed," he said. "I could never have imagined you without the long blonde hair – but you're more beautiful than ever." He looked at her black dress with the daisy buttons. "Orla said you looked like a model and she was right."

"You're right, Con, my hair and clothes have changed. But they're only outside things – I've actually changed far more inside."

"How?" he said.

"I've discovered things about myself I never knew. I've been studying at college and my marks are up at the top with every exam. I've helped to turn an ailing business around and put it back on its feet." She smiled. "And I've learned to live in a strange new country and stand on my own two feet without feeling I need a man to look after me. I've done all that completely on my own."

He reached over to grasp her hand but she pulled it away.

"Just think," he told her. "If you've done all that on your own, how much more we could do together. Orla and me are starting a new venture together in the New Year. We're opening up a store that will sell both decorating materials and furniture, and it will be all laid out in sections with Orla choosing everything from wallpaper to matching curtains and bed linen and lamps."

"It all sounds very promising." He had just described the kind of business that had done David's flat up. It had worked in London and it could work in Dublin. Con was a hard worker and so was Orla. They would put their mind to it and they would do well.

"But you could be part of it," he said. "Just think, if you were to do all the sewing and designing of the curtains and things – we could work around you." He looked deep into her eyes. "We had dreams together, Sarah, and it's not too late. We could pick up where we left off."

"We did have dreams together," she told him, "but it's far too late." She looked at her watch now. "I've given you the five minutes I promised, Con, and that's it." She moved her chair back.

"Don't go, Sarah, Please give me one more chance. You can see I've changed, I've learned. You can see I'd do anything to get you back . . ." His voice faltered and his eyes welled up. "Please . . ."

A wave of pity came over her and, without taking time to think about it, she reached over and squeezed his hand. "I do believe you've changed, Con. Sincerely, I do. But I've changed too and I know from the bottom of my heart that things would never work out between us. The thing is – I don't love you any more and I'm not sure I ever did."

She wanted to tell him that she never had the right type of

feelings for him but she felt she had hurt him enough. While she knew he was a hard worker and deep down a decent lad – she realised now she never had felt the necessary physical attraction towards him that would make a good marriage.

She never experienced the intense, overwhelming feelings with Con that she'd felt earlier with David McGuire. She never knew they existed. It made her wonder now if, had she understood Con's needs instead of getting angry with him, the thing with Patricia Quinn would never have happened. It was something she would never know.

What she did know for sure was that splitting up was the right thing. Fate had intervened in order that she could lead the fulfilling life in Newcastle that she now had – and she was grateful for it.

She stood up now. "I've got to go, Con. But I just want to say something before I do."

He moved to his feet. "Goodbye – is that what you want to say?"

"It's more than that. I want you to know that I forgive you for what happened, that it's over and done with, and I don't hold it against you any more." She smiled at him, amazed at feeling so calm. "I wish you all the best with your business and with everything else in your life." She lowered her voice. "Now, please walk out of the pub, Con, and let me get on with the rest of my life."

He just looked at her, shrugged and then nodded. "I can't expect you to be fairer than that. Good luck and God bless . . ." His eyes filled again.

She knew to kiss him would be too much, so she put her two hands out and squeezed his and then she walked back to her friends.

CHAPTER 40

The following Monday Lucy listened with rapt interest as Sarah told her all about the fashion show and all the shops they had visited in London. Then, when Sarah gave her the make-up she had bought for her, she tried it out and they had a great discussion about the logo design and packaging.

When Sarah brought the Bazaar and Biba carrier bags out, Margaret and Lucy were mesmerised with the things she had bought. They studied the stitching and the materials and the buttons and fasteners, and turned each garment inside out to see how it was made.

"There's a whole new world opening up out there in fashion," Sarah told them. "And when you see the designs for 1966 it's even more inspiring."

At one o'clock Lucy asked Margaret to hold the fort for them so she and Sarah could go to lunch together. When they came out of the shop Sarah automatically turned to the left but Lucy guided her in the opposite direction.

"We're meeting Peter in the Station Hotel," she said. "He has some news for us."

"About what?"

"Wait and see. Tell me about David. All about his shop and flat and this new girlfriend of his."

Sarah recounted every detail she could remember. "He was the most wonderful host to me and Jane and Camilla is lovely, a bubbly bright, intelligent girl. They're very well suited."

"And does he seem happy?" Lucy wanted to know.

"I think he does," Sarah said. "But he did say there are things about Newcastle that he missed." A picture of David flew into her mind and it brought back the incident in the pub which she had been trying to forget – when she realised her feelings towards him had suddenly changed from friendship to something else. Just thinking about him brought the same physical sensation back which made her feel all strange and awkward. She had lain awake the last night in London thinking about him, and she'd lain awake again last night back in the flat in Newcastle. She knew now, without a shadow of a doubt that she was in love with him. From the minute they had first met, she knew she liked him more than any other lad she had ever met, but she hadn't anticipated, after all this time, that those feelings would turn into such a strong passion.

She changed the subject around then and went on to tell Lucy about meeting Con Tierney.

"And you really felt nothing?" Lucy asked as they walked into the hotel foyer. "No anger, no resentment, no feeling of wanting to make him suffer?"

"Not by the end. It's all gone and we wished each other well." She sighed. "It's actually been a big relief. I feel I can go back to Ireland next year for Sheila's wedding, and to finally see James's little girl without feeling awkward about meeting him or his family. Orla will have told everyone they met me and it will all have died down by the time I see them next."

"I could see a change in you, when you walked into the shop this morning. There's something different about you, and now I know what it is."

For a moment Sarah wanted to tell her what the real change was, but she knew how selfish it was going to sound. Lucy would háve every right to tell her what a foolish, immature girl she had been to let David McGuire move away to London to get over her, and then change her mind when he was settled in a new life with a lovely girl like Camilla. She would also have to point out that Sarah was acting nearly as badly as Con Tierney, thinking she could cause hurt and embarrassment and then expect David to forget it.

Peter was sitting at a table waiting for them. He gave both women a peck on the cheek and then he gestured to the barman, who first brought over three tall thin glasses and then a silver ice bucket with a bottle of champagne.

Sarah watched with some confusion as the waiter opened the bottle and then poured the bubbly liquid into the flutes. Lucy and Peter waited until he had gone and then Peter lifted two glasses and handed one each to the women.

"We're here to celebrate something big today," he said. "The start of your sparkling new career, Sarah."

"Well, thank you . . ." Sarah said, looking from one to the other. "But I'm not sure I really understand."

"I think Lucy would probably like to explain, since it was really her idea."

Lucy took a deep breath. "For some time, I've come to think your talent is wasted in Harrison's, Sarah. You've outgrown us and you need something to challenge your talent and help it develop further." She glanced across the table. "I've discussed it with Peter and we think we've found the very thing."

"What do you mean?"

"Before you went to London," Lucy said. "I put an offer in on the old building next to the bookshop – you know the one that's been closed for the last few years?"

"Yes," Sarah said, "I do . . ."

"I heard on Friday that it's been accepted, and it's just a case of waiting for all the documents to be signed now." She looked at Sarah and smiled. "Aren't you going to ask what we're going to do with it?"

"I have no idea."

"It's going to be your boutique," Lucy told her. "A place where you can show and sell all your fabulous designs."

Sarah's hands flew to cover her mouth as she tried to take it all in. "But how? How can I afford to buy a building?"

"I've worked out all the financial details," Lucy said. "And I think you can actually afford it yourself. But I'm prepared to put up a share of the money or go as guarantor on the mortgage if there are any difficulties."

Sarah bit her lip. "But I don't know anything about owning a business and all that it involves. I don't think I'm up to it."

Lucy noticed Sarah was trembling and she reached over to reassure her. "But I know all about owning a business and so does Peter – and you actually know a lot more than you think." She squeezed Sarah's arm. "Harrison's is not big enough for all your ideas. We sold out of all the dresses and skirts while you were away and we've orders for more. The clothes side is taking over the sewing business."

"Well, we can leave the clothes," Sarah said. "I'm happy with the cushions and curtains. I'm happy in Harrison's and I don't think I'm ready for anything else just yet."

"You are, Sarah. You just need a little time to think it all over."

"What about you? Don't you still need me in the shop?"

"But you'll only be across the lane," Lucy laughed. "That's the main reason I thought of it. I was actually thinking of expanding Harrison's again to have a separate area for clothes, but then I realised that it's trying to mix two separate businesses. The shop is perfect as it is for the sewing end, and I would probably lose my older customers if we mixed them with all the youngsters who are only interested in fashion."

Light was starting to dawn on Sarah. It was beginning to make sense.

"I also thought that you could keep on the flat, and still take in alterations which would give you extra money towards your mortgage."

Peter leaned forward. "If you ladies don't mind me chipping in,

380

I think from what Lucy's told me that it would be wise for you – after the initial opening phase – to take on shop assistants to sell your designs in the boutique, while you spend your time sourcing all the materials and making them." He paused. "I've had a look at the building and it's not as bad as I thought. It's a case of repairing the roof and the outside of the building and then damp-proofing and plastering the inside and putting in central heating. It would be up to you then to decide on the décor and furnishings."

Sarah's mind suddenly began to tick over. She could already picture the inside of the boutique in her head – right from the colours down to the display furniture and accessories. Unconsciously, she had been planning all this when she was walking around the boutiques in London, absorbing all the details she would take from each and add to her own ideas if she were ever to own such a place.

"I wonder if I dare . . ." she said, looking at them.

"I'll help with any finances," Lucy reassured her. "My father left me quite a bit of money plus a house in London my mother owned, so I'd be delighted to give you an interest-free loan."

"And you have plenty of time to sort things out," Peter said. "It will take a few months to get it ready. I reckon the building could be sorted and your stock all ready in time for an Easter opening."

Then, as if a light bulb had suddenly been switched on in a dark room, Sarah knew. She knew she could do it. "I have quite a bit of money saved," she said. "and my brother gave me some when I moved over and I put it straight in the bank and I've never touched it." She looked a Lucy and started to laugh. "It's a brilliant idea!"

Lucy hugged her then and so did Peter.

"I've asked around, and everyone is saying that it's the perfect time to open a boutique like this in Newcastle," Peter said. "Everything is changing – the music, the fashions, people's views on things. The sixties are like no other time in history." He lifted his glass. "To Sarah," he said. "To her new business venture!"

They all clinked glasses and took a drink of the champagne, then Lucy put her glass on the table.

"There's one more thing," she said. "And I thought I would be thrifty and celebrate it while Peter's paying for the champagne."

Peter started to laugh and Sarah looked at them in a bemused fashion.

Lucy lifted her handbag and brought out a small box. She opened it to show Sarah the three-diamond gold band. "Peter and I are engaged, and you're the first one to know!"

Sarah stared at the ring and then she suddenly couldn't see it as her eyes were filled with tears. She hugged her friend tightly. "You deserve this," she said, "You deserve all the happiness in the world."

The glasses were topped up and a second toast was made.

"We're going down to Durham later this afternoon to show it to Charlotte," Lucy said, rubbing her own damp eyes. "And we're going to tell her she can be a flower girl at the wedding in November." She looked at Sarah. "Needless to say, you'll be making your own bridesmaid dress and hers as well."

"What about your wedding dress?" Sarah said.

"But I thought . . ." Lucy faltered for a moment. "I thought that you wouldn't consider making one again."

Sarah shrugged. "That was last year – this year things are different." She grinned. "I've seen some lovely short wedding designs. I have them back in the flat."

CHAPTER 41

Sarah spent Christmas with Lucy and Peter, who had married the month before, and this time all three went in the morning laden with gifts for Charlotte. The structural work on the shop was already completed and Sarah planned to go and pick wallpaper and furnishings in the January sales. She had also started collecting items for display and had built up a collection of mannequins, antique shawls, hats and jewellery, and a set of six old French chairs she found in an auction.

Harrison's was busier than ever and she was still working long into the night doing alterations and building up her stock of dresses and skirts and tunics for the shop.

Lisha and her mother were now helping several evenings a week, Lisha cutting out and sewing patterns and her mother tacking and pressing seams. Sarah had also taken on two new members of staff – Adele, a curly-haired blonde girl who was passionate about clothes and had experience of working in a boutique in London, and Diana, a brunette who was studying fashion in the evenings as Sarah had done. Lisha would now be working on a Saturday in the boutique and during her school holidays.

Sarah had struggled to find a name for the business, trying to find something in keeping with the London boutiques when Lucy said, "Why don't you just call it 'Love'? Apart from the obvious link with your name, it fits right in with the popular music and the style of the clothes."

Sarah looked at her. "You're right – Love it is!"

She had kept David up to date with her plans and they met up for a meal on Boxing Night. She had hoped that her feelings for him would have gone back to that of a platonic friendship, but when she caught sight of him outside the restaurant from across the road, her pulse quickened and she was tongue-tied by the time they were inside.

Sarah felt more relaxed after the meal and a couple of glasses of wine. They sat chatting over coffee and David told her all about the book business in London and then listened as she described her plans for Love.

"Pilgrims Lane didn't know what hit it when you arrived," David laughed. Then he suddenly looked serious. "I don't think I knew what hit me either. It's funny looking back at it. It seems like a long time ago. A lot of water has passed under the bridge since then."

Sarah decided to take a chance. "I don't know what I would have done without you when I first moved over," she said quietly. "I know I didn't show it, but I knew you were always there . . ."

"It's great that we're still friends," David said. Then he paused. "Did you hear from the Irish fellow again?"

"Con?" she said. "No. When I spoke to him then, I made sure he got the message loud and clear that there would never be anything between us again."

He looked at her seriously for a few moments and then he gave his customary wink. "Ah, you're very good at that, Miss Love. You certainly know how to keep us men in our place. The big fellow looked heartbroken. A year later and he still hadn't got over you."

Sarah felt her heart sink. "You know what happened there, David." She swallowed hard. "And anyway, I told him it was for the best. We were never really suited . . . If we'd got married we would have just limped along."

384

"I wonder if any of us know how a marriage will turn out," David mused. "I suppose it's like anything – a business, a gamble or whatever. You just have to look at the odds and then take a calculated risk."

"You sound very cynical all of a sudden, Mr McGuire," Sarah said, trying to make light of it. "Surely there are plenty of marriages that are sure to turn out well? Look at Lucy and Peter."

"True," he said. "Now there's an interesting story. Who would have believed that someone could change so much in just over a year?"

"People can change." She looked straight at him. "I've changed . . . I see things very differently to how I did when I first came here. You have to understand the circumstances in which I left Ireland and then all the difficulties of starting a new life."

He nodded. "Tell me about it – I know how I felt first in London. I was lucky that I had some family there and I've made good friends."

There was an awkward silence, then Sarah said, "How is Camilla?"

A smile came on his face. "She's great," he said. "She was promoted a few weeks ago. She's moved up a few steps from the dog shows."

Sarah forced a laugh.

"I don't see her so much," David said. "The romance thing fizzled out after a couple of months, but she's a great girl and we catch up with each other now and again."

Sarah's heart leapt. "So you're not going out with anyone?"

He shook his head. "I'm taking a leaf out of your book. I'm not going to get tied down with anyone for a while. It's a big world out there."

Sarah knew then that he held it against her. Blamed her that he had to move to get her out of his system. She knew now that there was no chance of them ever turning the clock back. David McGuire had moved on.

They sat for a while longer and the conversation lightened up a bit when David asked if she'd heard about the situation with Robert Wright – the new manager of Thomson's bookshop.

"No," Sarah said. "I didn't hear anything."

"Just last week," David said, "he got done for embezzling the books. It's going to be a big court case."

"Oh, God!" Sarah exclaimed.

He laughed heartily. "Can you believe it? Thomson's doesn't do bad for a bookshop, but it's not exactly a million-dollar business. You think he'd have gone and got a job in a bank if he was that way inclined."

They left the restaurant and David walked her back to the flat, telling her all about his new niece and about his granny and granddad's upcoming Golden Wedding. She thought about asking him in for a coffee, but didn't have the courage. What was the point? Even if he was still slightly interested in her, he now lived and worked in London.

As he bent to give her a kiss on the cheek, Sarah felt her whole body trembling and wondered if he noticed. If he did, he said nothing. They said goodnight. He waited until Sarah opened the shop door and locked it again from the inside, and then he was gone.

He couldn't have gone more than a few steps along the lane when Sarah collapsed over the counter, sobbing and crying. Then, when she composed herself, she checked the time on her watch and went over to the counter and picked up the phone.

Lucy was shocked when she heard the state her friend was in and took several minutes trying to calm her down.

"Wait there," she finally said. "I'll get the car and I'll be down in five minutes."

Sarah was in her dressing-gown, curled up in a chair in front of the gas fire when Lucy came in. She got up and went over to bury her face in Lucy's shoulder and she sobbed again. Eventually, when she could finally compose herself, she told Lucy the whole story, leaving nothing out.

"Why don't you tell him straight out tonight?" Lucy said.

"I can't," Sarah said, rubbing her eyes. "He's different, he's not as open as he used to be . . . and he's more or less told me that he's not interested in going out with anyone. He's broken up with Camilla and if he wanted to have anything to do with me again, he certainly isn't showing it."

"But, Sarah, look at it from his point of view. You sent him away . . . his work and life is down in London now. What a huge risk it would be for him to start seeing you again, travelling all the way up from London at weekends." She paused. "Are you certain about your feelings for him?"

Sarah sniffed and nodded. "More certain than anything I've ever felt before. We can talk about anything and we laugh at the same things and I like his family." She looked at Lucy. "I knew all those before, but what I've just discovered is that I feel something more that I never felt with Con or anyone else – I want to kiss him and lie in his arms – and wake up in bed beside him in the morning. I never understood or felt those things before. Now I can see how people get into all sorts of situations through being physically attracted to someone." Her eyes filled up again. "I've found the last – and most important – part of the jigsaw between me and David."

Lucy shook her head. "Dear God . . . all the opportunities you had with him and you discover now . . ."

Sarah's eyes filled up. "When it's all too late."

CHAPTER 42

Love's opening was planned for the first Saturday in April – just a week before Easter. Sarah decided on a six o'clock launch when all the other businesses were closing.

By the time the week of the opening came round Sarah was totally exhausted. She had finished work in Harrison's in mid-March shortly after the decorators moved out of the new boutique and then the preparations began. The shelves and the furniture had to be installed and Sarah was reminded of the renovations that had been made in the sewing shop the year before. There was one big difference this time – she was going it alone.

Lucy and Peter helped with anything they could do, but Sarah found she had to do the majority of it on her own. The vision she had for the shop was all in her head – pictures and images – and it was difficult to put it into words. She could only really tell if something was going to work when she tried it out. And only she knew when it was right. Sometimes it would take ten attempts at something, but she was compelled to keep going till she got the look that she wanted.

The first major thrill for her was seeing the plum-coloured flocked Victorian wallpaper going up and then the gold-sprayed shelves and mirrors. A huge, shimmering crystal chandelier took centre place and was complemented by smaller versions on the walls.

The green Chesterfield sofas, inspired by the ones in the London pub, were put in place outside the velvet-curtained changing rooms. Tall oriental vases with peacock feathers stood at strategic points and a wine-coloured chaise-longue was decorated with an antique shawl and a gold velvet tasselled cushion. The gold pigeon-holed shelves were filled with bags and scarves and hats, and colourful knitted berets that Lisha and her mother had made.

The day before opening, Sarah, Adele, and Diana, the girls from Victoria Street, Lisha, her brother and her mother started on the mammoth task of setting up the rails and displaying all the dresses and skirts and tunics, the tartan trousers and capes. Sarah was amazed at all the stock she had made and packed away over the last six months, and as she opened each box she got a thrill from seeing dozens of the items that she knew had never been on sale in Newcastle before.

They had a music system installed in the shop which would play all the Top Twenty hits, and Sarah and the staff would be wearing dresses from the rails instead of shop uniforms. The shop would officially open to the public at two o'clock, then at six o'clock the local business people who had been invited would arrive and Peter Spencer would do the opening ceremony with a bottle of champagne. Sarah had also hired a catering company at the top of the lane to do trays of finger-food and glasses of wine or Coke.

They worked at the shop, hanging clothes and pinning others to the wall for display, until eight o'clock on the Friday night. Then, when Sarah felt they couldn't squeeze in another item without it starting to look like a jumble sale, she called a halt. She took all the helpers to a café for fish and chips, deliberately avoiding the one with the juke-box that she'd gone to with David. Afterwards, she went back to the flat to have an early night so she would be on top form for the important day ahead.

* * *

On the Saturday morning, Sarah bathed and dressed and came downstairs just as Lucy was unlocking Harrison's door. They had a coffee together and when Margaret arrived they went across the lane to have a look at the boutique.

"It's amazing," Lucy told her. "And to think you've stitched every single item in it."

Sarah walked around the rails, seeing things with a fresh eye. "It's as good as it can be for now," she said. "I'll learn as I go along and I'll improve."

"Sa-rah!" Lucy said, her voice full of disapproval. "You need to know when you've done a good job and not keep trying to better it. There's not a shop like this in Newcastle and, when you look around these rails and walls, you should have a huge sense of achievement. Two years ago you were sitting in a little bedroom in Ireland dreaming of all this."

Sarah looked at her and then she had the good grace to laugh. "Okay," she said. "I'm glad I can always rely on you to keep my feet on the ground."

"Or to take your head out of the clouds!" Lucy said, laughing along with her.

* * *

Sarah went off to the hairdresser's mid-morning and had her hair trimmed and blown dry into a perfectly straight bob. When she came back to the flat, there were two letters waiting for her – both of them with Irish stamps. One was a Good Luck card from Sheila Brady and her fiancé on the opening of Love and the second one was a letter from her sister-in-law, Martina, informing her that she and James were expecting their second baby in the summer.

She went on to say that they wanted Sarah to be the godmother and that if they planned the christening around the same time as Sheila Brady's wedding, then they hoped she would be able to attend both. Martina went on to say that James and her brothers were building an extension on to the house, which meant they would have another bedroom. It would be finished in plenty of time for the summer, so she would be the first one to sleep in it. The letter even finished off with a PS wishing her all the best for her new shop, which Sheila Brady had told her all about.

Sarah walked over to the window with the letter in her hand and looked down onto the cobbles of Pilgrims Lane. She wondered what had brought about the change in her sister-in-law, but could come up with no answers. Then, as she saw a mother and a young girl of around eight walking along, she thought that motherhood might have softened Martina's attitude. She shrugged to herself. She didn't know and she didn't really care. What mattered was the fact that an overture had been made, which might help Sarah to be a part of the Love family again in a very small way.

She didn't want anything more than to be an auntie who came home from England every so often, to spend a few pleasant days in the area she grew up in. She knew she would never go back there to live. She had moved on. Newcastle was now her adopted city. It had looked after her and allowed her to grow and thrive when the situation she left back home had almost crushed her. The place of her birth would always have a special place in her heart, but Newcastle was now her home.

As she started to turn away, something about Thomson's bookshop caught her eye. It was the *Closed* sign on the door. She had heard rumours about there being financial problems after the scandal with Robert Wright. A wave of sadness washed over her to think that the shop had gone downhill so fast. It had been a popular, thriving business when David McGuire had been manager.

Sarah stared down at the bookshop for a few more moments, and then a terrible feeling of guilt replaced the sadness. If David hadn't left because of her, the shop would still be doing as well as ever. Because of her selfish actions, Thomson's might well be closing down, while Love boutique was just beginning. The thought almost overwhelmed her, making it hard for her to breathe. She went back over to the sofa and sat with her eyes closed until she heard Lucy coming up the stairs.

"I have a special delivery for Miss Love," Lucy said in a high, almost skittish voice. Sarah moved now and went to meet her in the hallway.

Lucy was carrying a huge bouquet of flowers. "Are you all right?" she asked when she saw Sarah's serious face.

"I'm grand . . . I was just having a bit of a doze." She couldn't start unloading all her miseries about David again. Lucy had made it clear that she had missed her chance and needed to get over it.

"These have just been delivered for you." Lucy carefully handed over the cellophane-wrapped flowers over.

"Gosh . . . I wonder who on earth has sent such a huge bouquet."

"Let me get the card for you." Lucy peeled the Sellotape off the side of the wrapper and then handed Sarah the small greeting card.

"It's from David, wishing me good luck . . ." She felt a lump coming into her throat, but forced the thoughts away. "Isn't that kind of him?" She bent her head to smell them.

"It really is." Lucy looked at Sarah. "Are you nervous about this afternoon?"

"Yes, I suppose I am."

"Don't be – everything is organised." She smiled. "You just have to go into Love's and pretend that you are still in Harrison's. It's the exact same process. You're just going to be selling clothes instead of wool."

Sarah smiled back. "Will you come across and see how things are going?"

"Of course! Try and stop me." She looked down at her conservative dress and cardigan. "I brought one of your earlier creations to change into. I didn't want to let the side down by being old-fashioned."

"Don't worry – we serve everyone – apart from Mrs Brown!"

Lucy lifted her eyes to the ceiling. "I don't think I'll ever be able to laugh about her."

"I wonder what happened to her," said Sarah. "She just seemed to disappear. I often thought I'd bump into her around the shops."

"Good riddance," Lucy said. "Now, I must go downstairs and

let Margaret go for her lunch, and I think you need to get all dolled up and go across to your new shop."

Sarah went into her bedroom, opened the wardrobe and lifted out a fitted black dress with elbow-length sleeves, which had a row of large white, heart-shaped buttons going down the front. It was one of the first dresses she made after her trip to London, inspired by the Mary Quant designs she had bought. She had a dozen of the same style on a rack over in the shop. She then pulled on white tights, then her black stretch PVC boots. She put on her dangling black cube earrings and a row of black plastic bangles on her arm, then tried some black and white beads, but quickly decided the hearts on the dress were enough decoration and took the beads back off.

She spent more time than usual on her make-up and realised she was definitely nervous when her hands were trembling as she applied a modest pair of false eyelashes. The huge spidery ones, finished off with painted lashes, which she had seen in London were definitely not for her. She finished with blue eye-shadow and a pale pink lipstick and then stood back to view herself.

She could see she had lost weight over the last few months and reckoned she would have to be careful not to lose any more, as she was just on the right side of slim as opposed to being skinny. From the blonde bob down to her fashionably flat black boots, she looked every inch like the fashion models she had seen on the runway in London. Hopefully, when the shop was up and running, she wouldn't have to spend so much time there, and she could go back to the more natural look she preferred for sitting at her sewing-machine.

For the time being she would enjoy wearing the clothes, the make-up and the jewellery as she knew it endorsed all the products she was selling.

* * *

There was a crowd of around fifty girls waiting outside Love when the doors opened at two o'clock to the sound of Wayne Fontana and The Mindbenders singing "Game of Love". Sarah was amazed

393

when they all rushed forward, as though it was a Sale day, and then felt gratified when they reached the middle of the shop and came to a sudden halt to look around.

She had no time to feel anxious or nervous as customers were coming up to check the sizes with her or to ask how many items they could take to try on. Adele was on duty outside the changing room to issue tags with the number of garments, and Lisha was standing at the opposite side watching for anyone who needed help with sizes or to reach up to the higher shelves. Diana was positioned behind the till with Sarah watching to see if she needed more help.

Sarah felt a great sense of pride when she saw the three attractive girls dressed in matching white tunics with wide black plastic belts, black short skirts and the popular flat, PVC stretchy boots.

The afternoon flew in and the stock flew out. Several dresses were favourites and the racks were soon empty and Sarah had to go upstairs and bring down more. By five o'clock several of the rails had no dresses on them with all the replacements sold too.

Sarah noted down the designs that were gone and was already planning a full day's work tomorrow to make sure she had more in stock for Monday.

The hats and scarves were a big hit too, since the spring weather was still on the cool side. Sarah kept a close watch on everything, checking which things were favourites and which ones were not hitting the exact note she had hoped for.

And then it was half past five and the last customer was served, giving the girls little time to tidy things up and get it ready for the formal opening at six o'clock. Lucy came across wearing a black A-line sleeveless dress which had a big daisy motif around the hem which stopped just above her knee. She wore a white skinny-rib top underneath and two rows of long black beads.

"You look fantastic!" Sarah told her.

Lucy leaned forward in a conspiratorial manner. "I had to make a special effort when my dear husband has been honoured by being asked to make such an important opening speech."

"Oh, don't!" Sarah said, "You're making me feel nervous talking like that."

"Relax," Lucy told her, patting her hand. "It will all go perfectly."

More and more people arrived, and Sarah found she would be busy chatting to one group and then she would feel a hand on her shoulder and turn to find another group waiting for her behind.

When it was busy enough, Sarah got Diana to bring out the trolley with the glasses and the wine to distribute to the guests. She then signalled to Diana and Adele to go around the crowd with bowls of cashew nuts and trays of cheese and pineapple on cocktail sticks, and round crackers spread with pâté and cheese-spread with shrimps.

Peter arrived and, after checking the microphone system for his speech, he and Sarah went through to the stockroom to get the champagne and the trays of flutes. When she came back into the shop, she was delighted when she caught sight of Harriet Scott making her way through the crowd, hand in hand with a short, stocky fellow with longish hair and a beard.

"This is Kevin," she told Sarah and Lucy, her eyes sparkling. "He's a pharmacist in the hospital. He couldn't believe it when I told him you made all these clothes yourself."

"If you knew the hours she puts in," Lucy laughed. "You wouldn't be surprised at all."

Kevin laughed and shook hands with them and both he and Harriet congratulated Sarah on the shop opening and gave her a card and a box of chocolates. Sarah got them wine and, after chatting for a while, Harriet dragged him off to look at the rails of clothes.

A short while later Peter made his way through the crowds to Lucy. "I think it's time to start the formalities now. I don't think many more people can fit in the shop."

Her eyes darted to the art-deco clock above the service counter. "Give me two minutes. I just need to check that everyone is here. You find Sarah and let her know you're ready to begin."

When Lucy came back she waved to Peter from the door and he took up the microphone.

Everyone fell silent, eyes fixed on him.

He started off telling the guests about a young girl from Ireland sewing in the bedroom of a white-washed cottage, dreaming of the day when legions of young women would be walking around wearing outfits she had designed.

Sarah kept a fixed smile on her face as she heard the sentimental description of her teenage years and wished this part of the night was over. She felt self-conscious at being the focus of everyone's gaze, but knew it was the business end of things that she would have to endure.

Peter went on for a while, explaining the work behind getting the building ready and the long hours Sarah had put into getting the stock ready for the opening. Sarah occasionally stole glances at the assembled crowd and offered up a silent prayer of thanks that so many people had turned up to support her. She looked at Lucy, whose gaze remained firmly fixed on Peter and felt both happiness and a slight touch of envy at her friend's good fortune in finding such a solid, supportive and kind man.

Her mind wandered off for a few moments as she wondered if she would ever find anyone like that to share her life. She had come across plenty of men in her time in Newcastle – the handsome doctors at the party, the men who eyed her up in restaurants, the businessmen she came in regular contact with. But none of them had raised the smallest spark in her. There was only one man who had managed to do that.

Suddenly, there was a burst of applause and everyone turned towards her. Then she realised that Peter was beckoning her up to the microphone to say a few words.

She held her hands up and shook her head, but still found herself being propelled towards the front. And then she knew there was no point and gave in.

She took the microphone and then stood for a few seconds gathering her thoughts.

Her voice wavered when she started off but quickly became stronger and clearer.

"I have many, many people to thank here this evening," she said, "but there is one person who I will never be able to thank enough for the help, advice and friendship she has so freely given since I came to Newcastle not that long ago. That lovely lady is the owner of Harrison's shop across the way – Lucy Spencer – and I'd like you all to give her a huge round of applause!"

She then went on to thank Peter for all his legal and professional advice and all the local business people who had been so supportive, the staff of Love boutique, giving a special mention to Lisha and her mother who had helped with the making of some of the accessories on sale. She gave a special thanks to the girls in Victoria Street who had put up with the whirring of her sewing machine at all hours of the night, and got a big cheer of delight from Vivienne, Anna and Elizabeth. She looked for Jane but couldn't see her and then, just as she was winding up with final few words of thanks, she spotted her friend at the door with a well-dressed dark-haired man.

It was when Peter popped the cork on the bottle of champagne and the crowd all cheered, that something made her glance over at the door again to where Jane had been standing. Both she and her partner had moved. Lucy rushed forward to hug her and then Peter came over to them with half-filled champagne flutes.

"Thank you," Sarah said, holding the glass up to them both. "You have given me the biggest support I've ever had in my life."

Lucy touched her glass to Sarah's. "You have lots of people – lots of friends supporting you here today." She looked over Sarah's shoulder. "And you've a special one coming towards you now."

Sarah turned and saw Jane making her way through the crowd with a big beaming smile on her face. "Congratulations, darling!" she said, throwing her arms around Sarah's neck. "This is the start of something very, very big. But then, we all knew that."

Sarah's eyes filled with tears. "Oh, thank you!"

Jane let Sarah go and, smiling, stepped to one side.

Sarah's heart suddenly stopped. "My God . . ." The words wouldn't come.

"Congratulations," David McGuire said, taking her hands in his. "I decided I couldn't miss seeing the fruits of all that hard labour."

She looked at him, unable to take it in. "I can't believe you're here . . . I'd no idea . . . you sent the beautiful flowers . . ." She turned back to Jane but she had disappeared again. And then she realised that Lucy had moved as well. They were standing on their own.

David guided her by the elbow over to a space at the side of the room.

"I'm here because I got a phone call from your friend, Miss Harrison."

"Lucy? When did she phone?"

"Last week . . . but I wasn't sure whether to come or not. I wasn't even decided when I ordered the flowers yesterday . . ." He took a deep breath and shifted his gaze to the wall just above her head. "I don't know how to say this. I didn't want to come because I didn't want to be like the big Irish fellow . . . I couldn't bear it again."

"David . . ." Sarah said, her hand coming up to touch the side of his face. "You're nothing like him."

He looked directly at her now. "She said you told her you have feelings for me . . . more than just friendship?"

She looked into his eyes and knew she had too much to lose to stay silent. "I do," she said, "And I realised it some time ago. I love you, David – I love you with all my heart."

He didn't react, but there was something in his eyes that made her continue.

"And I know the right thing would have been to have said nothing to anyone – but I couldn't." She closed her eyes for a moment. "It would have killed me . . . I had to let my feelings out. So I told Lucy." She swallowed hard. "I don't even know if you have any feelings left for me . . ."

"And – what if I have?" There was vulnerability in his voice.

"I'm willing to try anything," she said determinedly. "Anything at all to make it work. I know that your life is down in London and I'm up here – and that's all my fault – but I'll travel down at weekends. If things work out, I'd even move to London if that's what it takes." The intensity of her feelings could not be mistaken. "Just tell me what I need to do, David . . . and I'll do it."

He seemed to consider her words for a moment and then suddenly the rigidity went from his face and he broke into a smile. His arms came around her waist and his mouth came down on hers. As she returned his warm hard kiss, Sarah knew without a doubt that she had found the friend, the confidant – the one true love she hadn't known she'd been searching for. The crowd and the music, the celebratory noise and everything else just fell away. They stood wrapped together until at some point they both became aware of clapping noises behind them.

Sarah eased out of her arms to find Peter and Lisha, and all the girls from the house cheering and clapping while a single tear trickled down Lucy's face.

* * *

Later, back in Sarah's flat, they talked about how they would manage the future.

"I'll come back to Newcastle," David told her as they sat on the sofa, with their arms wrapped around each other.

"How?" she asked.

"I don't know exactly how I'll do it, and it may take some time, but it's the only way that will work."

"What about the bookshop in London?"

"I'll see about selling my partnership in it," he said. "I have a feeling that some of the family will be interested in it." He shrugged. "If it works out that I can afford to keep the partnership, then we'll just get a manager in my place."

"And what will you do up here?"

"I'll find something." He sounded confident. "I can live at home until something comes up. I have savings and my grandparents have always told me that there's money there for each of the grandchildren from when they sold the building business. They offered me it for the shop in London, but I managed to raise the money myself."

He squeezed her shoulder. "I'm not worried at all."

"You know Thomson's are in financial difficulties?" she said. "I've heard they might be closing permanently."

He smiled at her. "I heard that too." He raised his eyebrows. "It was another reason I came up here today. I'm going to spend a bit of time on Monday, finding out what's going on there."

Sarah sat up straight. "Do you mean you didn't just come up to Newcastle to see me?"

He glanced away. "How could I know what was going to happen? How could I know you were going to tell me all those things?"

"Oh, David . . ." She buried her face in his chest. "I'll never be able to tell you how sorry I am for treating you like that." She was silent. "What will your family think of me? Will they hate me for taking so long to realise? Will they understand how difficult it was for me starting all over again after what happened in Ireland?"

"They understand already," he told her. "Every time I went home or phoned home they kept asking if I'd heard from you yet. My granddad even had a bet with me that we'd end up together. After last summer I wouldn't have given tuppence for his odds – but now the old sod will probably be rubbing his hands together in glee . . ."

Sarah laughed and then reached up to kiss him playfully on the nose. "I have so much to find out about you . . ."

"And I," he said, suddenly grabbing her and laying her sideways on the sofa, "am looking forward to getting to know every single inch of you." He then moved until her was lying on top of her and Sarah was left in no doubt as to what he meant.

The last time she had been in such a position with Con Tierney, her heart had been racing for all the wrong reasons and her instincts had been to fight him off.

With David, she knew they both felt exactly the same. When she realised she loved him, it was because she knew that she wanted and needed him in all the right physical ways. When the subject of marriage came up, as she knew it would, she would tell him it would have to be soon. Very soon.

The sky was dark and the streetlamps were on as he was leaving. They walked across to Thomson's bookshop and looked in through the shadowy window.

"Wouldn't that be amazing if we ended up with businesses next door to each other?" David said.

"I couldn't imagine anything more perfect. It would be a dream come true." She hugged his arm. "I'll be counting the days until you're back in Newcastle."

He halted, thinking. "If all goes to plan, we'll end up married and settled here, but I've often wondered will you miss Ireland? Will you some day think you might want to go back there to live?"

"My home is here," she told him with great certainty, "but there's a part of my heart in Ireland – in Tullamore – and it always will be."

"We can go over for a holiday any time you want."

"Oh, we will," she told him, tightening her grip on his arm. "I've already got you lined up to accompany me to a wedding and a christening in the summer."

He pulled her closer to him. "We'll have to check out the dates – we don't want it to clash with our own wedding plans."

Sarah smiled. "I suppose I'd better get started on the dress soon."

The End

If you enjoyed *Sarah Love*
by Geraldine O'Neill why not try
Leaving Clare also published by Poolbeg?
Here's a sneak preview of Chapter One.

LEAVING CLARE

Geraldine O'Neill

POOLBEG

CHAPTER 1

April 1958
County Clare, Ireland

Rose Barry woke at half-past eight to a blue sky more suited to August than April, and the smell of bacon and sausages wafting through the small cottage that she shared with her parents and grandmother Martha, her seventeen-year-old brother Paul and her two younger sisters Eileen and Veronica.

One of her first thoughts was whether Michael and Ruairí Murphy would call in at Slattery's pub that afternoon. Most of the local girls had an eye for them but working part-time in the only pub-cum-shop in the area gave the dark-haired, eighteen-year-old Rose a distinct advantage. Well, if they didn't come in during the afternoon for their usual Saturday game of cards, they would definitely be there later on. The two lads spent most weekend nights in Slattery's, joining in with the music sessions – Michael on the fiddle and Ruairí on the accordion.

Rose smiled at the thought of the day ahead and threw the bedcovers back.

Martha Barry had been up and about a good hour or more before Rose stirred. Dressed in her customary cross-over, flowery apron, she had lit the stubborn old Stanley range and then set about cooking breakfast for the whole family as she routinely did at the weekends. Rose's mother, Kathleen – a dark-haired, good-looking woman who was an older version of her daughter – had left the house around eight o'clock as usual. She worked in the local

Guards' Barracks, doing all the cooking and washing and general looking-after of the Guards.

"You should have taken a bit of a lie-in for yourself," Rose told her grandmother as she sat down at the white-painted kitchen table. The comment was only perfunctory, as it would have been a sad Saturday if she had no cooked breakfast made for her.

"Ah sure, a young girleen like you needs a decent bite when you have a good walk ahead of you and then be on your feet all day at work." Martha put the plate of bacon, sausage and black and white pudding in front of her grand-daughter, then affectionately tousled her thick, straight hair. "You can make a start on that. I have a bit of fried soda bread and an egg still cooking in the pan for you."

Then she went back to the range where she would stay contentedly for most of the morning until all the family had been fed.

The twenty-minute walk down to Slattery's bar at the quayside was all the more pleasant since it was such a lovely sunny morning, and Rose called out or stopped to chat to various neighbours who lived in the whitewashed cottages along the way. On a fine morning there were always people around the houses, bringing in turf or emptying ashes or going in and out tending to the cattle.

Rose's Saturday shift started off on a high note when she arrived at the pub to find that the landlord and his wife were all dressed up and ready to head out for a day in Galway. Mary Slattery was bustling around in her good red coat between the bar and shop, her black court shoes tapping on the old stone floor, while Joe was huffing and puffing about being made to wear a suit and kept running his finger inside the neck of his starched white shirt.

"Will you leave your shirt alone, for God's sake!" Mary hissed as she went to the till in the shop with a bag full of copper which would be needed for change.

Joe looked at Rose, rolled his eyes to the ceiling and sighed loudly.

Mary put her hands on her hips and gave him a long look. "Get yerself out to that car and get it warmed up," she told him, "and don't be acting the eejit with me this morning!"

Joe shook his head and smiled. "You're easy riled, Mary Slattery, you're easy riled."

Mary banged the small sack of coins down on the bar counter and then turned to look at Rose with a resigned look on her face. "What would you do with an *amadán* like that?"

Rose just smiled. She listened carefully as Mary Slattery ran through a list of instructions for the day.

"Now remember, no tick in the bar – *under any circumstances* – for Noel Pearson, and no tick in the shop for the Mullens and the Foleys." She tutted loudly. "I could kill that Joe for startin' that racket off – letting them pay when they like! They think we're running a charity here!"

Rose nodded her head understandingly, although she had already been told by the landlord to give a loaf and a few potatoes to the two aforementioned families any time they were in need. But always to make sure his wife wasn't around.

Mary picked her handbag up. "I know you're a sensible girl, Rose, and I can trust you to manage things on your own like you did when we went to the wedding. And if I'm satisfied, there might be a little bit extra in your pay this evening."

With a final glance about the premises, she went to join her husband.

Rose stood at the door of the pub watching as the landlord's car disappeared off along the coast road, then she went back inside, delighted to have the place to herself for the day.

It was rare that Rose had anywhere to herself. It was very hard to be alone in the Barrys' house. Especially in the colder weather when everyone congregated in the kitchen seeking the warmth and comfort of the old range. Occasionally on a warm summer day, Rose would go into the bedroom she shared with her grandmother and younger sisters, to lie on her bed and enjoy a few minutes of cool solitude. But it never lasted. After a while the younger ones would come looking for her, and if she chased them out her mother would appear shortly afterwards to check that she was all right.

Rose never quite found the words to explain her need for a bit of peace and quiet, to have some time to herself just to think. It always came out sounding a bit strange and broody.

"As long as you're all right," her mother would say. "As long as there's not something wrong . . . something you don't want to tell us."

And so it was easier for Rose to keep smiling and pleasant and join in with the general hustle and bustle of the house.

As she entered her teenage years and was allowed a bit more freedom, Rose found that walking down to the shop or post office on her own allowed her to have the space and the peace that she couldn't find at home. The mile or so there and back – feeling the fresh sea breeze running through her hair and the warmth of the sun on her face – gave her exactly what she needed. There were times when she walked really quickly to allow herself a short break later along the strand. Rose loved that. She could lose herself in the sound of the waves and among the small sea-pools in the rocks on the shoreline.

As she closed the door of the empty pub behind her, Rose decided that the chores could wait. Instead she slowly wandered around the bar, pausing at one of the four windows to gaze across the street to the small post office and the grey stony hills of The Burren which stretched out far beyond.

Nothing stirred apart from a few cattle in the field opposite.

Drifting to the back of the pub, she looked out over the shimmering, bluish-green water of Galway Bay where local fishermen eked out a seasonal living.

Then the bell from the small shop rang out, shattering the absolute silence and heralding the first of the morning's customers.

Rose had completed most of the tasks on the landlady's list by the time Ruairí and Michael Murphy arrived in the bar. She was delighted to see them but her pleasant, casual manner gave no indication that she held them in any greater affection than the other local lads.

After she served them, Rose gave half her attention to the glasses she was rinsing and drying and the rest to the two fair-haired brothers as they played cards at the table by the window.

Time passed as she pottered about behind the bar. It was lovely to be able to do things at her own pace without having to keep watching out for Mary Slattery. She glanced over at the two brothers again and Ruairí, the younger, caught her eye. She immediately felt herself blush. They were both good-looking lads but it was Michael she preferred.

Ruairí held up his almost empty glass, the white frothy Guinness dregs sliding to the bottom. "We'll have another two pints when you're ready, Rose!"

The shop bell sounded.

"I'll be back in two ticks," Rose said, putting her drying cloth down on the counter.

She went through the door behind the bar and stepped down into the little shop.

Two thin, pale faces looked up at her – Patrick and Ella Foley. Around ten or eleven years of age, they were somewhere in the middle of a squad of nearly a dozen children. Like the other members of the family, they were inadequately dressed and to Rose's mind they looked too skinny and underfed.

"A stone of spuds, Rose," Patrick said, heaving an old battered shopping bag up on the counter. The handles of the bag had broken and were reinforced with pieces of twine.

Rose weighed out the stone of potatoes for them and piled more on top, just as Joe would have done if his wife wasn't in the vicinity to witness it. Then she reached under the counter to the tray of currant buns and gave them two of the staler ones, left over from the day before.

"Don't tell a soul I gave you them," she ordered, "or Mrs Slattery will take my life."

As soon as they were finished eating, the two children lifted the heavy bag between them again and Rose held the door and stood watching as they started the good mile's walk back home with their awkward load.

Rose was just putting the head on the pints of Guinness when the bar door swung open and a large group of lads came through, loudly discussing the match they were all heading for. Rose felt her cheeks immediately flame up, uncomfortably aware of being the only female in the place – and because she would have to serve them all herself. The fact that her younger brother Paul was in the middle of them didn't help. She would have the worry of him trying to sneak a glass or two of Guinness when he wasn't eighteen and risking the wrath of her father if he found out. As usual, he gave her the briefest salute of acknowledgement before disappearing into a corner with the noisy crowd.

She carried the pints over to the Murphys, earning two big smiles from them. When she came back she was inundated with orders from the other group and time flew as she drew pints and poured lemonade.

Eventually there were only three lads left leaning on the bar. She flushed as she realised one of them was Liam O'Connor.

"Rose Barry! The finest lookin' girl in Kilnagree!" he announced, his hands drumming lightly on the counter. "'*The Darlin' Girl from Clare*'!"

Liam O'Connor was the tallest and most athletic-looking of all the lads in the parish and was hugely admired for his skills on the hurling field, being the only one of them to have reached the level to play in the county team. He worked hard and he played hard. Like many of the local lads, he kept two jobs going, working on the small family farm with his elderly father and helping his brother out with deliveries in his greengrocer's shop in Gort. He also did bits and pieces of woodwork and often helped his neighbours out with complicated repairs on furniture and windows.

Rose took a deep breath. "Now, lads," she said, affecting a casual manner she didn't at all feel, "what can I get ye?" She lifted the bar cloth and started to polish a glass she had already dried and polished earlier.

"I wouldn't mind a kiss," Liam went on, winking at the other two, "but I suppose, since it's the middle of the afternoon, I'll just have to make do with a pint of stout."

Rose gave an embarrassed smile and shook her head. "It doesn't matter what time of the day it is," she retorted lightly. "It's only drinks I'm serving."

One of the other lads clapped him on the back. "By Jaysus, O'Connor, you're the boyo when it comes to the women!"

Rose turned away now and, as she stood on her tip-toes to reach up to the shelf for the three glasses, she felt suddenly conscious of her skirt moving up higher on her legs and the flush on her cheeks grew deeper.

"If you want to take a seat, lads, I'll bring the drinks over to you when they're ready," she told them, anxious to remove herself from the spotlight of their stares. Especially Liam O'Connor's stare. The close attention he gave Rose always made her feel slightly unnerved.

"Go on, you two," Liam told his companions with a nod of his dark curly head. "I'll be across in a minute."

The two lads moved away from the bar now, used to taking the lead from him.

Liam paid and Rose started to pull the pints.

"It's a fine day," she said, keeping her eyes well away from Liam's face. She nodded towards the windows at the back. "I see there's a few fishing boats out now, taking advantage of the good weather . . ."

"Rose . . ." Liam said, leaning across the bar towards her, his voice softer and his manner suddenly serious, "I hope I didn't offend you earlier . . . about the kiss? I was only coddin' – a bit of oul' banter with the lads. I would hate you to think badly of me."

Rose rolled her eyes to the brown, smoke-stained ceiling. "Ah, sure I'm well used to it, working in here! I don't pay any attention to half of what's said."

He nodded his head slowly, his face still serious. "I was wondering . . . will you go with me into Galway this evenin' to see an oul' film? I have the loan of my brother's van for the night . . ."

Rose took a deep breath, her mind working rapidly on an excuse as she lifted the first pint onto the bar. With any of the other lads she would have just laughed and fobbed them off but she knew it wouldn't work with Liam. He was a couple of years older than the others and she knew his loudness was only a front for the other lads and that behind it he could be serious enough.

"I'm working again tonight," she told him in a low voice, turning away to top up the second pint.

"How about tomorrow night then? Or a night through the week?"

"I think my mother needs me at home . . ." She gave a little shrug, then bent her head so that her dark straight hair formed a curtain, shielding her from his stare. "And I don't think my father would be keen on me going to Galway in a van with a lad on my own."

Liam paused for a moment, his tanned brow furrowed in thought. Then he nodded his head. "Ah, sure, fair enough . . ."

Rose lifted the second pint onto the bar now, careful to keep her hand steady so as not to spill it. She didn't know what else to say to him so she stayed silent. She knew there was no point in giving him any hope because, even if she wanted to go out with him, there was no way her father would allow it.

When she'd started working in the pub, her father had warned her about the way some of the men treated women in pubs, especially when they had a few drinks on them.

"I know what I'm talking about, Rose," he told her. "I've heard the filth that comes out of their mouths after they've drunk more than their share, and I'm not having any daughter of mine putting up with the likes of that."

"Now, Stephen," her mother said, "you know well that Joe and Mary Slattery wouldn't allow that to happen to Rose. They keep a close eye on everything that goes on in the bar and they'll make sure she always has someone sensible to see her home."

"I'm only warning her," he said quietly. He turned back to Rose. "Just make sure that you don't go making too free with any of them. There's no decent man that needs to be intoxicated to ask a woman out and, besides, you have time enough for all of that nonsense. You're only working in the place to make a few shillings, so make it plain to any of the young lads that spend half their week in Slattery's that you have no interest in any of them." He paused. "There's time enough for you to meet the right type of fellow who'll treat you decently and be able to look after you."

But, despite those strong words, she felt that her father approved of the two Murphy boys and that when the time was right he might even allow her to go out to a dance with them or to a concert. Even though he hadn't voiced anything of the sort, she had heard him say that the Murphys weren't just musically talented, they also had brains or they wouldn't have got the good jobs they both had in Gort.

But she knew he wouldn't allow the likes of Liam O'Connor anywhere near his family. And, actually, her father's strictness was a good excuse to get out of this particular situation. For all he was good-looking and confident – and for all that most of the other girls had an eye for him – Liam O'Connor just wasn't her type. He might be good on the playing field and a hard worker, but she was looking for more than that in a man.

411

"You'll be at the dance down in the hall next weekend?" Liam asked, as she put the third pint on the bar.

"Yes," she said, nodding her head.

"Well, keep me a dance, so," he said, his gaze still fixed on her.

"I will," she said, with a smile that didn't quite reach her eyes.

The shop bell gave a loud ring now, giving her the perfect excuse to end the conversation.

A short while later a small coach pulled in at the side of the pub. About eighteen lads came pouring out of it and they all made straight for the bar. They were supporters of the opposing team from a neighbouring village and they greeted the local lads they knew with a shout or a wave. A crowd this size arriving unannounced would have put pressure on the pub staff any Saturday afternoon but with Joe gone Rose felt overwhelmed – and more than a little self-conscious – as the crowd of lads tried to catch her attention and laughingly jostled with each other as they waited to get served.

Eventually Rose had served their first round of drinks and set about sorting out empty glasses before they returned in ones and twos for refills. Thankfully, the shop had been quiet but of course it didn't last. A small but steady stream of customers to the shop kept her busy going back and forth between there and the bar for the next hour or so.

At one point she was just returning to the bar when she saw Michael Murphy standing there waiting to be served and her heart skipped a beat.

"Last round," he told her light-heartedly, glancing up at the clock. "We'll all be gone after this for the match and you'll get a bit of peace."

"Sure, it makes no difference to me," she replied in a cheery tone. "The busier it is, the quicker the time flies." Rose looked up at the clock now and realised that she should have called drinking-up time nearly five minutes ago. "Is it the same?" she asked him, feeling a little flustered as she rang the bell under the counter.

"It is," he said, indicating the two empty glasses he'd put on the bar.

Rose was conscious of him watching now as she pulled the two pints of Guinness.

"Have you heard from that cousin of yours lately?" he asked. "The one from Offaly – Hannah, isn't it?"

Rose suddenly stiffened at the mention of her cousin's name. The last time she'd been down for a holiday in Clare, last October, the dainty, blonde Hannah had made a hit with all the lads – but this was the first time that Michael Murphy had shown any particular interest in her. Hannah had obviously made a big impression on him. The thought gave Rose a tight feeling in her stomach.

"She keeps in touch regularly," she said, trying to sound normal. "I got a letter from her last week."

"And how's she doing? She was talking about going over to England or up to Dublin at some point, wasn't she? Did she go yet?"

"Oh, that's Hannah for you," Rose said, raising her eyebrows to the ceiling. "She's always planning to go somewhere and do something – but she's never left home yet. And there was no mention about her going anywhere in the letter." She put the two pint glasses to the side now, waiting for the froth to settle before filling them up to the brim. "That's as far as she gets, talking about it."

A small frown appeared on Michael Murphy's face. "It's a mighty big step – going away from home. But sometimes it's the only way forward." He leaned his elbows on the bar now, a thoughtful look on his face.

"Will you be playing at the dance next week?" Rose asked. Chatting about the music was an easier, more subtle way of finding out if the two brothers would be there.

"They have a three-piece band booked from Ballyvaughan," he said, nodding his head, "but we usually end up playing a few tunes one way or the other. I usually have the oul' fiddle along with me just in case."

Rose felt her heart lift. There hadn't been a dance in the local hall since Christmas. This coming weekend would be the first one of the year and thankfully there was no sign of Hannah travelling down for it. Rose had been careful not to mention it in any of her recent letters and Hannah hadn't enquired if there was a dance coming up – so all was safe on that front.

"I believe your cousin can play the piano," Michael said now. "She was telling me she's been going for lessons since she started school. She must be a well-accomplished player after all those years."

Rose felt a stab of irritation now and hoped that it didn't show on her face, because Michael Murphy might interpret it as jealousy – and it certainly wasn't. It was sheer annoyance at the fact that Hannah complained non-stop about her mother making her go for music lessons, moaning about having to practise every night at home, and yet, when she had been sitting all cosy with the musicians at the last dance, she had made out that she was absolutely passionate about her music just to get their attention.

"I've not heard her playing for a few years," Rose said casually, "but, like you say, she must be good if she's been practising all that time."

"I'd love to hear her playing. We must get her out to the hotel in Kinvara that has a piano some evening and let her play a few tunes for us all."

Rose nodded her head. "That's a good idea. It would make a bit of a change from here."

After he left the bar, Rose had a heavy feeling in her chest. The sort of feeling she got when she heard bad news. Why did Hannah have to spoil everything?

There was a time when they were younger when she had really liked her cousin – but that had changed. It was hard to like somebody when you couldn't trust them. Hannah had shown herself to be a liar on a number of occasions. She had no hesitation in making a story up on the spur of the moment to get herself out of an awkward situation. And she had involved Rose on a couple of occasions without even warning her about what she was going to say.

Rose tried to get on with her work now and not let the fact that Michael Murphy had enquired after Hannah annoy her. As she briskly dried the glasses to a fine polish, she comforted herself with the knowledge that Hannah wouldn't be coming to the next dance in any case.

Rose couldn't put her finger on what she actually liked about Michael, because he was – and always had been – a fairly deep and quiet type. Of course the fact that he worked in a bank – which made him a cut above the other local lads – was certainly a factor. But an even bigger attraction was the fact that he could play almost any tune on the fiddle. Even the older men grudgingly admitted that he was the best player they'd ever had in the area. He was the best fiddle player for miles.

But it was more than that. There was something about Michael Murphy's eyes – a strange, almost sad quality – that made her want to put her arms around him.

A short while later the few older men at the fire were finishing off the last mouthful of their whiskies for closing time and the younger lads finishing the dregs of their pints when the shop door went again.

Trained to the sound, Rose turned automatically and was moving down the step when she saw the petite but striking figure glide inside, clad in her customary waxed green hat and coat. There were only a few people Rose dreaded serving in Slattery's bar or shop – and this was one of them.

The fifty-odd-year-old widowed Leonora Bentley lived up in Dublin and she drove down to Kilnagree in her white Mercedes every so often to visit her daughter Diana. A schoolteacher in Gort, Diana was married to the local veterinary surgeon and they lived in the oldest and largest house in the village, overlooking Galway Bay. There had been a bit of talk when they first moved to Kilnagree, as the Bentleys were Protestant, but Diana had taken 'instructions' in the Catholic faith before they got married and was now a practising Catholic herself.

When Leonora paid her daughter and son-in-law a visit, she would always be seen first thing in the morning striding along the circular coast route that took her from the big white house along the edge of the sea and then onto the small main road that led to Kinvara and back around to the house again. After dinner in the evenings she took the exact same route again – a good brisk walk which covered approximately three miles.

Dressed in her long Barbour coat and hat, Leonora Bentley greeted everyone with an abrupt "Good morning" or "Good evening", depending on the time of day. She never broke the rhythm in her stride to wait for a return greeting, but carried straight on as though heading for an urgent appointment.

On the odd occasions that she came walking down to the post office, she sometimes looked into the shop for a loaf of fresh bread or some fresh scones or cakes. But she could go six months between one visit and the next.

If her straight-backed, elegant figure was seen going into the post office, Mary Slattery was notified immediately and she would take up residence behind the shop counter, all prepared should Mrs Bentley deign to come in. Joe would be ushered into the bar just in case he did or said anything in front of the sophisticated Dublin lady that might just show them up. Rose would also be kept in the background, unless she was needed to serve another customer to allow Mrs Slattery to devote all her care and attention to the lady.

But Mary Slattery obviously had not heard that Leonora Bentley was in Kilnagree on this particular occasion, as she had left no instructions with her young charge as to how she should approach or serve such an important customer.

Rose took a deep breath and went forward into the shop. "Hello, Mrs Bentley," she said in what she hoped was a cheery but polite voice. "What can I get you?"

"Nothing for the moment." The older woman's voice was unusually low and had a slight tremor in it but the usual strident edge was still there. "You can attend to your business . . . I just need a few moments' peace and quiet . . . *please.*"

She moved backwards now until her legs touched the wooden bench under the window, then she sat down. She made a sudden 'oohing' sort of noise and pressed the palm of her hand up against her temple, inadvertently cocking her wide-brimmed green hat to the side.

Rose watched in alarmed silence, until Mrs Bentley looked up and caught her eye.

"Are you okay?" the young girl asked.

Leonora Bentley closed her eyes, then nodded her head. "It's probably a migraine. It came on very suddenly. I thought I would make it back to the house, but the pain is very intense . . ." She waved her hand towards the bar. "If you could get me a drink of water, I think I have some tablets in my pocket that will help."

The hurling supporters were all starting to leave the bar now as Rose came rushing through to pour a glass of water.

Liam O'Connor was heading towards the door when he saw her and made a quick detour over to the bar.

"You're sure you can't persuade your parents to let you out tonight?" he said.

Rose moved her head to look over his shoulder as Ruairí and Michael Murphy headed for the door, both giving her a casual salute as they went. She could barely conceal her irritation with Liam O'Connor for making her miss having a word with them before they went. "No," she said in a decisive tone. "I've told you already, I've got things to do at home."

Liam turned to see what she was looking at and his eyes narrowed when he realised it was the two brothers. He looked back at Rose and gave a small shrug. "I'll see you again, so . . ."

Rose went back through to the shop and saw that Leonora Bentley had her hat off and was holding her head in both her hands. Even in such a pose she looked elegant and her thick ash-blonde bobbed hair had hardly moved out of place.

"I have the water for you," Rose said in a voice loud enough to be heard but not too loud for her customer's painful head.

Very gingerly and with only one eye open, Leonora stretched her hand out for the glass. "Thank you, my dear," she said in a weary but grateful voice.

Rose moved back behind the counter. "If you need anything else?"

There was a few moments' silence as the woman put the pills in her mouth, took a gulp of water and then threw her head back to help swallow them down.

"A brandy," Mrs Bentley suddenly said, her usual commanding tone back in her voice. "And I think you'd better make it a large one."

Rose hesitated. The bar was officially closed now until five o'clock and she had been reminded by both the landlord and his wife to stick strictly to those hours. She quickly asked herself what either of them would do, if they were in this situation.

Two minutes later Rose came back out into the shop holding a glass with a good measure of Hennessy's brandy in one hand and a small jug of water in the other. "I'm not sure how much water you want in it . . ."

"The same amount of water as brandy will be fine."

"Is the pain in your head easing yet?" Rose carefully poured water into the brandy.

"Very slightly . . . but it's affecting my eyes as well."

Rose took the empty water tumbler from Leonora Bentley's outstretched hand and gave her the brandy glass. "If you sit for a while and give the tablets and the brandy a chance to work . . ."

"That's exactly what I intend to do."

Rose looked out of the window now and saw two local women approaching the shop. Instinctively she knew Mrs Bentley would not want to be viewed in such a position. If it were her own mother or grandmother they would be mortified to be seen ill in a public place.

"Mrs Bentley, I see some customers coming across to the shop . . ."

"Oh, good heavens!" she groaned and made to stand up, looking suddenly flustered.

"Maybe you'd like to sit in the bar for a few minutes?" Rose suggested. "There's no one in there and there's a nice fire on."

"Perfect."

She straightened her back, took a deep breath and then made her rather unsteady way behind the counter and into the bar.

As she passed by, Rose was struck for the first time by how small and slender the Dublin woman actually was. She couldn't have been more than a few inches over five feet, but there was something about her manner and attitude that gave the impression of a taller, formidable type of woman. She was very different to the other females in Kilnagree. She dressed differently, spoke differently and acted quite differently.

In many ways – particularly when she was dressed in her severe winter outfits – she seemed older than women of her own age. But when summer came, in her cream linen trousers and straw hat or flowery dresses and dark sunglasses, she suddenly seemed much younger – almost girlish.

And Rose and her mother and granny weren't the only ones to comment on this – she had overheard two of the men in the bar talking about Leonora Bentley when they'd had a few drinks, and their coarse comments left her in no doubt that she was still an attractive woman.

As she bustled about organising the bread and vegetables the two women had asked for, Rose glanced every now and again into the bar, but she couldn't see any sign of Mrs Bentley by the table at the fire.

When she went back into the bar the place was strangely dark. At first she thought there was no one there but when she looked more closely she saw a stretched-out form on the long bench by the window. It dawned on Rose that she had obviously reached up and closed the curtains to keep out the light.

Rose tip-toed over to the bench. She could hear the gentle sound of Leonora Bentley's snoring. The tablets and the alcohol had obviously done the trick.

Very quietly, Rose worked around the sleeping figure, lifting glasses and ashtrays across to the bar where she left them in a neat pile to wash later, lest the noise of the rickety old tap wake Leonora up.

She then went silently around the tables with a damp cloth and a polishing rag to clean and shine to the standard that Mary Slattery would expect when she returned.

She wandered back into the shop and tidied around there for a few minutes and was standing with her arms folded looking out of the window when she saw her mother's neat figure coming out of the post office and making towards the shop. Kathleen Barry often walked down to post things for the Guards or letters for herself or her mother-in-law. Rose moved quickly to open the door as gently as she could and then held it open to keep the bell mute. As her mother approached the shop, Rose pressed her finger to her lips to warn her to be quiet.

"What's wrong?" Kathleen whispered, her brow deeply furrowed.

"Mrs Bentley – Diana Tracey's mother – is asleep in the bar!"

"What?" Kathleen's face was a picture of utter shock.

"She has a bad migraine headache," Rose whispered. "She nearly collapsed when she came in so I gave her a drink and she took some tablets for it."

Kathleen leaned on the counter and stretched up on her toes to try to see into the bar.

"She's lying on the old bench at the window," said Rose. She motioned to her mother to move further down the counter so they couldn't be heard talking, just in case Mrs Bentley woke up. "She had a brandy as well – she said that sometimes helps."

"A *brandy*?" Her mother's face was truly aghast now. "A brandy at this time of the day? Good God! And her one of the Quality! Who would believe it?"

Rose shrugged. "She must be used to taking it for the headaches."

"She'll have a bigger headache waking up after drinking that at this hour of the day!" Kathleen shook her head in a bemused fashion. She had very limited experience of alcohol – the odd sherry at Christmas or funerals – and it always went straight to her head. "Of course, she's a Protestant," she said now. "They have their own strange ways . . ."

Rose didn't say that the brandy had actually been a large one, as she knew her mother would only disapprove further and might well gossip about it to her father or, even worse, the Guards down at the barracks. Since working in the pub, she had come to realise that her parents had a very puritanical attitude to drink.

Kathleen shook her head again and turned her attention to her daughter. "Anyway, one of the reasons I called in was to tell you that I got a letter from your Auntie Sheila yesterday. I meant to tell you last night but I clean forgot."

"And what did she have to say?" Rose asked, lifting the small soft brush from under the counter to wipe away a few stray crumbs from an empty cake tray.

"She said that Hannah is definitely coming down for the dance next weekend – won't that be nice for you?"

Rose suddenly froze, the brushing of the crumbs forgotten. "But how does she know about the dance?" Her dark, arched eyebrows were knitted together in annoyance. "I never told her about it."

"Oh, I mentioned it to Sheila a few weeks ago in one of my letters," Kathleen said airily, "and I told her to tell Hannah about it, since she enjoyed the last dance so much." She smiled at her daughter now. "I thought it would be company for you and your father won't mind you going if she's there with you. He can hardly stop you going if Hannah has come all the way down from Offaly and everyone else is walking down to it." She looked at the expression on Rose's face now. "Is there something wrong? Do you not want Hannah to come down for the dance? Have you had a row or something?"

Rose forced herself to smile. "No, no . . . it's just that I thought Hannah was saving up to move to Dublin or London. I didn't think she'd have the money to come down."

"Oh, there's no fear of Hannah going anywhere! She has it too comfortable at home with only herself there, now the boys have gone. And anyway, Sheila says she still has her birthday money saved from January and she's keeping it for the coach fare down. She said that Hannah was writing to tell you what coach she will be arriving on next Wednesday or Thursday. I suppose you'll get the letter Monday."

"That's grand," Rose said, trying to sound enthusiastic. She pinned a smile on her face now. It was obviously all arranged. Hannah would be there at the dance making big eyes at Michael Murphy and all the other lads – and there wasn't a single thing that she could do about it.

If you enjoyed this chapter from
Leaving Clare by Geraldine O'Neill
why not order the full book online
@ www.poolbeg.com
Poolbeg books

See page overleaf for details.